TRYSMOON

Book Two: Duty

By
Brian K. Fuller

TRYSMOON
BOOK TWO: DUTY

Copyright © 2014 by Brian K. Fuller
All rights reserved, including the right to reproduce this book, or portion thereof, in any form.

Edited by Jessica Robbins JessiLynRobbins@gmail.com

briankfullerbooks.com
facebook.com/briankfullerbooks

ISBN-13: 978-1502806123
ISBN-10: 1502806126

*For J.R.R. Tolkein and Raymond Feist:
Thank you for teaching me to dream.*

Chapter 24 - Maewen

The Chalaine hurried through the sunset-bathed hallway, hiking her dress up above her ankles so she could walk more quickly. Large, arched windows revealed a deep blue evening sky filled with puffy clouds and shards draped in the warm light of the dying day. Jaron trailed behind her, face grim. The shock of the demon's attack haunted her dreams, and she slept less and less every night, mind and spirit unsettled.

The Pontiff had delayed the betrothal while he and Mirelle worked to calm the chaos, heal the injured, and bury the dead. The Chalaine knew the ceremony would have to take place soon to restore the people's faith and confidence. Eight nobles from Rhugoth, three Warlords from Aughmere, and four Tolnorians died that night in the Chapel, and grief and fear wracked the people of Ki'Hal as the news spread.

But there was something else, as well. Gen's name ran through the streets like wildfire blown on a gale. While many had questioned and even opposed his challenge to the Ha'Ulrich, there were none who could fault his bravery before the demon.

The Pontiff saw to it that the Chalaine's deeds and those

of Ethris and Gen were heralded from every pulpit as examples of the triumph of light over darkness. Because of his performance at the Trials, his challenge of Chertanne, and his courage in the Chapel, Gen's fame swelled in the minds of commoner and noble alike. The Chalaine desperately hoped he would live to enjoy it.

At the first preaching of the events that occurred the night of the betrothal, many wondered what the Ha'Ulrich had done during the entire affair, for the Pontiff made no mention of him in his account, save to say that he escaped unharmed. But before long—though from whom, no one knew—the tale of the Blessed One, frozen in fear at the sight of evil and lying helpless in his own filth, circulated through the streets. The inaction and fear of the one sent by Eldaloth to be their leader and protector from evil eroded the confidence of the people. If the Ha'Ulrich could not bear the presence of evil as well as a Mage or even a commoner such as Gen, then how would he fare when faced with the greatest evil of all, even Mikkik?

Chertanne's supporters countered by calling the story of his weakness an obvious ploy of the Ilch, perpetuated to weaken the unity and strength that the people would gain from trusting the Blessed One. They even invented a little story of how Chertanne had shielded his bride-to-be from the demon's attacks. She snorted in laughter at this fabrication and her mother swore in disgust.

The falsified explanation sufficed for the common folk and settled the arguments on the streets, but the Chalaine and most of the nobles of two kingdoms knew the truth, and their doubts were far from dissolved, festering anew every day. Two weeks had passed since the attack, and the Chalaine knew of several clandestine meetings of confused nobles, though she wasn't sure what was said. Chertanne called other meetings, attended by those he trusted most, no doubt to plan something to strengthen his position or to inform him of any activity against him.

But the Chalaine cared little about these political maneuvers and manipulations, confident that her mother would handle them adroitly. She descended the steps into the courtyard where those working to restore the Chapel were retiring for the day. They stopped to bow before her; she went by without acknowledging them. Her mind was fixed. In the lower levels of the acolytes' chambers Gen and Ethris lay dying. Two weeks had passed and neither had awakened.

The Chalaine had come awake late the night of the attack. Her mother, Jaron, Cadaen, and Fenna circled around her. The Chalaine remembered a hundred questions flooding her mind, but the only one that came out was, "Does he live?"

They calmed her and fed her to help her regain her strength, reassuring her that Gen was alive, as was Ethris, but their faces told another story. It wasn't until the next day when she was permitted to see them, both lying pale and fevered upon the beds of acolytes, that she understood the seriousness of their situation. Runic wards, drawn in white around their beds, protected them from unseen evil, and Puremen waited constantly at their sides, guarding lives that continually threatened to flee.

They had healed most of Ethris's wounds, but many of Gen's remained. She tried to approach him, but the Puremen blocked her way and her mother held her back.

"You cannot, child," her mother explained softly but firmly.

"And why not?" the Chalaine said, her voice betraying her frustration. "Are they to save me and I do nothing?"

"Gen's wounds were many and deep, and I'm sure some of those you could heal. The Pontiff and the Puremen labored through the night keeping them both alive and healing what they could. Ethris's body they healed, and they will continue their work on Gen to its completion. But there is something, some poison of the demon, that works within them, gnawing at them. The Pontiff fears you could be hurt if you tried to heal them. Ethris and Gen have suffered more than bodily wounds, and even the Pontiff does not fully understand it."

"Surely something could be done." The Chalaine finally acquiesced, going to Fenna and placing her hands on her handmaiden's shoulders.

Mirelle regarded her softly. "I have sent for Maewen to see if elven lore can shed any light on this."

The Chalaine had seen Maewen but twice in her life. The half-elven woman looked no older than Fenna, but she had seen centuries pass. The great King Aldradan Mikmir saved Maewen's life during the First Mikkikian War. Since then, Maewen, a tracker of extraordinary ability, had served Rhugoth in its times of need. It was she that helped them find the Hall of Three Moons on the Shroud Lake shard, and it was she who would lead their caravan to it when spring came.

For two weeks the Chalaine had waited for Maewen, some answers, and some hope. Since seeing Gen that first day, she had gone every day, finding him steadily worsening. Fenna kept a nearly constant vigil at his side, holding his hand in hers and sobbing softly to herself or staring at him with a defeated expression. The Chalaine cried, too, though she was never permitted to touch him, for her mother and the Puremen did not trust her to not attempt to heal him.

Ethris fared better. His fever lessened gradually and his breathing came more evenly. By the time the first week passed, the Puremen had healed both of their bodily injuries, though each had massive scars where the creature's spikes and blades had punctured and sliced their chests and arms during the fight. For Ethris, the scars appeared to be the first he'd sustained. For Gen, they were several of many and not at all out of place.

Today came a brief glimmer of hope. Maewen had

arrived and would see them at once. The Chalaine fairly ran past the yellowing oaks and fall flowers, going in through the small doors of the acolytes' quarters at the rear of the Church and descending a narrow flight of stone steps. She opened the heavy door as quietly as the old hinges would permit, finding her mother and Fenna already at Gen's side. Cadaen looked on from a corner, and Jaron joined him as the Chalaine took a seat near her mother.

Maewen was there, studying Ethris, her mouth bent down in a frown. The half-elf was beautiful, her long, raven-black hair pulled back away from a delicate, oval face. Due to her elven heritage, her features were thin and elegant, ears slightly upswept, though her human side made her heartier than an elf would be. While her beauty would grace any noble's court, the Chalaine knew this half-elven tracker was made of iron and had endured struggles and fighting for years untold. She wore the colors of the wood, browns, greens, and grays, and her gear lay in a pile on the floor, the tale of long miles upon them.

"Maewen, this is my daughter, the Chalaine."

"Yes," Maewen replied, voice strangely accented but beautiful. "I remember well this veiled one. I see she has grown tall like her mother."

The Chalaine inclined her head to her. "It is an honor to see you again. You have served this kingdom long and well, and I hope you can shed some light upon this."

Maewen offered no reply at first but crossed to stand by Gen, considering him with the same grave look she had given Ethris. "I have served and will serve, but I will be of little help here." At this, Fenna lowered her head. "Though why so much care for this one? Who is he?"

"His name is Gen. He has served my house with great honor," the First Mother replied. "He is courageous and wise beyond his years."

"Ah," Maewen acknowledged, nodding her head. "Then this is the one whose name jumps like a deer from tongue to tongue. I've heard tell of him as far west as Jameth. He was more handsome and a little bigger in the tales, however."

Maewen returned to her seat. "Since you summoned me, I will tell you what I can, but first tell me what happened, in detail. I have caught pieces as I traveled, but I would have the whole of it, without exaggeration or embellishment."

"My daughter should relate the events," Mirelle suggested. "She was less affected than any of us."

The Chalaine told the story the best she could, trying to insert every detail she remembered. What was spoken between Gen and the creature was a blur to her, and she was only able to pick out a few words. Maewen listened expressionlessly, though her eyes revealed her interest. When the Chalaine finished, Maewen stood and paced about the room for several moments.

"Intriguing, and some of it hard to believe. May I assume that the Chapel had been cleaned, refinished, and reworked recently? In preparation for this betrothal?"

"Yes," the Mirelle answered.

"Then you would do well to look at your workers more closely next time. You were the victims of a Burka pattern, and a clever one at that. Done by someone powerful."

"A Burka pattern?" Fenna asked, wiping her eyes.

Maewen nodded. "When Trys was still unveiled and the war with Mikkik and his creatures raged, Mikkik's dark elf Mages were taught by their foul master how to summon beings from the Abyss and force them into battle. Human Mages clandestinely observed how it was done and began to do the same. They learned mental mastery over the demons, forcing them to fight against Mikkik's own host, evil against evil. They called the creatures using patterns, a different pattern for each type of creature. The patterns were named after the human Magician who first mastered them, Burka.

"When Mikkik found that the humans had copied the

trick, he used his power to create creatures in the Abyss itself, demons who could not be controlled using human magic. Instead, they had no mind of their own and were controlled directly by the will of Mikkik, like the puppets your children play with. Cleverly, he used a traitor amongst the humans to reveal to them the patterns for summoning these creatures. The humans learned the new patterns eagerly, hoping for a new weapon to turn the tide of the war.

"You may guess the rest. When the Magicians summoned them, they were unable to force their will upon them and were slaughtered along with hundreds of others. Few escaped.

"As time wore on, Mikkik's Magicians became more devious, learning to make patterns upon the ground or on a floor in advance and have them triggered by some event, such as the passing of a certain number of people or the speaking of the dwarven tongue. The Mage that created the pattern could be hundreds of leagues away when the trap was sprung. In your case, the pattern was inscribed into the tiles of the floor and activated by the third repetition of the chant.

"Fortunately for the war, a Burka pattern has two weaknesses. For one, the Underworld creature cannot move far from it, the pattern acting as an anchor to its home. The armies of dwarves, elves, and men learned to simply run from the creatures. The second weakness is that those who practice the religious arts can send the creatures back to the Abyss with relatively little effort, at least in comparison to how much energy and skill it takes to summon one.

"War parties took Puremen with them wherever they went. The enemy countered with other tricks. When the pattern in the Chapel was forming, you mentioned how you were frozen in place, unable to move. This innovation in the Burka pattern hindered its victims from fleeing, allowing the creatures to slaughter all those who couldn't break from the spell. Other patterns were imbued with magics to aid in their effectiveness. Again, the one used against you was created with the ability to destroy the exits from the Chapel and drop rubble around the altar and the Pontiff so the creature could do its work. You are fortunate that the Pontiff is as tough as old roots or you would all be dead or share the same fate as these two."

Maewen paused to let the information sink in until a voice from the door startled everyone.

"What I want to know is how these two were unaffected by the creature's paralyzing magic. Everyone else was, and it seems a bit suspicious to me."

It was Chertanne. All present twisted toward the entrance of the room where he had entered unnoticed. His face was angry and his arms were crossed over his chest. Dason stood behind him, clearly uncomfortable. All in the room rose and bowed, save Maewen.

"Welcome, Chertanne," the First Mother greeted him politely, trying not to further anger one whose manliness had recently come into question.

At hearing the name, Maewen bowed as well. "So you are the Ha'Ulrich. Forgive my ignorance, Blessed One. It is an honor to meet you."

Chertanne looked her over. "Thank you, Maewen. I have heard your kind was beautiful and I was not misled. I should like time alone with you to learn more about the elves."

"Certainly, your Grace," Maewen answered.

The Chalaine hoped she had time to warn Maewen before she undertook that visit.

Chertanne stepped into the room fully. "But please, Maewen, if you would address the question. It is rather odd that these two should be entirely unaffected by the creature's presence whereas all others were frozen with fear."

The Chalaine thought it odd that he excluded her, and for the first time she wondered how she had escaped the paralysis that incapacitated almost everyone else.

"It is not odd, really," Maewen replied, "at least in the case of Ethris. The magic meant to paralyze the victims of the pattern can be overcome by those of exceptionally strong will or through counter magic. Ethris is a Mage, and a powerful one at that. All Mages and priests of high skill must develop strong wills to shape the energies of magic that emanate from the moons Myn and Duam, as I'm sure you know. As a result of that training and years of practicing his arts, he is strong enough to resist the entrancement."

"And what of Gen, then? I sense you think something is amiss with him?"

The Chalaine put her arms around Fenna, whose tenseness betrayed the offense taken at the accusation implicit in the Blessed One's question.

"Yes. I was going to ask more about him. I understood from the tales that he was not noble born. Is that correct?"

"Yes," Mirelle answered. "He is a serf, a refugee from his war-torn kingdom, Tolnor. Though a serf, he must have had some learning, for he talks as though he were noble born and is learned. He was also trained as a swordsman and is most disciplined."

Maewen started to pace again. "The reason I ask is that the Chalaine mentioned that this *young* man had a brief dialog with the creature, using the words 'Umiel' and 'Elde.' The language is ancient, the words of the Gods themselves. There are two humans I know of who know some of that language, and Ethris is one of them. Even then, he has studied long to learn what he knows of it. That a peasant boy, not even twenty if I do not miss my guess, should know any of it is unfathomable, unless he has elven blood in him and has been alive longer than you know."

"That would explain many things," Mirelle replied

pensively. "Talking with him is like talking to no other man his age. No one as young as he should be as knowledgeable, disciplined, or as wise as he is."

A Pureman clearing his throat surprised them all.

"Forgive me, your Grace," he said from a corner of the room. "There are many documented cases in scriptural history of men and women being blessed with the gift of God's Tongue in times where they faced great peril. It is considered a miracle and a sign of God's favor. The words put fear into all things evil."

"Thank you for the insight," Mirelle said. "I do remember some tales where that occurred."

Maewen didn't appear convinced.

"What do the words mean?" the Chalaine asked.

"Umiel," Maewen explained, "is a command that translated roughly means 'Flee in the name of the Light.' Elde is the ancient term for God, the root of 'Eldaloth.' Most likely he was invoking the name of God to command the demon to return from whence it came."

Chertanne was displeased at this last answer, face turning red.

"What of the other words, the last ones spoken by the creature. 'Chak Diggat, chak Ilch Murmit Cho'?" the Chalaine pressed, hoping to further vindicate Gen from Chertanne's implied accusation.

"I wish you could remember the first part," Maewen replied. The beast's tongue is a corruption of the God's speech and harder to understand. 'Chak Diggat' means 'The Betrayer', another name for Mikkik. 'Ilch' you know well, I am sure. The phrase seems to say that Mikkik will punish the Ilch, though that makes no sense."

"I may have remembered it poorly," the Chalaine said. "Ethris will know if he wakes. He seemed surprised by what was said."

"This can wait until later!" Fenna cried out, emotions raw. "Is there nothing that can be done for them?"

"You can wait," Maewen answered a little unsympathetically. "The poisons of the underworld do not just flow in the blood and destroy flesh. They infect the mind and the soul, working evil there, as well. Through the aid of your Puremen, the bodies have been purged, but only Gen and Ethris can purge what agents work at their own souls. Each must find a reason to emerge from sleep while the poison shows them every reason not to. Now if there are no further questions, I need to rest for a time."

"Thank you, Maewen," the First Mother said. "Ask for Pureman Feldsman at the door. He will see to your comfort."

"Thank you. Honor to your house. May Eldaloth keep you Chalaine, Ha'Ulrich."

Maewen gathered her things quickly and left, Chertanne's eyes following her out. "Well, Dason, we shall leave the matter of Gen to another time, unless, unfortunate of unfortunates, he dies. What a shame that would be."

Chertanne left, but Dason lingered long enough to bow to the Chalaine, eyes pained. Jaron scowled at him. The Chalaine inclined her head slightly as he left, finding herself missing his company again. When Gen had fallen, she had expected that Dason would be reinstated as her protector until he could be healed, but Chertanne refused to release him from service, and Captain Tolbrook had taken over as Gen's replacement.

Silence reigned in the small room as the acolytes trimmed the lamps and returned to their somber vigil.

"Go, Fenna," Mirelle said kindly, stroking the girl's hair. "Eat and rest. I will watch for you. Take my daughter with you."

Fenna thanked the First Mother and she, Jaron, and the Chalaine left. The girls took the meal in the Chalaine's apartments. The Chalaine sorrowed to see how little Fenna ate and how the girlish exuberance that had always been a part of her nature had died.

When the meal was over, the Chalaine commanded the protesting Fenna to sleep in her bed.

"I will watch over Gen in your absence," she promised. "And take heart. He is strong. He will win the struggle against the poison, I am sure."

Fenna nodded and closed her eyes. The Chalaine stayed by her side until her face slackened and her breath slowed. Quietly, she donned her veil and stepped outside. For all her assurances to her handmaiden, she feared more and more for Gen's life.

Chapter 25 - A Way Out of Darkness

With Jaron in tow the Chalaine returned to the room where Gen and Ethris rested. She peeked through the crack in the door, finding that her mother still sat at Gen's side, absentmindedly tracing the pronounced muscles on his arm and humming sadly to herself. The acolytes, having done what they could, had gone to meditate and pray. The Chalaine ordered Jaron to stay with Cadaen outside the door.

"Mother?" she said quietly, door creaking as she pushed it open. Mirelle startled, turning toward her daughter, embarrassment rising on her face. "How does he fare?" the Chalaine asked, navigating away from the awkward moment.

"No better," Mirelle replied, turning back to Gen, face drawn. "Ethris improves with each passing hour. Gen, if anything, gets worse."

The Chalaine felt as if someone had punched her in the stomach. She joined her mother at Gen's bedside, taking her hand. "Are you all right, mother?"

Mirelle managed a weak smile. "No, I don't think I am.

If the truth be known, I've been quite taken by this young man."

"Mother!"

"Hush, child. I know my place. But you cannot blame me—you of all people—for loving him. For hours I sat in front of the Walls, peering out at the street watching lovers go by hand in hand. And there I was, year after year, hoping that the Ha'Ulrich could be found and I be wedded to the greatest, most noble man to walk Ki'Hal.

"Instead, my seventeenth year comes, and after a brief, horrible week with some lucky, beautiful man whose name I was not permitted to know, I was left to live the rest of my life forbidden to love until the return of Eldaloth. It was only your birth and raising you that gave me the sense that I was the First Mother and not a cow."

The Chalaine nodded. "I feel my life will be little different, save I shall know the name of the bull."

"I know, and I worry about you every day. I hid the truth of Chertanne's character from you for as long as I could to at least permit you pleasant dreams. You may not thank me for it, but I couldn't bear to see your hopes dashed so young. Your veil keeps others from seeing your sorrow, but I am your mother and nothing is hidden from me."

The Chalaine squeezed her mother's hand, finding her tenderly regarding Gen's face. "When did you know you loved him, mother? How did you know?"

Mirelle smiled. "I knew when I saw him step to the dais after ordering Chertanne to let you go. I trembled, and not from fear. We have no kings in Rhugoth, but if you ever wonder what one is like, then remember him on that night, brave, powerful, commanding—a judge of all. You have no idea of the agony I felt as I watched Chertanne force you toward the door, and I doubt you could understand the thrill of seeing you freed and watching Gen, calm as a summer's morning, behead that monster and return to stand with the rest of the dumbstruck apprentices—bleeding all over the place—as if nothing had happened!"

Mother and daughter shared a quiet laugh.

"Yes," the Chalaine continued in a lighthearted tone. "He seems so intent on not being noticed or showing even the tiniest bit of emotion. He hasn't done very well at the not-being-noticed part. His emotions, however, he hides well."

"That is annoying, isn't it? I took him to my apartments directly after the duel. . ."

"Mother!"

"Calm yourself! You and Cadaen have overactive imaginations. I took him to my room to talk to him—and to test him. When you listen to him, there is something about him that feels . . . old. Every time I have been in his presence, I feel at peace in some inexplicable way. Have you talked with him much?"

"I rarely see him since he is the night watch. When I do see him, I usually find myself stumbling for something to say. And he says practically nothing. Still, now that I think of it, I have felt safer knowing he is outside my door. Until recently, I thought him nothing more than another fine swordsman. But I see now that there is more. He has humbled me. I don't think it is his wisdom or his skill, but an inner strength I don't think is breakable. There is a deep sadness somewhere in his heart, though."

Mirelle regarded her questioningly, and the Chalaine explained what had happened in the library as she, Fenna, and Jaron watched him sleep.

"He has suffered more than should be endured by anyone," Mirelle said. "If he lives, we should work some way that Fenna can spend more time with him. I can see she cares for him a great deal. I hope he will return her affection."

"So does she. I like him, too, and I am sorry if it ever seemed otherwise."

"Fair enough. When I named him your protector, it was political suicide, though his actions have since vindicated my decision tenfold. I worried you would be angry over losing Dason. I know he made you laugh. Gen probably won't make you smile much, though if he should live, and may Eldaloth grant that he does, you must speak with him. As I told Maewen, he is wise and well-spoken. I think you would find comfort in his words."

"If Fenna can't figure out how to talk to him, I doubt I will have much success, either. I've little experience talking with people in general, much less someone as closed as Gen. It took no effort to get Dason to ramble on about anything."

"I think the key, my daughter, is to ask questions that begin with 'why' and imagine him with a mug of ale in his hand dancing and singing on a table."

The Chalaine smiled at the image, finding it hard to conjure up.

Mirelle took Gen's fevered hand in hers. "I have so many things I would like to ask him. Some that I'm afraid to."

"The scars."

"Yes. And perhaps how old he *really* is. If he somehow has elven blood in him and is older than me, then Fenna might have some competition after all."

The First Mother smiled, and the Chalaine knew she was joking—at least she thought so. They sat in silence for a while, listening to his labored breathing.

"Would you have me love him as you do, Mother?"

Mother fixed her eyes on her daughter, trying to penetrate the veil. "Of course not. But I would have you love *something*, Chalaine. Gen's training taught him to submerge his feelings, to ignore pain. I fear, however, that it also robbed him of the ability to feel pleasure or to truly serve anything except duty and abstract ideals.

"When I think back to him facing the demon, cowering

though I was, I see someone all too willing to throw everything away, someone who didn't love life enough to even attempt to survive. I see someone who doesn't even seem alive enough to accept the affection of a beautiful young woman, attention most men can only dream about."

"He has utterly confused poor Fenna."

"My point is this, daughter. Before us lies a man, and a great one, slipping away because when the night is gone, he can no longer feel the warmth of the sunshine on his face. And since meeting Chertanne, you have become much the same." Mirelle paused, letting the thought sink in. "Find something, anything, you can love and anchor yourself to it. It will bring you joy when the rest of the world seems cruel and unfair. And I can think of nothing more cruel and more unfair than seeing you wed Chertanne. You were the anchor for me, Chalaine. You brought me happiness, and I want that same happiness for you."

"Thank you, mother."

Mother and daughter embraced, and Mirelle rose.

"Do not stay too long, Chalaine. You need your rest, too. Gen will be none the better for us staring at him."

The First Mother left, closing the door behind her. The Chalaine sat at Gen's side and thought about her mother's words. Gen muttered something unintelligible and was silent. Sweat matted his brown hair to his scalp. Several scars crisscrossed his forehead, and the Chalaine reached out and pushed his hair aside to get a better view of them. They were even and straight, as if someone had been trying to make a pattern on his skin. With her finger, she traced a scar that ran the length of his face, starting at his temple and ending on his neck. Feeling foolish, she pulled her finger away, glancing around to see if anyone had noticed her.

Then it hit her. No one was watching her. No one could hold her back.

Quickly, she placed her hand on his head and leaned

near. Her awareness of the room faded as she bent her will toward finding Gen's injury. The light of his life burned low, and it took her some time to find it at all. But something was wrong, different from other times she had healed the wounded. She sensed that his body was perfectly intact, but still his life ebbed like a candle struggling to stay lit in a drafty room.

She moved her concentration to Gen's mind, seeking to find if the poison had caused some madness there that she could heal, but as with the body, she could sense nothing overtly amiss, although as before something just within the borders of her perception seemed off somehow. She returned to the life force and searched, trying to find what was extinguishing it, but while the feeling of wrongness persisted, it always lurked out of her grasp, like a memory half forgotten.

The Chalaine's hopes sunk, and in frustration, she did the only thing she knew to do: she poured her energy into the dying ember, striving to spark it anew. The life force flowed from her, and as it did, she saw something, a darkness that clenched around Gen's life like the demon's black-mailed fist, crushing it. While her attempts at healing revealed it to her, nothing she did could break it. But her energy cast light upon the hidden force, and with another attempt she was able to follow the source of the darkness to Gen's mind.

There, in her light, she saw what she could only think of as a door, a terrible door, from which rushed a river of black water. A sense of foreboding overcame her and she shrank from it. For several moments she thought of breaking her contact, something about the darkness shouting at her to leave. The Puremen's fear that something in Gen could harm her became horribly real. Whatever brooded beyond that door, whatever it was that was killing Gen, was powerful and alive, and she feared she could not overcome it.

But as she lingered at that portal to the mind, lost in trepidation, she realized that what she faced was no different than what Gen had done for her in the Chapel. Without hesitation he threw himself in front of an enemy he knew would kill him, and for what? Because that was who he was and it was his duty to do it. Skill at arms and courage were his gifts. And while she was to be the mother of God, she, too, had been given a gift, the gift to heal. She felt ashamed that she faltered because the way was fearful and dark, and before she could think of any more reasons to dissuade herself, she concentrated and ran headlong through the forbidding door and into a world of pain.

At first she could do nothing but reel in the force of the dark torrent, floundering in swirling eddies of emotion—guilt, worthlessness, sadness, and despair. Like a fledgling swimmer, she fought to stay above the powerful current while it relentlessly pulled her down. Her own feelings of depression and her sense of inadequacy began to weigh upon her. How could she be the mother of God when she was so ignorant, so *simple*? At once she loathed herself for ever thinking she was somehow above marrying Chertanne. Who was she? Nothing. He was the Blessed One, and a wretch like her should be glad to even be of notice to him.

And then it stopped. Quickly, she took stock of herself, trying to forget the feelings and thoughts that had overwhelmed her. She was outside the door again. The current of darkness had expelled her and left her gasping on the threshold. Undaunted, she readied herself again. She knew the enemy now, and again she plunged against the current and into Gen's mind.

The dark feelings returned, but with effort she fought them off, concentrating on Gen and not allowing her thoughts to turn inward, no matter how much her emotions begged for her attention. Struggling, she went deeper, searching, the sense of blackness deepening. There was a voice, faint at first, but as she pressed forward, it became clear. It was smooth, persuasive and powerful, and as it talked, images flashed before her to illustrate everything it said, images from Gen's life.

And what was shown shook her to her very core. Gen's iron mask of stoicism obscured pain and remorse she could not fathom. The voice droned the same message and the same images over and over again while she watched, a silent audience. Dimly she could sense Gen's consciousness watching too, and it was from his consciousness that the darkness flowed, a flood that drowned his spirit. The dam had broken long ago, and the victory for the dark voice won.

"See Gen," the voice intoned with unquestionable surety, "that your every effort is useless. I could have given you the power to stop the pain and suffering, but you would never listen! Rest assured that your failure to serve will only hurt you, for many already take your place!"

"So now you are left powerless without me, struggling and unable to even claim something as easy as a girl! What business did an orphan have even thinking about a merchant's daughter? At least pathetic Hubert could give her a name worth a little more than filth. What did you have to give her?"

The Chalaine could see her, a cute country girl with blonde hair. Regina. She could feel Gen's longing for her, his anger at her betrothal to Hubert. She could hear them talking at the well and suddenly knew why Gen was so fair-spoken. In all her imaginings of Gen's past, she would have never thought him a bard.

"And how easily were your supposed feelings of love set aside! You remember, don't you, how you let the Shadan's training overtake you until you had no care for anyone or anything at all?"

Flashes of Gen's "training" came in a rush, and the Chalaine felt herself go weak. She would have turned away from the blood and agony if she could, but instead she felt forced to watch every wicked blow from day after day of misery. She watched with Gen as Aughmerian soldiers led people from his town away to be killed and thrown in nameless graves. She watched his torture, his silent suffering, his attempt to take his own life.

"You ignored your old master and your love while they suffered and waited for just one kind word to fall from your lips. Was that your love for them? If it had been love at all, you would have never let your own suffering take you and ignore their need. Had you even one grain of feeling, perhaps you could have at least helped them escape from Tell, but instead you did nothing. I ask you, did you ever think that you could have helped them escape without you, or did you just think of yourself?"

A wave of intense guilt poured down the channel of darkness, and the Chalaine had to fight away her own feelings of guilt as it passed. The scenes before her were so poignant and so private, she almost felt as if she should leave, but the healer within her impelled her to stay, made her watch in hopes that she could find some way to help Gen build his defense again, as he had done for her.

"Then your feelings are suddenly resurrected when you see her in danger," the voice continued, "and what good did it do?"

The Chalaine watched in horror as Gen fought desperately to save Regina, only to fail. She felt his sense of inadequacy and uselessness. Never in her protected life had the Chalaine seen such depravity, and inwardly she pitied Gen for the unfairness and for the mercy that never found him.

The voice continued its cadence like a steady drumbeat of doom. She watched as Gen read the note from his beloved master explaining how he had killed himself so he could no longer be used to manipulate Gen. All the while, the river deepened as Gen's spirit failed.

"And so then you come by dumb luck into the service

of the Chalaine. Do you think she needs you, Gen? Were there not a hundred soldiers for fodder before, and will there not be a thousand after? Do you think you've redeemed yourself from Regina's blood because you saved the Chalaine from Chertanne's lust? What difference will it make? Whether she is forced to be with him now or later, she will be with him. She is his, after all. The only thing you've done is prolong the agony of her waiting for it to happen."

The Chalaine felt anger within her rise, and yet something about the voice's words rang true. Her agony was there, her dread of Chertanne growing daily. Had she not just told her mother the same? But the voice ignored what Gen had done. Given her dignity. While she didn't doubt that Chertanne would do his best to strip her of it if he could, she still had it and would ever retain a portion of it. The voice told Gen nothing of the respect and goodness he had inspired, the web of hope that was spun at every telling of his bravery and honor.

As the voice continued its parade of disparagement, the Chalaine grew more and more incensed and indignant at its distortions, omissions, and exaggerations. Fear gripped her as she realized that Gen believed every word, ever eroding his will and snuffing out his life.

Time was short, and in the darkness she spoke. She wanted to say a hundred things to express her sorrow and pity. She wanted to tell him of her saved dignity, of Fenna's love and devotion. She wanted him to know what he meant to those who knew him. But from the great mass of words, she could only find three to yell over and over in the darkness.

"I need you."

At her cries, the voice ceased. And then the Chalaine felt a presence, strong and evil, turn its attention toward her. What she thought was merely a part of Gen's mind was something else entirely, something awful beyond imagination. She felt its surprise at her presence, and though she could see no form, it saw her, grinning like a hunter who had at last cornered a fox after a long chase.

"And see, Gen," the voice scorned him, "that you will be the instrument of her doom, after all. For here she has come in her pity for your wretchedness!"

The Chalaine felt something grip her and hold her fast, pulling her further into the darkness. She fought it, trying to pull and thrash her way back toward the door, but the force was too strong. She began to scream as she came closer to the void, feeling the destruction that awaited her if she passed through.

And then Ethris was there. She couldn't see him, but she could feel him behind her, grasping for her. There were others as well, and she cried out to them. Pulling away from the evil presence with every ounce of will she had left, she reached backward, feeling a pull come from the other direction. A fierce struggle ensued, and she felt herself nearly torn apart in the contest of wills. Just when she felt all was lost, the darkness was shut away, and the Chalaine tumbled out of Gen's tortured mind.

She opened her eyes. Ethris, still in breeches from his convalescence, stood behind her with two Puremen, all with their hands on her head. Sweat ran down his hairless body, and were it not for the Puremen, he would have collapsed on the floor. Jaron, on seeing her awake, came to her side, face relieved. The Chalaine felt dizzy and sick and needed Jaron's help to stand. The Puremen helped Ethris to a chair.

"Mikkik nearly struck a fatal blow this night," Ethris said. "Foolish girl! Jaron, get her to her Mother and have the Pontiff examine her. Everyone leave. I need to be alone."

The Chalaine leaned on Jaron and he guided her toward the door. "Thank you Ethris," she said. "I thought I was lost."

"And so you were," Ethris replied crankily. "But thank me not. It was Gen who shut Mikkik from his mind. Without that, we would have all been lost. Now go. No one is allowed in this room anymore without my leave. I need to think."

The Chalaine let Jaron lead her away toward her apartments. Puremen were dispatched to find the Pontiff and her mother. All the while, she couldn't help but feel bitter about the irony; she had gone into Gen's mind to save him and had instead been rescued by him again. But Ethris's belief that Gen had forced the evil presence from his mind gave her hope that perhaps his life would strengthen and return.

Her mother was already at the apartments when she arrived, as was Fenna. Both frowned at her with worry as she came in and fell exhausted on her bed.

"What's wrong, dear?" her mother asked.

"I tried to heal him, mother. . ." And at this she found herself unable to speak as the memories of what she had seen and felt of Gen's life overwhelmed her.

When she came to herself, tears ran unchecked down her face. "It was awful, mother. Awful. The things he's been through are beyond anything I had imagined. The evil one himself came for him, sought to use him, and he rejected him to save me."

For several minutes, the Chalaine was quite unconscious of anything, only aware of a mother and a friend who grieved with her.

When the Pontiff arrived, she gathered herself as best she could. He wore a simple black robe and held a staff tipped with a clear stone. The wrinkled face regarded her with concern.

"The Puremen told me what happened, Chalaine. It is unfortunate that you ignored the counsel of my brethren and sought to heal him. It is obvious that the demon opened a way for the dark one to war with Gen's mind. It is fortunate he had the strength to close the link when you were threatened. An act of saintly virtue, indeed. And while you may have inadvertently saved his life, you must—must!—realize that you cannot take such chances! You are part of the salvation of this world, and no one—not even a faithful soldier like Gen—is worth throwing the world away."

The Chalaine nodded and held to her mother's hand, though she still felt no guilt over her attempt to save her protector.

The Pontiff exhaled and extended his hand to indicate she should sit in a nearby chair. "Now I must ensure that no taint of the evil one remains within you. The enemy has many tricks."

The Pontiff laid a wrinkled hand upon her head and chanted softly for nearly an hour. When he was done, he leaned heavily upon his staff.

"It appears you escaped harm, except a deep sadness which I feel upon you. Sadness, though, is not evil unless it overwhelms us. While it may seem hollow, child, be of good cheer. You have many that care for you and a great destiny that lies ahead of you."

After a short silence, the Pontiff shuffled toward the door, turning before going out. "We shall have the betrothal in two days. We can no longer afford to wait. Our enemy is clever and all the guards and walls have done little thus far to keep out the danger. I shall summon the Council of Padras to come to help protect you during the winter. Sleep well."

As the Pontiff left, Jaron and Captain Tolbrook poked their heads in.

"Is she well?" Jaron asked.

"She is fine, Jaron. Close the door, please," her mother ordered. Once they were alone, the First Mother removed the Chalaine's veil, placing it in the armoire with the others. Tenderly, she combed her daughter's hair while Fenna wiped away her tears and stroked her arm. Gradually, the Chalaine felt the sadness fade, turning into a dull ache. She felt worn.

Mirelle rubbed the Chalaine's cheek. "We will go, my daughter, and let you rest."

"Please stay with me tonight," the Chalaine begged. "There is a story I need to tell you, tell you both, about Gen."

The First Mother and the handmaiden sat on the bed where the Chalaine lay and listened as she began. "Where Gen lived, in Tell, there was a girl. Her name was Regina. . ."

CHAPTER 26 - MEMORY

Gen awoke, inhaling deeply. He lay still for many moments trying to dispel the fog from his mind. He felt hungry, but there was no pain or injury that he could detect. The struggle for control of his mind and emotions left him tired in spirit, but he felt unburdened, as if what had pulled him down for so long had been stripped of its weight. Pain for Rafael and Regina was still there, but overcoming the darkness forced him to put sorrow behind him that he might do his duty and find himself again.

Memories of being crushed by the demon rushed back to him, and in panic he wondered if the Chalaine, or anyone, survived. During the struggle within his mind he thought he heard her call to him, and it was that call that awoke within him a need to live, a reason to throw off the despair the dark presence conjured within him. But still, he couldn't tell if it was real. The whole experience seemed like a nightmare.

He opened his eyes and came to his elbows, finding himself in a small stone room, empty except for Ethris, who was dressed in white as if prepared for a ceremony. He sat on a chair at the foot of the bed, face determined. Within his eyes Gen saw a battle being fought. In his hand he carried the Truth Staff, and as Gen came to a sitting position, Ethris rose and came to his side, placing the head of the Staff on Gen's bare chest and pushing him back down. Gen was surprised at the Mage's intensity but said nothing, waiting for an explanation.

"Hold there, boy."

Ethris stared into his eyes, searching for something. Gen, while feeling hungry, felt fit and strong, and he knew he could escape, save Ethris's magic. But Gen guessed what Ethris was about, for Gen also wrestled with what the demon had said in the Chapel that night, and with what the dark entity that had sought to destroy him had revealed. It was a notion so preposterous that he had dismissed it as a trick of Mikkik's to increase his despair.

"I have sat here the better part of two days," Ethris began, voice steady, "and three times I decided to kill you where you lie. No one would have thought it odd that you died, for you were close many times. But in the end I couldn't do it, at least not before I talked to you."

"You heard what the demon called me," Gen said.

"Yes. 'Torka bilex ur madda Ilch! Ilch-madda fen-gur enea ko. Chak Diggat, chak Ilch Murmit Cho.' I shall never forget. While it was the first I had ever heard the corrupted speech in person, its meaning was plain: *You have left your master's way, Ilch. My creature is not my own. This betrayal will be punished. Death everlasting is yours.* The creature in the Chapel that night was a Rukatahm, a puppet demon of Mikkik, created long ago. The voice that spoke through it was the voice of Mikkik himself. But you knew that, didn't you?"

"How could I be the Ilch?" Gen protested, ignoring the question. "I do not bear the mark of prophecy, and I have risked my life for the Chalaine more than once! The Ilch is supposed to be some dark creature bent on her destruction. That is not me! I could have killed her and Chertanne a hundred times over by now."

"And that is why I could not kill you. But make no

mistake. I will kill you and anyone who seeks to harm the Chalaine."

"As would I."

"So you say. But listen well. You do not bear the mark of the unveiled moon upon your left foot as written, but there are many scars there, so it may have been removed to hide your identity. The Ilch was to have no mother and father, but rather be a creature created by Mikkik. You are an orphan. When the moon Trys is unveiled, great power will come into the hands of the Ha'Ulrich and the Ilch, their magic set against each other, one for good and the other evil. That latent ability is within you, Gen. I searched for it as you rested, and just as Chertanne, Savior of the World, will gain his magic on the return of the light of Trys, so will Gen, the serf orphan from Tolnor."

"But. . ."

"There is more, Gen, but you must now answer my questions under this Staff, or I swear that you will not leave this room alive."

Gen lay back as Ethris pressed the Staff down even harder, pinning him to the mattress. He could do little more than meet Ethris's stare, the Magician's mind intruding upon his own.

"Do you remember concealing the birthmark on your foot or have memory of anyone else doing so?"

"No."

"Has anyone taught you magic?"

"No."

"Has anyone instructed you to kill the Chalaine or the Ha'Ulrich?"

"No."

"Are you determined to fight Mikkik and his allies?"

"Yes."

"Will you protect the Chalaine with your life?"

"I have and I will."

Ethris lifted the Staff and shook his head in wonder,

returning to his seat.

"I do not fully understand how this can be, Gen, but somehow the prophecy has been turned on its head! The one destined to destroy the Chalaine now protects her with as much devotion as the Ilch was to have hate. It is unfathomable! Someone or something powerful has intervened in the prophecy through you."

"The simpler explanation, Ethris, is that I'm not the Ilch!"

The idea of being the Ilch seemed so wild to Gen, that he could not accept it. The fanged monster, servant of Mikkik, searching the world to tear apart the Chalaine was not who he was, nor ever could be.

Ethris ran a hand over his bald head. "I think you are, Gen, for there is more. I said I do not fully understand how this could be, but I understand some. When the Chalaine tried to heal you—a stupid thing to do, I might add—I had to enter your mind to try to pull her away from Mikkik.

"In my search for her, I found something—something I went to revisit later—as you slept. Someone of surpassing power has placed magical seals on certain parts of your memory, as if he wished to protect you from what was there or perhaps protect others from what you would become if you knew what was there. The seals are meticulously and skillfully done, meant to be hidden, and only accomplished Mages, of which there are few, would have even noticed them. They are warded completely against the sight of evil. No small feat."

"But what could they be protecting me from? How could a few sealed memories have changed me from harmless Gen to the infamous Ilch?"

"Not a few memories, Gen. Hundreds of them. Things that you've seen, heard, and done that you cannot remember. We all forget things, so it would be difficult for you to find the holes in your mind, but they are there."

"There are holes," Gen confirmed, something Ethris

said tickling his memory. "I remember being visited by someone, though who it was I cannot recall. It's happened more than once, but I cannot remember anything specific about what was said or who said it."

Ethris rubbed his chin. "There is only one way to know what was happening. I could remove one of the seals."

"Then do it," Gen replied without hesitation. "This must be settled."

Ethris nodded his agreement. "I will do it, and I will watch with you as you remember. My reasoning says I must destroy you, but something within me senses a greater power at work, and I am reluctant to kill without great need."

Ethris laid his hands upon Gen's head, and Gen closed his eyes.

It was a bright autumn morning. Gen was but a boy, having seen but ten harvests come and go. The house was cold, and the fire burned low. Rafael had gone outside in search of more firewood, though Gen knew there was none left. Rafael had told him he would teach him more about music that day, but the lesson would be miserable if they couldn't heat the house. Numb fingers could not play the lute, and for Rafael it was doubly worse; the cold stiffened his already aching joints.

"Well, boy," Rafael said as he entered, face angry, "it seems as if we have neglected the wood pile yet again. Jesten has gone to Sipton for the next few days, so we'll have to get some wood ourselves the old fashioned way. Get your cloak!"

Gen jumped at the chance to get out of the house. Most of his lessons required him to stay inside and read when other kids got to run around and play. He wasn't even old enough to be an apprentice, but Rafael had treated him like one ever since Pureman Millershim had given the old bard custody of him.

After leaving the house, Rafael grabbed the old, dull ax from the barn, fingering it and shaking his head.

"Well, Gen, it's going to be a long day. So while we walk, let's have a lesson or two. As you know, a bard must learn skill with words, to say things in different ways to evoke different emotions. Take this ax, for instance. If someone asked why it took so long for us to chop wood today, I could answer as any other person and say, 'my axe wasn't very sharp and it took me a long time to cut the wood.' A true statement, but a boring one. So, lad, we must spice it up. Make it humorous or tragic so that people can feel the levity or pain of the situation. Are you with me?"

"I think so."

"All right, then. Let's suppose that tomorrow we're walking through town and that layabout friend of yours, what's his name?"

"Gant."

"Yes, Gant. Suppose Gant comes up and says, 'Hey, where were you yesterday? I dragged my lazy bones by your house to play several times and you were never there.' You say, 'We spent all day chopping firewood.' Gant replies, 'Well, what took you so long?' What do you reply?"

Gen thought for several moments. "I would say, 'The ax was as dull as Hubert Showles's brain.'"

Rafael laughed. "Very good! The humorous approach worked to perfection. Now change it so the answer conveys a more serious, sad feeling."

"The ax was as dull as one of Rafael's history lessons."

Rafael kicked him in the seat of his pants, smiling in spite of himself. "Watch it, you little scamp. You show respect or I won't teach you anything and you'll be a rock-brain just like Hubert!"

"Sorry, master."

Rafael continued his lessons on artful language, having Gen describe the dew on the grass, the golden and red leaves of the trees, and various people in the town. In no time they were in the forest, hunting for deadfall among the fallen leaves at the edge of the trees. Rafael found a dead pine, still standing. He removed his cloak and began to chop it down.

"Well, while we're here, Gen, let me tell you a little about this place, and it'll be your history lesson for the day. A long time ago, before the Shattering, this forest didn't exist. It was grassy plain all the way to the sea, and its name was Aumat. No one lived on Aumat Plain, but during the First Mikkikian War, the races of the world were driven ever westward, Mikkik's forces sweeping across the land like the shadow of a dark mountain in the valley at sunset.

"Near this place, the elves and humans worked together under Aldradan Mikmir to build a fort against the coming tide of evil, throwing up great mounds of earth and using what little wood there was to fence it with. It wasn't beautiful, but it was strong, and when the Uyumaak, giants, gek, and demons fell upon it, the brave warriors and Mages managed to drive them off. Many were killed. Blood, black and red, flowed freely. It was the first battle of Aumat and the first victory for good in quite some time."

"Was there a second battle of Aumat, then?" Gen asked. Rafael stopped chopping and leaned on his ax.

"There was. On hearing news of the defeat at Aumat, Mikkik was furious and sent an army twice the size of the one that had been defeated toward the crude fort. When the elven scouts heard of it, they trembled with fear, and many considered fleeing southward for their lives."

"But to Aumat came a Magician, Morrinne. Without even speaking to human or elven generals, he laid a great enchantment on Aumat, and when the armies woke, they were encompassed about by trees. It is said that everywhere the west wind blew in from the sea, trees grew, and grew quickly. Morrinne then confessed what he had done and earned the name Morrinne Treemaker. I can only imagine the confusion of the enemy when they arrived to find

Aumat missing, engulfed in the great protection of trees."

"Undaunted, Mikkik's armies poured into the forest, but in the wood the elves had the upper hand and slaughtered the first wave to enter. The Uyumaak then sought to burn the forest down, but even as they tried a great wind and rain kicked up, thwarting their attempts. The battle lasted for days, but in the end, Mikkik and his creatures were routed. The armies of the enemy retreated east, and Middle Peace began.

Gen looked at the trees around him with new wonder and respect, imagining the brave warriors running between the great boles and killing the evil hordes.

Rafael leaned down and put his face close to his pupil's. "In fact, I bet if one were to look around and dig a bit, he might find a spearhead or even a link of armor buried here and there."

Gen needed no further encouragement, and with an eye to the ground began trudging about searching for a likely spot to dig.

"Don't go too far!" Rafael warned. "I'll need help carrying this wood . . . in a while."

The sounds of chopping faded as Gen walked about, kicking up leaves and pulling up rocks. Ahead of him he saw a hill with a thick copse at the base. In his mind's eye, he imagined an elven archer in its darkness, waiting for a hapless Uyumaak to wander by. And it was there that he started to dig. The soil was dark, cold, and moist under his hands, but after several minutes he found nothing more than bugs and small rocks.

Disappointed, he turned to leave when he found he could no longer move. Casting his eyes about frantically, he saw a figure, only partially visible in outlines created by the shadows between the light streaking through the branches. It was a woman, tall and slender, though her features were lost in shadow.

"It is time for your next lesson," she said. "When Trys is

unveiled, you will be filled with power. You must learn how it can be manipulated and used. Trys is, primarily, the power to create and transmute. While you cannot do it yet, you will in time. Take this dirt, for example. It can easily be changed into stone by changing certain properties of it. Imagine the armies of the Ha'Ulrich and the Chalaine marching proudly across a muddy field when suddenly they are trapped, their feet and their horses' hooves imprisoned in stone!"

Gen trembled. "But why should I wish to hurt the Blessed One or the Chalaine? They are to save Ki'Hal. That is what Pureman Millerhsim says."

"Remember you nothing of what I say? The time is too short to repeat the lessons! Through treachery this world's God was stripped of his power! The Chalaine and the Ha'Ulrich are a farce, a deception played by those who crave control. My master will free the races of this world from their bondage of ignorance and fantasy!

"While the Ki'Hal lauds the Ha'Ulrich and his wench, you know the truth! It will not be easy, but you must learn all you can. You must destroy the Chalaine before the Millim Eri can again set their hand upon the world to turn it here and there as they wish! You are chosen for leadership, for power, and a throne! While now you will be reviled, persecuted, and hunted, when the truth is known, you will be worshiped! Do you understand?"

"Yes," Gen replied, confused but cowed by the woman's vehemence, agreeing merely to silence her and speed her departure.

"Good. Open your mind. My master sends another lesson. He bids me tell you that dirt to stone is a simple beginning. There is so much more!"

The method required to do the spell was burned forcefully into his memory. When the instruction finished, his head hurt.

"Tell no one of this!" the woman continued. "You must

remain a secret to all until the time is ripe, for no one will understand. They are all deceived, save you!"

The personage faded, and Gen fell to the ground, weak and exhausted. How could the whole world have been deceived? They chanted praises to the Chalaine and the Ha'Ulrich every day. Were they really part of some plot by unknown powers? Had they been tricked too? Why was he chosen?

As he lay thinking, a robin fluttered down and landed beside him. Gen marveled that it would come so close to him, but he shrank back in fear as it transformed into a being that awed him to behold. The towering figure had ears and a face like the drawings Gen had seen of elves, but rather than being thin and delicate, he was strong and tall, taller than the tallest man Gen had ever seen. White hair hung loosely down his back, and his skin was so pale that it seemed that light came from it. He wore a green cloak open to reveal a cream robe cinched with a belt that was fashioned from woven bark. Despite his fear, Gen could not help but think that he was majestic and beautiful.

The Being reached down and touched him, and everything went black. The next thing he knew, he was helping Rafael carry wood back to the house, disappointed that he had found no artifact of the great battle or fortress of Aumat. Everything that had happened with the apparition was forgotten, as was the being that came after.

Gen opened his eyes. Ethris lifted his hands from Gen's head and sat down heavily upon the chair at the foot of the bed.

"It is extraordinary! They still live!"

"Who?" Gen asked, still worried that Ethris might end his life.

"The Millim Eri, what people commonly think of as Ministrants. They were the elf masters and servants of the Gods in ancient times. Their lore has long been clouded.

They all but disappeared somewhere during the First Mikkikian War, just before the rise of the human Mages. The elves refused to speak of them, and few humans know they existed at all, at least with that name. But I have seen one now, albeit by proxy."

"What do they want with me?" Gen asked, mind racing.

"Isn't it obvious? They still have a hand in the affairs of Ki'Hal, which I count as a great blessing. You are the Ilch, Gen, but in their wisdom they hid the persuasions and teachings of Mikkik, your creator, from you. Rather than grow into the evil instrument of Mikkik, you have grown to be one of his fiercest enemies. Ha!"

Ethris stood again, babbling in uncharacteristic excitement. "It is so perfect, so clever! Turn the enemy's weapon against him!"

"You will not kill me, then?"

"Eldaloth help me, no! I will not interfere with what the Millim Eri have done. In fact, I shall do my best to push it along beyond what they have accomplished."

Ethris pointed his Staff absentmindedly toward the table where new clothes, boots, and a sword had been set out in anticipation of Gen's awakening. Gen rose and began to dress.

"You see, Gen, Chertanne has had training in how to use Trysmagic since he was a boy so that in the day he comes into his power, he will be ready to use it in Eldaloth's cause. Mikkik provided you with the same training, probably better, hoping that you could use it in his, but it is lost to you.

"While I cannot practice Trysmagic, I can teach you the principles of it and point you to tome after tome of knowledge concerning it. You have little time to learn, but if you don't, you shall have no defense against Chertanne, for rest assured that he has not forgotten the shaming you gave him."

"Ethris," Gen said, "during my struggle with the poison,

Mikkik told me that there were many that would take my place. Will it really matter on which side I fall?"

"Mikkik is a liar, Gen. Your defection is a deep blow to him and his purposes. You are a unique creature—if you'll forgive the appellation—and not easily replaceable. If we can keep Chertanne interested in something other than himself for long enough, then there will be two powerful Mages to fight evil instead of one.

"That there are many other powerful ones who have been deceived and who serve him, you know well, as do I. But he created you to be his servant, and a powerful one, when the time comes. The Millim Eri have seen to it that you serve a different cause."

Gen picked up the black shirt of his uniform, noticing the two small circles representing the moons Myn and Duam pinned on the collar opposite the usual sword-Trys pin on the other.

"What is this?" Gen asked.

"We were named Defenders of the Faith during our unconscious convalescence." Gen saw the same pins on Ethris's robe. "The sword, Gen, is a gift from the First Mother as a reward for your bravery. The scabbard is new, but the blade is old and has magical properties. To protect Mirelle from undue protest and argument, I will tell you no more of it other than to say many would object to you carrying it."

Ethris stepped forward, and placed his hands on Gen's shoulders, forcing him to look into his eyes. "I hope you understand that what we have discussed here goes to no one else. No one! If anyone got wind of who you really were, no amount of persuasion on my part would keep you from certain and immediate death. And while I can see a wise hand in what the Millim Eri have accomplished, there is still danger. Prophecy has outlined your destiny, and Mikkik may yet try to bend you to his purpose. We shall see if what the Millim Eri have done can rewrite your fate."

Gen understood, though he still couldn't see how he could be the Ilch, the Destroyer, the Slayer. He doubted he would ever fully believe it.

"Now we should go," Ethris said. "The betrothal should have ended by now. If you are like I was when I emerged from sleep, you are strong but starving. You can get something to eat at the celebration. Your presence will lift the spirits of several who have missed you, especially Fenna. I hear the girl barely left your side."

Gen smiled for the first time in a long time. He knew Fenna had feelings for him, but his mourning for Regina had kept him from returning any affection. To discover that she had watched over him touched his heart unexpectedly, and for once, the feeling didn't disappear into an empty void. That emptiness seemed gone, and he hoped his control hadn't left with it.

Chapter 27 - Reward

Ethris opened the door and led Gen up the steps. Gen felt the air cool as they ascended to the main floor. As they walked out into the brisk evening in the courtyard he noticed that the trees had cast off most of their foliage.

"How long have I been asleep?" Gen asked.

"Almost three weeks. I awakened only a couple of days before you did."

"The demon struck you, then?"

"Yes. I've quite the scar to show for it. Of course, a scar is nothing new to you, is it? There is much more I need to inquire of you, but our meetings must be few and in secret."

The sound of a celebration on the castle grounds came from the courtyard in front of the Great Hall, but Ethris led him down a different path, a long way through gardens and guard stations that kept them from the crowds. The few soldiers they did see saluted them smartly, and after they passed, the soldiers whispered excitedly to one another.

"We seem to be inspiring a lot of chatter," Gen observed. He was surprised by Ethris's hearty laugh.

"Ah, Gen. You simply have no idea."

Gen shrugged off the odd comment as they entered the castle through a side gate and crossed the lawn to the kitchens. A lantern hung over a stone bench next to the door, and Ethris signaled for him to sit on it. After entering the kitchen for a few moments, he returned with a plate full of food—bread, venison, and sliced apple—and a mug of cider.

"Enjoy the meal, Gen. Captain Tolbrook has taken over your duties in your absence. If you want to relieve him when you are finished, you can, though I'm sure no one would blame you if you simply wanted to enjoy the evening. I will be along later. There are some new preparations I must make, and I will talk with you again by and by."

Gen dove into the food before Ethris could even turn to leave, each bite tasting better than he could imagine. Before long, the plate was empty and the mug drained, and he set his plate aside and relaxed for a few moments to gather his thoughts and enjoy the pleasant feeling of being full.

Realizing he would see Fenna, he went to his rooms beneath the Chalaine's tower to retrieve something he had been meaning to give her for some time. Some of the servants and guards saw him as he passed, and, as before, his presence inspired a great deal of chatter and excited whispering.

As he returned to the lawns outside the kitchen, several children raced out of the open door and chased each other around the yard. By their fine dress—crumpled, untucked, and untied though it was—Gen could tell they were noble born, no doubt escaping tedious formalities in search of some fun. They took no notice of him for a moment as he stood and watched them, but soon, a girl, whom Gen reckoned no older that eight, stopped and pointed.

"Look!" she whispered surreptitiously. "It is one of the Dark Guard!"

"Leave him alone, Jelenna!" one of the older boys said.

"He's probably on important business."

"No, he's not!" Jelenna returned petulantly. "He's just standing around."

She skipped over and stood staring at Gen, hands on hips and face set. This dark-haired, dark-eyed girl would be a proud and beautiful lady someday. She was certainly fearless. Gen stared back at her, amused at her bravado. Suddenly her eyes and mouth went wide and she gasped.

"Ian! It's that one we heard about in Church! The scarred one with the dead face!"

Before he knew it, Gen found himself surrounded by seven gawking children.

"What's your name?" Gen asked the girl, feeling a bit uncomfortable with a gaggle of children staring at him as if he were a statue.

"I am Miss Jelenna Magravaine," she replied with a perfectly executed curtsy, "daughter of Regent Julim and Lady Mergem Magravaine."

"My name is Gen."

"I know!" she said. "Is your face really dead?"

"No," Gen said. "Watch." He made several silly faces, ending in a scary one that made the kids cower in surprise, all save Jelenna.

"Then why do people say your face is dead?" she pressed.

"Well, Jelenna, does your mommy. . ."

"Her name is Lady Mergem Magravaine!"

"Forgive me. Does the Lady Mergem Magravaine let you giggle in Church?"

"No."

"Well, I'm not permitted make faces when I'm about the Chalaine's secret business." Gen gave them a furtive wink, and they all nodded in understanding.

"Is she pretty?" a boy with grass stained pants asked, feeling a little more brave.

"I suppose so," Gen replied, "though no man is allowed

to see her, so I don't know for sure. I'm not really supposed to talk about it, but I'll tell you a little secret." Gen leaned down and motioned the children in close. "I hear she has a big nose," he whispered.

"Un-uh!" Jelenna protested. The other children giggled. "You were just joking, weren't you?"

"Yes, Jelenna," Gen chuckled. "But I wonder if you might do me a favor."

"What?"

"I have to go on duty soon, which is a secret. But I want to see someone first. Do you know Miss Fenna Fairedale?"

"Yes," Jelenna replied.

"Could you tell her that one of the Dark Guard needs to see her and then bring her to me? Don't tell her my name, though. It's a secret surprise."

"Okay!" she agreed, bounding off into the kitchen. Gen shooed the other children off and entered the kitchen to return the plate and mug he had left on the bench. The first cook to see him was Marna, who had greeted him so enthusiastically his first day at the castle. She dropped a wooden bowl she was carrying and stared at him with much the same look Jelenna had given him. Then she charged, arms outstretched. Gen, hands full, couldn't defend himself from another powdery hug. When she pulled away, she was smiling, tears running down here face.

"Eldaloth be praised, Gen," she said, wiping her eyes. "We thought ya lost there for a bit. We prayed for ya, the forehead to the ground kinda prayin', that you'd be spared. Does my heart good to see you. But look! I've done it again!"

"Thank you Marna," Gen said, smiling as she swatted at the flower on his uniform, adding as much as she subtracted. "And it is good to see you. The food was more delicious than anything I can remember."

"Do you want some more? I'd give you the best right off the spit! Or will you be going in? What a celebration that will be!"

"I will go in shortly. Where do you want these?" Gen held up his plate and mug.

"I'll take those," she said, snatching them from his hand. "I'll take them home and put them on my mantle. The plate, mug, and fork used by Gen during his first meal after the demon attack! I'll be famous."

She turned to find somewhere to put them and the others in the kitchen started haggling with her for the individual pieces. Gen left as her fellow cooks tossed offers of money for the items. Exhaling nervously, he alternately sat on the bench and paced around the grass, finding it difficult to settle himself.

And she came, Jelenna dragging her by the hand. Gen realized he hadn't paid attention to how beautiful she was, and now, in the light of the lantern, dressed in a blue gown, brown hair pulled away from her face, she was as precious a jewel as Gen had ever seen. Green eyes led the change in her expression from sadness to joy, and she was in his arms laughing and crying so quickly that Gen could scarce take it in. After several long moments, she pulled away, wiping her eyes and straightening her gown.

"I'm sorry," she apologized. "This is most unseemly."

Gen took her hand and kissed it, motioning for her to sit with him. Fenna put her hands in her lap and looked at them, and Gen, sensing her nervousness, spoke first.

"Fenna," Gen began, fumbling for what to say, "I was told that you watched over me as I fought the poison for so many days. I want you to know that I am in your debt and that your devotion will not be forgotten."

She smiled and turned away embarrassed. "It was nothing."

"It certainly was something! Please accept my gratitude."

She nodded and silence reigned for several moments, save for the children playing and the banging of pots and pans.

Fenna finally spoke up. "Gen, the Chalaine told me about Regina. I am so sorry. It wasn't your fault. You did everything to save her."

It was Gen's turn to look away. Memories of Regina's death and his inability to save her ran across his mind afresh, threatening the new-found happiness he had felt since awakening. But Fenna was there, putting her arm around him and leaning her head on his shoulder. Her warmth drove away the dark thoughts, and he sat enjoying her company for many minutes.

"Fenna," he said, rising, "As much as I would love to have you to myself all evening, I think it is time I returned and resumed my duty after such a long absence. Did the betrothal go well?"

"Compared to the last one, I'd say yes," Fenna grinned. "But you should go. There are many who are anxious for your return. Shall I have the Chamberlain give you a grand entrance?"

"No!" Gen objected. "I don't like attention. I'll just slip in quietly and relieve Captain Tolbrook."

"Have it your way," she acquiesced. "But I thought bards liked the attention."

"She saw a lot of my life, then?"

"Not that she would tell," Fenna answered. "But I think we'd both like to hear you sing again."

Gen felt a tap on his arm. "You can sing?" Jelenna asked, appearing from behind a nearby bush where she had been spying on the couple.

"I used to sing," he answered, "but it's been a long time. Not much time for it now that I have my secret duties and all."

"Well," Jelenna said, sitting on the bench next to Fenna. "You've got time now, don't you? Sing me something since mommy, um, the Lady Magravaine, probably won't sing to me tonight."

Gen hesitated. He hadn't had it in his heart to sing

anything for so long that it felt like any attempt would be starting from the beginning.

"Yes, Gen," Fenna goaded, "sing us something! My mommy, I mean the Lady Fairedale, hardly sings to me at all anymore."

Fenna's eyes were playful, as Gen remembered Regina's to be.

"All right, then. Just one little song, and then I have to go. I'm a bit rusty though, so don't expect much more than caterwauling."

Gen crouched down and took Jelenna by the hand.

Old man winter, quiet and bitter,
Cradled a storm in frostbitten hands,
And with a breath from his icy lips
Blew it forth on the land.

With thick clouds and swirling snow it came;
With biting wind and ice it blew,
Old man winter enshrouding in white,
All that the summer sun knew.

But on some forgotten hilltop,
Struggling in a deepening drift,
An untimely crimson rose broke forth,
Blooming winter's springtime gift.

And old man winter, quiet with wonder,
Wept at the rose as the storm retreated,
For even the iciest heart can thaw,
When by beauty it is defeated.

Jelenna and Fenna clapped, praising him warmly. Feeling embarrassed, Gen stood.

"I really should be going, now, but," he reached into his coat pocket and retrieved Fenna's colors, "I am excessively late in returning this to you. I hope this is a special enough occasion."

Fenna looked on the verge of tears again as she took it from his hand. "It is."

"I thank you again. I look forward to talking with you soon."

"And I with you," Fenna returned. "The Chalaine is sitting at the table next to Chertanne, as usual. Tolbrook is to the left of the dais near the kitchen door. You should find him easily. I will come in before too long, but I wish to stay here for a while."

Gen bowed to her and went in search of Tolbrook, finding him watching from a shadowy recess where Fenna told him he would be. Owing to the loud celebration, he managed to relieve Tolbrook quietly and unnoticed despite the Captain's shock at seeing him. Gen settled in and took account of his surroundings.

In comparison to the feast held when the Blessed One first arrived, the one celebrating the betrothal was sparsely attended. Only high-ranking nobles and aristocrats had been permitted entry. A cadre of religious men sat against the wall, Prelate Obelard among them, displaying disdain at the revelry around them. The Pontiff was at one end of the head table, and across from him was an empty seat normally reserved for Ethris.

The First Mother chatted with Regent Ogbith and his wife, while the Chalaine stared off into the crowd. Chertanne busied himself with eating, carousing with the serving women, and bantering with Warlords from his own kingdom.

Also sitting near the Chalaine was a half-elven woman, and Gen immediately recognized her—Maewen Birchwood, daughter of Samian. So powerful were the desires and memories of the man who had shared so much of himself with him, that Gen had to exert all his control to keep from running up to the woman and gushing a hundred things Samian wanted to tell her. Gen wasn't sure how he would ever be able to do justice to what the man had felt for her, but knew he would have to try sooner or later.

With effort he turned his attention elsewhere, noticing the Dark Guard placed strategically around the room, though the apprentices were nowhere to be seen. Many other officers of the castle guard were present as well, and Regent Ogbith permitted them to mingle and celebrate with the crowd. After several minutes Fenna entered and squeezed his arm.

"They don't know you're here yet, do they?" she whispered. Gen answered by putting his finger to his lips. Fenna's expression turned mischievous and she mounted the dais.

"Don't you dare!" he said to no avail and watched as Fenna went and whispered in the ear of the First Mother. Mirelle squinted into the shadows and smiled at him, excusing herself from the table. Rather than come to him, Fenna and Mirelle headed out into the crowd, the Chalaine watching them as they walked away. To his dismay, he saw them find the Chamberlain by the door. Mirelle threaded her way back to the table, Regent Ogbith and her daughter questioning her as she sat. Fenna went to stand by an older man and woman whom Gen guessed were the Regent and Lady Fairedale.

After the First Mother sat down and the curiosity of the table was fully aroused, the herald slammed his staff onto the granite floor with three deafening taps, silencing the music and quieting the crowd.

"Chalaine, Ha'Ulrich, First Mother, Gentlemen and Gentlewomen, it is with the greatest pleasure that I direct your attention to the front of the room and present Gen, protector of the Chalaine, Dark Guard, Defender of the Faith, Demon's Bane, and newest Lord of the Realm. We thank Eldaloth for his recovery and exult in his return to service."

Reluctantly, Gen stepped from the shadows and raised his arm in salute. The thunderous applause nearly bowled him over. Raucous cheers and even singing broke out. Everyone stood, even a mostly unwilling Chertanne, and clapped.

Gen kept his face smooth, glancing about to find Fenna beaming. Gen resolved to ask her what had happened over the last few weeks. Only after he gave another wave to the crowd and sunk back into the shadows did the noise die down and the celebration continue. He noticed Chertanne staring daggers at him, but the Pontiff descending the dais blocked the view. Gen inclined his head as he approached.

"It is good to see that you have at last recovered, young man. You gave us a good scare."

"It is good to return, Holiness."

"Yes. As you can see, it has done much to lift the spirit of the people. For that, you are an invaluable ally to the purposes of Eldaloth in these troubled times. I shall speak with you again soon. Not many live to hear Mikkik's voice and survive unscathed. I would know more of the demon and your struggle with its poison that some provision might be prepared against them."

"As you wish."

"Bless you, my son."

Gen couldn't help wondering what it would do for the spirit of the people if they found out he was really the Ilch, should it prove to be true. He still couldn't accept it.

He settled back to watch the Chalaine who was signaling for Fenna to come forward. Once she did, the First Mother, the Chalaine, and Fenna came to him, cornering him in the recess.

The Chalaine bowed formally to him, but Mirelle embraced him warmly. "It is good to see you well, Gen."

"Thank you, First Mother."

"So," Mirelle continued, "what do you think of your

new titles?"

"Demon's Bane, I'm afraid, is a little much. Demon's Fodder would be more accurate. Titles don't suit me well, and plain old Gen will be fine, if you don't mind."

"You weren't impressed with 'Lord of the Realm'?" Mirelle pressed. Gen thought for a moment. That particular title had escaped his notice among all the others.

"What in the Realm, exactly, am I Lord of?"

"Oh not much," Mirelle said coyly. "Just a little elevation in rank, a tiny plot of land. . ."

"A tiny plot!" Fenna exclaimed. "More like an entire. . ."

"Hush, Fenna! Gen's barely out of bed and we don't wish to overwhelm him with insignificant matters. He can find out about what being Lord of Blackshire means later. But this we want you to know," the First Mother's tone grew serious and she pointed her finger at his chest. "If you haven't been able to tell, you are dear to the three of us and to many more besides, so don't go throwing your life away at every chance you get. Do you understand?"

"Yes, your Grace."

"Very well. We shall talk more with you later. Fenna, be sure to bring your mother and father to meet him."

Fenna kissed him on the cheek, and the First Mother hugged him again before they turned to go.

"Chalaine?" Gen said.

"Yes?"

"May I speak with you for a moment?"

"Certainly, Gen. In fact, if you could contrive some excuse to force me to leave, I would be in your debt."

"How much of my life did you see?" The Chalaine was silent, turning her head away for several moments before answering.

"Perhaps we should speak of this later, Gen," she said, voice unsteady. "I didn't see much, but what I did see fills me with great sorrow, and right now I cannot falter."

Gen glanced over her shoulder, finding Chertanne's eyes

boring into him, and for the first time since he awakened the reality of her betrothal hit him.

"I understand, Chalaine. When you are ready. I also wanted to thank you for coming after me, so to speak. I know the risk was great, and I will ever be indebted you. I will not forget what you have done."

"Gen," she replied, "I. . ."

"Your Holiness," it was Dason, breathless and distressed. Gen stepped behind the Chalaine as she turned toward her former protector.

"Dason?" she said, concerned. "What is troubling you?"

"If I could have a private word with you, Holiness. It will not take long. I believe the library is unoccupied."

"I, I suppose. If it is short. I cannot be gone long," the Chalaine agreed, voice unsure.

They left together for the short walk to the library, Dason apologizing profusely.

"Can you permit me a moment alone with her, Gen?" Dason begged. "I give you my word of honor as a Tolnorian that I will let no harm come upon her."

"No," Gen replied firmly and flatly. "What you have to say you will say with me by her or not at all."

Dason seemed torn for a moment, but he opened the library door and entered. No lamps were lit, and the moonlight provided the only illumination. The Chalaine sat on "Gen's couch" as Dason came and knelt in front of her, taking her by the hand, blue eyes pained. Gen stood just behind the couch.

"Your Holiness," he said, voice subdued. "I had to speak with you. Please, Gen, permit me to speak with her alone. If you would just move away a little space. . ."

"No."

"Please! You are my Tolnorian brother! You know. . ."

"Enough, Dason!" Gen interrupted. "Three weeks ago, a demon attacked the Chalaine. If after that you have some hope that I will leave her side even for a moment, then it is an extraordinary one. I give you my word that I will not repeat what I hear, but I will not move."

"Please go on," the Chalaine encouraged. "Gen is noble and trustworthy. We must hurry."

"Very well, though I protest, Gen, your not extending the trust to me which is due. Chalaine, I kneel before you as I did that day when I received the branding and beg you to forgive me. I failed the night I did not support Gen in defense of your honor. I did not know Chertanne's character then. I wanted to obey the Blessed One, as I had been taught. Please, I see I was wrong."

"Dason," the Chalaine returned tenderly, "I understand why you acted as you did. Do not fret. I do not hold you in lower regard for those choices. You have your honor."

"But I cannot proceed like this!" he plead. "I only wish to return to your service. Every hour I am with him, I can do nothing but think of you and the way it was before that night. Will you not speak to him and ask him to release me? He refused my request. Will you not also beg the First Mother to return me to the Protectorship? I have learned from my mistakes. It was my place to defend you from the demon, a place I lost because of my stupidity. Help me get it back."

"I will speak to Chertanne," the Chalaine said. "But argument with my mother will prove fruitless. I will try to convince her to let you back into service with the Dark Guard should Chertanne release you. It is the best I can offer."

Dason groaned and stood. "I have brought shame on my family and upon myself," he said, chidingly. "I thank you for your consideration, Holiness, and I await your answer. Should you ever need anything of me, do not hesitate to ask. You are ever in my heart, and I will not fail you again."

Dason bowed and left, door closing quietly behind.

"I have to get back," the Chalaine said, voice troubled

and hollow. She stood to go, wringing her hands. Gen took her by the arm and stopped her before she could get to the door.

"You cannot go back in there in this state," he whispered. "Take a few moments to collect yourself. Chertanne will question you when you return. He watched us intently as we left. If you can, you must appear as if nothing of consequence happened. If he gets a hint that you are upset, he may try to use Dason to manipulate you."

The Chalaine nodded, pacing about the room for several minutes before motioning for Gen to open the door for her.

Gen took up his position in the alcove near the table as they entered the celebration. Chertanne watched them enter, staring at the Chalaine until she sat. As Gen expected, he bombarded her with questions. Mirelle appeared anxious to talk with her as well. Dason was nowhere to be seen. Gen cursed him for laying his burden on the Chalaine on such a difficult night for her. While he couldn't hear the answers she gave to Chertanne, he was proud that she seemed relaxed and calm.

Fenna approaching with her parents forced him to clear his mind. He had to put aside his concern for the Chalaine for a moment to seek his own happiness even as hers faded.

Chapter 28 - Interviews

It was late. Chertanne dismissed Dason from his post as a travel-stained and cold Kaimas entered the room. Kaimas, gaunt and bald, removed his cloak, setting it by the fire to dry. Chertanne secretly feared the Magician but tried to assume an air of confidence and command despite the clenching of his stomach. Most outside of Aughmere didn't know what Kaimas did for Chertanne's father, but Chertanne knew the man's power and what deeds he had done to ensure that Torbrand Khairn's rule went unchallenged. He wore a white robe underneath a long open coat of deep red, embroidered with golden thread.

Chertanne eyed him, trying to discern what he was thinking. "Well, you returned more quickly than I thought you would, Kaimas. I trust you didn't overexert yourself on this matter."

Kaimas, who was warming his hands over the fire, shot Chertanne a displeased look. Wrinkles lined the sharp features of his thin, tall face, deepened by the exhaustion of his journey. Beady and intelligent hazel eyes met Chertanne's, and Chertanne signaled for him to sit across from the table from him. Kaimas strode over and pulled back the chair in front of the desk and sat down heavily.

"Exerting much effort on this matter simply wasn't possible. The tree was bare, so to speak, as is my stomach."

"I'll see to your comfort after I have your report," Chertanne said impatiently. He had just started his own meal but pushed it aside. "You learned nothing, then?"

"Nothing of much value, I'm afraid. Your father saw to that. He completely obliterated the young man's village and those nearby in the first months of the war. In fact, I could find nothing useful about him until I talked with the Shadan and Captain Omar."

"You talked to my father?"

"Yes, and you should be thankful I did or my mission would have been entirely wasted. He was quite excited to hear Gen was alive. As most suspected, your father trained him. The stories about his killing Cormith and defying you arrived soon after I did."

"How did he take Cormith's death?" Chertanne asked, blood starting to boil.

"His reaction surprised me. He was ecstatic. I got the feeling from talking with him that he considered Gen his 'master work.' In fact, the biggest news I have is that Torbrand has changed his mind and will accompany you to Elde Luri Mora come spring. Not out of any love for you, of course, but because he wishes to see Gen again. If you're lucky, he might kill Gen himself. I fear he has become rather bored with being undefeatable."

"If you could arrange for them to kill each other, so much the better," Chertanne growled. "To think my father was the one who trained him! I should have known only he could create such a monster."

"Gen's training was unique, according to Omar. Those scars he wears were all given to him to train him. Few consider the boy a monster, though. He's practically become a saint among all but your most loyal of subjects. If you wish to curry favor with the populace, you would do well to appear to feel the same."

"Is that all the mighty Kaimas can come up with?" Chertanne disparaged, frustration clenching his fist. "I sent you to find more about him so we could manipulate him, shame him!"

"That would be stupid. The way you've behaved toward him and indeed, all of Rhugothian society, is disadvantageous to you. I'm determined to winter here and correct your missteps. It will be difficult. You seem to have forgotten everything you've ever learned about this nation. Trying to bed the Chalaine before your wedding was the pinnacle of idiocy. Turning the Rhugothian challenge of honor into an Aughmerian challenge of possession was just as misguided."

"How was I supposed to know? Who has ever beaten Cormith?"

"I'm not here to discuss your mistakes; I'm here to fix them. You will do as I say or find yourself in dire trouble."

Chertanne folded his arms. "Just what is it that I am supposed to do?"

"My goodness, where to begin? First, you want to kill or shame Gen, but since you have failed to hide your dislike of him even in the least degree, if anything untoward were to happen to him, you risk the blame being leveled at you."

"So am I to smile and say, 'How do you do?' when I see him? Should I give him some reward for his deeds to show my 'gratitude?'"

Kaimas nodded. "I would suggest doing just that. In fact, while I was with your father, I came up with a possibility that would be an excellent token of appreciation."

"No! How can I bear it? Do you know what songs they're singing in the taverns? What the kids chant in the streets?

Gen defied the demon trance.
Chertanne turned pale and wet his pants.

Gen fought and bled and nearly died.
Chertanne fell on the floor and cried.
Chertanne can play and hold his beer
But cannot stomach demon fear.
The Chalaine's Chertanne's, as is his right,
But who stays with her every night?
Chertanne is grand when times are fun,
But come a fight, then Gen's the one.

"Sounds accurate to me," Kaimas commented derisively. Chertanne's cheeks flushed red as he trembled with anger.

"You remember who you're talking to, Kaimas!" Chertanne spat. "I may not have my power yet, but you'll end up dead if I say so!"

Kaimas stood, meeting Chertanne's gaze and intensity, and said a series of quick words Chertanne didn't recognize. Chertanne slumped back in his chair, body unable to move. He could feel Kaimas force himself into his mind.

"And you, Chertanne, need to learn that the party is over!" Kaimas's mouth did not move, voice pounding in Chertanne's brain. "You send me off on some waste of a mission simply because you're angry that you couldn't have your piece of the Chalaine before your wedding day! You talk and philander and stumble around as if the world existed just to tolerate you! I taught you better than that! The world is political, Chertanne, and perception matters.

"When you come into your power and the armies of all nations are at your back, Gen will matter nothing! But if you don't want to be on the battlefield facing down the hordes of an evil God all by yourself, then we have a lot of work to do. Some people will need to die, yes. But Gen should not be one of them."

Kaimas released his hold and Chertanne sucked air.

"Are you one of his admirers, too, Kaimas?" Chertanne seethed, taking stock of himself.

"His skill is certainly admirable, but that's not the point,

Chertanne." Kaimas returned to his seat. "Whether you like it or not, he has kept the people's spirits high. That works to your advantage. A dispirited populous would be much more difficult to rally when the time comes, especially if the Ilch starts his work in earnest and things get miserable. As it is, everyone is anxious to march off to war for the Chalaine. If you're smart, you'll leave Gen be. All he does is protect the Chalaine. There are others here that are much more dangerous to you than him. Those we must discover and deal with. But first we must improve your position among Rhugothians, the aristocracy in particular."

"I hardly talk to them at all, and I think I've been polite," Chertanne reported half-heartedly.

"Are you really that daft?" Kaimas retorted. "You offended the First Mother of Rhugoth! She is an extremely persuasive and devious woman. If she doesn't like you, then let me assure you that not a single one of the Regency will. From what I've gathered from my sources, she doesn't talk with you, she doesn't dine with you, she doesn't dance with you. Not even once, since your initial blunder. Is that true?"

"Yes," Chertanne answered sheepishly.

"I'm not sure we can repair that relationship, but we will try. We must think of some pretense for undoing your selection of Dason as your bodyguard. We can't have someone that loyal to the Chalaine close to you."

"That will be easy," Chertanne said. "The Chalaine asked me to release him a couple of weeks ago."

"Good. Your concubines will all be dismissed from your possession and sent home tomorrow. You will tell the people that you did it because the Chalaine's glory undid your desire for any other woman, or some other such nonsense. There will be no more wanton carousing and public drunkenness."

"But it's winter and there is nothing else to. . ."

"No objections, Chertanne. If you don't do as I say, I'll leave you on your own and let the Rhugothians do what they will to you when you've offended them beyond their ability to tolerate it! You've taken your position as Ha'Ulrich for granted. If you hadn't done so poorly in the presence of the demon, you may have had the privilege of continuing as you are, but not now. There is so much to do, but I do not have the patience or desire to review it with you tonight. Get a good night's rest. We start tomorrow. Early. Now, I need to go greet my brother, though my presence will bring him little pleasure, I'm sure."

Eldwena had long since fallen asleep, snoring loudly as she always had from her adjoining room. The lamp was trimmed low, and its light suffused the curtains around the Chalaine's bed with a soft yellow glow. Her own veil was off, blonde curls fanned about her head upon the elegantly embroidered pillows and her hands laid one atop the other upon her stomach. She fancied that this would be the position the Puremen would arrange her in were she to die, though even in death, she suspected they would make her wear the veil.

Sleep would not come, a crowded, noisy mind unsettling her and repelling every attempt at relaxation. She thought that once she had endured the betrothal she would find some sense of peace at having fulfilled one part of her duty and having the winter to try to forget about the marriage and to enjoy the company of her friends and Protectors. Instead, she felt worse. A strange blend of emotion squirmed inside her stomach, coalescing into a draining anxiety and depression.

For one, she felt guilty for the way she thought about Fenna. In the weeks since Gen had reawakened, Gen and Fenna had spent every one of what few free moments they could manage together, their friendship deepening. Gen's maturity helped the woman in Fenna emerge, and Fenna brought a light into Gen's eye and taught him tenderness.

Unbeknown to them, the Chalaine sometimes used the Walls to watch them when they strolled through the castle together, read books in the library, or just sat talking in the commons. Gen had even taken to teaching Fenna how to play the lute. While the Chalaine couldn't hear what they were saying, their mutual pleasure was evident.

The Chalaine knew she should quit invading their privacy. She knew she should confess to Fenna and Gen and apologize. Unfortunately, while she couldn't say why, she found watching them irresistible, even though every time she did it the dark canker of jealousy ate away at her. Fenna was living the Chalaine's dream. Gen wasn't the Blessed One or the Savior of the World. He wasn't destined to rule kingdoms or lead armies. He was simply a good young man, and that was all the Chalaine really wanted, and it was something she would not have in Chertanne.

Every time Fenna smiled at Gen and wrapped her arm in his, every time he sat beside her, gently showing her the proper fingering of the instrument, every song they sang together, every joke he told that had Fenna covering her mouth in shock and laughter stung her until she wanted desperately to turn away. Only she never did.

She realized that Fenna was now no stranger to jealousy. Gen's notoriety and reputation had spread, not the least of all into the hearts and minds of young women inside and outside the castle. In front of the Walls, the Chalaine found that she was little better than the scullery maid who shot longing looks at Gen whenever he came to get his meal in the kitchen.

Deep inside, the Chalaine felt happy that Fenna had finally won Gen's attentions, but the feeling was deep enough to be considered buried. The dissatisfaction and sense of loneliness took their toll on her mood, and the Chalaine wondered if Fenna divined her bitterness despite her best attempts to act as if all was the same between them.

Tonight after Eldwena retired, the Chalaine did the worst possible thing for her attitude that she could imagine: she used the Walls to spy on Chertanne. Watching him engage in yet another night full of drunkenness and debauchery sent her spirits spiraling even lower, and she wondered how it was that her own childhood had been one where her duty—and the rigid morality that was to enable it—were taught unceasingly, while Chertanne, it seemed, had grown up without a worry or care of any sort for duty, morality, or even a modicum of decency. The vessel Eldaloth would use to return to Ki'Hal was to come from him as well, so how did her strictness profit anything when his carefree indulgence more than destroyed any hope for a holy union?

As the memories of Chertanne's night about town resurfaced in her mind, she threw aside the curtains of her bed and stood, determined to find a way to distract herself. She knew it had to be a couple of hours past midnight, but Gen was awake, and her mother had wished that she would talk to him. Because of her despair, she knew the conversation would do no service to Gen, but any conversation at all, even if a fight, would be better than lying around contemplating marital doom.

As silently as she could, the Chalaine retrieved a veil from a drawer and pulled it over her head. Taking a deep breath, she opened the door. While Fenna succeeded in coaxing emotion out of Gen's face, the Chalaine wasn't surprised when Gen didn't even lift an eyebrow at her unexpected appearance in the middle of the night. Of course, he could sense her coming.

"Are you well, Holiness?" he asked. The Chalaine went to the wall opposite from where he stood and sat slumped against it, hugging her legs and putting her chin on her knees.

"Would you quit using the 'Holiness' honorific? It makes me feel like we never met."

"Of course, Chalaine. I apologize."

"And quit being sorry, too. People are always telling me how sorry they are for the stupidest things."

"Yes, Chalaine."

"And don't answer me like I'm Captain Tolbrook barking orders to a bunch of idiot apprentices."

"I see. I will limit my responses to hand gestures and grunts from this point forward."

The Chalaine tried to decipher his face. Irritatingly as ever, she couldn't make sense of it. She sat silently as Gen resumed his statuesque vigil without further comment. The Chalaine stared at him to annoy him and wondered if he could tell that she was doing it in the dim light of the hallway.

"So," she said suddenly and sharply, seeing if she could get him to blink. It failed. "Fenna tells me you are teaching her to play the lute." Gen raised his fist before him, moving it up and down at the wrist in a semblance of a head nodding 'yes.' As out of sorts as she was, the Chalaine couldn't help but smile.

"Stop it and talk to me," she said.

"I can't even say a simple 'Holiness' without causing offense."

"I bet you don't go around saying, 'your ladyship' to Fenna all the time except when you are having a little fun at her expense. You've known me almost as long as you've known her."

"True," he said, "but Fenna isn't the Holy Chalaine, either. In fact, 'Holiness' almost seems less formal than 'Chalaine.' That is a weighty title as much as it is your name."

"Then I shall need a new name for you to call me, one that won't weigh your tongue down so much. You know the ancient speech of the Gods. Give me a new name from

God's language."

Gen thought for a moment. "Very well. How about 'Alumira'rei Se Ellenwei'?"

"It sounds beautiful and it rhymes. What does it mean?"

"It means, 'One who picks fights when she should be sleeping.'"

"Alumira'rei knows she should be sleeping but has found that she can't. She has decided that she wants to go on a walk."

The Chalaine stood and started toward the entrance to the maze. Gen intercepted her in a heartbeat, blocking the way.

"No, Chalaine!" he stated firmly. "Night is the friend of evil. It is too dangerous to have you outside the tower wards, especially so soon after the demon attack. Those responsible are still uncaught."

"I am Alumira'rei, remember? Demons and scoundrels have no interest in her. And I am going. I will not stay cooped up in here a moment longer. You don't have to come, I suppose."

"Be reasonable, Alumira. I am charged with keeping you safe. I must suggest a course of action that will most likely keep you out of harm's way. I couldn't bear it if something were to happen to you on my watch."

"But it would be all right if it happened under Jaron's watch, I suppose? Then it wouldn't be *your* fault, right? In that case, your reputation and honor would be intact."

"That's not what I meant, Cha . . . Alumira, and you know it."

"Look, Gen, I am going out there. You can do one of two things. You can come with me, or. . ."

"Or what?"

"Or you'll have to lay hands on me and hold me here. Imagine the scandal!" With that she skirted around her Protector and resumed her course toward the entryway to the maze.

"Wait!" Gen said, hurrying forward. "You'll be the one starting a scandal walking around the Hall in your bedclothes. You need to change."

"Well, that's the first sensible thing you've said all night," the Chalaine returned tartly. "Do you have a cloak?"

"In my quarters."

"Well, let's fetch it and be on our way."

The Chalaine followed Gen to his room and he opened the door after taking a lamp from the wall to light his way. The Chalaine peeked in out of curiosity, finding the room as ascetic as his facial expressions. A mattress without a frame lay on the floor opposite an ancient armoire that had occupied the room since the first Protectors. Besides the lute that leaned against the wall and a couple of books by the bed, no other decoration graced the walls. Dason had spruced the quarters up nicely during his tenure, going as far as to hang a painting and a tapestry. Of course, he came from a wealthy family. Gen had nothing.

"Did they not issue you a bed frame?"

"No," Gen said. "Apparently the one that was here was Dason's that he had brought from home. It had some sentimental value. The mattress suits me fine."

"A bed frame with sentimental value?" the Chalaine commented, perplexed. "What could Dason possibly find sentimental about a bed frame? Who told you it had sentimental value?"

Gen shrugged. "The servants carrying it out. Why don't we stay here and summon some servants to give you an explanation."

"Nice try, Gen. Give me the cloak."

The Chalaine let Gen help her into the cloak he retrieved from the armoire. It was voluminous on her, but since they were of a similar height, it didn't drag on the ground. As they wound around the maze and out into the Antechamber of the Chalaines, the other Dark Guard snapped to attention, amazement and concern plain on their faces. The Chalaine ignored them. Knocking Gen off balance, for some reason, improved her mood and she wasn't about to stop. She led him over the bridge and through the long hallway filled with guards into the manor proper, entering the Great Hall through a side door near the kitchens.

Moonlight strong enough to cast clear shadows poured in through the high windows and into the hall. The large fires that normally warmed the room had long since faded to embers, and the Chalaine crossed her arms for warmth as she walked the length of the hall to her mother's throne and sat down heavily in it. Gen stood behind her where Cadaen stood when guarding the First Mother. The Chalaine sat restlessly, shifting positions every few minutes and exhaling roughly from time to time.

"Have a seat on Aldradan Mikmir's throne, Gen," the Chalaine said, signaling to the ornately carved marble throne behind her.

"I most certainly will not! That would be a great offense to your entire nation!"

"Have it your way. I think a great number of people have sat in it on the sly since his disappearance. What would you think of being a King, Gen?"

"Really, Chalaine. . ."

"Alumira!"

"Milady, we can have this conversation someplace safer. . ."

"Answer the question and don't nag me about safety anymore," the Chalaine commanded, trying to put enough weight into it to shut him up.

"I think I would find it bothersome."

"And why is that?"

"I would scarce have a moment to myself, if the First Mother is any indication."

"You value being alone, then?" the Chalaine remarked. "Strange."

"Not so much being alone," Gen returned, "as being able to have some say about when I am. Kings are always at the beck and call of others."

"But kings have all the say they want. You could command everyone away whenever you wanted and sit in your room all the day long and talk to your bed post—well, your mattress—if you liked."

"Good ones wouldn't do such a thing," Gen stated.

"Why not?"

"Because they never feel comfortable leaving anything undone, and there are no end of things to be done. That was my point in the first place."

"I see." The Chalaine stood, turning to face him. "Did you know that I am the second highest ranking aristocrat in Rhugoth?"

"Of course."

"Well, it doesn't quite seem like it, now does it?" She turned and started down the dais stairs, arms raised. "Behold! The High and Holy Chalaine, the Mother of God. She has no say in anything and has absolutely nothing to do but sit around and wait to marry a dog!" She got louder as she continued, heedless of the guards outside the doors that might hear her.

Gen followed her. "Please, Chalaine. . ."

"Here I am, the paragon of virtue and healing, beloved of all, but when my Aughmerian fiancé—no, he wasn't even my fiancé then—when some Aughmerian Warlord tries to drag me off to his bed a full year before our marriage in front of a room full of aristocrats and nobles who are sworn to protect my honor, who actually does something? A complete stranger! Some nobody serf from some nowhere lumbering town, from Tolnor! From Tolnor! My mother looks at the floor! Dason looks away! Jaron scowls but follows along!

"But is that the worst? Oh, certainly not!" Her voice was cracking now, and Gen stood silently as she yelled at him from several feet away, a shaft of moonlight dividing her into light and shadow. "Now everyone knows what Chertanne is! Some piggish, whoring drunk who wouldn't know decency, honor, or love if he tripped over them in harsh daylight! But not one person thinks I shouldn't have him, however wretchedly different we are. Will everyone just turn away on my wedding day, too? There's the prophecy, Chalaine! The child must be born, Chalaine. Chertanne must be the father, you the cow, Chalaine!

"So what is a fine, upstanding Protector like Gen to do? He saves my honor and my dignity so that I can have it for one more year and anticipate hour by hour the day Chertanne will strip me of it when he welcomes me into his wonderful family of filthy concubines.

"What does Gen do next? He throws himself in front of a demon to miraculously save me from a horrible death so a few weeks later I can stand hand in hand with Chertanne before the Pontiff and obediently promise my life to him! Eldaloth help me, Gen, are you protecting me or killing me?"

Rage dissolved into sadness and she stood sobbing in the middle of the floor, head down and hands over her face.

"Come on," Gen said, gently taking her arm and coaxing her toward the steps. "A little air will do you well."

She let herself be guided up the curved stairways to the balcony, where Gen opened the door to the outside. The midwinter night was chill, a biting breeze slicing through the protection of the cloak. The long balcony on the eastern side of the Great Hall looked out over Mikmir at the base of the hill below and was bathed in the light of the moons Myn and Duam.

Being late at night and late in the year, the weak light colored everything a soothing deep blue and gray. During the spring and summer, the balcony had many plant beds brimming with bright and fragrant flowers. All these were dead, wasted stalks twisted in a frozen tangle over each other. The smallish trees and shrubs were scraggly and bare, save one evergreen, the sole survivor of the season.

The Chalaine walked to the arched stone balustrade and stood rigidly in front of it, and Gen joined her there. She took several minutes to calm herself, reaching up under her veil to wipe her eyes. Gen observed her carefully, and under his compassionate gaze she felt tension slowly leave her muscles. At last she put her forearms on the balustrade and leaned forward, breathing deeply.

"I suppose you want your cloak back," the Chalaine commented, voice worn.

"I have no need for it."

"You don't feel the cold?"

"It's not that I don't feel it. It just doesn't mean anything to me, if you can understand that."

"I am sorry, Gen. I shouldn't have put you of all people through this. I should have stayed in my room and kept this—whatever this is—to myself. I am supposed to be the healer, and here I am yelling and whining at you like some three-year-old brat who can't get her way. I am not quite what you thought you had sworn your life to, am I?"

"On the contrary," Gen replied. "We commoners quite expect these outbursts from you unpredictable aristocratic types."

The Chalaine laughed quietly, sniffling as she wiped her eyes again. "You are not a commoner anymore."

"Once a nobody serf, always a nobody serf."

"Oh Gen, please don't take that comment about you being 'nobody from nowhere' seriously. You know I don't think that. You are an important symbol of strength to everyone, including me."

"Yes, but falsely, I think. The way the stories are told, I danced around on the demon's head before he broke every bone in my body with a lucky swing. All I want to do is protect you. Whatever is thought of what I do matters little, as long as you are safe."

"But it does!" the Chalaine contradicted, gripping his forearm and marveling at its strength. "And it's not just the demon. It started at the Trials. It continued with your defense of my honor. It serves you well to despise the fame, but never deny its importance! The people need something to believe in as dark times approach.

"Chertanne and I are only the potential of what may come. For now we are powerless and weak. People may love the idea of the perfect beauty and the savior of all, but they can't grasp it. I can't even grasp it, as you now know all too well. But your place in history all of us can understand. Your present actions and obvious virtues we can imitate. And you have inspired immeasurable goodness that you should feel proud to have fostered."

"Maybe," Gen said, "but you seem to have forgotten that you do the same." She released his arm and turned her gaze back out into the night.

"The only good I've done is either imagined or yet to come, so if I have some reputation, then it is certainly fabricated and not deserved."

"Not true. Do not protest! Do you know when I saw you for the first time?"

"At the feast, or did you see me at the docks?"

"Before then."

"Really? When?" she asked, curiosity piqued.

"I ask you to keep this to yourself, if you would."

"Of course I will."

"Fenna may have described to you my appearance and dress when I came to the tournament field as like 'someone straight from the Damned Quarter.' I was. I was in the Damned Quarter the day before the Trials, the day you came to visit the children."

The Chalaine's hand went to her mouth. "The Damned Quarter!? How did you end up there, of all places?"

"That is a story for another day. What I want to tell you

is that I watched you in secret when you came. You were nervous, but you had compassion and love for those wretched children. You sat with them, you fed them, you sang to them. You held them on your lap, uncaring of what it did to what you wore or what discomfort it caused you. It was then that I knew you *were* virtuous, you *were* kind, you *were* beautiful, and that you had more power to do good in this world than I would ever have. In short, that you were worth protecting, whatever it cost. Chertanne will be no boon to you, but you need not let him destroy that good part of you that I saw that day."

She sighed. "Sometimes I think he already has. Thank you, Gen. I will try to look forward with a bit more hope, and I promise I will never yell at you again. You certainly don't deserve to be the victim of my frustration."

"Feel at liberty to yell at me whenever you like. Whether you need a Protector or someone to verbally abuse, I am at your service."

The Chalaine laughed again, feeling lighter of spirit. There was something old about Gen, as her mother had said. Everything and everyone around him might writhe in tumult, but like a garden wall he stood calm, come sun or storm, abundance or want.

"I think Fenna would object if I took advantage of your good nature too often." At the mention of her name, Gen smiled, the first time the Chalaine had seen him do so in person. A wave of jealousy washed over her, and she fought it back with effort. "Is Fenna much like Regina?"

"In some ways. Regina, like Fenna, was beautiful and playful, though Regina was more devious and cunning. It was difficult to tell what Regina felt, but Fenna shows her emotion plainly, for which I am grateful."

"You may wish to return the courtesy of showing emotion plainly, if you want to win her. You do face some competition."

"Kimdan. I know."

"Yes. But other young men at court pay her a great deal of attention, as well. Even those who don't give her a good look when she passes by."

"I've seen them give you both a good look."

"This bothers you?" the Chalaine asked.

"Fenna I can understand, but you are always veiled and wearing a loose robe to hide your shape. For all any man knows, you might be bloated, scaly, and hideous."

"Thank you," the Chalaine laughed, though he seemed perfectly serious. "Well, she is quite a beauty. You should feel quite fortunate that she takes an interest in you."

"I do," he said and smiled again.

"Another smile from the dead-faced man. He must be stricken, indeed," the Chalaine quipped. Gen smoothed his face but answered nothing, and the Chalaine respected his silence. She felt grateful for her mother's advice. Talking with Gen gave her a stillness of mind and brought a smile to her face when but an hour before she would have thought both impossible. Her emotion spent, exhaustion prevailed upon her, and the chill made the warmth and comfort of her bed suddenly appealing.

"We should go," the Chalaine said, taking Gen's arm the way she saw Fenna do. "It's difficult to see through this veil in the dark, so if you could assist the Lady Alumira down the stairs, she would be in your debt."

"I would be honored to do so."

As they walked arm in arm across the dark balcony and descended the marbled stair, the Chalaine imagined the hall well lit and filled with the noises and smells of celebration. Ladies and Lords danced in bright clothing to lively music, while others feasted and talked of trivialities with each other. As she and Gen came down arm in arm and step by step, the dancing and music stopped. Voices hushed as all turned to watch them arrive. The assembled patrons bowed as she approached the floor, for here was beauty latched to strength; and while the ladies looked at her with envy, the men dared not look on her at all. When he was beside her, all were beneath her and she was who everyone thought she was—strong, beautiful, and divine.

The vision faded as they reached the door that led from the hall, the same door Chertanne had tried to drag her through so many weeks ago. The Chalaine reluctantly let go of Gen's arm as he opened the door for her. After he was assured the hall was safe, he let her through and took up his normal position half a step behind her. The Dark Guard were visibly relieved at her safe return, and she hoped she hadn't caused Gen any trouble with Captain Tolbrook or Regent Ogbith.

"Thank you, Gen," the Chalaine said, turning as she opened her door. "I am sorry I was so cross earlier. Please forgive me."

"There is no need. Sleep well."

The Chalaine closed the door, threw her veil in the corner, and lay down. Sleep came quickly, and when she closed her eyes to dream, she was running. . .

CHAPTER 29 - PADRAS

Cadaen cracked the door.

"Gen requests to see you, your Grace."

"By all means, let him in!" Mirelle replied happily. Cadaen swung the door open wide and Gen strode in and bowed.

"Your Grace," Gen said, genuflecting. "I am sorry to bother you so early this morning." Mirelle sat in front of the fire to dry her hair as her maid brushed through it.

"Quit troubling yourself with all that bowing and scraping, Gen," Mirelle said as he finished his bowing and scraping. "You may go, Kora."

"Yes, your Grace," she said, handing Mirelle the brush and leaving quickly. Mirelle stood. Her breakfast—sweet bread, jam, and cider—waited for her on a nearby table.

"Now, good morning, Gen," Mirelle smiled, crossing to him and embracing him. "I am delighted that you came to see me."

Gen received the embrace awkwardly, not quite sure why the First Mother showed him this tenderness so often.

She held his gaze with her bright blue eyes. "I can only hope you are here for the pleasure of my company and not because of some pressing matter."

"Your company is as pleasurable as it is difficult to find oneself in, but I do have something I wish to talk over with you, if you'll permit."

The First Mother frowned teasingly at him. "Well, that was certainly an unfortunate and diplomatic answer. Come, eat with me and let me know what is troubling you. And shut the door the rest of the way, Cadaen."

"But, your Highness. . ." Cadaen protested.

"Do it, Cadaen!" Mirelle commanded as kindly as her exasperation would permit, and Cadaen reluctantly complied. "I'm not sure what further stunt you'll have to pull to earn that man's trust."

"I think he fears I'll behave dishonorably toward you, Highness," Gen speculated.

"Dishonorably?" Mirelle grinned, sitting. "Do tell me more. And quit using honorifics when we are alone or in informal situations. I can tolerate such behavior from other people, but when you do it, it just annoys me. Now what dishonorable things is he afraid that you will do to me?"

"I hadn't anything specific in mind," Gen answered lamely.

Mirelle chuckled. "You are certainly Tolnorian. Please, sit. There is enough for two. Here," she said, breaking off a piece of sweetbread and pressing it to his lips. "Tell me if this isn't the finest sweetbread you have ever tasted." Gen chewed the bread and raised his eyebrows, Mirelle watching his reaction with pleasure. "Marna has some secret that elevates it above ordinary sweetbread to something more sublime."

"That is very good," Gen concurred. "I wonder that she doesn't serve it in the commons. She would earn everyone's undying good opinion."

"If you ask her, I'm sure she'll bake a loaf just for you. Anytime I see her, you are half of what she talks about. Now, what did you want to tell me?"

Gen leaned back in his chair and recounted her

daughter's outburst of the night before. The First Mother's levity disappeared instantly and she stopped eating as he talked, her face paling and turning grave.

"I don't know if she would object to me telling you this," Gen finished, "and you may know some of her concerns already. I don't think I have the influence and ability that you do to aid her in these struggles. I can help her with enemies of flesh and blood, but I think she needs you to see her through the rest."

"Do not doubt your own wisdom. You have done the right thing in telling me," she said. "I have not spent the time I should have with her. So much to do! You would think that preparing to relinquish one's reign would be easier. I have to see her, but the Council of Padras arrives today and I'm sure I'll be forced to meet with them until well after dark. Churchmen like to hear themselves talk."

"They are here to see to the Chalaine's protection, aren't they?"

"Yes."

"Then wouldn't they need an extensive overview of the grounds and every building on it?" Gen asked.

Mirelle's face brightened. "You are absolutely right! And I'll be damned if I'm going to lead a bunch of Churchmen around in the cold. But on whom do I lay this task? Since the lake was frozen over, they were forced to ride for over a week in the cold. They will be irritable and I suspect more than a little annoyed about being out in the freezing weather even more."

"Ethris is the obvious choice," Gen suggested. "He can rattle on for hours about anything, which will give you more time, and the Padras will be too intimidated by him to offer him much complaint."

The First Mother thought for a moment. "It's perfect," she said. "I may get the whole afternoon with her if Ethris can hold out that long."

Cadaen cracked the door. "A message, Holiness," he

said. "The Padras have arrived and await your attention in the Great Hall."

"Thank you, Cadaen," she acknowledged. "Shut the door. Curse it all, they are early. Can't I get just one meal with you where we talk about the weather, or music, or books? I am in your debt, as usual."

She stood and brushed through her hair quickly. Gen retrieved her cloak for her and helped her into it.

"I fret over my daughter excessively, and I do not want to leave her unsupported and motherless during this difficult time. And the next time she tries to go out during the night, you grab her and hold her there, scandal notwithstanding. I'll defend you in the matter. Your arm, sir."

Gen extended it and she took it, kissing him on the cheek and thanking him again. Cadaen fell in behind them as Gen escorted her over the bridge and into the tunnels underneath the Great Hall. Her scribe, Mafeus, met her there and started to outline her schedule for the day.

"Forget all that," she interrupted. "Cadaen, I want you to find Ethris for me and bring him to me immediately."

"I am your Protector, Highness," Cadaen protested. "Send Gen. He is off duty."

"Cadaen," she remonstrated. "Do as I say. The Padras specifically requested to meet Gen, and I will help get him through it quickly so he can get some rest. I will see you shortly."

Cadaen bowed stiffly and left.

"Mafeus, I will be with my daughter from lunch through dinner. Please have her informed."

"Yes, Highness," Mafeus said, following as the First Mother started forward. "But I received a request from the Blessed One. He wishes to dine with you this evening."

Mirelle stopped dead in her tracks. "What? Has Kaimas arrived, then?"

"He should still be two days out, as I reckon it," Mafeus

explained.

"Go check with the House Guard and see if he arrived during the night and bring me word. Go! Yet another unwanted distraction."

"What does Kaimas have to do with Chertanne's request to take dinner with you?" Gen inquired. Gen knew Kaimas served as court Magician for Shadan Khairn, though he knew little besides. Kaimas, due to his nationality, was not as well known as Ethris.

"Kaimas," Mirelle explained, "is Chertanne's 'handler,' for lack of a better term. He is also Ethris's brother. When we were in Aughmere last spring, Chertanne's manners improved considerably whenever Kaimas watched over him. He is a frightening man, but if he has arrived, we will likely see Chertanne behave much more 'nobly,' if the term can be applied comfortably in his case. It isn't anything to worry about. Let me introduce you to the Padras and see if we can't spare you as much boredom as possible."

Padras formed the governing council of the Church of the One. The council currently consisted of seventeen members, and together they held as much authority as the Pontiff himself. That the Pontiff would summon them all to the aid of the Chalaine evidenced his concern for her safety and his resolution to protect her at all costs. To gain a seat on the Council, a man had to be adept in at least one of the magical arts, possess an unwavering loyalty to the Church, and have lived an exemplary life. Padras were elevated from Prelates, chosen by the Council itself when a vacancy came free.

Gen felt a little trepidation about meeting all of them at once. The Council of Padras wielded a great deal of power and had historically not brooked any opposition to their mandates. Only Aughmerians flouted the Church leadership on a regular basis, and there was no love lost between Shadan Khairn and any Church leader in lands under his control.

Chamberlain Hurney straightened at the First Mother's approach to the doors, bowing deeply.

Mirelle smiled affectionately at him. "Are they here?"

"They await you within, your Grace. Let me announce you." The Guards pushed open the doors and the Chamberlain planted his feet, striking the tiles of the floor three times with his staff.

"The First Mother of Rhugoth, the Lady Mirelle, comes to her Hall. May I present with her Lord Gen Blackshire, Protector of the Holy Daughter."

Arm in arm, Gen and the First Mother strode into the hall. Mirelle slowed their pace to a casual walk, and she whispered to him, "Forgive a little posturing. It is good to let such as these know who is in power here."

The Padras stood as she entered. Two long tables with padded chairs were set before the dais, and at each of the seventeen places steamed a goblet of mulled wine.

Gen noticed several eyebrows raise at their approach, and he couldn't tell if it were due to the First Mother's leisurely pace or her company. Rather than let them sit immediately, she waited until she sat on the throne, Gen standing at attention behind, before she signaled for them to sit.

All appeared travel worn and a little cold. The Padras wore deep crimson robes with voluminous sleeves cinched at the waist with a golden rope. A purple stole, embroidered with complex designs, hung over each shoulder. On the left side of the stole the three moons, Trys eclipsed, were represented. One Padra's stole was different. On his Trys was uneclipsed like the other moons.

He approached the Dais but did not kneel. His face was long and thin with a hooked nose separating two closely set gray eyes. Black hair ringed his head in a perfect circle, and Gen judged that he wasn't an inch over five-foot six. Despite his diminutive stature and thin frame, his eyes carried a self-confidence and intensity that more than compensated for any lack of size. He appeared to be at least ten years younger than any other member of the Council, though his stole marked him as their head.

"First Mother," he began gravely, "it is unfortunate that inclement weather delayed our arrival. After we received the Pontiff's impassioned missive to arrive as quickly as possible, we had hoped the weather would warm and we could join you more quickly. When news of the disastrous events of the betrothal reached us, we were deeply angered. Clearly the Chalaine has not been cared for and protected properly. That a Burka pattern was inscribed inside your Chapel within the inner walls of your castle is inexcusable! That those who perpetrated the act are uncaught and unpunished bespeaks a bungling incompetence! Things will change, starting now!"

His voice, high-pitched and nasal, rang through the hall, his loud accusations echoing throughout the chamber. Gen watched the First Mother stiffen during this diatribe and feared she would say something rash.

"It is good to see you again as well, Padra Athan," Mirelle said pleasantly. "Was your journey tolerable, even if long?"

"Forget the journey," he replied dismissively. "We have business to attend to and we cannot delay. This must be Gen behind you."

"Lord Blackshire. Yes."

The First Mother answered dully. Padra Athan ascended the dais to stand directly in front of Gen. Gen returned his gaze unblinkingly and assumed his now famous dead face.

"I understood that you were young, but I didn't realize you were *this* young. I wonder why you are the Chalaine's night Protector when a more experienced soldier would certainly be advantageous and desirable, as evil is more active in the dark than the day." His eyes bored into Gen's. "Well, young man?"

"I am sorry, Padra," Gen said tonelessly, "did you ask

me a question?"

"Ah," he said, turning away. "You are arrogant and evasive, as I've heard. Just remember that what we won't say often says more about us than what we will."

"Ask anyone you trust," Mirelle suggested as Athan returned to the table and sat. "Gen is the best fighter on our soil and quite possibly all of Ki'Hal, excepting Shadan Khairn himself."

"I doubt that. He is too young," Athan disagreed. "The Pontiff has vouched for his bravery and moral character, but I can hardly believe he is the best sword fighter, even in this building."

Mirelle smiled. "He killed Cormith. What further proof do you need?"

"From what I heard of the event, Cormith lost because he was arrogant and stupid, not because Gen overwhelmed him with skill or experience. I think I would much rather have Cadaen or Tolbrook protect the Chalaine and have Gen assigned to some other post in the Dark Guard, protecting you in Cadaen's stead, perhaps."

"While I should certainly like nothing better than to have the pleasure of Gen at my side day and night, I will leave him where he is." Athan opened his mouth to object, but Mirelle plowed on before he could start. "I really do not think you should tender any recommendations to me about anything concerning the Chalaine's safety until you have been properly briefed by those entrusted with her care. Ethris will be joining us shortly and will thoroughly inform you about all you wish to know in this regard.

"While I had planned for you to meet Regent Ogbith tomorrow, I will have him brought this evening in company with Jaron, Captain Tolbrook, and Cadaen so they can vouch for Gen's skill-at-arms. If they cannot convince you, then I suggest you gather five of the best soldiers from the Eldephaere and let Gen beat on them until you are satisfied or they are dead. And—" The First Mother's tone grew serious and sharp. "—I love my daughter. I *never* want to see her come to the least harm. So do not come into *my* Hall and imply that I am not doing *everything* possible to see to her wellbeing. And do not within my hearing ever insult, dishonor, or demean Lord Blackshire. He has done more than any man living for the Chalaine's life and honor, and you had best show him the respect he is due."

Gen was impressed and wondered if there was anyone in Ki'Hal that could intimidate the woman. Unlike the majority of the other Padras at the table, Athan did not appear ruffled in the least.

"And so you know, First Mother, the Pontiff has afforded us some liberty in assessing the situation and implementing what changes we see fit to insure that the Chalaine and the Ha'Ulrich are fully protected and prepared for their important work. I will personally oversee the protection of the Chalaine and will require unfettered access to her chambers, her Protectors, and the leadership of the Dark Guard. Padra Nolan will do the same for the Ha'Ulrich. I will speak with all those you have indicated, though it will be difficult for them to satisfy me concerning Gen. I will, of course, want to interview him sometime today."

"By all means, assess and interview to your heart's content," Mirelle returned heatedly. "Lord Blackshire is my daughter's Protector and that will *not* change, even if you recommend or even command otherwise. If I find you are hindering him or Jaron in their duties in the least degree, I will pack the lot of you up, put you on the slowest carriage back to Mur Eldaloth that I can find, and pray for snow! I rule in Rhugoth, not the Church. The next time we talk, I suggest you address me with a great deal more respect than you have done this morning."

They were shocked. Athan's pale face bloomed red.

"Now," Mirelle said as she stood, voice calm, even flippant, "enjoy your wine. Ethris will be with you shortly."

Gen escorted her out, the Padras already chattering frantically to each other. Mirelle leaned in close. "And they were so pleasant and accommodating in the letter announcing their imminent arrival," she whispered. "Athan obviously has an agenda. I am going to write the Pontiff immediately. I wish he had never left. Let's go find Ethris. I'm afraid his job just became more difficult."

Chapter 30 - A Song at the Quickblade Inn

"So, where are we going, Gen?" Volney asked. Gen waited for him and Gerand to ready themselves to head into town. It was the afternoon of Sixthday, and Gerand and Volney had time free from their masters. As usual, the Dark Guard worked the apprentices doubly hard in the morning, and neither Gerand nor Volney seemed overly enthusiastic about heading back out into the snowy, cold afternoon. But Gen, who had slept during the morning, invited them to accompany him on an errand laid on him by Chertanne.

"We are to go to the smithy on Chadsbury Street," Gen answered as Volney retrieved Gerand's cloak and handed it to him before getting his own. "As a reward for my distinguished service to the Chalaine, Chertanne has commissioned a fine set of armor to be crafted for me. The smith, Morgan, I believe, is to take measurements this morning so he can finish it before the trip to the Shroud Lake Portal and Elde Luri Mora."

"Is it true that Chertanne disowned his concubines and sent them home?" Gerand asked.

"Yes," Gen answered. "He announced his decision just a week ago to the Chalaine and the First Mother."

"Was the Chalaine happy?"

"I would imagine so. It is difficult to say what she feels," Gen lied, hiding what he knew out of respect for the Chalaine. Mirelle had informed her daughter of Kaimas's interference, and the Chalaine viewed Chertanne's sudden concessions with a cynical eye.

"I was surprised when Dason returned to the Dark Guard," Volney added, opening the door to their room and leading the way into the hall. "It would seem an honor to be in the Ha'Ulrich's service, even in light of the ... difficulties. Chertanne does appear to be mending his ways a bit, though, which my father says is of great comfort to the aristocracy and officers alike. Who would have thought that he would stand and actually praise you, the one who defied him?"

Gen said nothing, and Gerand noticed his peculiar lack of response to Volney's comment.

"You see his changes as disingenuous?" Gerand prodded.

"To be diplomatic to my new benefactor, I will say only that I find it highly coincidental that Chertanne's behavior changed with the arrival of his adviser, Kaimas."

They walked out of the barracks into a gray afternoon. Low dark clouds dropped large, heavy flakes on the ground. The snow had started only a few hours before, but it had already covered everything in a fluffy blanket of white. There was no wind, and Gen speculated that the storm would linger throughout the day.

The fresh snow improved the city, covering the dirty sludge churned up from the snow that had fallen three weeks ago. The weather meant fewer people on the streets, and the soft covering muffled the harsh edges of city's usual din. Gen judged that a snowstorm might be the best time to venture into streets he usually found unpleasant, noisy, and crowded.

"Is this your first time outside the castle walls since you challenged Chertanne?" Gerand asked, coming to a sudden realization.

"Yes," Gen replied.

"Then bury your face in that cowl! We'll do the same."

"You fear I'm still in danger?" Gen asked. "I was under the impression that the whole situation had settled down, given recent events."

Gerand laughed wryly. "Danger?" he said, signaling to the guards at the gate before lifting his cowl over his head. "Not from assassins, friend. From a mob."

"Really?"

"Tell him, Volney."

"Well," Volney explained, "it goes something like this. . . Gerand and I go into town every Sixthday to relax, take in some entertainment, and in general enjoy ourselves after getting unfairly beaten about by our masters. What do we end up doing instead? Answering questions about you and telling every young woman in the whole of Mikmir that, 'No, we won't deliver a letter to Lord Blackshire.' I swear, if we would have brought even half back to you, you would find you had little time to do anything else but read them! We almost stopped going into town because of it. They have provided us with a great deal of tinder to start the fire with, for which we thank you."

"I had no idea I was such a celebrity," Gen remarked.

"Oh, please," Volney retorted disgustedly. "You can't be *that* isolated. Surely you get news of what goes on in the city."

"A little," Gen said. "But I don't seem to recall that a few amorous young ladies were important enough news to concern anyone in the castle."

"If you say so," Volney said incredulously. "Well, if you are in need of some entertainment, then we'll see to it that you get some today. Some of the letters are absolutely scandalous. Gerand actually blushed."

"You read them?!" Gen exclaimed. "I thought you said you refused to accept the letters or burned them?"

"I only read a few," Volney stammered. "And that was only because..."

"I had nothing to do with it!" Gerand said, obviously embarrassed. "He insisted on reading them aloud to me despite my objections. I would never..."

"Calm down," Gen soothed. "I don't blame you for anything. I doubt there was much to get excited about anyway."

"I hope so," Gerand said, "because a stack of them went missing a few days ago. We suspect Kimdan has them."

"And if Kimdan has them..." Volney interjected before Gen could comment.

"Then the Lady Fairedale will know about them as well," Gerand finished.

"I am not worried," Gen shrugged. "I can hardly feel responsible for letters I have not seen or answered from women I do not know who are writing me without any solicitation on my part."

"But you can be sure," Gerand added, "that Kimdan will cast them in the worst possible light."

"Is he very public, then, about his affections for Fenna?"

"Yes," Gerand answered. "I don't know how close you and Miss Fairedale are, but to hear him tell it in the commons, he feels he has nothing to worry about."

Gen smiled to himself and let the subject drop. The snow fell more quickly now, smaller flakes dropping faster and more thickly. They stopped several times to ask for directions to Chadsbury Street, Gerand insisting on doing the talking to keep Gen's identity a secret for as long as possible. Fortunately, Chadsbury Street was a scant mile away and situated against the Kingsblood Lake.

As they approached the smithy, the rhythmic banging of hammer and anvil rang out sharply over the frozen water where children laughed and played on the ice. The three young men spied a roughly carved sign of an anvil hanging on a fence gate and opened it, working their way around to the back of the modest one-story home made of white plaster and wood. There they found the smith.

Morgan was a monster of a man, blue-eyed with black hair just starting to gray at the temples. The forge was in a large room behind the house, and, unlike most smithies, Morgan's room was not littered with broken plows, spades, and pots. Pieces of armor and weapons of all types were stacked or leaned against corners. As they entered, he looked up from a conical helm he had been reshaping. Gen lowered his cowl, his companions following suit.

"Lord Blackshire!" he said, bowing. "I am Morgan the Smith. I welcome you to my humble home."

"Thank you," Gen said. "Please stand and be at ease. I have been a commoner my whole life and am not accustomed to being bowed to. I should introduce Gerand Kildan and Volney Torunne, apprentices to the Dark Guard."

"Welcome all," Morgan said. "I want you to know that I followed the First Mother's instructions and told no one you were coming."

"The First Mother sent instructions?" Gen inquired, curious.

"She did, Milord," Morgan answered. "She feared you would be mobbed if I told anyone you were to visit me. Though I would like to introduce you to my boy, if you would allow it."

"Of course," Gen said.

"You wouldn't happen to have any daughters, would you?" Volney asked. Gerand elbowed him hard in the ribs. Morgan's face scrunched in confusion.

"No," he answered. "It's just me and my boy here. His ma died birthing him. But I'll fetch him after we are done so we won't be interrupted."

For the next hour, Morgan grilled Gen about the style of armor he wanted, taking notes on a fresh piece of parchment. Gen was impressed; most smiths in Tolnor could not read, much less write. After Gen described the designs he wanted on his breastplate, arm greaves, and leg greaves, he had to argue passionately for several minutes for Morgan to accept that he did not want a helmet of any sort, as it would interfere with his vision and hearing.

Volney and Gerand poked around the shop while Morgan measured and scribbled. They commented on several items, speculating as to how the damage to the items had been done.

"This was obviously done with a blunt lance," Volney said after examining a deeply dented breastplate. Morgan stopped writing for a moment.

"Actually," he corrected, "General Harband was thrown by his horse and he landed chest-first on a fence post."

"Old Hardman Harband?" Volney laughed. "Oh I wish I could have seen that."

"Killed the horse directly after, I hear," Morgan added, turning back to Gen. Volney laughed again.

"No doubt. And for you foreigners," Volney explained, "General Harband is as brutal and coarse a person you'll ever find in our refined nation. He's grumpy and ugly and wiry and has this scraggly white beard and these sunken beady eyes that make him look like he's a hundred years old. My father threatened to send me to train with him if I ever did something bad. Terrible, terrible stories about that man."

"Surely he can't be all that bad," Gerand said. "Regent Ogbith would dismiss him if he were so uncouth and wild."

"I'm sure the Regent would love to dismiss him but is too scared to do it," Volney argued. "When Harband was just a lowly Captain, they say his Knight Captain threatened to court-martial him for some reason. Harband gets mad, and that night he walks four miles to town, gets some thread and a needle from a tent maker, and sews the Knight Captain inside his tent while he's sleeping."

"That doesn't sound so bad," Gen said, arms outstretched as Morgan measured from his armpit to his elbow. The name Harband was vaguely familiar, but he couldn't remember where he'd heard it.

"Then he set the tent on fire," Volney added.

"And not only that," Morgan continued. "Before he sewed the tent shut, he threw in a canvas sack full of squirrels, badgers, and the like."

"Really?" Volney said. "I hadn't heard that little detail."

"That's ridiculous," Gerand said. "They would have dismissed him for such an act, even in Rhugoth."

"Ah!" Volney returned, finger pointing in the air. "They could not prove that he did it and he would not confess."

"Seems it would be easy to prove it was him," Gerand said. "He went into town, and catching badgers and squirrels is dicey, noisy business."

"How would you know anything about catching badgers and squirrels, *Prince* of Tolnor?" Volney countered.

Gerand and Volney spent the rest of the time arguing the merits and fallacies of the fantastic story, Morgan interjecting from time to time with other exploits that proved that General Harband was capable of other gross forms of malice. Gen listened, amused, thinking the material perfect for a little barding, if he were ever to have the chance of it again.

"That is all I can do today," Morgan said, stowing his materials. "I'll need you to come back from time to time during the next few weeks to do additional fittings and adjustments. Your project is highest priority, though I'll need to repair the General's breastplate quickly, lest he become angry with me."

"I can certainly understand that," Gen said.

"Let me fetch my boy, if you'll permit. He's only fourteen and watched you at the Trials. I daresay he's imitated you a great deal in this very shop room. Scares me to death."

Gen smiled and nodded his assent, and Morgan jogged to the edge of the lake and shouted for his son, Emry. Gen watched them return. Emry, while not as bulky as his father, was still muscular and tall, even at fourteen. By his movement, Gen surmised that he was agile. The boy smiled affectionately at his father as they approached the smithy. Gen couldn't help but size Emry up as an excellent candidate for a fighter, as long as further growth didn't ruin his quickness and balance.

"Emry," Morgan said as they entered the shop, "these are Gerand Kildan and Volney Torunne, Apprentices to the Dark Guard. This is Lord Blackshire, Protector of the Holy Chalaine."

Emry's mouth dropped and he stood rooted in the doorway. Gerand and Volney grinned widely. Gen stepped forward and offered his hand. Emry took it and shook it, still stunned.

"Lord Blackshire!" he exclaimed. "Well, I should bow, right Pa?"

"Don't bother," Gen interjected quickly. "We are all friends here. Your father says you watched me at the Trials."

"Yes, sir!" he exclaimed, eyes brightening with the memory. "It was the best thing I've seen in my whole life. You were so fast. I ain't never seen anyone so fast."

"I'm glad I could entertain a little, at least. Here." Gen removed the dagger from his boot and handed it to him. It was thin and finely crafted, a silver rose etched into the ebony blade. "Find me in two years, and if you can throw the dagger and hit a target at twenty paces, I'll teach you a little of the blade."

Emry took the dagger reverentially. Morgan smiled and thanked Gen for the gift, as Emry was too engrossed in examining it to respond.

"Thank you!" Emry said after a helpful nudge from his father.

"You are most welcome. We had best be going. Just send word to the castle when you need me again. Good day."

Cowls up, Gen and his companions walked quickly back into the street. As they turned onto the road, they could faintly hear Emry yelling excitedly to his friends on the frozen lake.

"You are irritatingly good with people," Volney commented, "no matter what everyone says about your personality. I would have never thought to do that for his son. He has just become the most popular of all the boys on the street. Are you serious about taking him on as an apprentice after the prophecy is fulfilled?"

"Yes. He is built for it, as long as he doesn't lose his agility. He could still be trained to good effect, even so."

The snow had persisted during their visit and showed no signs of abating. Gen turned to go back toward the castle, but Gerand brought him up short.

"You aren't on watch for another four hours, correct?" Gerand asked.

"Yes. Why?"

Volney grabbed his arm and steered him in a different direction. "Then for your inaugural trip into town, we shall introduce you to a wonderful establishment called the Quickblade."

"Is that really a good idea?" Gen asked. "You warned me of being mobbed, and Protectors are not allowed to drink."

"The Quickblade is close to the castle and gets its name from the number of castle guard and Dark Guard who frequent it," Gerand explained. "So you won't be so put upon there as you would be elsewhere. Jaron is there often. And you don't have to drink anything but water if you don't want to. Jaron doesn't seem to mind a little ale now and then, though. Come on. You need to relax a bit. Besides, Volney has someone *special* there he likes to see whenever he gets the chance of it."

"Shut up, Gerand," Volney growled darkly.

"It doesn't sound like he's very excited about it," Gen returned. Volney studiously ignored them both.

"As it turns out," Gerand said, "there is a certain Innkeeper's daughter who, unlike the rest of the young ladies in the city, is completely unimpressed with *apprentices* to the Dark Guard. This annoys him greatly, especially as he is smitten by her."

Gen smiled. "And what about you, Gerand?" he asked. "I imagine a handsome princeling from Tolnor would have his pick of the ladies."

Gerand's countenance immediately fell. "I was promised to be married to Oelia Mukor, and I still hope to be able to someday."

Oelia was the younger sister of the Queen of Tolnor and was reputedly very beautiful. The war and Gerand's apprenticeship to the Dark Guard had thrown his hopes and his parents' plans into some difficulty. Gen sympathized with him, and he wondered if Torbrand's daughter, Mena, had heard that the man she hoped her father would win for her had won a place as an apprentice to the Dark Guard.

The Quickblade was a clean, bright, two-story establishment constructed of light-colored stones and mortar. It sat just south of the castle walls, puffing smoke from four of its eight chimneys. As it stood at the termination of a steeply ascending street, it possessed a Church-like quality. Friendly lights beckoned to them through clean window panes on a mid-afternoon turned mid-evening by glowering clouds.

"By the way, gentlemen," Gen said offhandedly to his two dispirited companions, "we have been followed all afternoon. Do not look! He followed us out of castle and is behind us about forty paces."

They went inside quickly, and a boy waited just inside to take their cloaks. As soon as he saw Gen's face, he grabbed the cloaks and ran into the common room shouting that Lord Blackshire had come. Volney rolled his eyes and Gerand shook his head.

"Might as well get this over with," Volney sighed, ushering Gen forward. Gen stepped inside slowly, not quite sure what to expect. The bard stopped playing, all talk died, and every eye turned toward the entryway. An impossibly thin man ran out of a door in the back, wiping his hands on a heavily stained apron.

"Lord Blackshire!" he said grandly. "Welcome to the Quickblade. We had so hoped you would come one day and, well, here you are! I am Innkeeper Cedric, and I am at your personal service!"

Gen was about to reply his thanks when the bard started playing a song. Everyone joined in the tune, and Gen guessed that all the servants and cooks in the establishment were abandoning their posts to rush into the common room and join in the impromptu choir.

Here's to the man of great reknown,
Who, when Chertanne sailed into town
And tried to have his sweet Chalaine,
Served him up a plate of shame.

Gen, Gen the dead-faced man,
Voice of thunder, sword in hand.
Chertanne's a King, or so they say,
But Gen's the one who gets his way.

Gen defied the demon trance.
Chertanne turned pale and wet his pants.
Gen fought and bled and nearly died.
Chertanne fell on the floor and cried.

Gen, Gen the dead-faced man.
Eyes of stone, sword in hand.
Chertanne's a King, or so they say,
But Gen's the one who gets his way.

Chertanne can play and hold his beer
But cannot stomach demon fear.
The Chalaine's Chertanne's, as is his right,
But who stays with her every night?

Gen, Gen the dead-faced man.
Nerve of iron, sword in hand.
Chertanne's a King, or so they say,
But Gen's the one who gets his way.

Chertanne is grand when times are fun,
But come a fight, then Gen's the one.

"They add a verse every couple of weeks or so," Gerand commented as the song ended in clapping and cheering. Gen waved to everyone and took a seat at a table near the fire. To his chagrin, he noticed several people leaving quickly and had no doubt that the Quickblade's patronage was about to double. He tried to settle in and be as nondescript as possible, although he had a difficult time ignoring the constant glances popping at him from all sides of the room.

A nubile young woman with chestnut brown hair and brown eyes sauntered to the table with a smirk on her face. Volney saw her approach and immediately pretended to inspect the fireplace to his left. His strangled, uncomfortable demeanor betrayed his feelings for the woman, and Gen grinned. To see an apprentice to the Dark Guard, a formidable fighter, reduced to such squirming was a pleasant reminder of the person beneath the uniform.

"Welcome to the Quickblade, Gerand and Volney. Would you like to introduce me to your new companion?"

"He doesn't need an introduction, for pity's sake," Volney grumbled, avoiding her gaze.

"But *I* do!" the young woman returned with asperity. Volney's face turned red.

"Lord Blackshire," Gerand said, standing, "this is Gina, the Innkeeper's daughter."

Gen stood. "It is a pleasure to make your acquaintance."

She stared at the scars on his face. Gen wondered if she heard him at all. "The pleasure is all mine," she finally said. "Forgive me for staring. It's just that, well. . ."

"No need to explain," Gen soothed as he returned to his seat. "I know my appearance is a little frightening."

"No, no!" she blushed. "It's not that. It's just there are so many stories and descriptions of you! It's hard to believe that one man could do as much as you have. I think everyone just wonders what someone is like who has done such amazing things! You guard the Chalaine! You've fought a demon!"

Out of the corner of his eye, Gen spotted the man who had followed them that day enter. He refused to doff his cloak, choosing to sit alone in a corner across the room. He was horribly conspicuous, and Gen realized the man could not be a professional spy—or if he was, he was extraordinarily bad at it.

"I assure you," Gen told Gina, "that I am quite ordinary."

"If you say so, though I doubt anyone here will quite be convinced of that. What can I get such a fine gentlemen today?"

Gen ordered water, while Gerand and Volney ordered ale, Volney speaking so softly that Gina had to prod him to speak up.

"Volney," Gen said after Gina left, "I thought you liked the girl. I hardly doubt that acting sullen will help you win her affections."

"You don't know what I've been through. What she said to me!" Volney whined. "You have it easy. You don't even have to try to get women to offer their attentions to you anymore. You're up in the castle swimming in a lake full of beautiful women begging for you to dive in."

Gerand shot Gen a look that Gen interpreted as, "Drop it." Gen turned his attention to the man in the corner. He hadn't ordered anything, sitting rigidly in his chair, face hidden in a cowl, the dark opening pointed in the direction of Gen's table.

Gina returned with the drinks, and, as Gen had predicted, people started filling the inn to overflowing. Soon Gen found he could hardly take a sip in between shaking hands and receiving compliments, congratulations on his elevation, and nervous curtsies from every young woman from every household within a comfortable walking distance to the inn.

"I'd better leave," Gen yelled to Gerand above the roar. "This is getting out of hand. Cedric will never want me to return."

"Don't be ridiculous," Gerand yelled back. "He's scraping up more money this evening than he earns in a week."

Gen stood to go anyway, and when he did, the bard launched into another rendition of "Gen's Song." The patrons stood and danced, swirling around and gradually pushing Gen toward the front of the room. The roar of so many voices and the smell of pipe smoke and beer were overwhelming, and Gen felt uneasy. Days and nights of solitude in the castle had unaccustomed him to such revelry. Gen managed to work his way back to his own table by the end of the last verse.

The bard, a plump, puffy man with fine pleated pantaloons and a multicolored shirt and hat rose from his stool and silenced the crowd.

"I know we are all glad that Lord Blackshire finally graced us with a visit to Cedric's fine establishment that has served as host to many men of renown and great courage through the years. I believe I speak for everyone when I say that we thank him for his service. I think we should have a speech! A few words, Lord Blackshire, if you please!"

Gen tried to wave off the opportunity, but the general clamor became so insistent that he felt compelled to say something or risk offending at least a hundred people.

With some prodding from the bard, Gen stood atop his table and stared into a sea of expectant, anticipatory faces. Gen cleared his throat and searched for something to say.

"Tell us about the demon attack!" someone yelled before he could squeeze a word out.

"Well," he said, "if you would like." A general shout of approval was the reply, and Gen launched into the story, feeling grateful for the chance to finally tell it like it was—the demon smashing him several seconds into the whole affair. While he began falteringly, Rafael's training returned to him, and before long, his gesturing, intonation, and vivid descriptions held his audience captive as he puppetted their emotions through the intense story. So enthralled were the patrons, that when Gen concluded, no one spoke for fear of breaking the spell.

"Well," Gen ended loudly, "it is close to the time for my watch, and I shouldn't keep the Chalaine waiting."

The man that had been following him slid out of his booth and walked quickly toward the door as the crowd expressed their disappointment.

"But you've got to tell us about killing Cormith!" Another roar of approval. Gen settled them with his hands.

"Some other time, perhaps," he said. "But I have some pressing matters to attend to, such as finding out why that man has been following me around all day."

Gen pointed to the man, who was almost to the door. All eyes turned to the stunned figure who yanked the door open and plunged through it.

"Get him!" someone shouted, and three burly off-duty soldiers bounded out into the night. Gen hopped down and a path was cleared for him, though Gen figured the inn-goers mistook his purpose. Rather than run to catch the man, he hoped to keep him from being attacked by his three benefactors. Volney and Gerand came quickly behind, as did half of those in the common room.

Outside, the snow was deep and all sounds muffled. It was dark enough that Gen couldn't see the man or the soldiers anymore, and he jogged ahead tentatively, the steep hill in front of the inn making for treacherous running. Most of those pouring from the common room held up just outside the inn, for which Gen was thankful. At the bottom of the hill, the three soldiers were returning, one with a bruised eye and another carrying a ripped blue cloak.

"Milord," the one with the cloak said, handing it to Gen. "He gave us the slip. Headed back in the direction of the castle, we think. Though it was very dark in the alley he chose to run through."

"Thank you," Gen said. The cloak was of rich cloth and was finely woven. "I'm sure it was nothing." The soldiers bowed and trudged back up the hill. Gen turned to Volney and Gerand. "I'll see if I can get to the bottom of this," he said. "I will let you know what I find out, if anything."

"We'll walk back with you," Gerand offered.

"We'll have to walk quickly," Gen said, "or I'll be late."

The streets were mostly empty as they hiked back. Gerand and Volney split off toward the apprentices' quarters as Gen jogged up the hill toward the castle. Once inside the walls, he entered through the kitchens, Marna greeting him warmly. It took a concentrated effort to keep her from feeding him and a strong dedication to resist the savory smells and sights around him in favor of being on time. He hurried out of the kitchens before Marna's entreaties and the promise of good food could lessen his opinion of punctuality.

A breathless soldier ran to catch him just as he was about to cross the bridge to the Chalaine's shard. "Milord, the First Mother requests you in the Great Hall immediately."

Gen dismissed him, curiosity piqued, and went to the Great Hall where the doors were open. A grumpy-looking First Mother, Ethris, and Regent Ogbith stood just inside the doors with a smug Athan standing with his arms behind his back, face flushed. Gen bowed to the First Mother.

"This had better be good, Padra," Mirelle said acidly. "I was with my daughter and do not like to be disturbed."

"This will only take a moment, Highness," Athan said, small eyes alive with glee. He walked with a slight limp as he approached Gen. "So, *young* man, you are aware, are you not, that as one of the Chalaine's Protectors you are not permitted to imbibe liquors, as it will dull your ability to perform your duty adequately?"

"I am."

"And were you not, just minutes ago, at the Quickblade Inn drinking?"

"Indeed, I was," Gen had to try hard not to smile.

"You admit it!" Athan crowed, ecstatic. "I would not have expected you to be so cavalier about your indiscretions! You must be suspended from your duties!"

The First Mother, Ethris, and the Regent wrinkled their brows almost in unison.

"I am sure he did not drink enough to impair himself," Mirelle argued, making light of the accusation.

"Even a small amount is grounds enough for suspension," Athan said. "And my reports say he had more than a little. Just how much did you drink, Gen?"

"I believe," Gen said honestly, "that I had three full tankards."

"Three!" Athan exclaimed. "There you have it, Mirelle! He is clearly unfit!"

"I don't see why three tankards would incapacitate me," Gen said. As he had hoped, Padra Athan eagerly took the bait.

"What? Are you some sort of braggart? Are you going to tell me you can hold your liquor so well that you can drink with impunity? I am sure you are quite familiar with the effects of ale, are you not? This isn't the first time you've gone drinking, I'm sure."

"Certainly. I've been drinking before, but. . ."

"No excuses! No explanations! You are dismissed!"

"You are going to dismiss me for taking three tankards of water?"

Athan froze. "What? You just admitted you had been drinking!"

Mirelle, who had gradually appeared more and more distressed, relaxed and grinned.

"Well, you have to drink water, too," Gen said, "unless someone has come up with a way to eat it. I suppose you could freeze it in weather like this, but is ice really still water in the traditional sense?"

"These are outrageous lies," Athan said. "My reports said you were drinking ale."

"With all due respect," Gen countered, "whoever you had follow me was so far on the other side of the common room that he could not possibly hear what I ordered or see what I was drinking. And here is his cloak. The patrons were rather spirited in their pursuit of him this evening." Athan turned bright red, ignoring the cloak Gen held out to him. "I would think the Church could afford better spies."

"Ethris!" Athan sputtered, "Give me the Truth Staff!"

"Please, Athan," Ethris said. "This is ridiculous. Don't exacerbate your mistake."

"Give it to me!"

"There is nothing to worry about, Ethris," Gen said. "Give it to him." Ethris shrugged and handed the Staff to Athan, who stuck it in Gen's face. Gen grasped the other end.

"Were you drinking ale this evening?" Athan demanded, concentrating.

"No," Gen replied.

"Were you drinking wine this evening?

"No,"

"Beer?"

"Nope."

"Mead?"

"That's enough, Athan," Mirelle said vehemently, pulling Gen away. "You have wasted our time with your stupid little crusade to discredit Gen. You no longer have my attention. Come, Gen. Escort me back to my daughter."

Athan stalked off mumbling coarsely to himself as Mirelle led the Chalaine's Protector away briskly.

"Why did you have to taunt him?" Mirelle asked as they crossed over the bridge and into the antechamber of the Chalaines.

"He seemed to be having so much fun I didn't have the heart to stop him right away." The First Mother laughed and Gen continued. "And besides, he deserved it."

"That he did," Mirelle agreed. "You certainly have a penchant for annoying important people."

"I hope I haven't offended your Grace or the Chalaine with my rash behavior."

"I can't speak for the Chalaine, but I have, thus far, found your rashness rather entertaining, though I think we both wish your antics were more conducive to keeping your head on your shoulders. You only offend me by not visiting me enough." Gen was unsure how to reply to that. "Oh yes," Mirelle said as they entered the maze, "I hear there is a song about you burning up the inns in our fair city. Do you know it?"

"I hear there are several different versions. It changes constantly. I heard one this evening. It is a bit rowdy and more than a little controversial. Your Grace might do well to simply avoid it."

"Excellent. I shall have a bard brought in immediately to sing it for me. I must be apprised of all things rowdy and controversial within my borders. I'm sure the House of Regents will demand to hear it, as well, if they haven't already."

Gen groaned inwardly.

"It is a gross exaggeration of my character and my reputation. Hardly worth your attention."

"I am surprised, Gen," the First Mother teased. "I thought you would know my character well enough by now to realize that the more you protest, the more likely I will want to have it played for me."

Jaron bowed as they approached the door. Gen apologized for his tardiness. Jaron, of course, cared little and headed off immediately.

"Thank you for the escort, Gen," Mirelle said, tapping on the Chalaine's door. "Let me know if Athan gives you any more trouble."

"Well?" the Chalaine asked expectantly. She and Fenna sat in front of the Walls, which currently showed Gen standing calmly on guard outside the door. "We could see that Athan was worked up about something. Did Gen tell you anything about the song they were singing, or the story he told this afternoon that had everyone so enthralled?"

"Really, Chalaine," Mirelle said quietly, "I think Gen might be a little offended that you and Fenna have been spying on him all afternoon. It is a bit childish, don't you think?"

"Please, Mother. You of all people shouldn't be lecturing me about spying, especially when you've been spying right along with us. Besides, Fenna is in a fair way to be in love with Gen and she needs to know what he is like when he's not on duty and in the castle."

"But you seem to be the one asking all the questions. Fenna has been quite silent. A little perturbed over all the attention he was getting from the young ladies at the inn, Miss Fairedale?"

"Yes!" she exclaimed. "Did you see how all the girls mooned at him and fawned over him and smiled and flirted. Absolutely disgusting!"

"You need a bit more confidence in yourself," the Chalaine placated. "It was plain that he didn't enjoy their attentions at all."

"How could he not enjoy it?" Fenna said. "He's a man. And then there are those letters he never told me about. Kimdan found some of them in Gerand's quarters. Absolutely shameful and forward, all of them!"

"Pout if you must," Mirelle said. "But I will tell you what happened with Athan. As for the song, I will have to arrange for the bard at the Quickblade to give us a little private performance."

CHAPTER 31 - THE ASH WITCH

In the afternoon before Gen's watch, Fenna and the Chalaine invited him to come to the Antechamber of the Chalaines to play cards with them in company with Dason and Eldwena as part of an informal celebration of Dason's release from Chertanne's service. When Gen arrived, they had already started and were so concentrated on the game that only Jaron standing guard nearby noticed his approach, nodding his head in acknowledgment.

Dason sat with his back toward Gen. Since his reinstatement to the Dark Guard, Dason had transformed almost instantly from a slump-shouldered shadow to his beaming, gregarious self. The only thing that hadn't changed was the tender, longing expression that fell over his face with his every glance toward the Chalaine. Gen thought the First Mother perfectly justified in her worry over Dason's feelings for her daughter and wondered how much of those feelings the Chalaine returned.

"Ah, Gen!" Dason greeted. "At last we shall cross swords across the card table!"

Gen genuflected to the Chalaine and took his seat next to Fenna, who kissed him on the cheek.

"You can see," Dason continued, "that we have a drink

ready for you, just water, out of deference to Athan." Dason winked. "I assume you know how to play Red Wheel?"

"It has been a while," Gen said, "but I think I remember."

"Excellent," Dason said, shuffling the cards and dealing them with a nimble skill born of much practice.

"I must warn you, Gen," the Chalaine said, "that Dason is very good, as is Eldwena. The rest of us can hardly win a round."

Gen noticed that Dason appeared hurt by the Chalaine's statement.

"I will do my best," Gen answered, assessing the cards Dason dealt him.

Gen played conservatively the first round, watching everyone closely. Fenna and the Chalaine played for fun rather than to win, while Eldwena was serious and eyed every card laid down. Owing to the Chalaine's comment, Dason purposefully lost, doing what he could to surreptitiously help the Chalaine. Eldwena won handily.

"You played very well, your Holiness," Dason complimented her fawningly. "But a card or two more in your favor, and the match would have been yours. And Gen, if you wish to do better, you will have to pay more attention to what cards everyone else has played."

"I'll keep that in mind," Gen said as Eldwena gathered and shuffled the cards for the next round. As Eldwena dealt and they started playing, Dason jabbered on with humorous stories of his card exploits of the past, eliciting laughter from the ladies who were clearly enjoying his company. Gen wondered how many hearts the handsome Prince of Tolnor had broken when he signed on to the Dark Guard. Gen was annoyed at Dason's smooth manner with the women and his affectionate glances at the Chalaine, so he exercised what Rafael had taught him about cards.

Many young bards survived on what they could win at

cards and dice because the poorer inns that journeymen frequented rarely produced much in the way of income from musical exhibition. After a few games in Tell, no one would play cards with Rafael anymore, and once Gen had reached the age of fifteen, Rafael finally thought him old enough to bestow all of his techniques—some rather underhanded—for winning the major card games played in courts and taverns alike. Despite this training, Gen never could consistently beat Rafael, and he suspected his master kept back some of his masterful methods for himself. Gen could, however, beat anyone else he knew.

In the next hour, Gen won all but three hands despite Dason changing games twice and abandoning his attempts to aid the Chalaine by losing. Dason poured all of his effort into strategy and examining every card Gen played. Eldwena started slamming her cards down and swearing near the end, and the Chalaine called an end to the games, claiming she was tired, when it appeared that Dason would force them to play until he managed to defeat Gen.

Everyone rose and left, Gen feeling quite smug, until Fenna gave him a cold farewell and left, escorted by Dason. The Chalaine dismissed Eldwena for the evening so she could spend time with her family, and the handmaiden shot Gen a withering look before stalking across the bridge.

"You know, Gen," the Chalaine commented as they rose and worked their way through the maze, "it is ungentlemanly to win so much. I think it would be doubly so in your own country."

"Among nobles, I suppose," Gen answered, realizing guiltily that he had let his desire to punish Dason ruin everyone else's fun. "Rafael taught me that in cards, there are no gentlemen, only winners and losers. I apologize for blemishing Dason's evening. I will simply excuse myself from playing from now on."

"I hardly think Dason will let you get away with that. He will pester you to play unceasingly until he has mastered you. There is another solution, however."

"What is that?"

"Tell me how you do it. You cheat, I imagine."

"It's not *all* cheating," Gen replied defensively.

"I'm sure. Tell me how to do it. I've got the cards right here."

"Why would Dason leave me alone if I taught you to win at cards?"

"Because he will be too distressed over being trounced by a woman. So what do you do? What did Rafael teach you? I want it all."

"You can't ask me to do this!" Gen protested. "I am not going to be the one who corrupts the *Holy* Chalaine by teaching her how to cheat at cards. What would the Padra Athan say about me then?"

"I thought I was talking to Gen, not Dason. You *will* teach me. I am so tired of Dason letting me win. If I can beat him all the time, he'll stop. If it helps your conscience any, just think of it as teaching Alumira—not the Chalaine—how to cheat at cards."

"As you wish." Gen rubbed his chin speculatively. "Actually, if you have two people chea—working—together in a game. . ."

"That's more like it."

"And you have the clothes for it," Gen continued. "You could hide fifty decks of cards in those robes, and the veil makes it impossible for anyone to see if you're nervous and shifty. You could be formidable indeed! But I do require something in return."

"Such as?"

"Such as putting in a good word for me with Fenna. I think she despises me right now."

"Done."

For the next several hours, Gen taught the Chalaine everything he knew about winning at cards, and she absorbed it enthusiastically. Her mind was sharp, and beneficially, she had dexterous hands. By the time she finally went to bed at well past midnight, Gen realized he had created a monster. He cautioned her not to start winning all at once, lest she arouse suspicion. He could sense that she was awake a good while before she fell asleep, no doubt anxious with anticipation for the next opportunity to smash her entire acquaintance at cards.

Near the end of his watch, Gen heard footsteps approaching, and they were too light and coming too quickly to be Jaron's. A servant emerged from the maze, huffing a bit as she delivered her message.

"Chertanne requests the Chalaine's presence and your own in the library in half an hour, Lord Blackshire. The First Mother was summoned as well."

"Thank you," Gen said.

The servant bowed and left as hurriedly as she had come. Gen knocked on the door and relayed the message to a sleepy Chalaine who yawned and promised to come shortly. Gen wondered what Chertanne was about.

As the First Mother predicted, since the arrival of Kaimas, Chertanne had changed his behavior a great deal. Gen saw him rarely, but when he did, the Ha'Ulrich forwent his usual unpleasantness and behaved with civility, if only a practiced one, toward the Chalaine and those close to her. Kaimas himself was rarely seen, but his influence hung palpably over Chertanne. The rough edges only surfaced intermittently, especially when he drank. While Gen doubted Chertanne had changed in a sincere way, even a feigned sense of propriety was better than none at all.

When a yawning Chalaine was ready, they left, meeting Jaron in the Antechamber. He took Gen's place behind the Chalaine and the Chalaine took Gen's arm and pulled him next to her.

"What do you suppose this is all about?" she asked quietly. "It is rare enough for Chertanne to summon you to anything, much less early in the morning. I am quite concerned that something terrible has happened. You haven't offended Padra Athan again or anything, have you?"

"No. Athan has avoided me since I disappointed him by not being sloshing drunk the other night. I am at just as much of a loss as you are."

When they arrived at the library, Chertanne and his new guard, a Captain Drockley, were there, Chertanne sitting on the couch where Gen usually read. He rose smiling, bowing for the Chalaine before taking his seat again. Mirelle and Cadaen sat across from him, and Athan frowned upon seeing the Chalaine escorted by Gen, though Gen noted a certain self-satisfaction in the way the Padra carried himself. Mirelle stood and greeted her daughter and Gen, offering her seat to her and taking her place at Gen's side.

"What is this all about, Chertanne?" the Chalaine asked.

"Patience, my dear," he said happily. "We await the Mages and Regent Ogbith."

They didn't arrive for several more minutes, and an uncomfortable silence hung over the small assembly. Ethris and Kaimas came one after the other, and Regent Ogbith, who had to be fetched from his residence in the city, entered last, eyes bloodshot.

"Excellent," Chertanne began, standing. "I apologize for the early hour, but messages arrived late last night that I was sure you would want to hear immediately." Gen caught the brief flash of surprise on Kaimas's face; Chertanne had not apprised him of the letters yet.

The Ha'Ulrich shuffled the papers in his hand. "The contents of the messages will affect Gen the most directly, so if you would like to sit. . ."

"No, thank you," Gen declined.

"Very well. The messages are long, so I will summarize. First, Tolnor has surrendered and is now under the control of my father." Gen's heart sank, and Mirelle tightened her grip upon his arm. "Your deposed King Filingrail is in hiding, but despite this, my father will allow the leadership of your duchies to remain under the control of the Dukes as long as they swear fealty after the Tolnorian fashion to my father and accept the presence of a Warlord to help direct the affairs of their respective regions. Even you, Gen, will have to admit that this is a generous concession, indeed."

Gen knew that it was, but he said nothing. The thought of Aughmere controlling Tolnor in any degree was abhorrent to him. While he knew it unlikely, he had hoped Tolnor would provide a fierce enough defense to force Khairn to abandon his war.

"As the new King of Tolnor," Chertanne continued, paraphrasing from the thick letter in his hands, "my father informed the Church that Tolnor is again ready to honor the Fidelium and that I will march in command of the full strength of the nations of Ki'Hal when the time comes for war against Mikkik. He expresses his regret over the lives he took in defense of the Fidelium."

Gen thwarted a strong impulse to laugh in derision at the Shadan's disingenuous piety.

"The second message is also from my father and concerns Gen particularly. Under my direction, and as part of my gratitude for Gen's distinguished service to my sublime fiancé, I asked my father and Kaimas to see if they could find any of Gen's friends or acquaintances from Tell that might have survived. I am happy to report that some were found." Gen's heart leapt in his chest. Chertanne continued, "It says in the letter that there are five persons: a Mr. and Mrs. Morewold, their daughter Murea, and two youths named Gant and Yuerile. He writes that Gen would know them well."

All eyes turned to Gen, who was fighting with conflicting emotions. "I do," he said. "I thank you, your Grace." For the first time since the day Chertanne arrived in Rhugoth, Gen genuflected to the Ha'Ulrich. Athan was visibly pleased, though his smile touched nothing but his lips.

"They are being conveyed to Rhugoth as we speak and should arrive before the end of the week. Well, that is all. I will leave this first letter with the First Mother and Regent Ogbith for further perusal so that they can fully understand the arrangement my father has negotiated during Tolnor's surrender."

Chertanne rose to leave, but Athan stepped forward quickly. "A moment, your Grace," he said. "I have an announcement of equal import, if you'll forgive me."

Chertanne, perplexed, took his seat.

"Say on, Padra."

"I am pleased to announce that our investigation into the Burka pattern has at last yielded fruit. We have caught the criminals and they will be executed in the Main Square shortly. I have riders spreading the news now so a sizable gathering can be ready. It is important this be as public as possible to restore faith in the people. The Chalaine and the Ha'Ulrich will not be permitted anywhere near the spectacle, of course. I am leaving directly to attend."

"What!" a shocked Mirelle burst out, releasing Gen's arm. "You order a public execution without my. . ."

"Athan!" Ethris said loudly, cutting the First Mother off. "Who did you catch? And how?" The worry in Ethris's eyes, reflected in those of Kaimas's, took Athan aback.

"My men were inquiring about town when a man tipped us off to the presence of an old witch living in the Damned Quarter. We raided the place late yesterday afternoon and found an old woman and a man there with several drawings of Burka patterns in their possession. We immediately ordered everyone out of Bainburrow Cathedral and imprisoned them in the catacombs under magical guard."

"What did they look like?" Ethris prodded impatiently.

"Fairly nondescript from what I heard. Both forty or fifty years old, dark hair. The man had one blue eye and one white. You know something! Out with it!"

A breathless Padra Nolan entering the room at a jog surprised everyone.

"Your Grace, a moment."

"Is this about the detainees?" Athan asked.

"Yes, your Grace," Nolan replied, wiping his brow.

"Then you can speak. They know."

"Very well. I was there when they removed the prisoners from the cell this morning. I don't understand it, but instead of an old woman, a. . ."

"A girl!" Kaimas exclaimed. "You fools! You have no idea who you're dealing with!"

"What!?" Mirelle inquired, a puzzled Athan shouting the same inquiry.

"Are they still headed toward the square?" Ethris questioned, ignoring everyone.

"Yes," Padra Nolan answered, perplexed. "We figured it Ilch's work."

"Mirelle," Ethris explained, voice barely restrained. "That square has to be cleared!"

"Who is it, Ethris? Kaimas?" Athan yelled. The two Magicians glanced at each other before answering in unison.

"Our mother."

"How could your mother be a girl?" Padran Nolan asked.

"Our mother has been alive since before the Shattering," Kaimas explained uncomfortably. "She dies every day. At sundown she crumbles to ash and is reborn a babe, aging throughout the day. It is the price of her immortality, a corrupt gift from Mikkik to her. The only time the cycle is stopped is when she is with child, as she was when she bore triplets, Ethris, Dethris, and I. She has children often simply so she can live normally for a while. I'd wager half the students in the academies of magic over the years were her bastard children."

"Your mother is a witch, then? An evil witch?" Athan exclaimed.

"She is a Mage, yes," Ethris said gravely, "the most powerful alive, I suspect. But explanations can wait. You must stop the carriage and clear the square. Now."

"But we have her under guard of three Padras!" Padra Nolan said. "Surely she is contained or can be killed!"

"No," Kaimas rebutted. "She is only caught when she wants to be caught. You take her to that square and she will kill hundreds, if not thousands."

"Then we should kill her while she is in the carriage!" Athan argued. "When she isn't suspecting it."

"You can't kill her!" Ethris said.

"Nonsense!" Athan objected. "She can die, can't she?"

"Yes," Kaimas said, "but it will take a Trysmagician or extraordinary luck to do it. You know the legend of the Ash Witch, don't you? *She* is the Ash Witch. Mikkik appointed her to be an Elda to sit in Owena's throne as goddess when he comes to power. He remade her a pureblood Mynmagician and Duammagician. My brothers and I are but half-blood. Your best Padra is likely quarter-blood at best."

"So are we supposed to just let her go?" Athan asked incredulously.

"If you are wise," Ethris answered, "you will do just that. Walk away. She will still kill, but not thousands as she will if you continue this course."

"I cannot in good conscience do such a thing! How could we face the people?" Athan said. He turned to Padra Nolan. "I will communicate to them to turn back to the Damned Quarter and the Cathedral. We will kill her there. You watch through Padra Gray's mind. I will contact Padra Tremain."

"It will fail!" Kaimas yelled. "Listen to me!" But Athan had closed his eyes.

"Your Grace," Ethris said to the First Mother. "Send

word to clear the square." Mirelle turned to Regent Ogbith, who nodded his head.

"I will see it done," he said, leaving quickly.

The room fell silent. The two Padras concentrated, faces serene. No one moved or even fidgeted, watching intently until the Padras' faces contorted in pain and paled. For several moments they didn't breathe. "They are under attack," Padra Athan uttered through clenched teeth. "We're trying to assist. . ." The words struggled from his mouth as his breath returned, laboring.

"Get the Chalaine out of here!" Mirelle commanded. The Chalaine stood and left quickly with Jaron behind.

"Perhaps I should leave as well," Chertanne said uncertainly. "Come, Drockley."

"Can you help them?" Mirelle asked Ethris after Chertanne left.

"I. . ."

Both Padras screamed, grabbing the sides of their heads as if to hold them together. As one, their eyes snapped open and they fell, shoved to the floor by some unseen force.

"Ethris?!" the First Mother exclaimed worriedly.

"The contact is broken, Highness," Ethris said calmingly. "They should revive momentarily." Ethris crossed to Athan, signaling for Kaimas to check on Padra Nolan. Both Padras lay still for nearly a minute before stirring. Blood ran from their noses and their hands shook as the old Magicians helped them onto the couch.

"Such power!" Padra Nolan exclaimed. "She attacked me through Gray's mind! Through my own link!"

"And me through Tremain's at the same time," Padra Athan added angrily. "We must get news of what happened."

"Regent Ogbith will see to that," Mirelle said. "I will send for the other Padras to attend you."

"So," Athan said, gathering himself and glaring at Ethris

and Kaimas accusatorily, "you two knew who inscribed the Burka pattern, didn't you? And the fires? Your mother is the Ash Witch, and here you are in the service of the Ha'Ulrich and the Chalaine! Merciful Eldaloth! You should be dismissed for this!"

"We did not know it was her for certain," Ethris returned with equal acrimony. "She was certainly a suspect, but there are others who could have done it. Joranne isn't one you can send soldiers out searching for, even if you knew where to look for her. Your three dead Padras will be evidence enough of that!"

"So Joranne is her name, then. Sounds harmless enough for someone of such frightening power. And who is the man with the strange eyes?" Athan asked, still incensed. "The Ilch? Some other Magician?"

"We have no idea," Kaimas answered.

"Wonderful," Athan returned, standing unsteadily. "We will have an inquiry about you two. I doubt even Mirelle wants you around after these startling revelations. You are practically Mikkik's stepchildren!"

"I doubt Mirelle is as stupid as you are," Kaimas growled.

"How dare you address a Padra in that fashion!" Padra Nolan yelled.

"Gentlemen!" Mirelle interrupted. "That is enough. Let us assess the situation. And Padra Athan, surely you must see that whatever their genealogy, Ethris and Kaimas are the best protection against Joranne we have. Ethris has served long and well, so calm yourself. Panic and accusations will do little good now."

"Come, Padra Nolan," Athan said, ignoring Mirelle. "We have work to do."

"We should head into the city," Kaimas said to Ethris. "We may be able to prevent further damage."

"Your Grace?" Ethris asked.

"Go," she said, running her hands through her hair.

"Come with me, Gen. I want to see my daughter."

CHAPTER 32 - CHANCE

"For pity's sake, Salem," Errin scolded quietly, "You could have laundered your robes before coming into the presence of the First Mother of Rhugoth and the entire Council of Padras—well, minus three."

Salem sniffed his robe and then scratched his pitted face, tiny chunks of detritus falling out of his scraggly beard. "I can't hardly smell nothin' at all anymore, lad. Is it bad?"

"Bad? Crippling is more like it," Errin complained to his plump companion. "I had to scrub mine for five hours straight after we buried that crusty old dead fisherman." Errin doubted he looked much better than Salem. Their ministry to the worst of the downtrodden took them outside and into the dirt. The sun had tanned Errin's pale skin, and his wavy hair was long, dusty, and unkempt. *My relations probably wouldn't recognize me.*

They stood outside the large oaken doors that led into the Great Hall of Mikmir castle. Salem continued sniffing his robes, finally shrugging his shoulders.

"Listen, acolyte," Salem whispered, and since he called him acolyte, Errin knew what came next would be a command. "You jus' lemme do the talkin' in there. A wrong word in front of the Padras'll earn ya' a defrockin.' I know my way 'round these uppity types."

"You forget," said Errin, "that I was an uppity type once before my blessed entrance into the Church and assignment to be your acolyte. I can safely say that the crowd in the room behind those doors will find your tales of vomiting sea monsters and your morbid analogies a little less than wholesome."

Salem cuffed him on the back of the head, raising the eyebrows of the Chamberlain and door guards. "I ain't as stupid as all that, *acolyte*. Jus' cause I never ain't had a tutor don't mean I got shmite for brains! But curse it all, this rope is a bit tight 'round me waist."

"You've put on weight since we've been in Rhugoth," Errin informed him bluntly as Salem pulled and twisted the rope. "You're actually going to have to untie and retie it one of these days." Errin rubbed the back of his head. "You just can't keep pulling it over your head."

"You can't untie this farging knot!" Salem exclaimed proudly. "It is a special knot taught to me by me first Captain. Once tied, you can only cut it off."

"Nonsense," Errin disagreed. "Every knot can be untied with enough patience. And what would you ever want with a knot you can't untie?"

"Remember that fella and the angry lobsters?" Salem reminded him gravely.

Errin shuddered and changed the topic. "You have those necklaces that belonged to Gen?"

"Yes," Salem said. "'Course I do. Just a misunderstandin' an' all. They're just cheap stones. Don't be lookin' at me that way. We see 'im, and I'll give 'em to him. I swear it!"

The doors opened, and several men they didn't recognize left hurriedly. The Chamberlain, face skeptical, signaled them forward, turning to face the assembly. The Council of Padras sat at a long table before the dais, the First Mother behind on her wooden throne.

"I introduce Salem, Pureman of the Church of the One, and Errin, his acolyte."

"Come forward, please," the First Mother commanded. Salem threw back his shoulders and entered with a swagger more fit for a dock than a Hall. Errin stared about in amazement. The Hall was as beautiful a place as he had ever seen, but once he turned his eyes to the First Mother of Rhugoth, nothing else in the room could beg for a glance. She was younger in appearance than he'd heard and beyond divine. Salem was either oblivious or unaffected by her stunning appearance.

"First Mother!" Salem intoned heartily, bending slightly at the waist, "and Council of Padras! We poor Puremen. . ." And then he saw her. Errin tried not to laugh as he gaped. His mouth still thought it had words left to speak, and it moved up and down silently in a fair imitation of a fish.

"Pureman Salem!" one of the Padras chided angrily. By his stole, Errin knew this had to be Padra Athan, head of the Council. Errin roughly elbowed the stunned Salem in the ribs.

"What? Oh, yes! But mighty Eldaloth!" Salem exclaimed. "Have you ever seen a fairer creature? Boggins and boddy ho!"

Errin had no idea what that meant and wished it the incantation of some spell to kill them both on the spot. The embarrassment would probably do it first. The First Mother's Protector did not appear pleased, and the First Mother was obviously not in good humor.

"Get hold of yourself, Pureman!" Athan roared again, standing. "Where is it you serve? Where is your congregation?"

"Ah, yes, your Grace," Salem said, recovering himself. "'Tis the road, the ditch, and the alley where we tread, 'mongst the congregation of the diseased, daft, and downtrodden, lendin' a hand an' a kind word when. . ."

"Enough. I understand," Athan cut him off, returning to

his seat. "It smells as if you brought some of your congregation in with you. Well, you can be in no doubt of why you are here, Pureman. You are the only surviving witnesses to the incident yesterday morning, and we would have your account of it, starting with why you were near the event in the first place."

"Yes, well," Salem began, "you see Errin, my acolyte here, and I often must go to Bainburrow Cathedral, bringin' in the disfortunate an' mistrodden, and it jus' so happened that we shows up that mornin' with this beastly old shnogger in our wagon who barks like Mikkik's own hound when he's not scratchin' himself and howlin' like 'es jus' got a swift kick twixt the legs. Found him outside this tavern, and the funny thing was he was crawlin' round on all fours, sniffin' around and liftin' his leg to take a. . ."

Errin elbowed Salem again.

"Right, well there we were at Bainburrow, bangin' away at the door for Prelate Shefston. Well, he never comes, so Errin an' I figure he ain't risen yet. So we sit to wait 'im out when from round back comes a prison coach and three Padras and a score of Church soldiers. We'd heard rumors of an execution, so we jus' sorta followed them from a discrete distance, thinkin' they had somethin' ta do with it.

"So there we was," Salem recounted, voice turning dramatic, "bouncin' along the Damned Quarter as pretty as you please when we notice somethin' suspicious!"

Salem paused. For too long.

"Out with it!" Athan demanded.

"A cat! An orange cat, no less, followin' along!"

Athan threw up his hands. "For mercy's sake, man! A cat? Acolyte, perhaps you'd like to finish the story?"

Salem scowled in disappointment and surprise.

"It is true, your Grace," Errin corroborated. "There was a cat and it was behaving strangely. And believe it or not, it is actually relevant."

"Yes!" Salem jumped in quickly. "You see, I ain't never

seen a cat follow anything fer that long, and then I see with me keen eyes that everywhere it steps it leaves black paw prints on the ground. So I comment to Errin here, who thinks I'm drunk—not that I get drunk anymore—till he watches the odd little beastie fer himself.

"Suddenly," Salem said so loudly and abruptly that the First Mother jumped. "The prison wagon stops and the crazy blighter we got in our wagon starts barkin' somethin' fierce, jumps out the wagon, and starts chasin' the cat down this alley. Well, me and Errin give chase, of course, hopin' ta reel 'im in afore he hurts 'imself. We find him at the end of the alley. The fellow's got the cat, and the cat is a screamin' and a scratchin' and puttin' up a ruckus. The man is thrashin' about until he sinks his teeth square in the throat of the animal. Then, poof!" He paused again.

"What? What!" Athan yelled.

"He burns to ash! Burns until there ain't nothin' left that the toddler of a wind can't carry away! Cat is jus' lyin' dead. Well, we scratched our heads on that one, you can be sure, but we hears this screamin' back from the street, so we run that way, and as I got some experience at not bein' stupid, we don't jus' go runnin' into the street. So we peek 'round the corner and all the soldiers and the Padras are shakin' 'round on the ground and thrashin'—and then they stop. Errin here, of course, wants to be runnin' out to see things, but I ain't that dumb.

"The back of the prison coach door opens and this man with Mikkik's eyes jumps out with this girl and they run off through the streets just as quick as can be. We wait a while longer. Folks start comin' outta houses and we go check on the Padras. Still alive, but slobbering and yabbering like infants. The soldiers was all dead."

"Is that all?" Athan asked.

"That be the whole of it."

"Doesn't tell us much more than we already knew," Athan said disappointedly.

"Except one thing," the First Mother interjected. "That they intended to use the cat as the focus of the attack. We owe a great deal to your 'crazy blighter.'"

Errin felt he could lose himself in that voice.

"We do at that," Salem agreed, smiling strangely at the First Mother.

"You are free to go," the First Mother said.

Salem bowed and turned to leave, but Errin held him back. "Forgive me, Highness," the acolyte began, Salem looking worried, "but we have something we need to deliver to Gen." Athan lifted his head from his notes. Errin continued, "It is nothing of much consequence, something of his he must have had when he escaped from Tell."

"Speak to the Chamberlain and he will see it delivered," she ordered, face questioning. "And while you are here, feel free to take a meal in the common room."

"Thank you, Highness." With that they left. It took some prodding, but Salem handed the necklaces to the Chamberlain, who signaled for a servant to deliver them. Salem would not miss an opportunity to overeat in the common room of the castle, and after they drained the food stores for nearly an hour, they walked toward the stables to retrieve their horse and cart.

A liveried servant approached them. "The First Mother has asked that you be escorted to the garden," he said. "She wishes to speak with you briefly."

While surprised, Errin was thrilled. Salem tried to straighten his robe and rope to no avail, and even stared into a barrel of rainwater to fix his wild hair and pick food out of his beard.

The gardens of the castle were bright with the reds, yellows, and purples of spring, and the First Mother awaited them on a marble bench under a flowering plum tree. Her Protector, clearly upset at the sight of them, stood behind her, arms folded. They bowed.

"I am sorry to trespass on your time further," she

apologized. "But I would like to know your connection with Gen and what it was you brought him."

"Yes, yes! I am delighted to serve your worshipful flower of gracefulness," Salem said. "It all. . ."

"Let me tell this, please," Errin requested with a fervent look. Surprisingly, Salem agreed. Errin started when they found Gen face down on the road and told her everything.

"I think they will be nervous and maybe even frightened," Gen commented to Fenna as they walked arm in arm through the brightly lit corridors. "Remember that these are simple country people, accustomed to small towns and small places! This all must be terribly overwhelming for them."

Fenna smiled. She wore her hair loose around her shoulders and was dressed in a fetching purple dress embroidered with gold thread.

"I'm sure having you near will comfort them. I look forward to meeting them."

"Is the Chalaine coming to this little gathering?"

"She said that nothing could detain her save Chertanne himself sitting on her."

"She said that?" Gen asked incredulously. "That's doesn't sound like her."

"I couldn't help but think it was something rather like you would say. Whatever the case, I think she, like me, is anxious to hear more about where you came from." Her smile turned mischievous. "And what you were like in your 'younger' days, since you aren't very forthcoming. Surely Gen in his tenth year wasn't so polished as he is now."

"I think you will be disappointed. There simply isn't much to tell! Life in a remote lumbering town is hardly inspiration for a ballad or a scandalous story."

Inwardly, he began rifling through his memory and found that perhaps there was material for a story or two, though he certainly wouldn't want anyone to hear them, especially not the First Mother and the Chalaine.

"Mmmhmm," Fenna teased. "We shall see. Refresh my memory. What were their names again?"

"The best friend I had in Tell was Gant, a woodsman's apprentice. With him will be Yeurile, his late master's daughter. They were going to be betrothed this past spring and married in the fall. The other three will be the Morewolds. They were Regina's parents. Store owners. Their youngest daughter, Murea, will be with them."

"It will be my pleasure to know them. Are you nervous?"

"A little," Gen replied. "A lot has happened since I last saw them. The Morewolds probably don't even know what happened to Regina. I don't know if I can bear telling them."

"You'll do fine," Fenna encouraged.

The luncheon was in a large drawing room, and, as they approached, two servants pulled the doors open for them. They stepped aside as two apologetic young ladies bore pots and pans away. The room, decorated in white, blue, and gold, felt wintry despite the emergence of spring. Two high arched windows let in the sun through gauzy light blue drapes. A fire burned cheerily in the fireplace on the east side of the room, and the servants had set up a long table and laden it with breads, cheese, wine, dried fruits, and tender meats.

Around that table sat his friends, accompanied by the Chalaine and the First Mother, Cadaen and Jaron standing guard nearby. As Gen feared, Gant, Yeurile, and the Morewolds appeared profoundly uncomfortable. Gant fixed his gaze on the table, and Yeurile examined her hands folded in her lap. Jeorge and Rena glanced uncomfortably around the room, seeming lost in all the finery. Only

Murea, ensconced sleepily on the Chalaine's lap, was clearly at home. Mirelle stood by the fire. Gen cleared his throat and all eyes turned. For a moment they all stared at each other, unblinking and unsure of what to do.

Gant rose and crossed to where Gen stood, studying him. "It is you! I don't know how, but it is!"

Jeorge and Rena stood as well, Rena covering her mouth on seeing the scars that ran across Gen's face. After a few stuttered greetings, the awkwardness broke down and Gen embraced them all and expressed his pleasure at seeing them again. As they approached the table, Gen genuflected to the Chalaine and the First Mother and helped Fenna into her chair. Gen was about to take his own when Mirelle pulled him next to her by the fire and put her arm around his waist. Gant raised his eyebrows.

"Gant, Yeurile, Jeorge, Rena and . . . Murea, yes," Mirelle said, addressing them individually. "I wanted you to know that Lord Blackshire, whom you knew as the serf Gen, is very dear to us and that we owe him a great deal more than we could possibly repay. The Gen you've heard about in all the stories is your friend and the one who stands before you now. As you are his friends, you are ours. We know circumstances are difficult for you, and it is our intention to ensure you are well taken care of, for his sake. If you are in need, I shall be offended if you do not seek my help. Is that understood?"

None of them could meet her eye, settling for mumbling "Yes, First Mother."

"Very good then," Mirelle continued. "I will let Gen sit, and we can talk and eat as we like." Gen pulled Mirelle's chair out for her. "I, for one, would like to know more about Lord Blackshire from those who knew him. He says little about himself, you see. Was he always so reserved and quiet?"

Gant looked at Jeorge to see if he would answer. Finding Jeorge studying a piece of bread carefully, Gant ventured a quiet, "No."

"Oh, really?" Mirelle prodded. "Quite a talker, then?"

"Couldn't get him to shut up, most times," Gant replied haltingly, the smiles blooming around the table finally dispelling the uncomfortable silence. Gant, encouraged by his success, continued. "You see, Gen here knew he was smarter than the rest of us. So he'd go flapping off words nobody in Tell ever heard just to make sport of us. Like that time you said to Jakes, 'Hey, you're an . . .' What was it, Gen?"

"An intellectual," Gen said, trying to hide his embarrassment.

"And he thought you meant something bad and chased you for two miles. You see, Jakes was a Showles, and the Showleses hated Gen. . ."

And from that point on there was no stopping him. Gen tried unsuccessfully to change the topic of conversation several times, but Mirelle, Fenna, or the Chalaine would always—and with apparent delight—steer Gant or Jeorge, who had joined in the festivities, back to Gen's exploits. To Gen's dismay, Gant and Jeorge remembered every one of his idiotic adventures, and with such engaging women egging them on, they would not stop until they shamed him completely.

"So you had difficulties with authority before your confrontation with Chertanne," Mirelle quipped after Gant told them about the time Gen put a skunk in the Showles's outhouse.

"Oh, they hated each other!" Jeorge laughed. "The Showleses got Gen good, too. There was that time Bernard stuck him in jail for ten days!"

"Wasn't fair, of course, but then again. . ." Gant said.

"Gen was in jail?" Fenna gasped, feigning shock. "My goodness! I had no idea I was consorting with a common criminal! What was his crime? Do tell."

"Well, we were playing White Sticks against Howen and

Jakes. They were so bad that Gen and I took to playing one-handed and hopping on one leg just to keep it interesting. Howen and Jakes, though, they don't take to losing real good, so I was in the Box and Jakes trips me. I fall and hurt my arm bad, but I get up and keep going, just managing to bat their bone away before turning to go find ours. Gen here sees that it's plain that the Showles boys are going to find their bone and score before I could, being in so much pain and all. So Gen rears back an' throws his bone at Jakes as hard as he can."

"Which is perfectly legal in White Sticks," Gen inserted defensively.

"Yep. So when Gen throws it, Jakes is facing away from him, bending down to get the bone. Just as he turns around, Gen's bone hits him end-first right square in the mouth." Fenna and Mirelle winced sympathetically.

"So Jakes's teeth come flying out his head, falling on the ground like hail in autumn, and Jakes lands flat on his back. Of course, Gen and I knew when to run, and we ran all the way to the Church, Howen hollering at us the whole time and swearing to give us a beating. So we get to the Church, and Pureman Millershim sends Gen back to find Jakes's teeth in the field, and when Gen gets back, Bernard accuses him of assaulting his son and sends him to jail, never mind that I'm standing there with a busted arm done on purpose by Jakes. Though as for that, Jakes certainly got the worst. He couldn't eat meat after that."

After more smiles and small talk, a silence fell about the table as everyone settled on food rather than stories. Gen felt uncomfortable. He found the Morewold's eyes on him more than once, the question in their eyes plain. Perhaps they held out hope of Regina's survival, but Gen hoped they knew better.

"What, what did Shadan Khairn do to . . . everyone . . . when the war started?" Jeorge finally asked.

"I escaped before it began," Gen answered, "so I cannot

be sure." Gen steeled himself. "He killed people continually through the winter. Your daughter was one of them. I am sorry."

Rena and Jeorge bowed their heads and Jeorge pulled his wife close. Murea, thankfully, had fallen asleep. Gen sorrowed with them, thankful, however, that they seemed to have expected his news. Fenna, however, when she saw Gen would offer no more of the story, opened her mouth. The Chalaine caught her before she could speak, and Gen could just hear the Chalaine say, "It is better this way." Fenna nodded and kept to herself.

At length, Mirelle raised her glass. "To Regina. From what I know, a young lady I would have loved to have in my acquaintance."

All joined glasses and drank, and for some time Jeorge and Rena shared memories of their daughter, Gen offering what remembrances were his and what comfort he could. Fenna took Gen's hand under the table, and Gen was grateful for her tenderness.

"Well," Mirelle said, as afternoon slipped toward evening, "it is time to have the Chalaine in her quarters, and I have several matters to attend to. It is my pleasure to save a little announcement for last. Jeorge and Rena, Yuerile and Gant, as you may know, I have awarded Gen a living in Blackshire when he comes into his majority—or when I decide I am done with him. I have arranged a living for each of you there so you can be near your friend when his duties with my daughter are at an end. You can be conveyed there when you like, but you can stay here for as long as it suits you. If Gant and Yuerile wish it, I can arrange for the Prelate to wed them before they leave."

Gant smiled lopsidedly and turned to Yuerile, who smiled in return.

"I'll take that as yes." Mirelle grinned. "I will send you word soon. I thank you all for shedding a bit more light on Lord Blackshire, and I will be pleased to provide a wedding dinner you won't forget. Now if you will all excuse my daughter and me."

Everyone rose and bowed, the First Mother smiling at Gen as she left.

"I think the First Mother must like you," Gant said after they had gone.

"She has been more kind to me than I deserve," Gen answered. "Too kind, by far."

Chapter 33 - Birthday

Gen,

Salutations from your former master. I do not expect anything other than hatred and loathing at word from me, but I thought I should attempt to barter some truce with you, for you and I will be face-to-face soon. From the tales I've heard of you and from my own knowledge of your character, I think it likely that you will challenge me to a duel when I arrive. I am sure you seek to find justice for the wrongs I committed against you and against the woman you loved while I wintered in your town.

I will not apologize for what I have done, for you would certainly perceive it as disingenuous. I will not explain why I did what I did, for you would not understand it. I will not try to offer any recompense for what life, love, or prosperity you lost at my hand, for I am sure that nothing I could tender for restitution would satisfy. And thus I am left only with the power of argument to convince you that you must not challenge me when I arrive, but instead you must put aside your vengeance for what I hope you will see is best for not only you and me, but for those with whom we are intertwined.

Before such arguments, I will say that I was impressed by your victory over Cormith. Cormith, before you, was my masterwork, and while he was certainly a better built fighter than you, it seems you have a double portion of intelligence and quickness that leant you the victory. Truly, I would like nothing better than to fight you to see just how far you could push me, but I will set aside my desire to be tested if you will put aside your desire to destroy me.

You must understand that whatever I took from you, you have me to thank for everything you are. You are now of noble class. You are a Protector of the Chalaine. You are in the personal acquaintance of the First Mother of Rhugoth. You are a legend. You have honor and position and power that most men of your previous station cannot grasp even in the most greedy and ambitious of their dreams. If not for my instruction, however cruel, you would be a second rate bard in a scabby town watching Regina wither at Hubert's side.

You may argue that I did not intend any of the good consequences and rewards that my training has since afforded you, and I cannot contradict the argument, but even one as evil as you must think me to be believes that fate pushes us together and pulls us apart in ways and for purposes we do not intend, and while what you once valued and loved was ripped away, what has replaced it is tenfold greater, greater not only for you, but for the Chalaine and for the purposes of prophecy.

My son and the Chalaine now face a dangerous journey, and, while I had not intended to travel with them, your emergence has taught me better. You and I are creatures fashioned for times as these, and it is time I put myself to the best service I can lend my skills to. If you will put aside your hate, those you now cherish will have my sword and my knowledge as well as yours. Out of respect for your previous losses and as a demonstration of my good will, I will protect whom you tell me to protect and kill any you call enemy.

Before us none can stand, Gen. Let us stand together. Just as I have broken your nation and welded it to mine to add strength where division subtracted, I broke you and would now add your strength to mine that we may most effectively accomplish the most important of purposes. You do not have to like my methods or me, but you do need to see reason. Remember what was taught in your training: even enemies must unite against the strength of a common foe, and so must we do.

I will arrive in Mikmir for the celebration of Chertanne's and the Chalaine's birthdays. I do not expect a reply, but I will be prepared for whatever you choose: vengeance and death or alliance and strength. The matter is yours to decide.

Torbrand Khairn, Shadan of Aughmere and King of Tolnor

P.S. I would like the return of the stones and the knowledge of how you escaped them, though I doubt you will feel inclined to surrender either.

P.P.S. I of course hold you blameless in crossing my son. If Kaimas tells the truth, he has been nothing but an embarrassment. I believe I shall force him to drop the name of Khairn and go by his prophetic title instead.

Gen folded the letter and threw it on the floor next to his bed. It was the third time he had read through Shadan Khairn's pointed message in the hours after the night watch ended with the Chalaine. The letter had come a month before, and—despite his resolve to ignore Torbrand and remain in the Chalaine's service—the words of his captor and trainer dragged back to the stage of his mind scenes he had fought hard to dismiss and silence. When he finally saw the Shadan today, he wanted to be poised and calm, but he knew full well that seeing the face that had tormented him day after day might break whatever resolutions he had formed in its absence.

He told no one of the letter, not even Fenna, who had left two weeks earlier to spend time with her family before leaving with the Chalaine on the journey to the Shroud

Lake Shard and Elde Luri Mora. Gen wished she were with him. Her brightness and affection revived him from his somber moods, and her presence would remind him why he wanted to cling to life and not risk it on vengeance.

Gant, Yuerile, and the Morewolds left a week after Gant and Yuerile's wedding. Gen enjoyed their association, though he had seen them little on account of his duties. The wedding the First Mother had thrown for them stunned them both, and the gifts of clothes, furniture, and money would provide them a living more comfortable than anything they could have expected. The Morewolds were similarly cared for. Seeing the happiness and anticipation in their eyes as they rolled south gave Gen peace, but Shadan Khairn's letter arrived a few days later, ruining his contentment.

Thinking of Fenna and his friends was all he had today to serve as support. Torbrand had arrived the night before and would attend the birthday party for his son and the Chalaine along with scores of Warlords from Aughmere, aristocrats from Rhugoth, and two Dukes from Tolnor. When the announcement of the party had come, Gen had hoped he would be blissfully excluded from the affair since Regent Ogbith insisted that it occur during the day, but the Chalaine had extended a personal invitation to him, and he could not decline.

Exhaling, he stood and donned his black dress uniform, buckling his sword and trying to forget who had taught him to use it. He grabbed the present he had fashioned for the Chalaine from on top of the stack of books at his bedside, and after stuffing it in his coat pocket went into the hall. Jaron stood outside the Chalaine's door; she was late for her own birthday party.

"Is the Chalaine coming soon?" Gen inquired of his counterpart.

"Her stomach gave her trouble earlier," Jaron explained, "but I believe she is over it now. I think it a matter of clothing at this point."

Gend nodded. "I felt the illness in her earlier, as well. A case of nerves, I think. I'll see you soon, then."

Gen navigated the maze, finding the First Mother leaning against the wall on the other side. No matter how often he saw her, her beauty always prompted a feeling of surprise, and today she had obviously put effort into being beautiful. The red gown she wore was one intended for a relaxed celebration rather than formality or regality. Cadaen—who stood a short distance away—would need a sharp eye today. Gen had to use all his control to not gawk like a dumbstruck fool.

Gen bowed. "Your Grace."

"Well if it isn't the young Lord Blackshire," she nodded, eyes playful. "It is good to see you. I see that you find me rather ravishing."

"What makes you say that?" Gen asked, fearful he had betrayed something of what he thought.

"Because if you don't, I think I might cry. What do you think?" she asked, executing a twirl. "Is the neck too low?"

"Being a decent sort of man, I didn't notice."

"Then it isn't," Mirelle frowned.

"I assure you, your Grace," Gen consoled her, smiling, "that you are more than stunning, and I may need to stick close to Cadaen to help him beat away your slobbering admirers."

"That is more like it," she said. "I was beginning to think my efforts had failed entirely."

"Is there a motive behind your 'efforts,' or are you just trying to make life difficult for Cadaen? I'm sure he must have a lot of worries already."

"My motives are my own, though I hardly need one."

"Of course, Milady," Gen replied, inclining his head. "I apologize for the intrusion. If you are waiting for your daughter, she is still readying herself. She felt ill earlier, but I am made to understand that she is currently selecting suitable attire."

"Thank you for the news; I did not know she was feeling unwell. However, I was loitering around waiting for you. The party is underway, and I found myself in need of an escort. Cadaen, if you could leave us. I need to speak with Gen alone. Meet me in the Great Hall, or you can get some sleep. I will have Gen watch over me in the interim."

Cadaen frowned. "As you wish, Milady," he said, bowing stiffly and walking back toward the Great Hall.

"Well?" the First Mother said expectantly. Gen swallowed hard and stepped forward, extending his arm. The First Mother took it and pulled him in close, talking in a whisper as they walked slowly by the sentries. She smelled intoxicatingly of some distracting scent he couldn't quite place, and her softness and warmth were quite unnerving.

"My motive, you should know, is to get my way. I find aristocrats and noblemen much more pliable when I dress to woo rather than to rule. And I need you to frighten those I cannot make pliant by my feminine gifts. There are some important matters to settle at this little party."

"A rather utilitarian use of your beauty and my ugliness."

"You are intimidating, not ugly. And since I am not permitted to love until my daughter weds and is with child, my beauty serves little other purpose than manipulating squabbling regents and abstinent Churchmen. Fortunately, my restriction will be lifted before the year is out, if all goes well. Perhaps I should start flirting with some eligible men. If I play things right, I can wed and have a man for my bed the day after my daughter announces the blessed conception of her Holy Child."

"I am sure you will have little difficulty finding a man who worships you, Mirelle."

"Thank you. I fear I shall botch any attempts at romance since I have only played at it for political purposes. Instead of asking for a kiss, I'll probably slip into old habits and ask for a boundary change or a tax increase."

"I wouldn't worry, Highness. Coming from you, most men would find talk of seed corn terribly enthralling. However," Gen said, trying to change the subject, "I'm sure that you didn't wish to speak with me about finding a potential consort. I take it you just want me to walk with you and act menacing."

"More or less. While you accompany me today, be all smiles and address me by name, not title. When I address one of the nobles or aristocrats in a matter of business, stand close at my side and turn unhappy every time they disagree with me."

"What if I disagree with you?"

"Then I shall have to turn my wooing arts on you, though it might take a concentrated, prolonged effort to affect one as stubborn as yourself."

Gen didn't know how to answer and settled on a noncommittal grunt.

"But what concerns me," she continued, "is a particular decision and a particular person I must convince."

"Who?"

"Torbrand Khairn. I'm sorry to cause you pain by speaking of him, but you will see him whenever he decides to grace the party with his presence. I know he hurt you, and you have every reason to seek his life. I need to know what your intentions are."

"I will not raise a challenge," Gen said. "We must ally ourselves to the same purpose for now. We need him on the journey."

"I hoped you would say that. I am much relieved."

"What is the decision that involves him?"

"When we were in Aughmere, Torbrand stated his intention not to accompany his son on the journey to Elde Luri Mora, much to the disappointment of Aughmerians. His absence, however, permitted Regent Ogbith to take leadership of the caravan. Khairn wrote me a month ago and informed me of his change of heart, going on and on about his new desire to serve the prophecy. I hope he didn't expect me to believe any of his babbling. In that same letter he stated his intention to take command, as is his right as father of the Ha'Ulrich and Shadan of Aughmere. He was 'gracious' enough to permit Regent Ogbith to serve as his second. I want to change his mind today. If it will cause you difficulty to be near him, I will understand and go it alone."

"I will stand with you, First Mother."

"Excellent. With my beauty and your reputation, we will make short work of the room and have ample time for other entertainments. I thank you and hope you do not feel ill-used. Did you bring a present for my daughter?"

"I did."

"It must be small. What is it?"

"You will have to wait and see. I doubt I will give it to her at the Presentation. It is a poor gift compared to those I saw being dragged in yesterday. I don't have my income from Blackshire yet."

Mirelle squeezed his arm. "Ah! You should have told me, Gen! I would have set you up with a nice sum. But don't worry too much. The gift giving is really a contest for the nobles to see who can outdo the other. It's actually quite annoying. By the way, when is your birthday?"

"I have no idea."

"You don't even know how old you are?"

"Not precisely. I am around the same age as your daughter, give or take a year or two."

When they arrived at the doors of the Great Hall, the party was in full gallop, a happy roar of music, laughter, and talk echoing into the hallway. Chamberlain Hurney introduced them grandly. Gen took the time to assess the room, noticing the Padras, Athan included, skulking about the fringes of the assembly, keeping to themselves. Both Ethris and Kaimas were absent, having left some days earlier, apparently in each other's company—which surprised Gen. Their manner toward each other had always seemed cold.

"You have more titles than I do," Mirelle observed as they walked inside to a great deal of bowing. Chertanne sat at a table against a wall, mug in hand. He looked nervous and out of sorts, and Gen wondered if his yet absent father had anything to do with it. Cadaen fell in behind them as soon as the First Mother entered the room, and Gen felt grateful for his presence. Several men in the crowd gaped at Mirelle with naked passion on their faces, and Gen employed his first few moments at the festivities shooting warning glances back. To his delight, his disturbing countenance and fierce glare proved more than adequate to discourage the lusty celebrants.

"I shall have to bring you along more often, Lord Blackshire," Mirelle commented after a few minutes. "Now that the world knows I can take a consort soon, I've spent great deal of time at these kinds of occasions fending off those hungry for power, my passion, or both. With you it appears I shall be left blissfully alone."

"Inform me if there is a potential consort out there I should refrain from scaring away."

"Scare them all."

After they greeted several of the Regency from Rhugoth and Warlords from Aughmere, the Chamberlain's voice rose again. "May I present the Most Holy Chalaine, Mother of God, Future High Queen of the World, the Healer."

All music and talking stopped as the congregation genuflected at her entry.

"Rise and continue," she said, and Gen noted the slight tension in her voice and wondered what was worrying her. She approached her mother quickly. She wore blue, the first time Gen had seen her in a color other than white at a public presentation.

"Mother, Gen, it is good to see you both."

"And you, Chalaine. Look who I caught for an escort,"

the First Mother said, pulling Gen in tight. "Shall I make him dance with me?"

"I need to borrow him for a moment, if I could."

"I think you should pay your respects to your fiancé first," the First Mother admonished, "or I think he will become upset and perhaps get drunk and loud rather sooner than usual. Kaimas left four days ago and I fear he is already slipping into old habits."

"Yes, yes," the Chalaine said distractedly. "You are right. I fear I may be too late. I will return as quickly as possible. It is important."

She walked away only to be thronged by a horde of admirers, and before long Mirelle and Gen found themselves entrenched in a spate of visits that required the same mechanical and polite conversation repeatedly.

Mirelle handled it deftly, managing to sound fresh at each new encounter, while Gen found the words 'thank you' coming out more gratingly each time someone would compliment him for his work. The First Mother did manage to take care of one of her items, denial of an annexation of property, during the brief visits.

A halt in the music and a call for silence gave them a welcome distraction from their conversations.

"First Mother, Gentlemen and Gentlewomen," the court bard said grandly, "it is with great pleasure that I present the Ha'Ulrich and the Chalaine who will dance to the Swallow's Wade for the court."

Gen knew the song and how to dance it; it was a tune for the young and in love, energetic and romantic.

"Interesting. Another one of Chertanne's stunts to prove his love?" Gen asked as the Chalaine and Chertanne took the floor.

"I arranged it," Mirelle admitted.

"Really? Your daughter will no doubt have words for you afterward."

"Perhaps, but I hope she understands why," the First

Mother whispered in his ear. "It is starting to get around, and I mean everywhere, that the two dislike and ignore each other, so I'm hoping this will help settle the rumors—well, the truth—a little bit. The rift between them will hurt the morale of the people, at least in Rhugoth and Tolnor. Besides, I didn't teach her to dance for nothing."

Gen nodded his understanding, amazed at Mirelle's ability to deal with so many issues at once.

The dance went by slowly to Gen's reckoning. Chertanne danced ably, though he looked a little ridiculous doing it, but the Chalaine performed each move perfunctorily and with no pleasure. Gen riveted his stare on Chertanne, hoping to remind him to behave, but even dancing with the most beautiful woman ever born could not wipe away the concern Gen had noticed on the Ha'Ulrich's face earlier. A weight pressed upon Chertanne, and Gen thought the sober result a definite improvement upon his character.

The dance ended to polite clapping, and after a formal bow, the two went separate ways. Mirelle bit her lip, face concerned.

"I doubt that helped allay any fears," she commented quietly. Gen nodded his agreement. The talk in the room had barely started afresh when again the court bard called for attention.

"It is my great honor to announce that the Chalaine has requested her mother and her escort perform a dance for us of her choosing."

Gen groaned inwardly and Mirelle laughed. The assembly clapped and shouted their approval.

"There's good girl," Mirelle whispered, leading Gen toward the center of the floor. "At last she has learned that turnabout is fair play. You know the Swallow's Wade, don't you?"

"Of course, but. . ."

"Good. We need to show them how it is done."

And show them they did. Gen had never danced with a partner as capable or enthusiastic as the First Mother of Rhugoth, and, while he felt reluctant at first, Mirelle's energy drew him into the dance. Nothing existed save her and the rhythm, and when the music stopped, the crowd applauded thunderously—the Padras excepting. The First Mother gripped his hand and they both bowed as performers would, after which Mirelle hugged him and kissed him on the cheek.

"She favors him overmuch," Chertanne complained nearby. "She hasn't danced with me at all, and I'm her future son-in-law!"

"That will give them something else to talk about," the First Mother said as they walked arm in arm from the floor. The Chalaine caught up with them quickly.

"I need to speak with him, mother. We will discuss my dance partners later."

The Chalaine came to Gen's side and took his arm. Gen realized he'd just left the company of the second most beautiful woman for the company of the first and started to feel extraordinarily fortunate. He thought the Chalaine would comment on the dance, but instead she directed him up the stairs to the balcony where fewer people loitered about. Athan watched them, face displeased. The doors to the outside balconies were open, the air refreshing and brisk. As was often the case in the spring, where the sun shone was warm and where it did not was chill.

"Gen," the Chalaine said, voice worried, "we will see Shadan Khairn today. How can I face him? I saw what he did to you and to Regina. How can I not hate him for your sake? And what will you do? Please do not fight him. I know it is hypocritical to ask it, but no good can come from it."

"I will not fight him, Chalaine," Gen answered calmingly. "We will need his sword and his experience. I will forbear my own desire for justice for the good of us all."

"Thank you, Gen," the Chalaine said, squeezing his arm. "I have worried so."

"As for facing your future father-in-law, just do the bare minimum to satisfy propriety, which isn't much in this case. Just approach him as you did the dance with Chertanne."

The Chalaine nodded. "I did poorly, then?"

"Far be it from me to tell the Holy Chalaine she danced badly. I will say, rather, that you did exactly what was needed to finish the task and no more."

"My mother certainly did more than what was needed 'to finish the task.' I suppose she was a bit more fortunate in her partner than I."

"Her partner had little to do with it. She is a spirited dancer."

The Chalaine replied with a dissatisfied 'humph' and pulled Gen back toward the stairs.

"So why blue?" Gen asked as they descended.

"Birthdays need color. I'm not required to be 'Her White-clad Holiness' today. When is your birthday?"

"I have no idea."

"Oh, come now. What day did you celebrate on?"

"Commoners in Tolnor don't celebrate birthdays. All this fuss, bother, and horde exchange is a game for nobility."

"And you are now nobility," the Chalaine said, "so welcome to our little game. We shall have to declare a proper birthday for you."

"You and your mother can work one out. She asked about it as well. But on the subject of presents, I caught a glimpse of some of the ones the servants stored yesterday. I think there is a statue in there somewhere."

"Another one?" the Chalaine asked unhappily.

"You have some already?"

"Yes. There's a whole room full of them somewhere in the castle. All of them depict me unveiled, fantasies of the artists, so they were deemed inappropriate to put in the garden or in the Square. Most are based on my mother."

"I would like to see them. Do any of them look like you?"

"Not really."

"Can I have one? My room needs decoration."

"No."

The music and talking stopped as the Chamberlain banged his staff on the floor again.

"May I present Torbrand Khairn, Shadan of Aughmere and King of Tolnor. Father of the Ha'Ulrich, master swordsman."

Gen's back stiffened. Torbrand strode confidently through the doors, in appearance much the same as he was the day he emerged from Bernard Showles's house—tall, confident and commanding. He wore all black save for red trim on his coat and pants. His sword in scabbard, etched indelibly in Gen's mind, hung at his side, and his eyes darted around the crowd.

At last they fell on Gen. Gen met his former master's eye, concentrating on controlling his thoughts and reactions. Khairn ignored the still-silent crowd and walked forward, a grin on his face. No one spoke. Gen wondered how much information about the nature of his training was known to those besides the Chalaine and her inner circle. Jaron rushed toward them and urged a reluctant Chalaine to follow him.

"Find me after," she said after acquiescing to Jaron's demand and Gen's insistence.

Gen nodded and tried to relax, knowing Shadan Khairn would sense his tension and see it as weakness.

"So, Gen," Torbrand said, hands on hips, studying Gen from top to bottom. "I must say you cleaned up well. You look fit. Should I take the Chalaine's departure as a sign that we are to fight, or have you seen reason and are being overly cautious?"

"There will be no fighting." The crowd visibly relaxed. "There is more important work to do and you will help me do it."

"Of course I will, but I've been wondering something."

Torbrand's hand darted for his sword hilt and Gen drew his own in an instant. The nobles gasped at the display of steel and the Dark Guard scrambled into a protective position around the Chalaine. Torbrand laughed heartily and resheathed his sword. Gen followed suit, feeling foolish.

"You are still fast. Wonderful," Torbrand effused. "My apologies to the First Mother if I have offended her Court. It was merely a test for my student. Where is Chertanne?"

The people parted to reveal the Shadan's son, who had turned a sickly pale color from drink, fear, or both. He turned even whiter on seeing his father. Torbrand strode forward until he stood in front of him, examining him for several long moments in much the same way he had Gen. Chertanne stood as straight as he could, but he had difficulty meeting his father's eye.

"Chalaine," Torbrand said, turning back to find her in the crowd. "I am truly sorry. If you'd like, I'll burn a black circle above Gen's eye and you can marry him. Why is it so quiet in here? I thought this was a party."

The musicians began haltingly as Torbrand went in search of food and conversation with his Warlords, affronting Rhugothian aristocracy by his complete disregard for the First Mother. Chertanne exhaled, angry but relieved.

"Thank you again for your forbearance," Mirelle said, taking Gen's arm. "Insufferable man. Thus you see how men who fear nothing behave."

"I'm sorry," Gen said, "for drawing my blade again in your Court."

"No apology needed. Torbrand is capricious and I don't fault you for defending yourself from his feint. Are you ready for me to own you for the next couple of hours?"

"The Chalaine wished for me to find her after talking with Lord Khairn."

"She can wait. Remember, address me as Mirelle and try to relax, except when they disagree with me, of course."

Chapter 34 - Sticks and Stones

For the balance of the morning Gen went with the First Mother from noble to aristocrat and watched as she "got her way" with every matter on her agenda. Her skill with persuasion and even coercion taught Gen to fear and respect Mirelle as a leader more than anything she had done hitherto. Her skill rendered his dark looks virtually unnecessary, and he used them only as accent to Mirelle's masterful diplomacy.

Mirelle doted on him the entire time, lavishing him with more feminine affection than he thought entirely necessary to accomplish her purposes, though he hardly felt like complaining. She always had at least one arm in his, pressing into him so closely he could smell her hair. Whenever she spoke to him, her blue eyes were alive with affection, and he called up his training to quash the feelings rising within him. She was just using him as a tool, after all.

"We are almost done, Gen," she said, glancing about the room. "The midday meal approaches and I would like to be finished before then. Unfortunately, our toughest assignment remains."

Gen knew she meant Torbrand. He had felt the Shadan's eyes on him more than once as he and the First

Mother worked the room. Torbrand stood completely relaxed against the wall next to the great doors of the Hall, watching everything unconcernedly. To Gen's surprise, he actually executed a bow for the First Mother of Rhugoth.

"First Mother," he said, coming upright. "You are certainly a pleasant view today and a good reminder of why we veil women in Aughmere. But I must say, the way you favor Gen here is certainly provoking a bit of conversation."

"I thought I would be sharing my affection with my future son-in-law, but things haven't turned out so well on that front, as you may have heard. So I have all this tender feeling saved up and have to expend it somewhere. It would be a shame to waste it."

"Indeed. You be careful around this woman, Gen," the Shadan said, face serious. "She's a devious one."

"Why, Lord Khairn, I'm harmless," Mirelle countered innocently. "However, I must confess that I do not come to you for social reasons. We need to talk about leadership of the caravan to Elde Luri Mora. Knowing your character, I will be direct. I want Regent Ogbith in command when we march out of Rhugoth."

"What say you, Gen," Torbrand asked, "Regent Ogbith or me? Which should command the caravan?"

"As a matter of honor," Gen answered, well aware of Khairn's disdain for the concept, "it should fall to Regent Ogbith. You turned down command early in the planning by stating your intention of not going, and Regent Ogbith has done all the work of preparation. It would be an insult to him to remove him now and ungracious of you to commandeer the post after abdicating it."

"Honor again. Oh, very well," Torbrand said. "If Gen says it should be Ogbith, then Ogbith it shall be, though I shall want to be on the Leadership Council and attend any meetings from this time forward."

Gen was shocked at his carefree relinquishing of

command, and he worried that the wily Shadan was up to something. The First Mother quickly masked her surprise as well.

"Of course, Shadan. Your experience and knowledge will aid us greatly. We thank you for your understanding in the matter. I must beg leave of you now. There are several things I must look into for the Presentation of Gifts after midday meal. Gen, you are free to see to the Chalaine's request, though I should like to dance with you again. Good day."

Torbrand watched her go, face serious. After a few steps she turned back and threw Gen a smile before continuing on.

Torbrand shook his head. "I tell you again, boy. You watch yourself with that woman. She will use you until there is nothing left, and you will love every minute of it."

"Do you insult her?"

"Not at all," Torbrand said. "I admire her more than you know. I would never take her for a wife, though; she would slit my throat in the dark. Speaking of wives. . ." He reached into his pocket and pulled out a sealed letter, handing it to Gen. "Give this to Gerand Kildan for me. It concerns Mena. Now if you will excuse me, I need to harass my son with a few questions he probably cannot answer, which will then force me to get the information elsewhere. Then I'll probably leave. Rhugothian parties are a bore. No fighting at all."

Gen stared at the letter addressed to his friend for a moment before stuffing it into his own pocket. He had completely forgotten about Torbrand's promise to Mena that he would give her to Gerand in marriage upon winning the war. He didn't look forward to giving the letter to Gerand and wondered how he would react. By law, he could not refuse the offer, but Gen was certain the brooding young man would take the news ill.

Mind unsettled, Gen went in search of the Chalaine,

finding her dancing a popular group dance, the Autumn Fall, with Dason. He waited for the dance to end, but her pleasure at talking with her former Protector was plain, and Gen decided to let her enjoy him while she could.

Now that his business with the First Mother was concluded, the day was shaping up to be long and tedious, and he again wished Fenna were around. Everyone appeared content to talk about him rather than to him, so he wandered about studying the tapestries until servants brought in several long tables and laid mounds of food upon them. Aristocrats, Dukes, and Warlords retreated to the dais to be served while lesser nobles sat at tables, taking places upon the balconies and the floor.

Ignoring protocol, Gen went to the table and took a plate and filled it for himself, the servants smiling at him—in the kitchen he was beloved. Gen took his plate upstairs to the balcony, placing it on the wide balustrade and watching the children play in the castle yard. He chuckled to himself, noting that despite the dense grass on the field, the children had somehow located mud, and more than one pair of nice pants was decorated with smeared hand prints.

Gerand and Volney striding onto the field caught Gen's attention, especially the large sack Gerand carried over his shoulder. As Gerand dropped the sack on the ground, Volney looked up and Gen waved to catch his eye.

"Gen!" Volney yelled. "Are you on duty?"

"No! What are you doing?"

"White Sticks!" Volney answered dumping the contents of his bag on the ground.

"I'm coming down!"

Gen gobbled down the rest of his food in a rather indecorous fashion. To avoid a scene, he went through the kitchens and out into the yard to his smiling friends. He'd had scant occasion to talk with either during the winter, though he had delivered the news of Tolnor's fall to Gerand. He had taken it well, glad that the fighting had ended.

"Before I forget, Gerand, I have a letter from Shadan Khairn for you."

Gerand's expression turned dark, and Volney sidled in next to Gerand as Gen surrendered the letter. Gerand turned his back to a disappointed Volney, breaking the seal and reading. When he finished his arms slumped to his sides. After a moment he folded it with trembling hands and stuffed it into his coat. When he turned, his face was pale, eyes burning with a controlled rage.

"Well, what did it say?" Volney asked tentatively.

"I am married."

"What! To whom?" Volney's exclaimed.

"One of Torbrand's daughters, Mena. This letter is basically a 'deed' transferring her possession to me and naming her my 'first' wife." Abruptly, Gerand turned his face upward and yelled to the sky. "I hate that man. I hate Aughmere. And I will hate this woman!" He closed his eyes and lowered his head, voice barely audible. "My family is already whispered about due to Dason's dismissal from the Protectorship. Now this! It is intolerable! How am I to live saddled to a stupid slave girl for the rest of my life? I will be a shamed laughingstock!"

"She is not stupid, Gerand," Gen informed him gently. "She is an intelligent, beautiful woman, Torbrand's favorite."

"You know her?" Volney exclaimed. Gen briefly summarized his visit to the Ellenais shard and his interactions with Mena. His information didn't ameliorate Gerand's indisposition.

"Is she to come to you?" Volney asked his angry friend.

"No," he answered evenly. "She awaits my orders. She can rot in Aughmere. Let's play."

Gen swallowed hard, feeling for Gerand but unable to think of anything to say to comfort him.

"Can you stay long?" Volney asked. "Even with you,

we're still short a player."

"I can stay," Gen answered, removing his coat and draping it over a tree limb. "The nobles will present their gifts, and that will take until dinner, at least."

"Don't you have a gift for the Chalaine that you have to present?" Volney asked, face concerned. "It would be a dishonor if a newly appointed noble such as yourself did not give something after being invited."

"I will," Gen replied, "but I'll do it personally. I won't have the income from my land for some time, and I am not about to give my poor gift in the midst of such treasure. You would understand if you saw the riches delivered to the castle yesterday."

"What is your present?" Volney inquired, face curious.

"I'll keep that to myself," Gen returned.

"Oh, yes," Volney stammered. "My apologies. Look, it's Kimdan."

Kimdan jogged forward, a smug smile on his face.

"I was about to take lunch in the commons," he said as he approached. "I couldn't help but notice you were a player short. I certainly hope, Gen, that your sword training with Khairn did not include White Sticks as well?"

"No."

"Have you heard from Fenna?" Kimdan asked offhandedly as he shed his coat. "I wrote her just after she left and received a return letter today."

Gen felt a stab of guilt. He hadn't written at all. She was only to be gone a month, and Khairn's letter had pushed almost all other thoughts out of his mind.

"What does she say?" Gen asked, ignoring his question.

"That she is doing well and anticipating the journey to Elde Luri Mora with excitement. I, of course, begged her not to go, for her safety. I am sure you did the same. So, how shall we team up?"

Gen teamed with Gerand and Kimdan with Volney, creating an instant rivalry between Tolnor and Rhugoth.

Even before they started, Gen noticed a gathering of nobles along the Great Hall's balcony, and after the first two matches, money was changing hands.

Gen had never played such an exhilarating, frenetic game. Playing against small town boys paled to playing with intelligent nobles trained to the peak of their physical prowess. His opponents threw bones with alarming accuracy. Gerand played like a man possessed, using the game to vent his frustrations. Kimdan noticed his anger, but Gen counseled him against inquiring about it.

Gen took a few bruises. Kimdan, as always, taunted them nearly constantly, but Gen didn't care. For the first time since coming to Rhugoth, he felt carefree and relaxed, laughing at success and failure. Before long, off-duty castle guards and even members of the Dark Guard itself joined in the fun. Gen even played a round with Kimdan on his team. This continued even as night came on, the spotty lantern light adding an element of fun and danger to their game.

It was with great reluctance that Gen pulled himself away from the game at the approach of the sixth watch. Puffy dark clouds blowing in from the south hinted at a night rain to come, and he regretted that he would be trapped indoors. A walk in the rain appealed to him for some reason, and he thought Samian might be to blame. Gen had no time to eat anything despite the hunger the activity put into him, but the mindless fun proved far more valuable than food.

"Let me know if Fenna writes you anything!" Kimdan goaded as Gen retrieved his coat, waving in reply. He went to clean up in his quarters before finding Jaron and relieving him. As he entered the Great Hall he stopped in amazement. On each side of the dais lay a great pile of riches of all varieties—jewels, fragrant woods, tapestries, gold, and silver. Two marble statues, one of the Chalaine and one of the Ha'Ulrich, stood over the Chalaine's treasures, heroic and of austere design. The artist tactfully eliminated the girth from Chertanne's likeness. Servants started carting off the statues as Gen approached.

The Chalaine still sat at the table on the dais, and Gen took Jaron's place behind her, noting that she wore an exquisite diamond necklace. At once, he felt the inadequacy of his gift and reconsidered giving it; he needed to find something better or risk offending the Chalaine. He wondered what Chertanne, who sat beside her, had offered as a gift. To Gen's chagrin, the Ha'Ulrich turned to him and spoke, voice loud.

"Well, *Lord* Blackshire, they have obviously not schooled your peasant mind enough in the matters of Rhugothian Court. I had to learn all the silly rules, and so should you! You were invited to the party by the Chalaine herself and yet you left to play a little game. Protocol dictates that you be here to present a gift for the Chalaine at least, if not for the Ha'Ulrich! Did you forget to bring one or did you just wish to snub the Court?"

Mirelle, face concerned, broke her conversation with Regent Ogbith and approached the gathering. Silence fell at the Ha'Ulrich's words.

"I do have a gift for the Chalaine," Gen said. "My gift to you is to keep your bride safe."

"Then let's see your gift for my fiancé!" Chertanne prompted. "We are all curious."

"I will give it to her later."

"So you did forget, then," Chertanne teased.

"I have it."

"Then out with it, man!"

Those nearby voiced their encouragement and approval, and Gen was dismayed to see the greater part of the remaining attendees gathering around the dais upon noticing the commotion.

"It's all right, Gen," the Chalaine said expectantly. "You can give it to me."

He had no choice now, and he reluctantly drew forth his gift from his coat pocket. The nobles gasped disdainfully. Gen held an unremarkable smooth stone, flat and egg-shaped, dangling from a woven thong. Just a hint of bluish-green tinted its surface. Chertanne laughed out loud in derision, and Gen saw disappointment on Mirelle's face. He could only guess at what the Chalaine felt.

"Let me explain," Gen said loudly, trying to get everyone's attention.

"Yes, please explain!" Chertanne said. "Did it cost a tin piece at a street merchant's booth? I think the Chalaine will get along nicely with the necklace she has."

"It is an Ial Stone," Gen answered.

"And, pray, what is that?" Chertanne asked snobbishly.

"It is elven craft." Gen spun at Maewen's voice, watching her approach as she came in through the kitchen. Her travel stained clothing and unkempt hair set her apart from the nobles all around her, but so powerful was her presence that even the most nattering of propriety-mongers said nothing. Maewen came forward and retrieved the stone from Gen's hand.

"It is very well crafted," she announced after examining it. Those close by 'oohed' as the stone changed to the color of her hand, and those who could not see craned for a better look.

"What does it do?" the Chalaine asked. "Is it magical?" Gen opened his mouth to explain, but Maewen jumped in ahead of him, and he realized the half-elf thought he knew nothing of it.

"It is not. It is completely natural. It is not precisely a stone, either. It is made by collecting the sap from an Ial tree, what humans know as the frost pine. You add various herbs and spices to it, as well as the secretion from the Elne bird, which gives it the color-changing properties. The sap hardens over the space of few weeks into something nearly as hard as stone that can then be carved into a variety of shapes. The thong is woven from the bark of a fragrant Rail bush, which is worked until it is as soft as silk. While watching it change colors is interesting," Maewen moved it over her green cloak and the sleeve of the Chalaine's blue dress as demonstration, "its chief virtue is its smell, and not just from the bark. Hold the stone enclosed in your hand for a few seconds, Chalaine." She complied. "Now smell."

The Chalaine put the stone underneath her veil and sniffed while the assembly waited for her verdict.

"It is delightful!" she exclaimed.

"If you wear it close to your skin," Maewen continued, "the warmth of your body will release the smell constantly. Where did you get this, Gen? This craft hasn't been seen in over two hundred years."

"I . . . made it," Gen explained haltingly. "I realized that all the elements needed could be found within the Castle walls—the Chapel gardens, mostly."

Maewen furrowed her brow in skepticism and curiosity. A question came to her lips, but a group of nobles swarmed around the Chalaine, asking for a smell or to watch it turn colors. It took a forceful demand from Mirelle several minutes later to break up the throng. As part of his new security measures, Athan ordered the Chalaine safely quartered precisely at the start of Gen's watch. Mirelle and Regent Ogbith cornered Maewen as Gen helped the Chalaine out of the door and into the hall.

"I am sorry Chertanne was baiting you again," she said, warming the stone in her hand and smelling it, "though, as usual, it turned to his detriment. I wish Kaimas would return. Chertanne was almost tolerable while he was here."

Gen nodded. "I am sorry if I offended you by not staying around for the Presentation."

She sighed. "I forgive you. It is terribly tedious. I wish I could have watched your 'little game.' The nobles and even aristocracy certainly found numerous excuses to ascend the east balcony. I don't think I've ever seen so many people in need of fresh air."

"I assume Chertanne gifted you the diamond necklace, then?"

"No. That was Dason. It was one of the crown jewels of Tolnor. It must have been quite a feat to get it out of the country."

"Impressive. What about Chertanne's gift?"

"The statues," the Chalaine said, tone disparaging. "Why did you not come to find me after your 'work' with my strangely behaving mother?"

"I did, but you were busy."

"I was?"

"Yes. You were dancing."

"You should have waited. I had hoped to dance with you."

"You were happy with your partner at the time."

"Dason?"

"Yes."

"That man has an insatiable appetite for dancing. He quite exhausted me."

"For a dancing companion," Gen commented, "you could certainly do worse."

"And I certainly did on a couple of occasions, which is where I needed you to step in and save me," the Chalaine said, stopping in front of her door.

"I offer another apology for my dereliction of duty."

"I would accept it, if I thought you were sincere," the Chalaine responded. Before he could protest, she quickly added, "I want to ask what inspired you to craft this for me?"

"I know you worry a great deal and have difficulty sleeping," Gen explained. "I sense you pacing the floors late in the night. The scent of the Ial Stone is said to soothe the mind and relax the body, so I thought it might help. Wear it next to your skin as you sleep and breathe deeply."

The Chalaine slipped it over her head and dropped the

stone underneath her dress.

"Sleep well, Your Grace," Gen said, inclining his head. As he straightened, the Chalaine put her hand on his cheek and held his eyes for a moment.

"Thank you, Gen," she said. "You are very thoughtful. For a man. Goodnight."

The Chalaine closed the door behind her and removed her veil. To her horror, both statues gifted to her by Chertanne stood at the foot of her bed. No doubt her mother had ordered them delivered as a joke. Sighing, she removed Dason's rich gift from around her neck and fastened it around the neck of her stone likeness.

After reading for a few hours, she drifted off to the sweet evergreen scent of the Ial Stone, and for the first time in weeks had a deep and dreamless sleep.

Chapter 35 - Sweetbread

"I have placed many protections upon the wagon," Ethris explained, proudly pointing out the details of his work. Gen examined the runes, etched silver and black into the dark wood, wondering at the purpose of each. The Chalaine, Jaron, Mirelle and Cadaen stood nearby as Ethris lectured on about how the wagon could withstand crushing, burning, and magical attacks of several varieties.

Despite the impressive charms laid upon it, it was simply built, a dark wooden box on wheels. The craftsmen, acting on very specific designs from Regent Ogbith and Ethris, used oak wood the thickness of a hand and studded with iron bands to construct what most nearly resembled a prison wagon. Barred, narrow slits, one on each of the four sides, provided the only ventilation and light.

It had been constructed in a large outbuilding used for storage. Servants had worked through the early winter to clear and clean the large room, and the craftsmen had started their work as the snow fell deep. Today, servants of all varieties bustled about, loading wagons or preparing the four powerful black horses that would pull the heavy monstrosity. The dust kicked up by their stirring converted the diffuse morning sunlight into well-defined, slanted shafts from high windows to the floor. Summer approached, and the time to undertake the long journey to Elde Luri Mora had come.

"Now," Ethris continued, as happy and enthusiastic as Gen had ever seen him, "what you may not realize is that the lock upon the door is only visible to those that have the brand. All others will be blind to it. Quite the feat, really. I will give one key to Gen and the other to Jaron, who will have sole charge over entry to and exit from the wagon while on their watches. Even if they were to be killed, however, the enemy would see nothing to place the key in!"

"What if both Jaron and I are slain and dragged off with our keys?" Gen asked. "Is there any way to open the wagon in that circumstance?"

"I can open it with magic," Ethris replied.

"And what if you're dead, too?" Jaron asked before Gen could.

Ethris stroked his chin, face perplexed.

"Let us hope it does not come to that," Mirelle filled in during Ethris's contemplation. "If you three are dead, it will likely be better the Chalaine not get out. Let's get the Chalaine's things in the wagon and get the horses hitched. We leave in an hour. The parade will slow us down, and we are already late."

Mirelle left, Cadaen—and a still pensive Ethris mumbling to himself—trailing behind. Normally Gen would use the morning to sleep, but the First Mother had asked him to sit atop the Chalaine's wagon during their crawl through Mikmir so the people could see him. Gen didn't want to do it, but he acquiesced at Mirelle's insistence.

"I wonder what could be keeping Fenna?" the Chalaine thought aloud. "She was supposed to meet us here for Ethris's exposition about the wagon. Do you know where she is, Gen?"

"Yes, Holiness," Gen replied. "The First Mother asked

her to ensure that the bard Geoff was taken care of. He arrived from Tenswater last night."

"Why did Fenna get chosen for that particular duty?" the Chalaine asked.

"As she made me understand it," Gen continued, "the bard requested her specifically. He wanted to talk with someone close to the Chalaine and somehow knew of her. What his purpose could be, I do not know."

The Chalaine nodded. "Geoff has played here several times. Quite good. He is familiar with the members of the Rhugothian court—and all others, I suspect. No doubt he remembered Fenna was my handmaiden."

Their conversation was interrupted by a skinny, tall young man looking firmly and determinedly at the floor. He held a small chest in his arms.

"H-h-h-holiness? I have the first of your things. I, um, I was told to put them inside the chest in the w-w-agon, if you, well, of course not you, of course, but someone could let me in?"

The Chalaine smiled and tilted his head up with her hand. "What is your name?"

"I, well, my name is Rolf, your Grace," he managed after a shocked silence and a great deal of blushing.

"I thank you for carrying that down. Gen is not on duty and will open the wagon for you. I would like to get a look inside myself."

Gen unlocked the door quickly, hoping to spare Rolf as much discomfort as he could. The inside of the carriage did little to recommend itself to any occupant. A chest sat on the floor at the far end of the dark interior, and nothing of art or craft had been worked into the design to cheer a potential rider. Rolf clambered inside and started transferring the contents of the smaller chest into the larger one.

The Chalaine stared inside for a moment, hands on her hips. "Help me up, Gen. I want to get a look at my new accommodations."

Gen proffered her a hand, but the wagon was tall enough that he had to practically lift her into it. She inspected the inside, knocking on the wood and staring out the barred slits in the walls.

"Leave it to Regent Ogbith to design a wagon. Am I being protected or punished? I don't think I'll even have enough light to read at full noon! I won't even mention how hot it will get in here."

Despite her complaints, Gen could sense her excitement at finally undertaking a journey that would lead her outside the confines of the castle. Her mood had gradually improved since the end of winter, and he thought it due to her anticipation of the road and adventure.

"And where were my Protectors when this was crafted? Surely this is something I need protected from? By the time I get to Elde Luri Mora, I shall probably be little more than cured meat. If they put any salt in here, I shall be sure of it."

"We regret our negligence, Highness," Jaron apologized. "We should have inspected the wagon sooner."

The Chalaine turned back toward them. "I was only kidding, Jaron, though if you could cut a few more windows into this without Ethris noticing, I would be grateful."

"I'm afraid Ethris will notice every scratch, Holiness," Gen said. "I'm sure in the event of an attack he will check to make sure you are safe very soon after checking the wagon."

Jaron cracked a rare smile and the Chalaine laughed. She ran a finger along one of the runes on the doorframe. "I hope I am worthy of a wagon that can resist hail, lightning, and battering rams while never becoming soiled."

"It is with the wagon as it is with all other things," Gen joked. "Of all that is good about the wagon, you are worthy. Of all that is bad, you are most undeservedly afflicted."

The Chalaine was about to say something when Rolf cleared his throat to indicate he was ready to get out of the wagon. The Chalaine turned to see where he was, and as she did her foot slipped from the edge and she fell. Gen caught her before she hit the ground, spinning to keep his balance and to redirect the momentum.

"Are you all right?" Gen asked.

"Of course. Unhand me, knave," the Chalaine teased, and set her feet on the ground. For a several minutes they were subjected to every variation of apology Rolf had at his disposal, some bordering on actual eloquence. Despite the Chalaine explaining that he was guiltless, he would not relent or leave until she explicitly forgave him twice.

The rest of the loading—consisting mostly of clothes, cushions, and blankets— took little time as the Chalaine only wished to bring but few of her possessions. Pureman Obard arrived with a small stack of books for her and bid her farewell. Fenna came soon after, the bard Geoff at her side.

Geoff was much younger than Gen expected, in appearance not even thirty. Large hazel eyes sparkled on a lightly tanned face framed by shoulder length hair the color of straw. The corners of his mouth seemed permanently pegged upward, and so cheery was his demeanor that he practically bounced at every step. As he talked with Fenna, his gestures were as broad as they were lively.

His clothes evidenced his success at his craft, a fine green coat with golden buttons and yellow hose, accented by a green cap complete with the feather of some exotic bird. He and Fenna had just shared some joke together, and they were laughing as they entered. Gen felt a stab of jealousy. Both genuflected before the Chalaine.

"Chalaine," Fenna introduced, "I believe you are familiar with Geoff of Tolnor, master bard."

"I am. Welcome. We are glad to have your considerable

talents with us on this journey. I'm sure you will make the long miles more enjoyable."

Geoff bowed again, flourishing his yellow cape and bending to the point where his elbow nearly touched the top of highly polished black shoes with pointed tips curling upward.

"It is my honor to entertain and to chronicle this historic event. I couldn't have been less deserving or more blessed to garner such a position! That the rest of the world will see the event through my eyes is a weighty responsibility, but I am so overcome with gratitude that I feel it not. I assure you, that I will strive to be accurate and not exaggerate. I hope you will not mind if I ask you some questions from time to time?"

"Certainly not, master bard," the Chalaine replied.

"Excellent. And you must be Lord Blackshire? Correct? Hard to miss a face like that."

"I am."

"I have so many questions to ask you, I hardly know where to begin!" Geoff said. "Winning the Trials, slaying Cormith, battling the demon! I feel a song coming on every time I think of it! And besides all that, the Lady Fairedale informs me that you were but a winter away from starting your life as a journeyman bard! From songs to swords! What a story that must be! I insist that you sing with me some time. Fenna says you have a delightful voice."

"Lady Fairedale is too kind," Gen said. "I would certainly be a frog in the swans' pond singing next to you, if your reputation is of any substance."

"You are too modest, I'm sure. Have you heard him sing, Chalaine?"

"I have not, though I would like to."

"That settles it then, for you cannot ignore the wish of the Lady," Geoff concluded. "We shall have a song from you before this journey's over. Well, the lovely Lady Fairedale is to show me what my accommodations are,

Chalaine, before she returns to your service. I could hardly be blessed with fairer company or a finer day to be in it. Are those plans acceptable to you, Holiness?"

"That will be fine," the Chalaine agreed. We should leave soon, however, so do not be over long. I would have Fenna with me so I may have some company in my cage."

"Excellent!" Geoff said. "I look forward to speaking to you again. Chalaine, Lord Blackshire, Jaron." He bowed and extended an arm to escort Fenna. Before they had taken four steps, Geoff had Fenna laughing again.

"No offense to either of you," the Chalaine stated matter-of-factly, "but that is a handsome man."

The swinging open of the large wooden doors of the building filled the silence that fell after the Chalaine's comment. Mirelle, sidesaddle on a beautiful black horse, led a riderless horse of the same color. Cadaen gripped the reins of the animal, leading it toward Gen.

"Did you see Geoff, my daughter?" Mirelle asked. "Gorgeous man! Quite the talker."

"I had just commented the same to Jaron and Gen."

"So how did *you two* find the bard?" Mirelle asked Jaron and Gen as she dismounted.

Gen glanced at Jaron.

"He had bright clothes," Jaron said, flatly.

"I agree wholeheartedly," Gen concurred. The First Mother glanced from one to the other, expecting further comment.

"I see," she said. "A little jealous, perhaps?"

"Not at all," Gen answered quickly. "We only fear that with men about such as Dason, Kimdan, and now Geoff, only the scraps of womanhood will be left to squander their love upon us, especially as we are afflicted with a persistent case of ugly. What say you, Jaron?"

"Speak for yourself, lad," Jaron said. "I've won the heart of a barmaid at the Quickblade—you know, the sickly widow with three children and crooked teeth?"

"Oh, right," Gen replied. "Does she have a sister?" Mirelle and the Chalaine laughed, Cadaen grinning behind.

"Well, Lord Blackshire," the First Mother said, coming close and throwing Gen a sultry look, "if the barmaid's sister doesn't work out to your satisfaction, you always have me."

Gen swallowed hard and forced himself to smile in return.

"Mother!"

"Merely teasing, Chalaine. Gen, I have changed my mind. I wish you to ride beside me behind the wagon. Crescent is a gentle horse and you should find him to your liking."

"May I ask why?" Gen said. "It seems it would be better if I were on the wagon."

"You will still be close to the wagon and in some ways better prepared to protect the Chalaine. A man on a horse has the advantage over one on foot, as you well know."

Gen nodded in deference. "As you wish, Highness."

The rest of the preparations were finished in a chaotic rush, people running in all directions and shouting reminders and instructions to each other. A cadre of squires fitted Gen into the new armor Chertanne had commissioned. The silver breastplate, arm and leg greaves, and pauldrons were burnished to a high shine, each decorated with golden filigree. The breastplate bore the symbols of the lioness and the rose, devices of the First Mother and the Chalaine. Black leather gloves, sword belt, and scabbard completed the ensemble. Gen had ordered the armor fashioned as light as possible, wanting to retain the advantage of speed, and he pulled his brown hair behind him, securing it with a leather thong to keep it out of his eyes.

The First Mother watched him approach and mount Crescent with a pleasantly speculative smile on her face. Gen tried to ignore it. Fenna returned just as the Chalaine was about to despair of her arrival. Gen smiled at Fenna from atop Crescent, and she winked in return as she climbed inside the carriage. Jaron locked her and the Chalaine in before climbing up to sit on a small platform fashioned on top of the wagon for the Protectors. Gen nudged Crescent over by the First Mother as men opened the rear doors of the building, a large train of wagons pulling up from behind.

"What kind of protection has been arranged for Chertanne?" Gen inquired of Mirelle over the din.

"Nothing extraordinary. He will be surrounded by a detail of his soldiers. That is all. It has always been felt that the Ha'Ulrich should not be hidden, as it would make him appear weak and fearful."

"Who won the argument over which nation's soldiers will be in the vanguard?"

"We did," said Mirelle. "Regent Ogbith is in command of the train. Our soldiers and our flag will march at the front. As a compromise, Chertanne and his colors will be the vanguard on the return journey. Of course, at that point there will not be a separate kingdom called Rhugoth. Speaking of Regent Ogbith, he told me of your idea for traveling to Elde Luri Mora. Do you really think this caravan is a bad idea?"

"I do," Gen opined. "While the scouts have returned little notice of danger, a lumbering caravan is slow to move and easy to find. I recognize that the people need ceremony, but what wisdom I have tells me a small group should have left in the middle of the night two weeks ago and let the caravan follow as bait."

"And what did Harrick say to that?"

"That I was too young to know anything about such matters."

"Did you tell Maewen of your plan?"

"No."

"She suggested much the same. It worries me that you

both agree on this point."

The First Mother frowned pensively until the building's front doors swung open. The driver of the Chalaine's wagons, a weathered horsemaster named Ulney, urged the horses forward, and the wagon emerged into the sunlight. It took nearly half an hour to get the caravan situated in the castle courtyard. Rhugothian horse soldiers, two hundred and fifty strong, led the procession, though Chertanne's smaller company of soldiers came directly after, in front of the Chalaine. The full complement of Aughmerian soldiers brought up the rear after the supply wagons, a formidably equipped horse regiment dressed in red with burnished bronze breastplates.

"Gen? I mean, Lord Blackshire?" Gen turned to see Marna at his stirrup, the plump cook flushed from exertion.

"Marna." Gen grinned. "It is good to see you."

"I've barely caught ya, but I wanted to give ya something afore you left. I know the food they pack can wear on the tongue a bit, so I baked you this to give you a bit of sweetness when the meals get dull." She handed him a loaf of sweetbread wrapped in a light cloth. It smelled delicious and was still warm from the oven. "The crust'll get hard, but the rest will keep if you don't leave it uncovered!"

"Thank you, Marna!" Gen said. "You are most thoughtful and kind."

"You're welcome, sir. All of us in the kitchen love you! Take good care of yourself and the Chalaine and remember us when you come into your own at Blackshire. Some of us have always wanted to live in the country!"

"No you don't, Marna!" the First Mother said, leaning over. "You will not escape my kitchens that easily! Gen deserves whatever we can give him, to be sure. But he shall not have my cook!"

Marna curtsied. "As you wish, your Grace."

"Farewell, Marna!" said Gen. Marna waved and walked away toward the castle.

"You will be sharing that, of course," Mirelle said. "It smells lovely."

Gen placed the bread in a saddlebag. "Share what, your Grace?"

"Don't toy with me, Lord Blackshire. If you don't share, I will let it drop within Padra Athan's hearing that you taught my daughter to cheat at cards. She needs a bit more practice, by the way."

At last the castle gates swung open, an enormous crowd of onlookers, barely checked by guards, thronged about the caravan clapping and shouting as Regent Ogbith led the long line of soldiers out. Gen shook his head at the folly of driving the Chalaine through a mob of people. Settling himself, he concentrated on sharpening his senses, taking in everything around him. Only when he passed through the castle gates did he realize the enormity of the danger.

More people than he had ever seen in his life crammed the streets and buildings to overflowing. Swarms of celebrants milled about the alleys, windows, and rooftops, all festive and carefree. The noise rose and fell in waves. Festive bunting hung from rooftops and windows, and performers were everywhere, singing, juggling, and blowing fire. Merchants sold every kind of trinket imaginable, from moon medallions and wooden shakers filled with pebbles to kites, beaded bracelets, and carved replicas of the luminary personalities of the caravan. Little boys held up small wooden Gens as he rode by, many sporting wooden swords at their sides.

As Chertanne and the Chalaine passed, great shouts of adoration rose, but Gen was surprised when he found his name chanted in company with "Long live the First Mother!" Young ladies from every walk of life waved sashes at him, leaning forward so that he might grab them if he would. Gen ignored them, keeping his eyes forward. Mirelle leaned close.

"You see that there is plenty of womanhood left for

you," she yelled. "You might want to wave or salute."

The ebullient crowd swirled about them, but Gen didn't dare let himself get distracted. His eyes roved everywhere. He hoped the Chalaine had enough sense to stay away from the windows of the wagon. As it was, the guards could not keep the onlookers from crowding the road, and the people seemed to take it as an honor to touch the wagon as it rumbled by. The mob forced them to stop several times to wait as soldiers roughly cleared the way.

Once they turned and left the city center, Gen hoped the situation would improve. Instead, he found the broad road leading east just as thick with people. As they crept slowly forward along the lane, Gen felt increasingly uneasy. The buildings here were lower and the crowd more rural. He caught sight of more than one bow among the crowd, along with the occasional spear and club. Beer and ale flowed freely from taverns lining the way, and drunken revelers reeled about, yelling in slurred voices. A commotion in the street brought the caravan to a halt.

"It will take us the better part of the day just to leave Mikmir at this rate," Cadaen shouted from where he rode just behind Mirelle. "The mob grows more unruly."

As the First Mother turned to address her Protector, Gen caught movement on the rooftop on her side of the street. Someone fell from the roof of a nearby house, hitting the ground with a thud. A similar sound on the opposite side of the street let him know that someone else had fallen. People screamed, and Gen snapped his eyes up to the roof. A man drew his bow and fired from the position vacated by the victim of his shove.

Grabbing the First Mother's shoulder, Gen pushed her backward. She flailed, and the arrow passed inches in front of her face before sinking into Crescent's flanks. Gen knew another arrow was coming from the opposite direction but could do nothing as Crescent reared in pain. Gen heard the second arrow impact the horse's shoulder, and he threw himself from the saddle before the floundering horse could fall and crush him. His head hit the stones and his vision blurred for a moment. The people shied away as he threw off his disorientation and jumped to his feet. Drawing his sword, he scanned the rooftops. The men had vanished.

"Gen!" Cadaen yelled to him as he helped a pale Mirelle from the saddle and toward the wagon. "Unlock it!"

Gen sprinted to the wagon as the rest of the Dark Guard rode forward and surrounded them, swords at the ready, eyes darting about. Mirelle was visibly shaken. Cadaen practically threw her inside the wagon with her daughter, pulling himself in after and closing the door. Gen ran back to Crescent, finding him dead, two arrows protruding from his flesh. *Poisoned*, Gen reasoned.

Working quickly, he pulled the shafts from the horse for evidence. By the time he had finished, Regent Ogbith, Ethris, and a large contingent of soldiers had pushed the people roughly away from the scene, curses filling the air from both sides of the altercation.

"What happened, Gen?" the Regent asked. As Gen told the story, Geoff came forward and dismounted. In moments he pulled his book, quill, and ink bottle from his leather bag and began writing, balancing the ink bottle on the opposite page as he wrote. Harrick ordered that a message be sent back to his son, the acting Warden of Mikmir, and that the two arrows be taken as well as descriptions of the men. Before the messenger could leave, Maewen arrived, bow in her hand, and asked to inspect the arrows.

"Do you think the other arrow was meant for you or the First Mother?" Regent Ogbith asked.

"It is difficult to tell," Gen replied, "though I would wager it was for me. From the angle, it would have either hit me in the head or the First Mother in the side or leg. You may wish to inspect the horse. The arrows appear unremarkable, but any poison that can kill a horse that quickly would be rare. It was likely silverberry, dead thorn, or elver weed. None of them are easy to make. Was anyone else targeted?"

"I have not heard from the Aughmerians," reported Regent Ogbith, "but no one else from Rhugoth. Have you heard anything, Maewen?"

"No."

"Very well," said the Regent. "We need to get out of the city as quickly as we can. Let me have a few words with the First Mother, Jaron?"

As Regent Ogbith spoke to Mirelle through the bars, Maewen probed the horse's wounds. Gen watched her, wondering what Samian would think.

"Dead thorn," she said in Elvish.

"The wound turns black, then?" Gen asked in her language.

"You know your poisons as well as your Elvish," she said, standing and regarding him gravely. "Yes. The wound turns black. It still could be something else, or a combination of things. This whole caravan idea is folly," she said, fuming as she stalked back toward the head of the caravan.

Retrieving Marna's gift from the saddle bags and thanking Eldaloth that the horse hadn't fallen the other way, Gen waited until Regent Ogbith was finished before climbing up to join Jaron. Mirelle was assuring her daughter that everything would be fine.

"A quick piece of work there, Gen," Jaron said as the caravan began moving again. "Cadaen owes you a debt. If the First Mother were hurt or killed on his watch, I don't think he would forgive himself. At this rate, you will be a rich man when the time comes to call in favors."

The caravan moved much more quickly afterward, the soldiers guarding the route brooking no interruptions or worshipful surges toward the Ha'Ulrich or the Chalaine. The Dark Guard remained in formation around the wagon,

Captain Tolbrook unapologetically ordering them to attack anyone who got close.

At length—and to everyone's relief—they passed out of the city and into the countryside. Their caravan was followed by another of equal or greater numbers. Provision wagons stretched back as far as his eye could see, and as they passed by less populated roads, others fell into the line, having assembled beforehand, prepared to follow the Ha'Ulrich and the Chalaine to Elde Luri Mora.

"Regent Ogbith won't like this," Gen said. "We can't protect all these people."

"He won't protect them," Jaron said. "He knew this would happen and had an announcement taken to the merchants and outfitting companies within the city. I doubt most of them have any idea what the road will be like. I don't like the mercenary rabble they bring, either. Anyone could be in that caravan. After the assassination attempt, Regent Ogbith may order the Portal to Shroud Lake closed to everyone but those in this caravan."

As the numbers of people on the side of the road dwindled and civilization gave way to open plain, Gen relaxed. The day was cloudless, bright, and warm. A stiff but soothing breeze blew in the smell of grasses and wildflowers, dissipating the dust from the passing of the horses. Sometime before the sun fell, they would arrive at the Pearl Bridge that spanned two large shard sections. They would camp before crossing. The journey to the Shroud Lake Portal in Three Willow would take a week.

"You had best get your rest," Jaron said. "You will need to be sharp tonight. There's no telling what kind of people are tagging along in those wagons behind us. You might want to get your forehead looked at."

Gen brought his hand up, tenderly probing the scabby, shallow cut. He hardly felt like sleeping, but saw the wisdom in it. He hopped down from the perch atop the wagon and went toward the covered wagon that had been prepared especially for him and Jaron.

"Good work, Gen," Tolbrook praised his former apprentice as he passed. Gen saluted him and waved to Volney and Gerand before catching the side of the wagon and swinging himself inside. The accommodations were simple—several blankets and one chest each for him and Jaron. During a brief halt, Gen summoned a squire to help him with his armor. Once the young man finished, Gen dismissed him and spread some blankets before opening his chest to place the bread inside. To his surprise, he found a note from Ethris along with several texts of ancient appearance.

More reading for you, the note said simply. Gen thumbed through the books briefly, excited to read more about Trysmagic. He had found the books Ethris had loaned him over the winter fascinating and a little frightening. Trysmagic was unlike the Duammagic and Mynmagic that Ethris practiced, and all the stories of Mikkik's horrors during the Mikkikian Wars became vividly true. Many reminded him of the dreams and visions that had tortured him when he had worn the training stones.

If the power of creation revealed the soul of the caster, as one book said, then Mikkik's was truly black. Walking fire, amalgamated corpses crafted into monstrosities of flesh, diseased mosquitoes, poisoned waters. Every horror imaginable and unimaginable came to life in the pages of the books. The most horrifying were the tales of men and women slain in battle and then reanimated again to return and slaughter their unsuspecting loved ones.

Gen shut and locked the chest, closing his eyes and settling in on the blankets. He wondered what kinds of things Chertanne would do with the power or—more importantly—whom he would do them to. The early Trysmagicians among the humans found themselves worshiped and revered by the people, for the Trysmagicians were the only ones who could stand against Mikkik's most malicious creations. Despite their importance to the battle—or perhaps because of it—pride infected the ranks of Trysmagicians, inciting division and destruction. Only when the plight of Ki'Hal turned its most miserable did they set aside their self-importance to unite around a shared desperation.

Sleep finally claimed him as the caravan lumbered forward. Gen awoke an hour before sundown, finding Mirelle sitting with her legs dangling over the back of the wagon. Her hair was loose about her shoulders, but there was tension in the stiffness of her posture and the tilt of her head. Cadaen rode a short distance behind, countenance upset. Gen straightened his clothing and came to sit by the First Mother.

"How may I serve you, Mirelle?" Gen asked.

"Saving my life was plenty for today, thank you. Or have you done so much now that you don't expect anyone to notice or care about further acts of courage?"

"There's an adage among bards that says, 'play the same song thrice and none will listen but the mice.' But you certainly haven't come here to lavish me with gratitude."

"Haven't I?" said Mirelle.

"No," he said. "The expression on your face seems more indicative of an impending rant."

"Would you prefer the gratitude first?"

"The rant will be much more interesting, I'm sure."

"Very well," Mirelle said. "Seeing that I am predictable, I will begin. Have you puzzled out the mystery of our would-be assassins? Do you know who ordered the attack?"

"Well, it seems that. . ." he began.

"I'll tell you who it was, Gen. It was that idiot of a future son-in-law that ordered it! Of course, I have expected something of the sort to happen for some time, since you are certainly not his friend—whatever he may be pretending now—and I have put forth no effort at all to hide my displeasure for him or my preference for you.

"But the sheer stupidity of it! Already the tale of the 'Ilch's attack spreads through the caravan! The Ilch! So people are expected to believe that the Ha'Ulrich rode exposed through a busy street, but instead of attacking him or the Chalaine, the Ilch decides to unleash his assassins on two people completely irrelevant to the prophecy!

"If Chertanne had even a diseased shred of intelligence, he would have at least paid an assassin to kill someone near him so it would appear as if he were a target, as well. As it is, he might as well have stood up on his horse and yelled, 'Heap all suspicion on me!' I half wish the Ilch would show up and take a chunk out of Chertanne. Eldaloth knows he has some chunks to spare, and a fright would do him good! How dare he try to kill me on the streets of my own city!"

"Mirelle," Gen said, keeping his voice soothing, "you cannot with certainty lay this to his charge. The day I defied Chertanne for the Chalaine, I made many enemies, even in Rhugoth. When you named me the Chalaine's Protector, you made some of your own. While most Rhugothians now fall on our side of those events, most Aughmerians do not. This is the first time in months either one of us has traveled away from secure places, the first chance that assassins had to reach us."

"Perhaps," Mirelle replied, "but I feel the answer in my heart and it angers me. I haven't been this upset in some time."

"First time to face your own mortality, then?" Gen asked.

"Yes. I'm not quite so practiced as you."

"And I hope you never are. But I have something that might help." Gen reached back and pulled the sweet bread from the chest. "Do you like the heel?"

"No," she answered. Gen took his knife from his boot, cutting the heel for himself and slicing a generous piece for the First Mother. The bread was still warm and moist.

He handed her the slice. "See if that doesn't taste better

than you remember. Once you get over the initial shock of almost losing your life, I think you will find you have a keener appreciation for simple things. 'Spring would only be half as beautiful if winter weren't before,' as they say."

The First Mother ate in silence as the sun, light diffuse in the dust of the wagons behind, sank into the faint outline of the city Mikmir. While her muscles relaxed, the anger around her eyes did not fade, and Gen feared what she might be planning and he hoped the plan wasn't rash. Determination in the hands of the powerful, intelligent, and vengeful created disaster as often as not, and the First Mother wasn't the type to give up when her mind was set to a purpose.

"Your watch approaches," Mirelle said, licking the crumbs and sugar from her fingers, "so I had best get on to the gratitude."

"There is no need, Your Grace."

"I meant for the bread."

"Oh, of course. You are welcome."

"As for the other matter, there must be some reward. You can't save an aristocrat's life and get nothing. Honor requires something be done."

"You have already given me rank and land beyond what I could ever expect. No more is needed or required. It is my pleasure to help you however I can."

"Well," she continued, taking his hand and kissing it, "it is by your hand that my house has its honor and its health. It will be my pleasure to reward you when I decide on something suitable. Do come talk to me when time permits. I will not be so busy on this long trip and could use someone to talk to."

The caravan slowed and turned off the road before the sun fully sank. The wagons circled, forming a protective ring with the host of soldiers surrounding the outside. Once stopped, the caravan exploded into activity. Horses were unhitched, watered, and fed, and servants unloaded tents and cooking equipment. An angry Regent Ogbith wandered around barking orders.

"You should sleep in the wagon with your daughter, Your Grace," Gen suggested. "For all we know, the assassins might be in the caravan behind us."

"Cadaen already requested I do the same. I will not cower. Do I have any crumbs on my lips?"

"No."

"You didn't look," Mirelle said.

"Yes I did."

"If you say so. . . Have my daughter heal that wound. I will come and clean the blood off your face momentarily."

"A servant can do that."

"Then I will be your servant. Cadaen! See to the tent. Make sure we are next to Ethris. Help me down, Gen."

When Gen arrived at the Chalaine's wagon, Geoff was there helping Fenna out of it. Jaron locked the door behind her.

"How are our accommodations, Gen?" Jaron asked.

"Plain and functional, just like us." Gen quipped.

Jaron slapped him on the back on the way by. "Excellent."

"Gen!" Fenna exclaimed, embracing him. "Is it true? One of the arrows was meant for you? How awful! Who would do such a thing?"

"We may never know, Fenna."

"Saving the First Mother," Geoff said, extending his hand. Gen shook it. "Yet another item on a long list of brave deeds. At this rate I will need to compose two or three songs to proclaim them all. Perhaps I shall divide them pre- and post betrothal. The betrothal, or rather the failed one, will be a song by itself. Did the First Mother visit you to offer her thanks?"

"Yes."

"Oh! I must have every word!" In an instant his book and quill appeared. "Did she cry from gratitude or perhaps sob from the awful memory? A hug or royal kiss? Promises of wealth?"

"You don't know the First Mother very well," Gen answered.

"Oh, come now! Don't be so close-mouthed. It should be recorded for history!"

"It was a private conversation. Suffice it to say that she thanked me and we shared a bit of sweetbread."

"You have sweetbread?" Fenna asked. "From whom?"

"Marna." Gen answered.

"Who is Marna?" Geoff inquired, scribbling quickly. "Is she the beautiful daughter of a Duke or Regent giving you a token to remember her sweet embrace by?"

"Well, no, Geoff," Gen grated, starting to feel irritated. "She is the rather plump cook of the castle. She has five children and a husband who love her dearly. I really must be about my duty."

"Come, Geoff," Fenna said, taking the bard's arm and steering him away. "I will tell you about how Gen first met Marna. Quite funny, actually. I will see you soon, Gen."

Fenna waved as she led Geoff away. Gen thanked her silently, breathing out and standing at attention in front of the wagon door. The day was finally starting to cool, and the settling of the dust was of itself a reason to rejoice.

"Hello, Gen," came the Chalaine's quiet greeting from behind the wagon's bars.

"Good evening, Chalaine. Are you well?"

"Because of you, I am," the Chalaine said. "I could not bear to lose my mother, and I owe you a great debt. I have always known the danger is real but never really felt it. I hope I can manage all this worry."

"You will do well."

"I am not like you or my mother. I am not strong in the way you two are."

"You have never had to be," Gen said, "and I hope you will never have to be."

Silence passed between them for many minutes as the activity of the caravan continued noisily around them.

"I do have a question, Gen."

"Yes, Holiness?"

"Where is the sweetbread?" the Chalaine asked.

"I don't know what you're talking about."

"Oh, you are a liar now? A shame to tarnish your reputation so soon after polishing it up, don't you think? You're lucky I'm trapped in this wagon. You bring me a piece of Marna's sweet bread tomorrow or we will have words."

"Yes, Holiness. Provided there is any left. Jaron may smell it and devour the whole loaf before sunup. He has quite the appetite."

Gen realized the bread would not last long and resolved to eat a large chunk of it as soon as possible.

"He will be severely punished if that is the case," the Chalaine said. "So what did my mother say to you?"

"Just the standard things aristocrats and nobles say when someone saves their lives. Nothing out of the ordinary."

"Humor me."

"She said, thank you. I answered, there is no need. She said, yes there is. I said, no there isn't. She said, there is too. I said, I assure you there isn't. Then she said. . ."

Her hands were on the bars now. "Will you stop it? Did she give you some reward?"

"Well, she said, I must reward you. I said, there is no need. She said, yes there is. I said. . ."

"Can't you just give a straight answer, Gen? In the name of Eldaloth and the vow you took to obey and serve me, I command you to give me a straight answer!"

"Answers, like roads, are the most fun when crooked."

"But just like travelers, listeners get frustrated when the journey takes too long!" The Chalaine sighed. "You are a private person, aren't you? Did she flirt with you again?"

"Not really."

"So, a little then?"

Gen chuckled. "Hard to say. Flirting is at its most successful when the recipient can neither confirm nor deny it."

"Confirm or deny it? 'If the barmaid's sister doesn't work out to your satisfaction, you always have me.' And that look! Not hard to confirm that, now is it?"

"Don't confuse flirting with jesting, Holiness."

"Don't be coy," the Chalaine said. "I know my mother. I have never seen her act the way she does when she's around you. She's up to something. She's never been so . . . relaxed . . . around any other man."

"Is it so hard," Gen said, "to believe I could make a woman feel . . . relaxed?"

"Yes."

"Why? I have ample evidence to the contrary. Fenna, Mirelle, Marna, streets full of crazed, ravenous young women. Maybe it's just you."

"We're not talking about me. We're talking about you."

"Actually, we were talking about your mother. Don't worry. Mirelle doesn't often get the opportunity for levity or idle conversation. I sense the burden of leadership leads to a great deal of loneliness, and I provide her with a bit of entertainment from time to time. That is all. Though, if she were seriously flirting with me, I could certainly do worse."

"I will have to tell Fenna that."

Gen winced. "Please don't."

"And speaking of our mutual friend," the Chalaine said, "have we moved beyond friendship yet?"

"You and I or you and Fenna?"

Her grip on the bars tightened, blood draining from her fingers. "So help me, Gen. . ."

"All right, all right. I would say yes, but we have agreed not to pursue things too aggressively while your marriage and the birth of God stand before us. We will both be busy and in more than a little danger. It is best not to get too attached in such times."

"That's what she said," the Chalaine said, "though it is terribly wrongheaded."

"So why did you ask me?"

"To see if you would say the same thing as she did. You must be the one who came up with the idea."

Gen was about to counter when he noticed Chertanne approaching. "Oh blessed day. Here comes your fiancé."

Chertanne, obviously saddle sore, waddled awkwardly toward the wagon. The sun had burned his face a deep red, and dirt covered the white outfit he had worn for the ceremonious parade out of Mikmir. A contingent of his guard, Captain Drockley in command, encircled him.

"Let me see her," Chertanne growled, exasperated.

"Yes, Milord," Gen said cheerily, unlocking the door for him. Drockley and another guard moved to help as Chertanne's girth prevented him from taking the high step up easily. Gen followed him inside and shut the door.

"What are you doing in here?" Chertanne barked. "We're to be married for pity's sake! Give us a little privacy!"

"No unbranded man is to be allowed alone with the Chalaine. We could arrange for Ethris to. . ."

"It's all right, Gen," the Chalaine said. "He and I should talk."

"Very, well. I will be outside."

Gen jumped down, drawing his sword at the same time. Most of Chertanne's guards stumbled backward in surprise, two actually falling over themselves. To his credit, Drockley didn't move but instead carefully examined the exposed blade. Gen held it at the ready.

"Forgive me," Gen apologized. "I must be poised for action with so many armed men around the wagon."

The conversation within was shorter than Gen expected, almost brief enough to be considered instantaneous. Chertanne rapped on the door to be let out and left as quickly as his soreness would permit.

"So what was that about?" Gen asked after Chertanne left earshot.

"Brace yourself," the Chalaine answered from behind the bars. "He came to express his concern and give comfort about the recent attempt on my mother's life."

"I'm stunned. Kaimas is doing a capital job."

The Chalaine laughed. "For the record, Gen, that was very cynical. Maybe Kaimas would offer you some lessons on social etiquette, too, since you still treat your Savior like an incompetent stable boy. He's the Ha'Ulrich, Gen!"

"I know, but I see his gut and I just forget."

"That's my future husband you're talking about," the Chalaine said, stifling her laughter as best she could.

"I'm sorry," Gen apologized. "I, of course, wish you every happiness."

"Thank you. As for his gut, I am counting on the meager fare of our journey to whittle it down to a more acceptable size. Once its rotundity is no longer blinding your vision, perhaps then you will remember your manners."

"Maybe," Gen replied noncommittally.

Mirelle approached carrying a small basin of water and a towel draped over her arm. Cadaen followed, asking her to let him carry the items. She refused, and the sight of the First Mother of Rhugoth in the attitude of a servant humbled Gen. She smiled sincerely at him as she came near and set the basin on a ledge at the rear of the wagon. The odd sight drew the attention of those nearby.

"Sit down, please," she said. Gen complied, sitting on the ledge of the wagon. "I see you haven't asked my daughter to heal you. Chalaine, can you reach Gen and heal him?"

"I did not know he was hurt!" the Chalaine exclaimed, pulling open a slot in the door that allowed meals and other items to be passed to her. "Why didn't you say anything,

Gen?"

"It is a trifle," he replied.

After an exasperated sigh, the Chalaine reached through the slot and touched his arm, and a few moments later, the wound had healed completely, leaving only dried blood and dust on the side of Gen's face. Mirelle dipped the towel in the water and washed his face, his arms, and his hands tenderly. When done, she kissed him.

"Thank you again," Mirelle said.

"Thank you, Mirelle." For several moments she locked her eyes on his, Gen ignoring the interested expressions all around them and trying to see what he could find in the woman before him.

"I would like to talk with my daughter," she finally said.

"Certainly, your Grace."

Gen unlocked the door and helped her in, closing it behind her. Cadaen stood at his side, and Gen resumed his stance, thoughts of the First Mother running confused through his mind.

"Look, Gen, I. . ." Cadaen started, his voice quiet and subdued.

"Cadaen," Gen interrupted, "please. There is no need to say anything. I tire of people being in my debt. I care for the First Mother as much as you care for the Chalaine. We are brothers in our devotion to them. We watch out for each other and for each other's charges. I was in the right place to help today, and I did my duty as you would have done in my place."

"I thank you all the same," Cadaen said. "I have not honored you with the trust you are due. You have more than earned it, but I am stubborn. I have watched over her for nearly twenty years, and I have made . . . mistakes. If she were hurt because I was not ready or able, or because I was forgetful or not alert, I would take my own life, I swear it."

"No one doubts your devotion or your ability, Cadaen.

Your careful service does you credit," Gen answered.

Cadaen seemed to want to tell him something, but he decided against it, and they passed the time in silence.

Nearly an hour went by before servants brought meals for the First Mother and First Daughter. Mother and daughter talked in low voices, and Gen did not try to pry into their conversation.

Peeking around the wagon, he glimpsed the Pearl Bridge for the first time. His eyes required several seconds to take in the structure. The bridge defied comfort or comprehension, spanning an impossible distance between two shard fragments. Its length and the yawning gap between the shards gave it a fragile feeling, and Gen could understand why some people in Rhugoth dared not to cross some of the longer bridges; Pearl Bridge emanated vertigo, even at a distance.

The First Mother stayed with her daughter for her meal, and, as she descended from the wagon when finished, she handed the empty plates and mugs to Cadaen.

"Take care of these," she ordered. "I need to speak with Gen briefly."

"Yes, your Grace," Cadaen said, retrieving the items without complaint. The First Mother waited until he was out of sight before turning back to Gen and, embracing him again, whispered in his ear.

"Keep talking to my daughter. You lighten her spirit, and she will need more of that every step we get closer to Elde Luri Mora. She tries to be brave, but she is frightened."

"I will," Gen said as Mirelle pulled away and straightened his hair with her fingers. Her nearness was exhilarating.

"I think the wind will win that battle, Mirelle," he said. "Perhaps I should wear a hat like Geoff, though I doubt I would find more than a crow's feather out here to garnish it with."

"No," Mirelle said. "A crown for that head or nothing. Good night. Talk to me soon. There are several measures I want put in place for my daughter's safety."

"As you wish, your Grace."

Cadaen arrived, and the First Mother left for her tents. Night descended on the camp. Regent Ogbith—motivated by the attack earlier that day—ordered double the active patrols they had planned for their journey. Gen caught Shadan Khairn wandering about, face reflecting a childlike glee, though Gen had to believe he was disappointed about not getting to kill anyone that afternoon.

"So, Chalaine," Gen said, "what did your mother say to you?" He waited, hearing the Chalaine walk to the front of the wagon before sitting by the slot.

"Just the standard things mothers say to comfort their daughters," the Chalaine replied. Gen smiled.

"Humor me."

Chapter 36 - Soul Jumper

The trip through the heart of Rhugoth took the caravan past the Royal Mountains, towering, stark and gray. The tips of the four peaks that comprised the principal mass of the range thrust upward, sharp and edgy like rough stone spearheads jammed up through the crust of the ground and into the blue body of the sky. The caravan camped within view of the peaks the second night of the trek, in the verdant tree-covered hills at their base the third night, and then pushed hard the next day to arrive at the small farming village of Kitmere, a pleasant town happily situated on a bend of the Buckwater River.

Gen thrilled at the country air, the sights and smells of the outdoors, and the considerably improved mood of both the Chalaine and the First Mother. The Chalaine stood nearly all day, hands clamped around the bars, staring at the world around her with wonderment and an infectious joy. When Gen would arrive on duty at sundown, she filled his ears with all the things she had seen that day that surprised, awed, or inspired her, and there were many. On the first night the Chalaine had declared the stars and shards—seen unobscured by city lights or smoke for the first time in her life—the most regal of Eldaloth's creations and hassled

Gen endlessly about their names and formations when she discovered he knew somewhat about the order of the skies.

Gen enjoyed chatting with her until late into the night. She asked him to teach her words in the old tongue and tell her what he knew of the places they would see along the trail. For the first time in many months her mind was clear and her spirit light, and she was determined to learn all she could. Despite the expansive knowledge Gen had gained from his contact with Samian, Elberen, and Telmerran, Gen thought that given a few weeks at the Chalaine's blistering pace of interrogation, he would have nothing left to say.

After leaving Kitmere they passed over another shard-spanning bridge into Odred, though the bridge was considerably shorter and far less magnificent than the Pearl Bridge they had traversed four days before. From Odred, they skirted the edge of the Willow Wood and rode into the lumbering town of Three Willow late that night. All were anxious to take advantage of the last civilization they would see for at least two months.

As with Kitmere and Odred, Three Willow brimmed to overflowing with the curious and festive, and even the lateness of the caravan's arrival did little to trim the numbers or the ebullience. Gen cautioned the Chalaine to stay away from the bars, and he kept his senses sharp. As a result of the attempt on the First Mother's life, the Dark Guard brooked no attempt to approach the wagon in which the Chalaine rode; Regent Ogbith had sent messengers ahead to warn the people beforehand to prevent unnecessary violence. After some concentrated persuasion by Ethris and Gen, Mirelle finally relented and agreed to ride in the wagon with her daughter when they entered into the towns along the way.

As they passed the rural throngs and the raw log buildings of Three Willow, memories of Tell flooded Gen's mind; woodsmen, it seemed, dressed and talked the same wherever they were found. The rough speech and rough homes, weathered faces, and loud brawny boys turned Three Willow into a surrogate home for the one he had lost. He half expected to see Bernard Showles turn the corner and shout some insult at him, or to see Gant lazing about on the steps of the Church with a set of White Sticks on the ground at his feet.

Revelers from every town nearby set up tents and lit fires in any space they could find on the edge of road and forest, and the wood smoke thickened to near fog-like consistency the deeper they went into the town. Gen wished for a wind to clear some of the smoke away and improve visibility, but calm air, unusual for the season, let the smoke settle and hang, clinging to tree boles and buildings. The Willow Wood was an old forest, thick trees with giant trunks thrusting into the night above them, branches weaving together to form a dark canopy thick enough to cloak the sky.

Despite its familiarity of spirit, Gen calculated that Three Willow was nearly three times the size of Tell, though the dark probably obscured even more buildings back in the wood itself. As with the small towns before, the principal inn, rather unoriginally dubbed Three Willow Inn, had benefited from some remodeling and fortification. Besides metal-banded wooden walls that encircled the inn and the addition of a heavy wooden gate, the high sloping roof, wooden walls, and unkempt grounds showed the improvements of craftsmen sent from Mikmir to repair and renew them. Glass windows accented new slotted shutters, the slightly slanted porch had been righted to exactly level, and crisp thick grass grew softly underfoot.

The fighting elements of Aughmere encamped outside the walls, while Rhugothian soldiers walked or rode inside. Ulney drove the wagon around the circle drive where Gen suspected that cobblestone had recently replaced rutted dirt. In the center of the circle stood the namesake of the town. Three immense willows, thickly leaved—limp branches nearly touching the ground—formed a dome underneath that the officers started claiming for their tent sites.

As they rounded the corner toward the door, Gen spotted two men standing by the stairs, undoubtedly the town Magistrate and the Innkeeper, the only two allowed inside the walls during the Chalaine's stay, and then only for a quick greeting. Cookmaster Broulin and accompanying servants would commandeer the building shortly after their arrival.

Ulney stopped the wagon near the steps, and Gen climbed down and opened the door for Mirelle and her daughter, Cadaen helping them out. They waited by the wagon until Regent Ogbith and Ethris arrived with the party. As one, they ascended the steps to the nervous smiles of Magistrate Polemark and Innkeeper Cheswick. Both were awkwardly clean, new clothes and a fresh trimming of hair setting them apart from the townspeople heard reveling outside. Both men went to their knees as the First Mother and the Chalaine approached.

"Please rise," Mirelle instructed.

"Thank you, your Grace," the Magistrate said. He was a stout man with thick, graying hair. Muscles had gone to fat, but a lot of strength was left in his frame. Cheswick, much the same in appearance, was terrified and said nothing. The Magistrate continued. "Welcome to Three Willow. We are thankful you chose to stay with us. I am Magistrate Polemark, and this is Innkeeper Cheswick. Will the Blessed One be staying with us?"

"I am here!" Chertanne, eyes watery and itching from the smoke, strode into the light of a lamp secured to a support beam of the inn's porch. Kaimas and Captain Drockley came after, and the Pontiff and Padra Athan followed only a few steps behind. Polemark and Cheswick again went to their knees.

"Blessed One!" the Magistrate intoned reverently. "We welcome you to our unworthy establishment. We hope everything is to your satisfaction."

"My satisfaction?" Chertanne laughed. "I have seen better. . ."

"What his Grace wishes to say," Kaimas interrupted, "is that we could expect no better inn anywhere and that it is no doubt more than adequate."

"Yes, yes," Chertanne reversed. "A fine establishment, indeed. Please stand."

"We should go inside," Gen interjected in the silence that followed. "I do not want the Chalaine out-of-doors, especially in the darkness and smoke."

"Of course," the Magistrate agreed, getting to his feet. "By all means, Lord Blackshire. It is thrill to see you, as well. Tales of your deeds have. . ."

"Been greatly exaggerated," Gen finished for him to general laughter. Gen signaled toward the door. "Please, if we may?"

The Magistrate turned toward Innkeeper Cheswick, who took several seconds to realize he was to do something. Frantically pulling the keys from his belt, he unlocked the front door and the assembly went in. The main room was comfortable, clean, and cheery. A bright fire warmed the room from an ample fireplace. As everyone settled into chairs and trunks from the wagons were brought in, Innkeeper Cheswick unlocked the rear door for Cookmaster Broulin and his cadre of servants.

The exhausted Pontiff, helped by Athan, went directly to his rooms, asking that a servant be sent with his food when ready. Kaimas and Ethris followed suit, both claiming fatigue. Everyone else chatted idly as the clanging pots, staccato of hurried chopping, and the eventual smell of meat roasting set mouths to watering. Dinner arrived late tonight.

"Geoff!" Chertanne piped up after a lull. "Favor us with

something to make the slow march toward dinner more tolerable!"

In a few short days, Geoff had become a favorite of Chertanne's, and—Gen noted glumly—Fenna had become a favorite with Geoff. As a consequence, Fenna, Geoff, and Chertanne were often in company together. Geoff rose and bowed, but as he started toward the fireplace, he noticed Gen behind the Chalaine and remembered something.

"Ah, yes!" Geoff said enthusiastically. "I just remembered that Lord Blackshire promised the Chalaine that he would sing for her!"

"I promised nothing of the sort," Gen contradicted.

"Oh come, now," Geoff entreated. "The Most Holy Chalaine said she would like to hear you sing. You cannot deny her request! What say you, Holiness?"

The Chalaine turned toward Gen. "Of course I would like to hear him. But I would not force him. He may do as he chooses without causing me any offense."

"Do sing for us, Gen!" Fenna joined in. "You sound wonderful!"

"I am on duty," Gen said. "Perhaps. . ."

"I'll take over for you . . . for a wee bit," Jaron offered, stepping forward.

Gen threw him a dirty look. "Traitor."

More encouragement came from the rest of the Dark Guard and their apprentices, who had entered a short time before. Seeing the battle won, Geoff clapped and handed Gen his lute, sitting close to the front with Fenna, both smiling grandly. Gen sat, stretching his fingers. Mirelle grinned nearby while the Dark Guard seemed disposed to break out laughing at any minute. Chertanne folded his arms and tried to appear as disinterested as possible. Only Regent Ogbith and Shadan Khairn, deep in some conversation, seemed uninterested.

"I will play the Lay of Pelewen and Nerena," Gen announced.

Geoff's countenance darkened and he appeared about to comment, but Gen started playing before he could protest.

*Pelewen still wanders the night
Under the canopy of long-dead days,
A knight sword-sworn to duty and might,
A knight faith-sealed with truth and right.*

*Nerena still wanders the misty eve,
Under the canopy of long-dead days,
A witch evil-sworn to lies believe,
A witch dark-sealed to darkness wreathe.*

*What brought you, knight, to wander that wood?
What brought the thieves who cut you down?
Where, dark witch, did you find the good,
To succor he who for goodness stood?*

*With secrets whispered in secluded shade,
She healed you, knight, your life returned,
With kisses, witch, the first he gave,
Your soul was healed and holy made.*

*Love, you too we see this night
Under the canopy of long-dead days;
A blessing sworn to the good and right,
A love that sealed a witch and knight.*

*What partings made upon the morn,
Under wind and sun and forest song:
One body whole and one soul born,
Four eyes wet and two hearts torn.*

*What drove you, Knight, to the distant glade?
What drove you to confess, dear maid?
Why, Knight, did heart turn horse 'round again?*

And why, Pureman, could you not forgive her stain?

One maid burned at morning's light.
One horse rides through ash at night.
One soul to tell the Knight the tale.
One Knight upon his sword impaled.

Death, you too we see this eve,
Under the canopy of long-dead days;
A death dark-sworn to love bereave,
A death dark-sealed to sadness wreathe.

"Well, that was depressing," Chertanne derided just before Gen strummed the last gentle strain of the song. "We'll stick with Geoff on the journey, Gen. No offense, of course."

Gen said nothing and stood, laying the lute down carefully on the chair. Geoff sprang from his seat in the difficult silence and threw his arm around Gen before he could return to the Chalaine.

"It was a sad song, indeed! But how about a little applause for our near-journeyman bard here?"

There was subdued clapping all around, and more than enough frowns for Chertanne from more than one quarter. Gen retreated gratefully to stand behind the Chalaine as Geoff launched into a more cheery tune to dispel the gloom Gen's had invited. Jaron patted him on the back before he left.

The Chalaine signaled him closer so she could talk to him over the din. "I am sorry for Chertanne's rude behavior, Gen. Do not listen to him. You sing very well, indeed. I should like to hear more when we are in . . . polite . . . company."

"Do not feel you have to apologize for him, Chalaine. You need not do that until you are properly married."

The food arrived soon after, and everyone ate happily,

all chatting excitedly about seeing Shroud Lake shard for the first time on the morrow. Jaron watched briefly to allow Gen to eat when most were finished. After eating a bit himself, Geoff played for the relaxed crowd. The Chalaine, Fenna, and Mirelle sat around a table playing cards with Dason, who, after the first few rounds, was clearly befuddled by the Chalaine's newfound skill.

"Holiness," Dason commented, "you are quite undoing us all! I must say, you are uncommonly improved. I will have to concentrate more completely! Eldwena must have given you a lesson or two."

"You are too kind, Dason," the Chalaine demurred, "but I'm just having a run of good fortune."

Mirelle winked surreptitiously at Gen, who couldn't decide whether to feel proud or ashamed of his accomplishment. He could, however, take satisfaction in the Chalaine's skill. She was a perfect cheat, for just as those who usually tell the truth are the best liars, those presumed innocent are the best cheaters. He was especially gratified that she noticed that Dason had begun paying an inordinate amount of attention to the cards she was playing, so she backed off of cheating and relied on the stratagems Gen had taught her.

Boots on the porch outside turned Gen's attention from the game. He could barely discern the muffled muttering outside and then the departure of whoever had come. A knock in a prearranged pattern on the door brought Tolbrook to his feet. The protocol was established, and the Chalaine rose, Fenna with her, and was escorted by both Gen and Jaron to her windowless room upstairs. Jaron went inside and Gen stood without. Captain Drockley passed by them, a slightly inebriated Chertanne stumbling behind. After letting a complaining Chertanne enter an adjacent room, the Captain stood guard just down the hall.

The door to the common room was unbarred and unlocked, and just as the hinges squeaked to open, a tremendous explosion shook the foundations of the building. Debris slammed into the front of the inn, pattering and clanging on the roof for several seconds afterward as chunks of armor and flesh fell about the inn.

Outside, men and horses screamed, and in the common room chaos erupted. Ethris, Kaimas, and Athan burst from their rooms and ran down the stairs, faces grave. Regent Ogbith was yelling, trying to order someone to shut the door.

"Is Tolbrook alive?" "Has the inn caught fire?" "Where did it come from?" "Get back in the kitchen, you dolt!" "Has someone secured the kitchen door?" "Why isn't that door closed yet?"

"It's off its hinges," Cadaen yelled, "but the board will hold it in place. Get it!"

"Wait," this was Shadan Khairn, entering from outside. "I'll help you!" A scrape and slam indicated the door was shut.

"I said *back into the kitchen*!" Regent Ogbith yelled again.

"Back away! What are you doing!" yelled Cadaen, and Gen craned his neck to see what was happening downstairs. There were frantic footsteps.

"Stand back, I say!" This was a voice Gen did not recognize. "And don't think about magic or I kill her. I can tell when you're doing it. I can! That includes you, Churchman! I only want to deliver a message."

"Stand down!" Cadaen yelled. "Do not hurt her, or I'll. . ."

"Shut up, idiot! Bring Gen. Bring him to me!"

"Lord Blackshire?" Regent Ogbith questioned, voice quavering. "What does this have to do with. . ."

"Bring him! Now!"

"Gen! Come here," Regent Ogbith ordered. "Horace, take Gen's place." Gen waited until Horace, Gerand's Dark Guard master, stood in front of the door before taking several steps at a time to the bottom. As he entered the common room, it took several moments to digest the macabre scene. Debris—wood, glass, and dinnerware—littered the ground. Although the front windows were shuttered, every one was broken, holes and breaks riddling the shutters' slats.

Two bodies, one badly burned, the other an unconscious Tolbrook, lay near the back of the room opposite the wall where the explosion had blown them. A Dark Guard worked furiously to stem blood flowing from Tolbrook's body from several deep gashes. The other was dead. Smoke from a fire outside filtered into the room, and from the bright orange light coming through the shutters, Gen surmised that the willow trees had caught fire.

Everyone, however, was focused on Mirelle, a kitchen servant behind her with a knife to her throat. The First Mother was rigid and bent slightly backward, face composed but sweating. Cadaen stood exactly opposite, face angry and desperate. Kaimas, Ethris, and Athan stood to the side of him, standing very still. Shadan Khairn, clothes and hair singed and sooty, had drawn his sword, and Gen knew that if the slightest opportunity presented itself he would strike.

Gen surveyed the situation. The servant's eyes were calm and collected, and he smiled maliciously at Gen as he approached. He was young—in his twenties—with stringy dark hair, thin lips, and a pale face. Gen had noticed him several times before. That he should attack the First Mother and claim to know of magic seemed ludicrous, but Ethris, Kaimas, and Athan did nothing, taking the threat seriously. The attacker held the knife rigidly and to the side of Mirelle's throat, increasing the probability that even if he were incapacitated, the knife would find a mark.

"What is your message?" Gen asked calmly, trying to read the man's eyes.

"Well, you are just as she said, thinking yourself quite clever and important, arrogant after all your 'accomplishments.' My message is to you alone. You will leave this room and start down the road to the Portal. My friends will tell me when you have arrived, and I will release the First Mother and depart. If you are followed, she dies."

Gen glanced toward Regent Ogbith, who nodded *no*.

"My duty is to the Chalaine," Gen said. "I will not leave her."

"I was told you would say that. Very well, then. Joranne sends her best to her sons, who may have figured out by now how she sent me here."

In a quick motion, he slit Mirelle's throat, Khairn leaping forward to strike as Mirelle slumped to the ground. Gen saw the young man's face go slack just as the Shadan ran him through, eyes locking on Gen's. Gen wanted to walk forward, but an ice cold shock wrenched his body and he stumbled. In an instant, he could no longer control himself, feeling as he had when the masters in the Training Stones had taken control of him. But there was no push or struggle for his mind; it was his own and he controlled his thoughts but nothing else.

Let's go, said a voice only he could hear.

"It's passed to Gen!" Kaimas warned, and every eye turned. "Contain him!"

Gen was only a spectator as what controlled him dove for a shuttered window. The shutters broke easily under his weight and he tumbled out onto the patio. Standing quickly, he sprinted into the yard. Bodies, blood, and carnage lay everywhere, the three willows, now smoldering, had been blown down and away from each other, a small crater in the center marking the focus of the explosion. Smoke wreathed everyone and everything. Soldiers wandered about confused, yelling orders. None thought to stop Gen. The door creaked behind him. He was almost to the front gates, which hung crookedly, providing a small hole through which soldiers clambered in and out. Outside the walls, people gathered, trying to glimpse what was going on within.

Ethris incanted, and the ground in front of Gen gave way. Gen landed hard in the bottom of a hole, struggling against what possessed him to no avail. Whatever controlled him rose, pulling himself up and kicking against the dirt wall to propel himself out and over. As he finally scrambled over the ledge, a fierce wind slammed downward and pinned him to the ground.

"Do it, Athan!" Ethris yelled. Gen was relieved that he was stopped, though the pressure of the column of wind sent a fiery pain down his back. Athan concentrated and incanted.

"It is done," Athan said, sweat beading on his brow. "It cannot pass to anyone else. I can hold it for a little while. Fetch the other two Padras. Together, we could probably hold him for an hour, maybe more."

Three members of the Dark Guard, faces grave, came and took Gen by the hands and feet. Kaimas released the wind, and the soldiers half carried, half dragged a struggling Gen into the inn, tying him securely to a chair with thick ropes.

"Get everyone out of this room, everyone but Ethris and Kaimas!" Padra Athan ordered. "Do it now! Regent Ogbith, hold on a moment. Be sure to check the kitchen!"

A spent Shadan Khairn passed by Gen first, eyes angry, and went outside. The Dark Guard carried a groaning Tolbrook up next, the First Mother ordering them to take him to the Chalaine.

"I will stay," she said, rubbing a thin scar on her neck where Shadan Khairn had healed her. Mirelle remained rooted to her spot despite the objections of everyone else. Regent Ogbith waited nervously by the door, clearly out of his depth.

"What am I to do, Padra?" he asked tremulously.

"I've little time to explain," Athan said, remaining focused on Gen. "The enemy has used soul jumping to get here. A soul jumper can pass to any person in sight, displacing the spirit of another. When the soul jumper leaves, it kills the victim. Have your men make inquiries in the town. See if anyone has died recently and if you can trace the occurrences. If we can find the soul jumper's body before my ward fails, we can kill him for good. He is likely somewhere out of the way, in the woods or in a locked room. It will appear as if he is asleep, but he will not wake. Kill him immediately if you find him. Go!"

Regent Ogbith left hurriedly. Mirelle's distress captured Ethris's attention.

"Is Gen dead, then?" she asked, tears welling in her eyes.

"If we cannot find the soul jumper's body before he leaves Gen's body, Gen will die," Athan stated flatly. "But there is hope. You should go to your rooms. What we have to do may be unpleasant. We should prepare to leave as quickly as possible. As we are short-handed, perhaps you can be helpful and get everyone organized."

Mirelle nodded distractedly and went quickly upstairs.

"Let's move him to the kitchen," Kaimas said. "No need for everyone to see or hear this."

The three of them hoisted the chair and Gen into the kitchen. Ethris closed the door to the outside, which stood ajar, drowning out the sound of Cookmaster Broulin commanding a frightened group cooks to pack up.

Whatever they do to me, the voice said, *you'll feel it too. Do not worry, though. We were prepared for this turn of events.* The other two Padras entered next, eyes wide at the scene before them. Ethris filled them in quickly.

"I will tell you when I am starting to fail," Athan instructed, already showing signs of strain. "When I do, you take over first, Marin, and then you, Orviss, when he fails. We need to get as much information as we can. There is some plot against us here. Kaimas, Ethris, I leave it to you to find out what you can. Do whatever necessary. Gen isn't nearly as important as whatever the jumper knows."

"On the contrary," Ethris disagreed. "The first question is why Gen was chosen in the first place! Joranne is clearly behind this, but she can only know Gen by reputation."

Gen figured that Joranne knew that he was the Ilch. Why hadn't she exposed him? Kaimas came forward, placing his hands on both sides of Gen's head. Exhaling, he closed his eyes and concentrated. "Speak! Who are you? What do you want with Gen?" Gen was dimly aware of the struggle. It was not with his mind, but with the jumper's, whose will was strong.

"Mother has warded his mind," Kaimas said, releasing his hold. "I will need your help, brother."

Ethris nodded, standing behind Gen. Both men placed their hands on his head, and the war of minds continued. Several times during the struggle, Gen felt fear from the jumper—the brothers' combined strength was staggering. The jumper focused his own mind as the wards failed and fought hard. Gen's body tensed, teeth clenching with the effort to repel the men. Suddenly it stopped, and the jumper laughed, Ethris and Kaimas releasing their hold.

"Curse that woman!" Kaimas swore. "She is too strong!"

"And she is coming," Gen heard himself say mockingly. "You have nothing left to fight her with. You have wasted your strength."

"You're bluffing," Ethris countered, sweating and shaking. Kaimas closed his eyes. The jumper focused his attention on Athan, sensing an opportunity.

"He isn't," Kaimas said, voice distant. "She is near. "

"Marin," Athan ordered, face red and eyes wide. "He is trying to jump. Take over." The plump Padra stepped forward and concentrated, Athan slumping back against the wall.

"We should get the Chalaine away from here," he gasped. "Tell everyone to say nothing of where we are going until we are well out of Gen's earshot."

Kaimas concurred, closing his eyes. "Joranne is coming in from the woods behind the inn. She is some distance off, still. I will remain behind to stall her approach, if I can."

Ethris furrowed his brow. "Are you sure?" he asked concernedly. "You will be of little use now. I must stay with the Chalaine and cannot help you."

"I will do what I can, Ethris. Hurry!"

Kaimas opened the back door, shutting it behind him and yelling at Cookmaster Broulin to clear everyone out, pots and dishes packed or no.

"Orviss," Athan said weakly, "you stay with Marin and hold the jumper here for as long as you can. If it appears you will fail, do not release the hold until you are out of his sight or he'll jump to you."

"Yes, your Grace."

"Let's get them out, Ethris."

By the time Marin's strength failed, the noise in the common room had faded. Gen heard the First Mother and the Chalaine and others coming down the stairs and leaving in a rush. Regent Ogbith poked his head in and told the Padras that horses would be left for them and that Athan would contact them mentally with instructions. After a brief glance at Gen, the Regent left. Orviss, Gen could see, would not last as long as his predecessors, nervousness sapping his strength.

The jumper was perfectly content. *She will come and free me,* he thought to Gen. *She is at the doors.* The sound of Kaimas howling in pain nearly broke Orviss's focus. He said, "I cannot hold any longer, Marin."

Marin nodded and both men backed toward the door, Orviss hanging on until the door shut. *She is here. Fear not. You are not to die.* The door at the rear entrance of the kitchen opened. Unexpectedly Kaimas entered, back rigid. His face was pale, waxy, and slack, and only the whites of his eyes showed. As Gen watched, blood poured from his eye sockets and dripped from his mouth. He coughed and gagged, staggering about spitting blood on the wall before vomiting and collapsing. Flecks of blood spotted the lantern on the table as Joranne, in appearance a wrinkled old woman, shuffled through the doorway.

"You have done well," she said, addressing the jumper. "I will release you."

"Into whom?"

"I am afraid no one is available, and I don't have time to take you back to your body."

"Betrayer!"

"Hardly. Gen is more important than you, and I must speak with him."

"No!" The jumper tried to release himself from Gen and pass into Joranne, but Joranne grinned mischievously as he failed. Frustration and fear gripped the jumper, sending him into desperation. He pulled and twisted Gen's arms against the ropes and the chair, bruising and rubbing raw his flesh. Joranne closed her eyes. "Kill him, Dethris."

"You'll pay for this, Joranne!" the jumper yelled, thrashing.

In a moment, Gen felt freed, regaining control of his mind and his body. Joranne smiled pleasantly at him, as a grandmother might smile at a grandchild who had just arrived for a visit.

"At last," she said, "we get to talk. It is hardly fitting that someone who practically raised you should not be able to find herself in your company without all this effort. But I understand now how deeply you were interfered with and that you do not know what gratitude is owed me or what place in history awaits you. Of course, I have gleaned from Kaimas that the magic used to hide the knowledge and teachings from you is powerful, but I'm sure with a little effort I can overcome. But first, I need information for my master."

She stared at him, and Gen felt her push into his mind easily despite his attempts to shut her out. She quickly sifted through his memories, going further and further back, his life a blur. The first memory she could find, the furthest back Gen had recollection of, was when as a child he had been stumbling through the woods of the Alewine forest by himself, cold and wearing nothing but a ragged shirt. His feet hurt as he trod through on the rough, dry ground. They were scarred. He heard a strange noise in the woods ahead of him and climbed a tree out of fear and curiosity. There were men in the clearing before him, the first he could recall seeing, chopping at a tree with heavy axes. One looked up and saw him. The memory vanished.

"So they concealed my care for you," she stated bitterly. "Then you will need some of my memories before you really understand. Learn from whence you came."

As with the memories of the three masters of his Training Stones, Joranne's thoughts played out before him as if he were her, watching through her eyes.

She waited. It was the night appointed by the Millim Eri for the Ha'Ulrich and the Chalaine to be born, and it was the night Mikkik had chosen—out of spite—for his servant to come forth. The ground before her was muddy and soft from the rain that had fallen on the twisted, thorny trees of Goreth Forest in sheets during the day. The perpetual mist that stirred between the boles threatened to conceal the spot where she had buried the seed that Mikkik had given her. She used her magic to clear the mist so her view of whatever creature was born from the seed would not be obscured.

The seed was little bigger than an acorn made of what appeared to be molten glass. Mikkik had given the task of planting the seed her, not trusting his followers, the Mikkik Dun, with knowledge of its whereabouts. He had slaved over the stone for months. She understood only dimly what he had done. From what she knew, Mikkik had not created the stone, but rather modified it, changed it somehow to suit his purpose, struggling to complete the work in secret as his power failed. When complete, he had found her and brought her to Goreth, entrusting her with the seed and the animon before disappearing into hiding. With Trys eclipsed, Mikkik was only a pinch more powerful than she was.

During the night, she jammed a stick into the mud and worked it around until she had a hole big enough to drop the stone into, covering it once complete. Now, with night ending, she held the animon for the new creature clutched in her hand. The animon would be the creature's life force, for Mikkik did not trust the creature to have life unto itself. Joranne thrilled in anticipation. She could hardly fathom what kind of creature the Ilch would be or what the manner its birth would entail. She had simply followed instructions and dared ask no more. Here would be one that would join her on the thrones of Elde Luri Mora in eternal splendor. Surely Mikkik would choose his own form or that of the Millim Eri for his servant.

She checked the sky. Any time now. Joranne's body was that of a youth as it always was when dawn was near. She was grateful she would have the day to arrange things before she was returned to dust to be reborn. If the creature were born while she was yet an infant, she feared it would overtake her in her weakness.

The dirt before her stirred with the faint signs of dawn, the first strong rays of light piercing through the gloom of the wood. She cast a spell to illuminate the still dim spot, light diffusing eerily in the mist. Slowly, strands of dirt writhed, at first giving the appearance of a mass of worms squirming just beneath the surface. Gradually, the dirt churned faster and took a more definite shape—it was humanoid, a child. Joranne was surprised. Why not create the Ilch fully grown? The brown and gray of the dirt changed into the white hues of bone, the red of muscle, and the peach-white of flesh. The eyes and ears formed last. A human child. A boy. It lay lifeless in the hole created from the material of its creation.

Joranne looked at the animon. The glass ball in her hand now glowed in the center, and she stretched out her hand and touched the chest of the infant with the animon, the flame inside bending toward the body. Muscles stirred as the power of the animon ignited the life of the Ilch, and in the pre-dawn chill, it bellowed, voice a clarion call through the trees. Mikkik's servant was born with a power for Trysmagic to rival that of his creator.

Joranne pocketed the animon carefully; breaking it would kill the child. She wrapped the baby in her cloak and comforted and quieted him as best she could. It would be a couple more hours before she had breast enough to feed the child, and Goreth forest was not a safe place. She could not disappoint her master by letting a wolf or a Gek destroy his creation before it took but ten breaths on Ki'Hal. Pulling him close, Joranne found her bearings and walked southwest. Goreth was no place to raise a baby.

The vision ended and the room returned to focus, Joranne stopping so her face was close to his. "And so it was, Gen. I took you south to the warm Plains of Ellinin. No one lived there but you and I by the river. I brought you up from a babe. You sucked my breast, slept on my shoulder in the afternoon, and learned the true nature of things as I taught you to speak. But in your fourth year the Millim Eri discovered me and took you and your *animon*. Do you want to know how it was? I have found those seals upon your mind, quite cleverly concealed. Let me release the first. . ."

As she bent forward to place her hands upon his head, her eyebrows scrunched together and she pulled back, casting about fearfully.

"My time here is at an end. Remember what I have shown you. Remember this most of all: the Chalaine and the Ha'Ulrich are not what you believe. You can master them both."

Joranne fled, flinging open the door and darting out into the night. Gen breathed out heavily, feeling the air in his lungs for the first time he could recall since coming under the control of the jumper. Kaimas's body lay still on the floor, blood settling around his head.

Gen struggled against his bonds, casting his eyes about the kitchen in search of a knife or sharp edge he could rub against to slice them. As he turned, he saw runes as shadows on the wall behind him. They read, "He has already won."

Turning back toward the lantern, Gen saw that the spittle of blood sprayed by Kaimas had dripped and streaked to form the message on the lantern panes. Gen shivered at the malice that would send a man to such a death.

Clearing his mind, Gen turned his attention toward freeing himself. He guessed that the Chalaine and her party could not be more than twenty minutes gone. He assumed they would push as quickly as they could to the Portal, as it was fortified. For such a large company to pass through the small Portal would take the better part of a day, and he could arrive in ample time to join them before they sailed across the lake.

Only after searching for several frustrating minutes and failing to get hold of something to help him did he realize that the chair he sat in had become rickety from all his scooting about. Leaning forward, he got to his feet and rammed backward as hard as he could into the wall. The chair held but was weakened considerably. Finding the stonework stove, he slammed into that next. The chair splintered and fell apart, but he fell awkwardly, hitting the back of his head on the edge of the stove. His vision swam, and he lay still on the stones, trying to fight off unconsciousness. Wings flapped somewhere nearby.

Chapter 37 - Shroud Lake Shard

"You can tell them nothing of what Joranne showed you," Ethris counseled Gen, standing well away from the rest of the column as it passed through the shimmering Portal. The advance riders had found Gen lying face down in the middle of the road the day after the incident, unconscious and bruised from the night before. The entire column had stopped in the middle of the wood a good half-mile away while Ethris and Athan rode forward to inspect him and ensure that he was himself and no longer compromised by the enemy.

Despite Ethris's proclamation of his health and self-possession, Athan had ordered Gen quarantined from the rest of the caravan for observation for at least three days, dismissing all objections leveled against the measure. Mirelle and Fenna were allowed to inquire after him, but only at a distance. In return, Ethris demanded that Gen not be questioned until he had eaten and been healed. Athan agreed, and a Pureman had been fetched to care for his scrapes and bruises. Once the Pureman had gone, Ethris pulled Gen aside and Gen told him everything.

"I am smart enough to know to conceal that," Gen answered, feeling anxious. "The question is, what do I tell Athan and the Padras? They'll be back to inquire about the whole thing soon enough, and if I lie they'll know it."

Ethris rubbed his chin. "There is much of the truth to be said, and we can only hope that will suffice. Just say she had my brother Dethris kill the jumper, interrogated you magically to find information about what we are planning, and then fled unexpectedly. That should do it."

Gen nodded his assent. One hint that he was the Ilch would see him dead in an instant, no matter how ridiculous the notion would seem to everyone else. He hoped the rush of getting the caravan through the Portal would spare him deep questioning. The Shroud Lake Portal was small and relatively unadorned, its size slowing the passage of the caravan. A rough stone arch was constructed to mark the Portal's location, a rutted road leading to it and not beyond. Gen thought it ironic that the entrance to the most important shard should be so plain and narrow. The Chalaine's wagon had been constructed with the Portal's dimensions in mind, and it barely fit.

To complicate matters further, the Portal opened onto the middle of a lake on the other side, and since its discovery two years ago, a hand-chosen group of craftsman had labored unceasingly to construct a large floating dock and a host of barges to convey the Ha'Ulrich and his party across the immense Shroud Lake, a water journey of four days to the east shore. Gen had heard about the floating dock and the mist-covered lake in the council outlining their plan and was anxious to see them, but as the Padras Athan, Orviss, and Marin approached in company with Regent Ogbith and Shadan Khairn, Gen felt his chances slim. All were severe—all save Torbrand, who looked festive.

"Gen," the Shadan said happily, giving his former student a slap on the back, "good to see you in control of yourself. I hope you noticed that I saved your First Mother for you. She hasn't shown me nearly as much gratitude as she showed you for similar service, but I suspect she'll warm to me sooner or later. She's had a pretty rough trip so far, wouldn't you agree?"

"Enough of this banter," Athan growled. "Tell us what happened, Gen? We don't have much time for this."

Gen rehearsed the events as Ethris had instructed, noting the general lack of surprise that Kaimas was dead.

"I felt Kaimas' passing," Ethris explained after Gen finished and asked. "Kaimas, Dethris, and I have always been connected in that way, despite our differences."

"What I would like to know," Athan continued, "is why go to all the effort to secure Gen in the first place? As devastating as the attack was, the whole purpose was not, as I reason, to do any physical harm to the First Daughter or the Ha'Ulrich, but to capture Gen. What does Joranne want with him? Did you get any sense of her purpose, boy?"

Gen remained as calm as he could. "She wanted to use me to gather information for her 'master,' as I said earlier. There was more she wanted to do and say, but something frightened her off before she could complete her interrogation. She wants to use me, but I do not know to what end."

"And how did you end up in the middle of the road ahead of the party?"

"I have no recollection of what happened after I tried to break the chair to escape," Gen answered truthfully.

"This business vexes me greatly," Athan grumbled aloud, dissatisfied. Gen was grateful, however, that the questioning appeared to be at an end.

Athan stared at Ethris. "A great deal has happened to the Chalaine of late, and at each turn of events Gen is at the center of it. I want him accompanied by you, Ethris, or one of the Padras, at all times for the next three days. We will examine him again at that time. If it were up to me, Gen would be left behind, but a certain aristocrat is against it. Gen, I implore you to abandon the caravan for the good of the Chalaine and whoever else you count as friend. You are drawing danger to them rather than the reverse."

Athan held Gen's eyes for a moment before walking away.

"That went as well as can be hoped," Ethris commented after everyone had left. "One of these times he will want to inspect your mind himself, and that would likely be the end of you—and of me, for that matter. Do try to keep out of trouble from now on, if you don't mind. It is obvious that despite his pronouncements after the first betrothal, Mikkik is anxious to recover you, unless Joranne is acting alone."

"Why doesn't she simply expose me? I would be on the run and more accessible."

"She may do just that, if it comes to it," Ethris speculated. "But your position is advantageous to her, and to Mikkik. If they could convert you to their purpose while you are still in a position of trust, the damage you could wreak would be immense, indeed."

"Do you still trust me?"

"You have given me no reason not to," Ethris said catching his eye. "I have examined your mind and your character deeply, and I find no shadow of wavering. Even if Joranne were to unlock the seals in your mind, I doubt you would turn."

"Athan is right about one thing," Gen said. "I may need to leave the caravan voluntarily to guarantee its safety."

"I doubt it will come to that. Just serve the Chalaine, Gen. Whatever you were born to do, protecting her is the best use of your talents and your forthcoming power. Eldaloth and an increasing number of people know that Chertanne cannot do it."

They were the last to pass through the shimmering field. The Portal Mage, clearly exhausted, shut the Portal down after following them through. It was midafternoon on the

Shroud Lake shard, a few hours ahead of the Rhugothian shard cluster. Gen glanced about, impressed by the floating dock, which was twice the size he had imagined it to be, nearly ten thousand square feet. Great sections of wood were lashed together, forming a solid platform stable enough for horses and wagons.

"The first small section was the hardest to build, given the size of the Portal," Ethris recounted. "They were quite enthusiastic once they completed it and quite disappointed the next day when they stepped through the Portal and fell into the water after it had drifted away during the night. It is well-anchored, now."

Gen and Ethris walked forward to where they could watch several barges departing laden with supplies. The soldiers had sailed first to form a protective ring about the Ha'Ulrich and the Chalaine on the water.

The day was hazy but calm. The Portal was in easy viewing distance of a large cliff a mile away, a towering limestone wall with scraggly plants and trees gouging a living from the rock. Looking east, Gen tried to make out the Chalaine's carriage atop one of the barges, but it had already passed out of sight into the mist.

"We'd best hurry," Ethris said. "The last barge is for us."

To Gen's dismay, Athan stood among the bags of supplies awaiting their arrival. The thought of spending the next four days in the company of the overzealous Padra made him suddenly fond of swimming.

"I thought I should be near at first in case I think of anything I neglected to ask previously," Athan explained defensively, though arrogantly, at noting their displeasure.

As they pushed out into the water, Gen wormed around the supplies to the front of the barge, peering forward into the hazy afternoon while the bargemaster pounded a steady beat on a small drum for the rowers. Ethris joined him and both expressed a wish for a good wind to clear the way ahead. The limited visibility was discomfiting, and—while Gen could sense in which direction the Chalaine's barge pushed across the lake—he felt uncomfortable not being near her or able to help. Of course, he didn't know if she, Fenna, or the First Mother would feel comfortable in his presence after his actions the night before.

Fortunately, Athan either thought of no more questions or declined to ask them. An hour before dusk approached, all the barges were pulled together and lashed one to another. Gen found his barge on the outer edge, even beyond the last ring of soldiers, though he could now just barely see the Chalaine's large wagon in the distance. Much to the relief of the entire crew of the barge, Athan left and did not return that evening.

For the next two days, Gen grappled with boredom. The oppressive mist and haze never lifted from the lake, and everyone on the barge complained of being smothered. To pass the time, Gen started taking turns rowing, spelling some of the burly men who pulled the oars day after day. At first they simply said, "Nobles don't row," but after Gen's diligent nagging and the promise of a song or two, they relented and let him try it, impressed with his endurance. On the second day, Gen even took over the bargemaster's job from time to time, chanting ridiculous impromptu limericks with the beat.

By the third day on the lake and his confinement to the barge, the bargemaster reclined among the supplies smoking a pipe, for Gen, by popular demand, had usurped his position. Gen, feeling more levity than he had in some time, was grateful for the employment; it helped take his mind off Athan and the dull trip. To liven things up, Gen invented a rhyme and taught the oarsmen to chant it loudly when he steered them within earshot of other barges:

Row and row
Row and row

We are fast
You are slow
Water splashes
Water swirls
We row like men
You row like girls

While not the cleverest of rhymes, owing to its impolitic nature they enjoyed several spirited races with other barges during the day, though the oarsmen were exhausted by the end of it.

Athan returned that evening, and—after another examination from Ethris and a series of mistrustful questions asked with the most pointed stare he could muster—Athan gave Gen permission to leave the barge the next morning and resume his duty to the Chalaine the next evening. Gen had difficulty sleeping, excited to be able to see his friends and his charge again, and when the morning came he wolfed down his meal and bid farewell to the disappointed barge crew. He set off across the great collection of barges, Ethris accompanying him, in search of Regent Ogbith and the First Mother.

The mist was thick that morning and the barges wet, and Ethris had difficulty getting over the myriad of barge rails they crossed on their journey toward the center of the floating conglomeration. They found Regent Ogbith first, and after a quick greeting, Gen left him with Ethris and continued forward, hopeful to gain the Chalaine's barge before the order came to break up. Her wagon appeared and disappeared in the fog only a few barges away. He could just make out Jaron or perhaps Tolbrook—whose life the Chalaine had saved—sitting atop of it.

As he crossed to the next barge, Regent Ogbith yelled the order to unlash the barges and row forward, bargemasters echoing the command. Gen hurried as fast as he could, jumping, dodging, and throwing himself over barge rails with enough agility and lack of concern for others that he elicited both awed stares and annoyed grumbles. His last leap from one barge to the next as they separated was truly acrobatic. He landed and balanced on the next barge rail—one barge short of his intended destination—and received a round of applause from the bemused oarsmen.

"What is going on?"

Mirelle stood from where she sat behind a pile of supplies which had been worked into a rough hut. Gen's face nearly fell upon seeing her, and he quickly substituted a smile for his look of surprise. The First Mother's countenance had always reflected command and energy, whether in heated argument, moments of levity, or even sitting absolutely bored through some pontification of one of the members of her court. That life had withdrawn, a gravity and worry taking its place. Cadaen turned with her, and her unhappiness reflected upon him as well. Gen executed a bow from the barge rail.

"Good Morning, your Grace," Gen greeted her in a bardly voice. "You see that I have gone to great lengths to sail with you today."

She smiled wanly, a little life returning to her eyes. "You were set for the Chalaine's barge and your lovely Fenna, though I appreciate your revised motives." She signaled him forward. "Get down from there. It will be our pleasure to entertain Lord Blackshire, Captain of the Shroud Lake Racing Barge, for the duration of the day."

Mirelle pulled her damp hair back and secured it behind her with a leather thong. Gen greeted Cadaen, who mumbled a quiet, "Welcome." Gen found it strange that Mirelle hadn't given him her customary embrace, but upon seeing her haunted face staring blankly at the commotion around her, he took the initiative. She returned it and held him close for many moments before letting him go.

"Thank you," she said warmly but dispiritedly. "What

was that for?" She invited him to sit next to her on a cushion laid out for her use, probably the poorest accommodations she had ever had—there had been no time to build comfortable barges for the aristocracy. Cadaen wandered off toward the back of the barge, leaving them alone at the front.

"After Athan deemed me worthy to return to service last night," Gen said, "I admit that I was anticipating a warm embrace from the First Mother of Rhugoth. I have become accustomed to it these past months. Seeing that you weren't in the humor, I thought I would risk being a little forward. Even if you are offended, I doubt you could slap me hard enough to inflict sufficient pain to make me rue the pleasure."

"Do you ever tell the truth?"

"Only when it isn't obvious or boring."

"And which is it in this case?"

"Obvious, I believe. Mirelle, you are always so full of life and passion, and you seemed so empty this morning when I saw you. I doubt I could say much to return your humor to you, but you at least should know that I am with you and at your service. I also feel badly that I placed you in danger. I'm sure Athan has told you repeatedly that the entire attack at Three Willow was an attempt to secure me. I thank you for not allowing him to dismiss me, though there is reason in the suggestion. If I am a liability to you or your daughter, I will run as far from you both as I can."

"You are hardly a liability, Gen," Mirelle said, leaning her head on his shoulder and staring at the Chalaine's barge fading before them. "What Athan doesn't want you to know is that an attack to capture you only points to your growing importance in the affairs of this world. The enemy takes you seriously, and so should everyone else."

"Barge racing notwithstanding?" he joked.

Mirelle smiled. "I sometimes forget how young you are. It was, perhaps, beneath you, but endearing yourself to those of lesser station is not an unwelcome trait in a leader. I must confess, however, that hearing Athan complaining about it in council last night was the only bit of cheer I have felt in days, especially when he repeated your rude little rhyme, expecting outrage and receiving laughter instead."

"Perhaps," said Gen, "court jester is my true calling."

"You can be whatever you want to be, Gen. Some people seem born to a profession, others are so blessed in character and intelligence that they must choose. The one is miserable until he finds his calling, the other miserable until he has tried them all. You are the latter, I think."

"I think some are both," Gen added. "You were certainly born to rule, though you have every gift to do anything your heart desires. But as of this morning, you don't seem quite yourself, if I may be so bold."

She stared out at the lake, eyes distant. "You cannot understand what these past few days have done to me, Gen. I am a woman who needs to feel in control, and every mile we travel away from Mikmir weakens me and clouds my mind. I have never felt so vulnerable! That I should nearly die twice in one week despite every precaution for my safety has unnerved me. I am at the mercy of forces beyond my ability to understand or manipulate. I don't feel safe. I don't feel confident. I don't feel happy. I have never been this way, and yet I must be strong for my daughter."

"It is perfectly normal. . ." he began.

"Please, Gen," the First Mother said, "don't tell me it is normal to feel this way after such deadly encounters. I've heard it enough."

He took her hand and tried to will strength into her. "It is true, Mirelle. You will be yourself again. You must at least hope for that. Until then, you lean on your friends and on your faith. It may be distasteful to one as capable as yourself to use a crutch, but there is no shame in it. When we give our friendship to others, we agree to accept both the blessing and the burden of tying ourselves to another person's life. You have many friends, Mirelle. Do not fear to be weak before them. They will leap to your aid and only love and respect you more for confiding in them."

"It isn't that simple," she returned. "A woman as scrutinized as I must live continually in reference to everything and everyone around her. A misplaced frown or a misspoken word from me can cause avalanches of unintended consequences, and if I appear weak, there are those who rejoice and sharpen their knives. My daughter is terrified, and if I show her that I am too, she may very well turn this caravan around. Cadaen flogs himself at every opportunity for his failure to protect me and has begged me to replace him. If he knew fully how I felt he would probably do something stupid like kill himself or leave. If I appear diffident for one such as Athan, he will trample all over me. So, you see, I cannot take the crutch."

"Have you shared any of this with Regent Ogbith or Ethris?"

"No. My daughter and I save these deep troubles for your ear alone." Her grin was affectionate, though touched with sadness.

"Very well," Gen laughed softly. "I'm not sure what I will do with all these dark secrets, but if I can help lighten your spirit, then speak on. You can even call me names if it helps. The Chalaine called me a 'nobody serf from some nowhere lumbering town' that night during the winter."

"Did she now? That's a bit tame for me. I have much sharper words at my command. I thank you for your willing spirit. I do hope to feel more at ease soon, though I think I would be much improved if I could sleep. Every time I close my eyes I can feel the knife at my neck. That, and I can't stop thinking about how I now owe my life to Shadan Khairn. I'm not sure which is more distressing. Do you think Fenna will be much put out if she catches me napping on your shoulder?"

"She is the jealous type, but not to worry. I've told her all about us."

"Good."

Mirelle leaned against him and closed her eyes, and in minutes she fell asleep to the steady drumbeat of the bargemaster. Cadaen checked on her from time to time, eyes angry and pained. Owing to his lack of rest the night before and the soothing undulation of the oar strokes, Gen nodded off soon after, awaking a couple of hours later to the shout, "Land ho!" followed by a the sound of splintering wood far ahead of them. Mirelle's eyes popped open. The oarsmen slowed the barge to a stop as quickly as they could.

"Curse it all," she yawned dreamily. "Why is it that good dreams always attract interruption? What has happened?"

They waited, hearing scattered reports of a barge slamming into a cliff face. Shroud Lake was completely encompassed by a canyon wall save for one beachhead to the south. Regent Ogbith's barge sidled up to Mirelle's and she stood, greeting him and Ethris who both stood at the rail.

"We've drifted too far north," the Regent informed her. "The lead barge has hit the canyon wall, though it is salvageable. We're having a devil of a time getting our bearings in this fog. We'll need to back a safe distance away from the cliff face and turn south. If we back away too far, we waste time. If we don't, we risk slamming into the wall again. If we see ahead of us for a space, we could proceed with more confidence."

"I think I can help," Ethris offered.

The old Mage closed his eyes and concentrated. At first it was just the whisper of a breeze, but as Ethris started chanting, the breeze grew to a wind and then swelled to a gale. The enshrouding fog leapt away from the barges, revealing a towering white cliff wall, some fourteen hundred feet high, looming ominously over the fleet. For the first time since the water journey began, everyone could see everyone else, and several minutes were taken by all just to stare.

"It will not last long. Get your bearings and move," Ethris ordered.

"Let's get to the Lead Barge and see if they've figured out where we are."

Regent Ogbith's barge pushed forward at double time, and in a quarter hour all the barges pulled around to face south and a little west. Within thirty minutes, the fog returned.

"An aptly named shard," Mirelle commented as the gloom enveloped them.

"Yes, and more than a little insipid," Gen added. "Though I hear the sights are more grand—a few weeks in."

"Well," she said, "if I had known I would have you to myself for a while, I would have asked the Chalaine to lend me her playing cards. She and I have played cards every night with Fenna, Dason, and Geoff. She has improved at every session and is uncommonly good now, underhanded methods or no. You must be a good teacher."

"I don't think so," Gen disagreed. "I am afraid that your daughter is a gifted cheat and had a previously untapped talent for gaming. Let's not let Athan know about my involvement in that discovery, shall we?"

"Indeed, not," Mirelle whispered. "And, speaking of Athan, I think the man is spying on me. I believe half the oarsmen on this barge are Churchmen in disguise. So if you have any insulting tirades for him or past indiscretions to confess to me, say them quietly. I am, however, particularly interested in your past indiscretions, so say on."

They spent the balance of the day in pleasant, idle conversation. Gen had to settle for the fact that he would not see the First Mother's natural humor return quickly, no matter what his assurances or his attempts at lightening her mood. She slept a little more during the afternoon, leaning on him as before.

As evening approached, the fog broke up in the face of a natural wind. To their left, the cliff still loomed, though it was declining rapidly, and the shards and moons lurked behind scattered, gray clouds that thickened with every oar stroke forward. The improving vista brought a palpable relief across the fleet, and many passengers stood and watched the landscape slide by.

Just as darkness fell, a drizzle threatened to dampen their spirits again, but ahead of them guttering torches and fires burned on the shore—the landing was in sight. A general hurrah was raised as everyone prepared to debark. The landing site they steered for was a small, treeless strip of beach a mile wide between two cliff walls. A half-mile behind the beach, a grassy hill sloped up, climbing gradually with the cliff that formed its edge. An earthwork mound, fortified with wooden walls, had been built just shy of the hill in the months previous to the start of the journey, forming a crude but effective defense meant only to buy escape time. On either side of wall, tents sprawled away into the darkness. Several regiments of soldiers were encamped permanently there, and most of the men now lined the beach to offer help with horses and supplies

As planned, the soldiers debarked first, followed by the Ha'Ulrich, the Chalaine, and then everyone else. The drizzle turned to a downpour as Gen escorted Mirelle to the Chalaine's wagons where she decided to sleep that night.

"Chalaine!" Mirelle called. "Look who I brought back with me. Let me in, Tolbrook. I'm soaked clear through already."

"Gen!" Fenna and the Chalaine said in unison.

"Move out of the way, you two!" Mirelle commanded as Gen helped her in. "He still looks the same!"

Fenna leaned out to kiss him anyway. "So how was your little vacation?" she teased as he closed the door and she opened the slot.

"Refreshing," Gen said. "All I lacked was the company of my friends, though I did get to spend some time with the First Mother today."

"We are both sorry and glad you had to return to 'work,' then," the Chalaine piped in. Gen could sense the uneasiness in her voice, her words attempting a buoyancy of emotion that her heavy heart did not feel. "Especially after your adventures as barge captain."

"That's getting around, is it?" Gen asked.

"Oh, yes," Fenna answered. "Geoff has written the whole thing down, including your little rhyme. He says it adds a bit of—what did he call it?—'lightening spice' to what has been a rather troubled tale, thus far. Oh! And he has asked me to be his assistant to help him organize his notes and record the history of the trip! Isn't that wonderful?"

"Fabulous," Gen returned stiffly. "I'm sure you'll enjoy it a great deal."

"And learn a lot, too," she enthused. "Did you do much writing when you were a bard's apprentice?"

"No. Tell had little to write about, and I enjoyed the telling of stories more than the writing of them."

"Well, Geoff insists that a biography be written about you, so he'll likely be asking you a lot of questions about your past. I've already told him some of the stories we learned from your friends."

"Great."

Fenna talked to him for nearly an hour, and despite her frequent mentions of Geoff, Gen was glad for her happy mood that seemed untouched by the horrors of Three Willow. She left for her tent after the rain subsided, though it intensified again soon afterward. The Chalaine and Mirelle had a whispered conversation he could only snatch pieces of. The camp was full of activity until well after midnight, supplies, wagons, and horses all arranged and accounted for.

After the camp had settled, Gen enjoyed the quiet and the soft rain that tapered off during the middle of the night. He glimpsed Maewen ascending the hill to scout forward and wished he could go with her. Beyond the rise awaited the new and unfamiliar where few but the half-elf ranger had trodden for hundreds of years. And somewhere in the distance awaited a city of legend where the great work of the prophecy would begin.

Chapter 38 - Into the Unknown

The next few days held few distinctions. Due to the downpour of the night before, they were unable to ascend the steep, muddy road that had been hastily excavated from the hill during the summer months. They ascended the third day and headed northeast over a pleasant plain between the shard edge and the cliff. It waved with tall green grass and purple wildflowers that shocked the nose with a rich, pungent smell. Once they cleared the shard edge, they turned due east, the lush plain giving way to stunted, yellowing grass, the moist winds from the lake replaced by a stifling, humid heat.

Due to the water needs of the caravan, they planned to press due east until they found the Khell River, which they would follow until it met up with the Dunnach River. The Dunnach River would take them into the Far Reach Mountains and the ancient Dunnach River Bridge. Regent Ogbith explained that the water would also provide a natural barrier of protection against attack. At the bridge they would resupply with food and animals brought in during the spring and take the Mora Road to Elde Luri

Mora. The scouts reported that the road was intact and easy to travel.

Going was slow despite the clear weather. The heat forced long stops to rest the horses and foot soldiers, and Regent Ogibth had to ration the water before they found the river Khell near sundown two weeks later. While everyone desperately wanted to stop and enjoy the abundant water, Regent Ogbith permitted only a watering of the animals before he demanded they press on. The river Khell disappeared into the dense Kord Forest to the south, and the Regent wanted a good mile between the caravan and the forest before they camped. He preferred the open fields they had traveled through, for they afforded high visibility in every direction. The forest could hide an entire army.

Given the composition of the caravan, Gen knew that the Regent's decisions were for the best. The First Mother and Regent Ogbith had sent knights and soldiers to the shard months in advance to clear the way, and the advanced scouts had found nothing. Since over five hundred soldiers currently marched in the caravan, it was unlikely that they would unexpectedly encounter a force of threatening size along the way.

If anyone wanted to get to the Chalaine or the Ha'Ulrich, however, their best strategy would be to send a small, quick attack group to sneak or streak past the outer perimeter. Thus, Regent Ogbith kept to the open plains and short grass as much as possible, steering clear of even the smallest copse that obstructed the horizon.

As Gen waited for the sun to sink and bring another scorching day to a close, he still thought that the best plan to get the Chalaine to Elde Luri Mora over hundreds of miles was not in a lumbering caravan; it was with a small mobile group on fast horses. As it was, any enemy within miles could mark them easily by the dust thrown up from their passing, and besides being slow, if rain came, he feared the Chalaine's heavy carriage would sink into the mud so deep it would be beyond hope of extraction.

Gen had proposed his plan to Regent Ogbith a month before they left, but the Regent rejected it, thinking they would arrive to find the road to Elde Luri Mora held against them despite the lack of evidence of enemies. Gen tried to explain that if the enemy blocked the way to Elde Luri Mora in numbers, five-hundred soldiers would be just as ineffective as five. The Regent had waved the idea off, grumbling about Gen being too young to understand.

The Regent's plan had worked so far, however. Their eastward crawl across the plain proceeded without the slightest sign of menace or danger. Faces that had been twisted with worry two weeks before relaxed with every mile forward, and laughter echoed through the camp with increasing frequency. This was doubly true wherever Geoff went. The young bard's infectious good mood and impeccable talent added flavor to the long, monotonous days.

The hurt and anxiety Gen had found in the First Mother faded as the weeks passed, and the Chalaine gained confidence in stride with her mother. Fenna was as bubbly as ever, though she was constantly with Geoff and brought him with her when she came to visit so he could record more of Gen's life. Gen's annoyance mounted with every visit from the exuberant bard. Whether Geoff's continual inquisition about Gen's past, his unrelenting flowery attitude, or his obvious feelings for Fenna, Gen didn't know. Maybe it was the way Fenna smiled when Geoff doffed his hat to her and winked. But whatever it was, Geoff bothered Gen like a rock in his boot during a long march.

As Kord Forest faded behind, Gen sat up from his bed in the wagon, put his shirt on, and grabbed his sword. The carriage he and Jaron shared for a bed bounced around more than usual as the ground grew harder and more strewn with rocks washed down with the river. Gen hopped off the wagon and walked backward past half of the Dark Guard and their apprentices.

Volney saluted him while Kimdan scowled down at him from astride his spirited bay. Gen returned Volney's salute and wished him well. The mess cart assigned to the Chalaine's party was only a few wagons behind. Since they weren't stopping until after dark, Cookmaster Broulin would have nothing hot in the pot tonight. Gen settled for raiding the sacks for bread and wrinkled apples, taking several ladles full of water before walking at a leisurely pace several yards away from the sweat of horses and the dust of wagons.

The low sun beat down against his neck, and the cool shadows of the Kord Forest beckoned to him in his memory. The wood had thick new growth along its edges, an excellent place to hide but a hard place to get out of quietly. Ahead of him, the land was still flat and featureless, though he knew it would turn hilly and finally mountainous once they joined up with the noisy Dunnach River.

Tactically, the passage along the river Dunnach presented a perilous and unwelcome challenge. To their right would run the swift, rocky river, roaring down toward Lake Mora. To their left would rise the steep slopes of the Far Reach Mountains, vast and not well known, even by Maewen, who had traveled them before the Shattering. She told Gen that the thickly wooded ravines and passes were too risky to be explored alone, and she usually traveled alone.

Their only other choice was to build a bridge across the Dunnach and go through several tricky mountain passes until they arrived at the abandoned fortress of Echo Hold and Echo Road, which connected to the Mora Road. Such a course was abandoned. There simply wasn't time to build the bridge across the deep water due to the difficulty of transporting men and supplies.

Out of a habit he supposed belonged to Samian, Gen ate his entire apple, including the core, and spit the seeds upon the ground. The bread was tasteless and made him think of water again. He turned to jog back to the supply cart when he noticed Geoff and Fenna riding up the column in that general direction. Gen turned away, hoping they hadn't seen him, but the beat of horse hooves behind him indicated he had not escaped their notice. Talking with Fenna and Geoff at the same time was like trying to woo a girl while her talkative, drunk father sat on the porch between you.

"Lord Blackshire! My good man!" Geoff greeted him enthusiastically. "We're heading into dangerous territory now, aren't we?"

Gen made sure his face was a cold expressionless mask before looking up at the handsome bard whose long blond hair flowed from underneath his smart, green cap—complete with feather—that seemed impervious to the wind and dust. Fenna rode on the other side of him, face flushed and happy. She greeted Gen with a smile and a wave.

"Yes," Gen answered. "Miss Fairedale." Gen bowed to Fenna. Geoff waited for more of an answer but got nothing.

"Well, I was just telling Fenna how anciently ships floated lazily down the Khell, sails burning in the dusk while lords and ladies, elves and men, danced on their festive decks. Those were the days to be a bard! Sure, they still do the same on Kingsblood Lake, but something about a river accompanying my voice sets an atmosphere and a tone that strikes the heart. Our companions will need a performance tonight, I'd wager, now that we're headed into a great mountain range full of creatures and enemies unknown, mysterious, and dangerous! Can you feel the excitement, Gen? Lands unexplored for hundreds of years! New songs to write and sing! My blood quickens at the thought! I'm sure you feel it yourself, as you have the heart of a bard."

"Actually," Gen replied, "I can't help but feel that every step brings us that much closer to disaster. The Far Reach Mountains are not the type of place to inspire a jaunty tune, Geoff."

"You talk to Maewen too much," Geoff replied. "She seems about as happy as you are about the whole prospect of seeing a land that was once so full of wonders. The Dunnach River Bridge, Gen! Can you imagine?"

Gen said, "Maybe she's tense because she's the only one in this caravan that's traveled these lands extensively. Do you know what the place we're walking on right now was called in the days of the First Mikkikian War?"

Geoff screwed up his face into a mask of concentration, snapping his fingers as if to coax forward the memory with the sound. Gen thought it was an act to cover up his complete ignorance of the topic.

"It's just not coming to me at the moment."

"This place was called Akrikuh Mikkik, or in the common tongue, Mikkik's Fury. After Eldaloth was killed, Mikkik's armies drove men, elves, and dwarves across this plain in a great slaughter, unleashing for the first time the foul creations he'd been breeding in preparation for many years. Near where we met up with the river is where the elven general Alemwei fell, head crushed by the club of a Gagon. Alemwei was a Mage-fighter more powerful than any single person in this caravan, and he died with one blow and was swept down a river tinted red with blood before the Uyumaak dragged his body to shore and ripped it apart. Those of his army unable to get across the river fought till death and were then eaten for dinner as part of a grand celebration."

"Gen!" Fenna exclaimed, eyes aghast and hand over her mouth. Geoff's face slowly drained of blood.

"So you see, Geoff," he went on, "there is no thrill in

every footstep forward for me. And there shouldn't be for you either. If I listen to Maewen too much, you listen to her too little."

"Yes, well," Geoff said, working up as much levity and calmness as he could, "I see your point, but there is a ray of sunshine in every storm! I intend to find it and live every moment in it. We should be off, however. Fenna here is going to accompany me on a song I am singing around the fire tonight. She really has a lovely voice, you know."

"I do," Gen replied, flashing her a smile. Fenna blushed.

"Of course you do. You must also accompany me some time, Gen! Come Fenna. One more practice and we're ready!" Geoff galloped off. Fenna held back for a moment and said, "I will see you later tonight, Gen! I promise!"

Gen waved. "Nice talking to you!" he said sarcastically, but he wasn't sure if she heard as she rode away after Geoff.

Gen opened his clenched hand to find he had inadvertently crushed his bread into the size of a small egg while Geoff droned on. The upside was he was able to push the whole piece of bread into his mouth and finish it quickly. After he made a quick stop for more water, the sun finally sank behind the horizon and he went to find Jaron. To his dismay, Torbrand Khairn had fallen back to the Chalaine's carriage and was talking with her day Protector. To make matters worse, Chertanne joined them as Gen strode up.

"You are going to have to ask Gen," Jaron was saying, voice exasperated. "He's on duty now."

Jaron climbed down from on top of the carriage and inclined his head to Gen. Gen grabbed the bars and swung up to stand on the ledge at the rear of the wagon, awaiting a familiar conversation.

"Gen," Chertanne called to him, voice dripping with concern. "We must insist that you let the Chalaine join us around the fire! You are torturing her by cooping her up in there."

"I am well, Chertanne," the Chalaine interjected through the bars. Gen knew very well that the Chalaine was not 'well.' The magical brand on his chest let him know that her head throbbed terribly. Days inside the thick wooden wagon were hot, miserable, and lonely. Gen sympathized with her but didn't feel he could risk letting her out as the journey went deeper into dangerous territory.

"You want the Chalaine to come out and sit by a *fire* at night?" Gen chastised. "Have you completely forgotten the Three Willow Inn? Honestly, Lord Khairn, did you teach your boy nothing?"

Khairn's eye twitched. Gen enjoyed baiting the Shadan almost as much as he enjoyed baiting Chertanne.

"Gen," the Shadan said, controlling his anger, "we all know about the danger, but I would have to agree with Chertanne—and that is rare. We have the finest sword fighters in Ki'Hal in this camp, not to mention enough Mages and Church folk to burn down the entire country of Rhugoth. They've agreed to ward the camp strongly. The Chalaine isn't going to be more safe inside this box than she is around the fire."

"No," Gen stated firmly. Chertanne threw Gen his hundredth exasperated look of the week while the Shadan settled for rolling his eyes up in his head.

"Really, Gen," Chertanne went on, "I would like a little of my bride left to enjoy once we get there. If you jail her much longer, she won't even be able to stand!"

Gen stood as still as a statue until they capitulated and rode back to their normal position well in front of the Chalaine's carriage.

"Hello, Gen," the Chalaine said weakly once they'd gone.

"Good evening, Chalaine." Gen replied, removing the strain from his voice.

"Alumira, remember?" she said. Gen admired her

strength. There was no bitterness in her voice, though he could tell that she wanted out of the carriage almost as much as she wanted to run away from Chertanne and hide forever.

"You don't get to be Alumira until well after dark when everyone is asleep. One moment." Gen turned and caught Volney's eye, signaling him forward. Volney had just been released from duty for the evening and came forward, eyes expectant.

"My Lord!" he said, slapping his forearm across his chest and bowing at the waist. "I am ready to serve your will. How may I serve you and the Lady?"

Gen hated how Volney always lapsed into formalities when he got within twenty feet of the Chalaine. The Chalaine hated it, too.

"Could you fetch a Pureman for me?"

"Forthwith, Milord!" Without Volney, Gen thought he might be able to forget he was nobility now.

"What are you doing, Gen?" the Chalaine asked.

"Taking care of that headache."

"You really shouldn't bother. A little headache isn't important enough for a Pureman to deal with."

"I sense the pain you feel, and that is no 'little' headache. Besides, it is hypocritical of you to turn away healing when you insist on healing me if I so much as stub my toe."

"I do not," the Chalaine objected. "I'm sure everyone else in this caravan has a headache, too. It's been a sweltering day. A sweltering month, actually. If the Puremen went around curing every headache in this camp, they would. . ."

"Will you shut up and take the healing?" Gen realized what he had said and was about to apologize, but the Chalaine was laughing.

"Did you just tell me to shut up, Gen?"

"Chalaine, I'm sorry. I didn't mean. . ."

"Only my mother dares do that! Everyone else thinks

the Chalaine shouldn't be talked to in that manner!"

"And you shouldn't be. My tongue slipped. It has been a long, frustrating day," Gen ended lamely.

The banging of the wagon across a patch of rough rock drowned out any further conversation. Gen had to steady himself as the carriage swayed back and forth. The first star winked into the crystal clear sky as the Pureman arrived, and a cool breeze from the north cut through the stale air, bringing welcome relief. Full dark had come by the time the Pureman finished the healing ritual for the Chalaine while sitting on the back of the bouncing carriage. The caravan pressed on for two more hours, leaving the edges of the Kord Forest well behind them in the dark.

Finally, Regent Ogbith called for a halt, eliciting a chorus of grateful mumbling. The horses were cared for and a fire built in the center of the ring, casting a cheery light in the darkness. The cookmaster distributed a meal little better than what Gen had scrounged for himself to those inside the circle.

Geoff's rich voice could be heard everywhere, and Gen gritted his teeth every time he heard it. Lighting a fire was bad enough, but each night Geoff ensured a general ruckus that Gen was sure would announce their presence to even the deafest Uyumaak within fifty miles. Gen expected the carelessness would continue until an Uyumaak arrow taught them better; Geoff lifted weary spirits, and that service meant more, apparently, than security or stealth. Gen climbed down from the roof of the carriage and sat on the small ledge by the door.

"Fools." It was Maewen, speaking in Elvish. "They will kill us all. Wild places are not for loud voices and bright fires." She approached from outside the circle, face turned down in a frown and with a bow in hand.

"You read my thoughts," Gen replied in the same language. "They still pressure me to let the Chalaine come into the firelight." Maewen sniffed indignantly.

"The Chalaine would be safer, Gen, if you and I were to take her to Elde Luri Mora alone. Mark my words. I have some bad news."

"What is it?"

"The deep scouts are two days late. They were to scout all the way to the Dunnach River Bridge and make contact with the advance party there. Regent Ogbith insists it is nothing to worry about. I worry. Be wary, Gen. I am increasingly uneasy, and that feeling should not be dismissed when it comes from one as old as I am."

"My ears are turned to you and the wind, Quaena," Gen replied. "I wish you led this caravan not only in direction but in comportment."

Maewen's sharp look startled him. "Did you call me *Quaena?*" she asked, face tense.

"Yes, I suppose I did. It seems to fit you," Gen improvised. Quaena was Samian's nickname for his daughter, the word meaning 'leaf daughter.' Maewen regarded him narrowly.

"Try not to use it again," she said, marching stiffly toward the fire. Gen shook his head and chastised himself for letting his tongue slip for the second time that evening. He took special care to not say much when Mirelle came over, Cadaen in tow, to chat a little with her daughter.

While Mirelle never questioned Gen's decision to keep the Chalaine confined, he couldn't miss the pain on her face over her daughter's plight. After she left, Gen heard the Chalaine settling near the door slot, opening it as she often did in the evening so they could talk. Since Fenna's night visits were increasingly infrequent, the Chalaine and Gen talked more than they ever had.

"What did Maewen say?" the Chalaine asked. "I couldn't understand it, but it wasn't happy."

"She worries, as I do, that we are being too careless. Fires and singing in lands so unknown is foolish. She also says the scouts sent ahead to the Dunnach River Bridge have not returned and are two days late."

"Do you think something has happened to them?" the Chalaine asked, and Gen could detect a hint of nervousness in her voice.

"I think so," Gen replied. "The terrain is easy and the weather cooperative. Unless they greatly misjudged the distance to the river, which I doubt, then I see little excuse for them to be as late as they are."

"Maybe they got lost."

"If the best scouts in Rhugoth got lost following a river, then we really are doomed."

The Chalaine remained silent for some time. Geoff played music and told stories to the delight of everyone. Even Shadan Khairn seemed to enjoy himself, though Gen found his former master's eyes on him more than once. Fenna sat to the right of Geoff, clapping and dancing as the bard played his lute to perfection. Gen suppressed a wave of professional jealousy; if Torbrand had left Tolnor alone, Gen thought he would probably have been a lot like Geoff, minus the annoying qualities. Of course, he also would have never come to know Fenna or the Chalaine.

"So, how are things with Fenna?" the Chalaine asked when Geoff took a break.

Gen shrugged. "How would I know? I could tell you, however, every one of Geoff's thoughts. I swear the man never shuts up, and he never leaves her alone. She doesn't seem to mind him, though. Quite the opposite, in fact. I can't blame her. Geoff's a handsome man, even if he is a little old for her. And he is the best at what he does. He plays the lute much better than I ever. . ."

"Gen!" the Chalaine interrupted. "You're rambling."

"Sorry. All I'm saying is that compared to Geoff, I must seem drab and boring."

The Chalaine chuckled. "Oh, yes. Gen, one of the best sword fighters in the world, Protector of the Chalaine, gone from serf to noble for facing down demons and dastards.

You're a bore a minute. Look, Gen," the Chalaine continued, "you hardly have the chance to see her anymore, so it's natural that you feel that she is getting away from you. But every morning when she comes to spend time with me, the first question she asks is, 'How is Gen?'"

"And then she spends the rest of the hour gushing about Geoff, right?"

"No! My goodness, Gen. You really are out of sorts this evening. I won't say that she doesn't talk about him, but she still cares for you Gen. Make no mistake."

"I thank you for the reassurance. I'm sorry for my mood. I'll try to be more controlled."

Gen realized the admission of his insecurities might lessen the Chalaine's confidence in him during a difficult time for her, and he didn't need the Shadan staring at him to make him remember that the slightest weakness could be used as a wedge for others to move him out of his place.

"Please don't," the Chalaine commented unexpectedly. "You telling me to shut up earlier was probably the high point of my trip thus far."

Gen shook his head. He couldn't remember a single story or poem where a woman was cheered by being told to shut up. Whatever the Chalaine said, Gen wasn't going to lose his control, not over anything. He couldn't afford to do it. He slid off the back of the carriage and stood at a rigid attention, turning his concentration outward.

"Oh," the Chalaine continued, remembering something. "This may not be the right time to tell you this, but Fenna mentioned this morning that Kimdan had renewed his attentions to her, too."

Gen beat down the feelings and let them slide away, leaving himself calm and self-possessed. The Chalaine offered no further comment.

Away at the fire, a new song started, and Fenna's voice—clear, if unpolished—rose into the night. Gen recognized the song Geoff had chosen for the duet:

Emereth's Journey, the tale of a young woman who went to find a warrior husband who had not returned from a bloody battle, and, after finding his body, fell in love with the Pureman who was preparing it for burial. Geoff and Fenna sang short stanzas in counterpoint to each other as their grief over the slaughter of war gradually changed to love. Gen doubted Geoff's song selection was an accident.

They finished to much applause, and both Mirelle and Geoff gave Fenna enthusiastic hugs. Maewen stood at the edge of the firelight, scowling at the proceedings.

"I had no idea she could sing so well!" the Chalaine exclaimed.

"With training, she could be a great bard," Gen replied, "though I think her station precludes it from being a possibility. She remembers the words and doesn't forget a tune if she's sung it once."

Fenna gradually broke away from the crowd. Gen pretended not to notice her approach.

"Well?" she asked, face beaming. "What did you think?"

"Miss Fairedale has a most luxurious voice," Gen complimented her, bowing.

"It was wonderful!" the Chalaine followed enthusiastically. Fenna smiled at the praise and had Gen help her stand on the back of the wagon so she could whisper through the bars to the Chalaine. While Gen couldn't hear everything they said, the name Geoff came up more than once with a couple of Kimdans thrown in for good measure. Gen tried to ignore their talk, and soon it was over. Fenna gave him a peck on the cheek and with a hasty goodbye practically sprinted back to the fireside where things were starting to pick back up.

"So, Chalaine," Gen asked, "how is Fenna doing?"

Chapter 39 - Thrashings

By the time the sky lightened the next morning, Gen felt very cross and not the least bit tired. While he preferred to sleep, his training allowed him to go for days without doing so, and today was going to be one of those days. When Jaron relieved him at sunrise, he went to find something to eat before everyone awoke. A few soldiers milled around the supply wagon, but it was Maewen packing her backpack that caught Gen's attention.

"Where are you going?" Gen asked her in Elvish.

"To scout ahead. I will return by nightfall. I cannot put my mind at ease and need to go have a look for myself."

An idea leapt into Gen's head. Getting away from the caravan was exactly what he needed. "Let me come with you."

He knew it was a long shot. Maewen wasn't fond of company in general, on her excursions doubly so. Her face registered surprise, then contemplation, and then, to his delight, she agreed.

"Do you have to get permission?" she asked.

"Yes. From Regent Ogbith."

"Well, let's go get it. I'll bring enough provisions for both of us and we'll take turns with the pack."

Regent Ogbith tented with his soldiers, and they found him there shaving his square face with a sharp knife. He eyed them questioningly as they approached.

"Good morning. Looks like another hot day ahead. What do you two need?"

Just as Gen opened his mouth to ask the question, Maewen spoke. "I still feel ill at ease and want to scout forward today. I would like to have Gen's sword at my back. We will return in time for his nightly watch."

Regent Ogbith wiped his knife on his pants. "Really? Do you think there's a need? I know the long range scouts haven't come back, but we just had our short range scouts return without report of anything for miles in front of us."

"Men on horses miss much, Regent," Maewen said. "I would like to settle my mind about the road ahead."

Regent Ogbith clearly felt that the whole thing was unnecessary, but he relented. "As long as you get him back in time and in shape to do his duty, he may go. Anything else?"

"No, Regent," Maewen replied.

Gen felt elated as Maewen led him back toward the caravan proper.

"Can you shoot a bow, Gen?" she asked.

"Yes." Samian had been an absolute master, and Gen felt he could hit a sparrow at a hundred yards in the dark.

"Talk to the weapons master and procure one while I pack more food. Then let's get going. The sun is already higher than I like."

In short order Gen had the bow strung and around his shoulders. Maewen took the pack first, and with a wry grin turned to him. "Let's see if you can keep up."

Turning her face to the rising sun, she sprinted along the edge of the caravan and Gen kept pace. Heads turned as they whipped by like the wind, and Gen couldn't help but grin with satisfaction as Geoff, having already found Fenna before she began her duties with the Chalaine, looked at him with a hundred questions plainly written on his features.

Gen knew he'd have to steel himself to answer every one of those questions when he returned, but after a quick smile and wave to an equally puzzled Fenna, Gen put the caravan behind him and reveled in the rush of the warming wind around his face. They ran for nearly an hour before Maewen stopped for the first time.

"That is better," she said, taking in the emptiness around them.

"Much better," Gen agreed, stretching his legs to keep them loose. "I tire of the caravan with each passing mile."

Maewen smiled at him, dark hair streaming around her face in a stiff morning breeze. "You run well, Gen. I fear, however, that with our departure the caravan is bereft of anyone with sense."

Gen laughed. Maewen didn't.

"Ethris is a smart one," Gen said. "He'll keep them from doing anything incredibly stupid."

"Ethris is indeed a smart man, but he is not an outdoorsman. The greater part of his life has been spent in damp towers with his nose in books."

"True," Gen agreed, Maewen offering him swig from the waterskin. "Are we looking for anything in particular out here?"

"You tell me, Gen. You seem to know more than anyone your age should. What do you think we would be searching for?"

Gen thought for a moment. "If I were planning to ambush the caravan along this route, I would, obviously, want to make sure the scouts returned thinking the way was clear for as long as possible. I wouldn't try to mount an assault in this open plain, but secrete a large force, on foot, where there was a narrow passage thick with trees or scattered rocks so that the effectiveness of the horses and the mobility of the caravan would be limited. If the enemy has scouts along this route watching our progress, they are no doubt pleased that everyone seems so carefree."

"Exactly," Maewen concurred. "And if one of the caravan's scouts saw something, you would prevent them from returning."

"So we look for signs of their scouts more than our own."

"Yes. It is hard to hide anything out here, but the Uyumaak skin camouflage transforms even this barren terrain into a field ripe for a harvest of trouble. I have little hope of finding anything, but even if I can turn up a ten-year-rotted Uyumaak skeleton, I will drag it back just to see if it can scare some thinking into Regent Ogbith."

Gen grinned.

"Whether our little trip does the Regent any good," he said, "it has already done wonders for me. I thank you for allowing me to come."

"I wouldn't have agreed if it had been anyone else but you. You are a rare one. It has been a pleasure having someone in camp that speaks Elvish. The human tongue grates on me. You speak Elvish so well, in fact, you could probably pass for one in the night. How did you learn it? Not as a bard in a backwoods town, I think."

Gen's mind raced. He still hadn't decided how to tell her about Samian. "It is a long story that deserves more time than we can comfortably devote to it now. I will tell you later."

"Very well," she said, and Gen was grateful she did not press the matter. From Samian, he knew such patience was a common quality in elves, born of their long lives.

"Let's see how well you can run with the pack on your back."

They ran at a brisk pace for over an hour. The terrain changed slightly the farther they went, showing more character than the less varied miles behind. Hills, depressions, and clumps of trees more frequently lay about their path, and Maewen would sporadically dart off their eastward track and scout around before turning back to the main path. Shard shadows moved over the landscape as they passed overhead, providing temporary relief from the sun beating down on their necks.

It was nearly midday when the half-elf pulled up abruptly, signaling for silence. Catching Gen's eyes, she directed his vision northeast. At first Gen couldn't see anything out of the ordinary, but as Maewen led him forward another hundred yards, he spotted a thin wisp of smoke coming over a low hill, barely visible even in broad daylight.

Maewen crouched low and helped Gen remove the pack. Leaning close, she whispered, "Someone with some lore lit that fire. It is well masked. We'll approach quickly. I can see no lookout on the hilltop. Let's go see what we can see. Remember where the pack is."

Gen nodded and they sprinted quietly toward the tendril of smoke. They covered the last yards on their bellies, scooting forward to peer over the summit of a low hill. What they saw brought little comfort.

Ahead of them a depression formed a shallow bowl, the hill on which they lay forming the highest lip. In the bowl a company of Uyumaak milled around in the brutal sun. Some slept, others walked about aimlessly, and some huddled in tight circles. A small cook fire boiled a viscous brown liquid in a dark cauldron while two Uyumaak took turns stirring it. Gen marveled at them. Their color-changing skin challenged his vision, complicating a quick understanding of the scene.

Gen noted the elements of a typical Uyumaak company. There were eleven Hunters, long wiry Uyumaak that could run like the wind. Seven Archers—like Hunters, but with thicker torsos and greater strength—sat together fletching arrows for longbows polished a dull black. Eleven Bashers, armed with crossbows, shields, and axes, were mostly asleep. They were short, bulky, and strong, bred to break shield walls and cut down horses. Then there were the eleven Uyumaak Warriors, a blend of speed and strength, possessing more intelligence than the others.

An Uyumaak Shaman stood outside a tent fashioned from dark hides. He watched his charges, slapping his chest in their mysterious, percussive language. Noticeably missing was the Chukka, a dark elf ranger that most often led Uyumaak companies.

Maewen signaled to Gen and they scooted backward. Again she leaned close. "Normally I would leave now, but with you at my side I am a bit more bold. The Chukka is missing, but if we could kill the Shaman, it would be a heavy blow. If we fail, however, the Shaman will make things miserable for us. Even if we succeed, we will have to fight off the Hunters. We should be able to outrun the others. It would be good to get some token of this place to show the caravan."

While the wisdom of Samian and Elberen told him this course of action was foolhardy, Telmerran wouldn't have hesitated to wade into the thick of trouble. Dealing a blow to the Uyumaak might aid the safety of the caravan, and Maewen was right; while their word of an Uyumaak company might be enough, if they had some tangible evidence to show, it would put a definite end to the reckless, carefree behavior that had grated on him for so long.

"All right," he agreed. "I'll split off to the left and shoot first to draw their attention. That way, the Hunters will come for me. If I hit, retreat and cover me when the Hunters come for me. If I miss, it will be up to you to kill the Shaman. One shot each, and we run."

Maewen smiled, but not the kind of smile that invited one in return. Gen scooted away, taking his time and going slowly. The sun beat down on him like a forge hammer, Gen's lips sticky with thirst and sweat dripping off his nose.

Finding a thick clump of blond grass, he unlimbered his bow and pulled out an arrow. He wiped his hands to dry them, and, after setting arrow to string, turned his head to see if Maewen was ready. She was on her knees a little farther back down the hill, watching him intently.

Gen nearly lost his grip on his bow. Coming up behind her, ghost-like, was the Chukka. He floated silently over the grass, his dark green cloak semi-transparent. Gen had been shown this ranger's trick when he had worn the Training Stones. It was windwalking, a completely soundless way to move from one point to another. He was almost upon her, a dark blade coming to his hand. Gen knew the Chukka would have to solidify completely before attacking. He had no way to warn Maewen short of yelling, which would bring the whole camp on them. The Chukka edged closer, and stopped.

Gen leapt to his feet, pulled the arrow to his cheek, and let the arrow fly. Maewen's eyes widened with shock as Gen's arrow sprung toward her, but comprehension dawned quickly and she threw herself to the ground just as the Chukka solidified, dropped to the ground, and swung his knife. Maewen's sudden movement proved enough to send the knife wide. The arrow slammed into the Chukka's upper chest, throwing him sideways and onto the ground with a thud. He screamed, and Maewen was on him slashing with her knife.

Gen turned back to the camp as he pulled and strung another arrow. The Uyumaak were standing dead still and looking up the hill, and just as they caught sight of him, Gen loosed an arrow at the Shaman. Sounds of Uyumaak thumping and tapping split the air. The Shaman noticed his assailant at the last moment, tossing aside its staff as he dove away. The move saved its life, the arrow sinking into its meaty shoulder instead of his head and driving him to the ground. The Hunters rose up and sprinted up the hill at Gen.

Memories of Hunters charging were plentiful in Gen's mind, but to see one directed at him in broad daylight awakened within him a real sense of danger. The Hunters moved fluidly and with heart-stopping speed. He fled, finding Maewen already at the bottom of the hill, turned toward him. Her cloak was spattered with black blood, and Gen hoped none of hers mixed with it. He chanced a look back to see all eleven Hunters cresting the hill, closing on him at an alarming rate.

Maewen's bow sang, and an arrow whistled by Gen's head, catching the lead chaser in the throat. It fell hard to the ground, tripping up two of the Hunters behind it. Maewen shot twice more before Gen reached her side, both her arrows dropping their pursuers. They ran as fast as their legs would take them, but Gen saw that they would not be able to escape without a fight.

"Keep running and turn to cover me if you can," Gen yelled in Elvish.

Maewen nodded. He waited until a Hunter was nearly on him and then spun around with a hard slash from right to left. It was the first time Gen had swung the sword Mirelle had given him against an enemy, and after the stroke, he thought he had missed—the blade met no resistance. Gen nearly lost his balance, but he sprang back defensively, awaiting a strike from the enemy he thought he had failed to mark. As he did, the Uyumaak fell neatly in half at the midsection where he had slashed.

Gen had little time to think about it as two Uyumaak bowled over their dead companion and came for him. Two others came behind those, and the remaining three streaked after Maewen. Gen knew he had to be quick. Lanky arms with claws groped for him, and he whirled the blade about him furiously, and wherever the blade struck, whether thick hide or soft underbelly, it went through just as easily as if cutting through a thin fog.

Limbs fell about him, and black blood stained the blond

grass as each Uyumaak fell in rapid succession. As he killed the last, he saw the archers and warriors crest the hill, churning toward them, skin matching the color of the grass.

Gen turned and ran. Maewen had taken down two Hunters with her bow before the last reached her, and she was trying to fend it off with a long knife that was ill-suited for battling with the long-limbed monster. Fortunately, Maewen was close and Gen was quick. With a vicious downward slice from behind, Gen bisected the Uyumaak cleanly. Maewen gathered her bow and sprang away as arrows began to whistle down on them.

Gen ran behind Maewen to protect her. The Hunter had clawed her arms in several places, blood drenching her sleeves. Time seemed to slow as they fled, as in dreams where the goal waits just out of reach and every step forward takes you no closer. An arrow nicked his upper arm, and with the quick reflexes imbued by the Training Stones, he batted away another aimed at his head, though he got a nasty cut across his right hand for the effort. In dismay he realized he couldn't move his fingers, though the pain didn't bother him.

With one last sprint, they passed the effective range of the archers and arrived at the spot where they had left their gear. Maewen grabbed it quickly, shouldering it and bounding away.

"Are you hurt?" she asked, gasping for air.

"I can't shoot the bow, but I can still run and use the sword."

"Let's see if we can outpace the Warriors!"

Gen glanced west to see all eleven running in a line behind their leader. They carried great clubs and large shields that seemed to float in the air beside vague shapes in the distance. While the Warriors could not run as quickly, the delay caused by the Hunters' assault proved just enough for the beasts to get directly in Gen and Maewen's westward path of retreat—their enemies knew which way the caravan lay.

"We cannot turn west," Maewen shouted. "They can outlast us, and they run well in the dark, but they cannot outrun us with that heavy gear. We must keep running south as fast as we can until we can get around them!"

Gen grunted in understanding and ran on behind her, her blood and his dotting the ground as they ran. After several minutes and a small separation from their foes, Maewen halted. They drank hastily, and Maewen discarded all the food to lighten the pack. Behind them, the Uyumaak persistently advanced. They had thrown aside their shields, lightening their load so they could run more quickly. Exhausted, Maewen led Gen farther south. The yellow grass diminished as they came upon harder and flatter ground, making for good running. Sweat stung Gen's wounds, and he felt his legs weakening from a week's worth of exertion churned out in a few hours time.

"Let's make our break!" Maewen yelled, turning abruptly west.

Gen came to her right so as to be the first in the melee should they fail, and fail they did. The Uyumaak put on a sudden burst of speed upon seeing their quarry change direction. The Uyumaak line was strung out over the space of a hundred yards, the quickest and hardiest pressing forward swiftly. Again Gen told Maewen to run on, and he saw fear in her eyes for the first time.

Gen drew his sword with his left hand and stopped in the path. This sudden defense brought the first Uyumaak to a halt as Gen leapt forward and decapitated it. Before the corpse could hit the ground, he sliced off the leg of the second one in the line. The third raised his club and arced it over its head with a heavy overhand stroke. Gen met the blow with his sword, splitting the club down the middle and chopping the Uyumaak down in one movement.

The fourth and fifth thumped furiously on their chests, beating out some plan in their percussive language. Two

Uyumaak barreled toward Maewen who had stopped and knocked her bow. The rest did not press the attack until their companions arrived, and then they came with fury.

Gen struggled, falling backward to keep them from encircling him. He was dimly aware of the thuds of arrow impacts as Maewen finished the two other Uyumaak off, and he hoped she would have time to turn her bow to his defense as an Uyumaak rushed him. Unexpectedly, one of his enemies threw its club. Gen went to block it with his sword, but the blade cut through it without throwing it off course and the club head hammered him square in the chest, knocking the wind from him.

In his effort to stay standing, he wrenched his ankle, recovering in time to impale the first Uyumaak as it attacked him. The others weren't far behind, but quick, painful cuts that severed away pieces of club and flesh demoralized them and they backed away.

Then all five bull rushed him at once.

An arrow took one down, and as the wall was about to crash into him, Gen dove at them, body low, slashing at their legs. Writhing Uyumaak fell atop him, and he tried to roll away. Sticky Uyumaak blood poured over him as he struggled like a fish caught in a scaly net. With a yell he pulled himself free, wiping his eyes clear and trying to get his sword up, but there were no more attackers. Feathered arrows protruded from the pile before him.

"Gen!" Maewen said, running forward. "You live! Are you hurt?"

"I've sprained my ankle and I'm having a hard time breathing." Maewen ripped open his shirt with her knife, revealing a dark bruise. She frowned.

"Can you move?"

"I think so," he said, "just slowly."

"Then let's go. I doubt they would have the Bashers pursue us, but they could catch us if we are forced to walk."

Gen nodded and limped westward as Maewen collected

the Uyumaak leader's head and stuffed it in a leather sack from her backpack.

"If we are not evidence enough," she said, explaining herself.

"Next time," Gen suggested, "perhaps we shouldn't throw rocks at the hornets' nest."

"My father used to say that," she replied with a weak smile. "I suspect, Gen, that there will not be a next time for you. We will both be in plenty of trouble when we return, though for me it matters little. For your sake, I could change the story to where they ambushed us. It's mostly true."

"With the Pontiff and Ethris in camp, I think our best defense lies in the truth. Let's just stick to looking as pathetic as possible and hope that sympathy carries the day."

Maewen grinned and drank deeply from a waterskin before handing it to Gen. "I'm sorry to have gotten you into this mess. My hatred for Uyumaak sometimes gets the better of me. One thing we can be sure of, though. No one will call us unskilled or cowardly. Killing one Chukka and twenty-three Uyumaak. . ."

"Twenty-two. I think the Shaman survived."

"A pity, but twenty-two between the two of us is nothing to scoff at, even with Aldradan Mikmir's sword." Gen's eyes widened in surprise. She furrowed her brow. "Didn't you know? They never told you?"

"No!" Gen was shocked. Aldradan's sword was legendary, having many magical properties in the tales. Uyumaak had come to fear Aldradan and his sword in the days when he aided those fleeing Lal'Manar. Gen wondered how many of the fantastic tales of the blade were true.

"Ethris told me many would object to me carrying it and wouldn't tell me more of it."

"Indeed they would," said Maewen. "It is not to be touched by any until Aldradan comes again, though I assure you he is quite dead, as I helped bury him. This is the second time that sword has come to my aid. There will be time for the story later, if we hurry. The secret of your blade is safe with me, but I think it will not be a secret for long."

They arrived in camp well after dark. His ability to ignore pain didn't make his ankle or his lungs work any better, and even with Maewen shouldering the pack and letting him lean on her as needed, they made slow progress. By the time they passed the first outlying patrols, Gen's entire body ached, his ankle was uncomfortably tight against his boot, and he felt sick. Maewen was pale and exhausted, and they both stank of Uyumaak blood and their own sweat.

Gen could hear Geoff's clear voice a mile away, and as they finally strode into the circle of clapping, festive nobles and soldiers, the celebration came to an abrupt halt. With what Gen thought was excellent dramatic timing, Maewen let the bloody, scowling Uyumaak head roll out of her bag and into the middle of the crowd just as they all went silent. Firelight glinted off its row of tiny eyes, the sharp teeth of the round mouth open wide in its rictus.

Geoff's eyes shot open and he covered his mouth. Mirelle and Fenna came running forward from the direction of the Chalaine's wagon, and Gen watched as their faces went from horror, to anger, and then back to sympathy and concern when they noticed his injuries.

Regent Ogbith stood. "Boil some water to clean and heal them, then the fire goes out. There will be no more fires on this trip! I want Gen and Maewen and all leaders in my tent immediately. Fetch the Chalaine as well. I suppose the bard will want to write all this down, too."

"Gen's wounds need attention!" Maewen objected.

"He's made it this far; he'll last another hour," Regent Ogbith grunted before stalking off. Mirelle followed him, but Fenna ran to Gen's side, face full of concern.

"Are you all right?" she asked, staring uncomfortably at the bruise on his chest.

"I'll live, Fenna. Don't worry."

"All I've done all day is worry! When nightfall came and you hadn't returned, just like those other scouts, well. . ."

"I am here. We survived."

Fenna humphed, hands on her hips. "Well, I'll have more words for you later. I think the First Mother will, too."

Gen stumbled a bit on his bad ankle, and Maewen was there putting his arm around her shoulder and helping him along.

"This is poor reward," she said in Elvish. "They should see to our wounds before making us talk."

"I'll help him," Fenna offered.

"Let her do it, Fenna," Gen replied. "We are both a bloody, foul mess." Fenna frowned darkly at Maewen and walked off in the direction of the Chalaine's wagon.

"She's too soft for someone like you, Gen," Maewen commented.

Gen grunted as his foot hit uneven ground. He said, "It's nice to have something soft around when everything else is so hard."

They reached the tent after a painful walk, exciting all kinds of comments from the people they passed. Regent Ogbith and Mirelle were there, along with Captain Tolbrook and Warlord Maelsworth from Aughmere. Mirelle stood by Regent Ogbith, arms crossed, and Gen felt her stern gaze upon him. Geoff, face a bit piqued, was fumbling with parchment and ink. The Pontiff and Ethris arrived, talking rapidly to each other. The Pontiff examined them, face showing alarm.

"Why was the cleaning and healing of these people not seen to?" he asked pointedly.

Regent Ogbith answered, "We need to know what they found as soon as possible to assess the threat. Neither is mortally wounded."

The Pontiff frowned, displeased. "I shall fetch the Puremen. They can at least start the work of cleaning them up. He stepped outside briefly and then returned. Two camp chairs were forthcoming, and Gen sat down heavily. The Chalaine and the Ha'Ulrich entered last, the Dark Guard surrounding the tent. She immediately came to examine their wounds.

"Don't touch them, Chalaine!" the Ponitff warned. "Remember last time."

"These wounds are from Uyumaak, not demons, your Grace," she replied.

"Even so, you should save your strength. My Puremen will care for them."

"Save my strength for what?" she complained. "To lie in a rolling fort for days on end? Let me help them!"

"Chalaine!" Mirelle interjected sharply. "You should not talk to the Pontiff in that manner. Obey the Pontiff."

The Chalaine acquiesced, moving to stand behind Gen.

"Where is Shadan Khairn?" Regent Ogbith asked, voice impatient.

"Here, my good Regent." Torbrand entered, face amused. "Well, Gen," he said, inspecting his former student, "didn't I teach you any better than that? I hope there were at least a hundred of them, or I will be very disappointed. You could have at least invited me along." The Shadan looked around, and upon finding a room full of frowns, feigned innocence. "Merely a jest between warriors, my good people!"

"Let's get this going, Regent Ogbith," Mirelle prompted coldly.

"Very well. Gen, Maewen, which of you would like to tell us what happened?"

"I will," Maewen volunteered. "It was my expedition."

Gen tried to relax as Maewen unfolded the tale. During her explanation, a Pureman with a bucket of water entered and knelt beside him. After removing Gen's shirt—the bruise on his chest eliciting a wince from even the angry First Mother—he inspected his wounds. Gen heard the Chalaine gasp at seeing the cuts on his hand and shoulder, both caked with blood. The entire proceeding came to a halt when the Pureman cut Gen's boot and sock off to reveal an ankle swollen purple and black. Another Pureman cleaned the Uyumaak scratches on Maewen, the only wounds she'd received.

Maewen was honest and forthcoming, though she gave little detail on their battles to hide the secret of Gen's sword. As the tale went on, Mirelle became even more livid than before. Her blonde hair was pulled away from a face as severe as a pretty face can be, and her eyes bored into him. Geoff wrote furiously, and at the tense spots, the Puremen stopped cleaning their charges to listen intently.

"Let me get this straight, Maewen," Regent Ogbith said when the half-elf finished. "You find a group of Uyumaak, and instead of running back to warn us and get help, you decide to assassinate their Shaman and fight off the Hunters? What? Just needed a little fun? The caravan a little too boring for you?"

"The two of us killed twenty-two Uyumaak and lived. For me, that is a good day," Maewen countered with such stern defiance to silence everyone. "This caravan has been careless for too long and my warnings have been ignored! The issue is what you're going to do now that you start to feel your peril. What Gen and I did, we did and are done. What you do now will determine if this little parade manages to roll the rest of the way to Elde Luri Mora or not!"

Maewen's fire was enough to turn the conversation away from a critique of their decisions and onto what was to be done to protect the caravan. From Mirelle's stare, Gen knew she wouldn't forget their folly so soon.

While the assembled nobles argued the finer points of

getting a large procession of people and supplies through hostile territory, the Pureman finished his cleaning, wrapping Gen's ankle in a towel and instructing him to see him afterward. Another towel was given to him and Maewen to dry themselves with.

The Chalaine touched Gen's shoulder and bent down to whisper in his ear. "I think healing you will be in vain. My mother is going to kill you."

Gen agreed. He closed his eyes to calm his mind and let the tension of the day seep out of him. After a moment he could feel the pressure in his chest lessening and he could move the fingers of his right hand again. He realized the Chalaine still had her fingers on his shoulders. He considered forcing her stop, but decided against it since it would likely create a scene. He quickly used the towel to cover his chest and arm, keeping his right hand closed. Before long the pain and exhaustion had fled, and the Chalaine backed slowly away.

"Chalaine," Regent Ogbith said as the meeting came to a close, "This will be the last time we can risk you out of your carriage. I am sorry."

"I shall bear up well," she said, "since it was also the only time."

"Very good. Captain Tolbrook will take Gen's place tonight while he is healed."

Mirelle fixed her eyes on Maewen and Regent Ogbith and pointed at Gen. "This one goes on no more little jaunts into the wild, understand?"

Both nodded their assent, and people filed out of the tent.

"Well, Chalaine," Chertanne said as she came close to him. "Not much of a Protector, is he? Nearly got killed by a few dirty Uyumaak!"

Shadan Khairn smacked his son in the face, and all chatter died.

"You show respect!" the Shadan said vehemently. "A

hearty group of squirrels could see you dead for all you know of the blade!"

Chertanne did not back down from his Father's fiery stare. "When I come into my power, we'll see who's alive and who's dead!"

He left quickly as Torbrand seethed. Jaron rushed the Chalaine from the tent during the confrontation. Maewen helped Gen up, though he didn't need it, and he faked a limp as they left the tent and headed toward the Puremen's camp. A sudden shove from behind nearly sent him to the ground.

"She healed you, didn't she?" It was Mirelle, face angry in the light of the moons.

"Yes," Gen confessed sheepishly. Maewen laughed and continued walking.

"I'll make sure they give you a good burial," she teased in Elvish.

"Thank you," Gen answered back in kind.

"Follow me, Gen," Mirelle commanded.

"May I get a change of clothes first?"

"Please do. Meet me at my tent when you are a little more presentable."

Gen arrived at his wagon to find Jaron just settling in.

"Gen! You had us worried. How are you?"

"I am well, though I was worried there for a while, too." Gen opened the box that held his clothes. "It was my first time to face down a Hunter charge. Stories don't do it justice."

"I faced one on the Daervin's Wild shard in my younger days. I had fifteen soldiers with me, and it was a close thing. Facing it with but two, and one a woman, would be several times worse."

Gen removed the pins from his old shirt and affixed them to the new. "Luckily, Maewen is as good a several men when it comes to the bow. Good night, Jaron." Gen grabbed his last shirt, pair of pants, and boots and left.

"Good night, lad."

Gen bathed quickly in the chilly river and half considered finding something else to do besides attend his interview with Mirelle. He had received permission to go on the expedition from his commanding officer, so technically, she should yell at Regent Ogbith. In the end, Gen couldn't bring himself to disobey her. Mirelle had always supported and cared for him, so he steeled himself and walked the short distance to her tent.

Cadaen stood guard at the entrance, and Gen thought he could detect a hint of a smile on the corners of the Protector's mouth as he pushed the tent flap aside for Gen. Mirelle's tent had only a chest and her bedding, and she invited him to sit near the door as she sat opposite him.

It was hard for Gen to know how he should think of her. On the one hand, she was old enough to be his mother; on the other, she was young enough and pretty enough not to be. She usually treated him as a friend, but she could switch from friend to First Mother in an instant. Tonight they had clearly moved beyond the First Mother and liege relationship and stepped into 'foot and bug' territory. She stared at him for a long time before speaking, eyes glinting with boiling anger.

"Before I get to my several points, Gen, there's really only one thing you need understand and remember if you forget everything else I may say to you tonight. The thing is this. Regent Ogbith may be your 'commander,' but when it comes to where Gen goes and where Gen doesn't go on this trip, there are only two people: me and me. The next time you kill an Uyumaak, my daughter better be close enough to watch! How dare you go running off without my knowing! Don't give me that stone-faced look of yours! I want to see you're sorry! And in case you're all smug about killing half a company of Uyumaak, let's just review all of your *stupid* decisions today, shall we?"

For what seemed like half the night, Mirelle laid waste to

anything Gen might be thinking good about himself and pointed out repeatedly that she was before Eldaloth himself when it came to Gen getting permission to do anything besides stay within earshot of the Chalaine. He was fairly sure she would have impugned his parentage for all of his faults if he had any parentage to speak of. At one point, he thought she might actually make up some parents for him just for that purpose, but mercifully, she did eventually tire and tell him to get out of her sight.

Gen felt more exhausted than ever as he left the tent, but still far from sleep. Cadaen clapped him on the back in an understanding gesture, and Gen glanced back to see a wide grin splitting his face. For a moment he stood and wondered what to do. He couldn't go back to his own wagon since Jaron would be sleeping there. The moons' positions in the sky told him that Mirelle had only berated him for a little over an hour. His stomach rumbled, and he raided the supply wagon for something to eat before returning to the Chalaine's carriage to attempt to relieve Captain Tolbrook.

"You are to rest tonight, sir," Tolbrook objected. "You've had a long day and probably have a good bit of healing to do yet."

"I am fit, Captain. The First Mother herself just told me to not leave the Chalaine's side without her permission, so I am trying to obey her orders. Trust me, Captain, I am ready for duty. If you think otherwise, come check on me in a couple of hours to be sure."

Tolbrook thought for a moment. "Well, I wouldn't want to cross the First Mother if she's told you to watch her."

"Indeed, you wouldn't."

"Very well, then. I will check in on you. I need to run Kimdan through a few more drills before I let him sleep. I don't see how you could be ready to watch through the night after what you've been through, but you're an extraordinary one, so I'll give you a chance."

"Thank you, Captain," Gen replied as Tolbrook walked off into the dark. The camp was quieting down, though the soldiers had started riding patrols around the edge of the circle of wagons. The night was again clear, the stars and moons brilliant in the sky, the shards drifting silently by.

After Mirelle's scathing, he supposed he should feel guilty for what he'd done, but he couldn't dredge up the feeling. Now that he wasn't dripping blood, running from Uyumaak, or hobbling on a bad ankle, the memory of the experience invigorated him. Gen thought of how when he was a child he couldn't stop playing with Rafael's small statuette of an Uyumaak even though it gave him bad dreams. If he'd had any idea as a child of what Uyumaak were really like, he would have buried the thing.

"I see you survived my mother's wrath. I could hear some of it," the Chalaine said from behind the small opening in the bars.

"She knows you healed me, so you are likely next in line. If she tells the Pontiff, you might want to consider feigning deafness. I hope your mother can see fit to forgive me."

"Don't worry, Gen. She only does that to people she really likes."

"That's comforting. I never thought I would hear that kind of language coming out of a woman's mouth. She could outdo any woodsman I ever knew."

The Chalaine laughed. "My mother does know some choice words, doesn't she? I think the way she found out about your absence accounts for a lot of her vitriol. The missing scouts worry her greatly. She had no idea you and Maewen had embarked on a scouting mission and were late in returning until she came at sundown to talk with me and found Jaron still on duty. I told her where you had gone. Fenna told me earlier about your 'running off' with Maewen."

"An interesting choice of words."

"Yes. You may find that your little getaway with a pretty

half-elven woman may have helped in other matters. Fenna was out here pacing around the carriage nearly all day. She actually told Geoff to 'run off and sing a song or something' at one point."

"He must have been crushed."

"Probably, but you know Geoff—always hunting for sunshine in the storm. I'm sure he will be after her all the more tomorrow."

"You were kidding about Kimdan last night, right?"

"No. But unfortunately for him, he's on duty all day and off training with the Dark Guard half the night, so unless he gets a little more time, I think you won't have to worry about him for a while."

Gen shook his head. This trip had proved more complicated than he could have imagined. "Thank you for healing me, though I must note my objection for any record that Geoff may write up about the incident."

"You are welcome. It makes me furious when they tell me I can't heal someone, especially you. Healing is one thing I *can* do during this lousy trip. If I can't even heal my own Protectors, then what good is my talent?"

"You just need to learn to be more like Chertanne," Gen suggested. "He's perfectly comfortable contributing nothing whatsoever. He didn't say one word while they decided the strategy of the caravan! The only thing he ever puts any effort into is trying to disgrace me."

The Chalaine's voice dropped to a whisper. "He's not doing very well on that front. Watching his father slap him has replaced you telling me to shut up as the high point of the trip thus far." They shared a laugh at the memory of Chertanne's bewildered look upon being hit, probably for the first time in his life.

The sight of Fenna striding briskly forward brought an abrupt end to their mirth. She stopped in front of Gen, and for several moments Gen couldn't tell if she would hug him or slap him. Thankfully, she settled on the former before stepping back and putting her hands on her hips and scorching him with the same kind of look Mirelle had tortured him with for the last hour.

"Well, I certainly hope Mirelle put you straight, *Lord* Gen. I bet you thought it was really funny smiling a little smile and waving a little wave to poor little Fenna as you go running out of the camp with that pretty little half-elven hussy!"

"That's not fair, Fenna. She is not a. . ."

"It's not your turn to talk, Gen. Don't you think that just because we haven't had much time together lately that you can just start fraternizing with whomever you please and that there won't be any consequences! I am not to be trifled with! I have feelings, too! Do you have any idea how we all felt when you didn't return? Sick, that's how. You only bother to tell Regent Ogbith where you're going, like the rest of us don't care that you're off on some dangerous mission where you almost get killed! I obviously don't mean enough to you for you to even tell me. I just get a quaint 'See you later, Fenna' smile as you run by!"

"We didn't know it would be a dangerous mission, and you're the one that's been preoccupied with Geoff every second of the. . ."

A stinging slap brought his argument up short.

"Don't you dare think that this is my fault! I wouldn't run off with some gorgeous ranger without telling you what I was up to. I've noticed you and Maewen talking lately, always in Elvish, as if you have your own little secrets to keep from the rest of us. I'll tell you this, Gen. My heart belongs to you. One day, I hope yours will belong to me."

She marched off without looking back. If he weren't on duty, Gen knew the right thing to do would be to follow her, pretend he was wrong, and apologize.

"Don't worry," the Chalaine said. "She only does that to people she likes."

"Very funny, Chalaine. Do you show this wicked edge

of yours to everyone or just me?"

"Just you, I'm afraid."

Gen put his arms behind his back and clasped his hands. "Well, if you have anything nasty to say to me, go ahead and get it over with. It would be most efficient to get all the abuse taken care of in one day."

"What should I say?" the Chalaine whispered teasingly, coming close to the bars. "Your reckless self-endangerment has saved both my dignity and my life. I could hardly tell you to stop now out of respect for the good incurred by your past insanity. But," and her voice grew soft and serious, "please don't do anything like that again."

That was the last remark Gen heard directed at him that evening, and he was grateful. He figured he would be the laughing stock of the camp tomorrow since the Dark Guard and half the camp had heard both of his thrashings. But the night was quiet and starry, the wind soft, and he enjoyed the silence until the sun bathed his face in light.

Chapter 40 - Murder

Gen couldn't help but think that the skirmish with the Uyumaak had somehow been the catalyst that changed the prospects of the caravan from good to ill. In the days that followed their discovery of the Uyumaak company, fierce winds howled from the north, kicking up dust and dirt that bit when they hit exposed flesh. Soldiers and drivers had difficulty controlling the horses, and they could only see for short distances in front of them.

For once, Gen mused, the Chalaine could feel grateful for her carriage. While dust still came in through the bars, she was not exposed to the full fury of the wind. The Mages, including Ethris, rode patrols around the camp, using their magic to ease the effect of the gale and to help the caravan lumber forward.

The winds would usually die down when the sun fell, something for which all were thankful, but Uyumaak bands began making raids in the night, launching arrows into the camp from their hiding places in the dark. Two soldiers had been killed, a few others injured, though many more Uyumaak found death for their boldness.

Regent Ogbith sent skirmishers forward night and day to clear the way and bring advance warning of any attack.

The terrain, hilly and dotted with trees and rocks, provided many shadows for ambush and assassins. Any sound out of the ordinary turned heads and moved hands to weapons, but as yet, the Uyumaak had attempted no open confrontation. Even so, the creatures' rhythmic and distant pattering in the night foreshadowed conflicts yet to come.

On the fourth day since Gen and Maewen's excursion, the quick-moving wind brought clouds with it, along with a light rain. The change from blistering heat and stinging wind was welcome, but as morning changed to afternoon, the rain picked up and the wind intensified again. It was in that wind that the long-missing deep range scouts were found, swaying from the branch of a dead pine, mangled so horribly that Gen felt sick despite the hundreds of brutal visions he'd seen during his training. Regent Ogbith ordered them cut down and given a proper burial. Their enemies had clearly left the corpses to unnerve the caravan, and thankfully the bodies were hidden from view well before the Chalaine's carriage passed.

Night fell, and still it rained.

The Chalaine spoke with Gen for nearly two hours, whispering her concerns in the dark, seeking strength as fear settled in the camp. To distract her from her troubles, he got her talking about Fenna and Geoff and her mother, throwing in a few jokes about Chertanne. By the time his watch was over, Gen was thoroughly drenched, his toes squishing in water pooled around the socks in his boots.

"I scared up a dry blanket for you, Gen," Jaron said as he climbed atop the wagon. "I would appreciate it if you would return the favor this evening."

"Thank you, Jaron," Gen returned. A dry blanket and his Trysmagic books sounded very inviting, and he jogged away toward his wagon. Maewen waited for him a little ahead of the wagon, backpack resting on her foot to keep it out of the mud. She wore no hood or hat against the rain and seemed heedless of the weather. Even with her black hair matted against her head and face, Gen thought she still carried an air of nobility that court-bred women with their carefully crafted hair and meticulously painted faces could not match.

"How was the watch, Gen?" she asked, always in Elvish. He hoped Fenna was nowhere nearby, since she scowled at him every time she saw Maewen talking with him.

"Long and wet, though uneventful."

"And the Chalaine?"

"She is understandably a little scared, but clinging to hope. She spends most of her time giving me advice on how to navigate the troubled waters stirred up by Mirelle and Fenna."

Maewen smirked. "I've lived a long time but cannot offer any aid there. You have done your duty and earned your respect by it. You haven't lost my respect for what we did."

"I would hope not, since it was your idea. But I doubt you're loitering around here waiting to tell me about your respect."

Maewen's face sobered. "No. I thought you should know that I had a talk with Ethris. He tells me what I had already suspected. The weather is the work of magic. The Uyumaak are trying to slow our journey and interfere with our ability to look around us. Ethris feels that the magic is too powerful to be the work of just the one Uyumaak Shaman we saw, so we are likely facing more than one Uyumaak company, or a very strong Magician."

"I prefer the rain over the threat of arrows in the dark," Gen said.

"They are toying with us. I fear they have a large force to set against us, and I have an idea of where they will loose it upon us. The farther we get into rough territory, the less our strength of numbers or provisions will help us. If you feel like defying everyone, convince Jaron to come with us, and we will take the Chalaine to Elde Luri Mora quickly."

Gen knew Maewen was serious, but she didn't have to report to anyone when it was over. Gen wasn't sure Maewen's plan would work anymore, anyway. The Uyumaak appeared to have intelligent leaders, and if there were significant numbers of them in the wilderness, they would be deployed to keep anything from slipping by them unnoticed. Strength and speed coupled together were what they needed to survive the Uyumaak, and the weather ensured that speed could not be had.

The question Gen had heard on the lips of leader and soldier alike was what had happened to the large force sent to clear the way for them. They were to guard a store of provisions at Dunnach Falls, and two days would see the caravan there unless the carriages and wagons became so mired as to prevent any progress. So far, the ground had held firm, but if the rain continued, it would only be a matter of time before the earth was over-saturated and the wagons would sink.

"I'm afraid we're stuck with the caravan for good or ill," Gen replied. "Besides, we would have to take the Blessed One with us if we absconded with the Chalaine, and I don't think I could stand being in close quarters with that man. Of course, if we left and he were killed, we could return home."

"Then the world would be doomed. He has many faults, but we cannot do without him."

Gen nodded but thought privately that they were all doomed, especially with Chertanne at the head of the human nations—unless the war were to be won by philandering and inebriation.

Gen said, "I'd best get some rest. I think I'll need every last wit I have in the coming days. I see they've granted you permission to scout ahead."

Maewen smirked. "I don't need their permission or their blessing, though I let them think I do as a courtesy—sometimes. I want to see if I can find any sign of the soldiers who were to meet us at Dunnach Falls for reprovisioning. They refuse to send any more scouts forward—as they tend not to return anymore—but I think I can manage. I do wish you could come, though. I could use that sword of yours."

"If you find the rest of that Uyumaak company, don't attack them without me. They've caused me quite a bit of trouble, and I should like to exact the price from them."

Maewen grinned and shouldered her backpack. "When this is over, you should travel with me. I could show you places that would cure you of any longing for cities or human company."

Gen was stunned by the offer. "No doubt you could, but I imagine I will spend the rest of my days in the service of the Chalaine."

"I don't think you shall be in the service of the Chalaine for much longer at all."

"Why?" Gen asked, surprised.

"Once the Chalaine marries Chertanne, she will be a member of his house and he will be the King of all the race of men, including you. Considering the way he feels about you and Rhugothians in general, he will place her under the protection of his guards and have the Dark Guard dismissed. If I read him right, he will have you killed the first chance he gets. If he is wise, which he isn't, he will at least wait till you help get him home. If I were you, I would enter no stronghold of his. You've made him look the buffoon twice, which is twice more than anyone alive has done. If you step one foot into Aughmere, I will be at your funeral within a week."

She paused, letting it sink in. "Of course, he'll order Fenna to stay with the Chalaine and order you to stay away first. He knows you have feelings for Fenna and will do whatever he can to make you miserable."

Gen felt numb. He thought his appointment to the Chalaine's guard would never end, at least as long as Mikkik still threatened her. The realization that what he thought would last the better part of his lifetime would be over in a few weeks made him instantly feel as gloomy as the weather.

"I'm sorry to be the one to tell you," Maewen said upon noticing his distress. "I thought you would already know, though you might have thought the Chalaine would have some sway with Chertanne on the matter. When it is time, Gen, I will come for you, and you should come with me. Soon, I think the only service you will be able offer the Chalaine or Fenna will be to stay alive and not grieve them. Chertanne will want your blood, and I know every good place to hide. Think about it, but tell no one."

Gen nodded his response as Maewen squeezed his arm and sprinted away into the rain-drenched hills. Gen exhaled heavily and went to the rear of the wagon.

Fenna sat inside, arms around her knees and eyes burning with anger. Unexpectedly, Geoff was nowhere to be found.

"Did you have a nice little talk with Maewen?" she asked, voice cold.

Gen clambered up into the wagon. He didn't feel like talking at all. "No. She had nothing good to say."

The bitterness in his voice was more than he had intended to show. The effect on Fenna was remarkable. Her face immediately changed from anger to concern.

"Gen, what's wrong?" Fenna asked as he removed his sword.

"For one, there are likely more Uyumaak arrayed against us than we previously thought. And they have Magicians. This storm is their work."

Gen pulled his shirt off and began to wring it out over the edge of the wagon.

"We always knew that was a possibility, Gen. Something else is bothering you. The look on your face when you came around the corner of the wagon was darker than any

I've ever seen you wear, though you rarely have an expression at all."

Gen pulled off his boots and socks and lay back on the bedding. Fenna shifted to look at him.

"If you must know," Gen explained, calming his voice, "Maewen is of the opinion—and unfortunately I agree with her—that once the Chalaine is married to Chertanne, elevating him to be the Lord and ruler of us all, he will have the power to dismiss me from the Chalaine's service, if not kill me outright."

Fenna's face saddened. "If he had any respect for the Chalaine, he wouldn't."

"We both know how much respect he has for the Chalaine."

"He will probably dismiss me, as well."

"That is the other thing. Maewen seems to think he will send me away but order you to stay and serve the Chalaine because he knows I love you and will keep you from me to hurt me."

"And do you?"

"Do I what?"

"Love me?" Gen regarded her closely and steeled himself. He knew what he had to do, even if it was unfair to Fenna.

"I do," he said softly. "If I didn't, I would have run off with that little half-elven hussy a long time ago."

Fenna grinned warmly and punched him in the ribs before laying her head on his shoulder and remaining quiet for many minutes. "I suppose," she finally said, "that I should act like I hate you from now on so that he won't think to use me against you."

"On the contrary! You should act like you love me more than ever. As if you can't stand to be without me."

"One might think that a self-serving answer." Fenna grinned, coming up on an elbow. "Though that wouldn't require an act on my part. But you are serious, aren't you?

Why?"

Gen held her eyes with his. "Listen, Fenna. When the Chalaine marries Chertanne, she will be utterly alone, kept from everyone she knows or cares about. If there's anything we can do to trick Chertanne into letting you stay with her, then we should do it. It would be hard on you, too, I'm afraid. You will end up in Aughmere miles from home and I'll be running for my life and won't be able to do so much as write. We could only hope that when Eldaloth returns to the world, he will put things right, both with Mikkik and Chertanne, and we can become Lord and Lady Blackshire."

Fenna lay her head back on Gen's breast. They listened to the rain patter against the canvas covering above them and the voices of soldiers preparing their gear for the next leg of the journey.

"You are right," Fenna finally agreed, voice resigned. "I couldn't bear to see her alone like that. I will help her, even if it means I can't be with you for a while. But how do we get Chertanne to do it?"

"First, the Chalaine must know nothing. She is stubborn and self-sacrificing and would do her best to scuttle our plan. As for the rest, I'll be as annoying as possible to Chertanne, which I can do without trying, and we should also announce our intention to marry and try to be seen as much as possible together. Of course, to make it convincing, I'll have to kiss you from time to time, which I haven't got much practice doing."

"I think we can work on that."

By the time Fenna left to spend time with the Chalaine, Gen felt confused and sick despite Fenna's sincere affection. None of the scenarios for rule under Chertanne ended pleasantly for him, and if he wasn't careful, things wouldn't end well for Fenna or anyone that cared for him, either. How Chertanne would react to the wedding announcement was not guaranteed to play out as Gen foresaw it, and everything Shadan Khairn had taught about enemies exploiting those he held dear to him were slowly and awfully coming true.

Gen shoved the worrisome thoughts away. Fretting would only weaken him. To distract himself, he removed the Trysmagic book from his travel chest and began to read. As it was written in a language only he, Maewen, and Ethris understood, he wasn't worried someone might discover it. If someone did find out it was a book about Trysmagic, however, it would invite a lot of questions he didn't want to answer.

Since he had begun studying some months ago, he had learned that Trysmagic greatly differed from Mynmagic and Duammagic and that it was staggeringly flexible and powerful. Whereas Magicians of Mynmagic and Duammagic had to memorize specific, discreet incantations and gestures to perform their magic, Trysmagicians did not. Trysmagic had no set spells and was limited only by the imagination and power of the Magician. This flexibility came with a price—Trysmagic required a stronger will to perform and tended to exhaust the caster more quickly than the others, and, from what Gen had seen, Myn and Duam magic quickly drained the power of even puissant Magicians.

To counter this weakness in Trysmagic, the book he was reading taught that a Trysmagician must use wit to accomplish tasks with a minimal effort. Gen read,

Take, for example, the case of bringing down a mounted rider. It is often the mistake of the apprentice to want to be ostentatious. Therefore, they expend great effort and time to turn the entire animal into stone, exhausting themselves unnecessarily and leaving them ill prepared to deal with any other danger that may arise by and by. Furthermore, anyone who witnessed the event would be immediately alerted that a Magician was nearby. While the result may be spectacular and impressive, approaching the problem differently yields a better overall result.

A Magician in this scenario would be wise to think, "What is the least I need to do to unhorse the rider?" There are several answers, of course, depending on how much injury you wish to inflict upon the rider. But instead of turning the horse to stone, why not simply weaken the material of the saddle buckle so severely that it breaks? The rider would fall, little effort would have been expended, and the victim would not think a Magician the culprit, but rather a poor craftsman.

The most important thing Gen had read, and what Ethris told him to understand—even if it meant suffering ignorance on every other topic—was protection from Trysmagic's transmuting power. Trysmagicians could take an object, including a living thing, and with a subtle spell protect it from transmutation. The protection was as strong as the will of the Magician, and only a stronger will could break it down. Gen knew that his first task upon the unveiling of Trys would be to protect those he loved against any pettiness that Chertanne planned to inflict upon them.

Since Trys would be unveiled slowly, its power would grow slowly for Gen and Chertanne. Gen wasn't sure how many people he could protect at first, but the Chalaine and Fenna were obvious choices for his immediate consideration. Mirelle and Ethris would follow as quickly as he could.

The more Gen read, the more he realized how complicated protection could become. While persons could be protected against having their flesh transmuted to stone, the protection could not keep a Trysmagician from transmuting the air above them into a huge slab of iron or the ground at their feet into a gaping pit.

Gen read how most Magicians would create and maintain a globe of protection around themselves when they thought danger was near. It took stamina to keep such a protection active, and only extraordinary Trysmagicans had power enough to create items that would do the work for them. Creating magical items was second in difficulty only to creating life, both feats involving imbuing something with a self-maintaining force. Few Trysmagicans had ever mastered the former, and even fewer the latter.

But somewhere within those pages lay the secret of Gen's creation, the answer to what Joranne had showed him. There were two types of creations Trysmagicians could fashion, animations that had no spirit or essence, and vivifications, whole beings with spirit. Gen wondered what Mikkik had done with the seed Joranne had planted in the Goreth Forest.

Gen studied protections for a while longer and then put the book away. He knew Chertanne had likely read translations of the same books he had and probably more. Thinking of what Chertanne would be able to do to any of them in a few short weeks sent a chill up Gen's spine. Trysmagic in the hands of a spoiled, self-indulgent brat could only lead to misery for anyone connected to him, and Gen doubted the Blessed One would ever have a will strong enough to impel Mikkik to do more than laugh at him. Mikkik was a God, and Gen didn't see how any mortal Magician could ever have sufficient strength to overpower him. Even Eldaloth, Mikkik's master, had not been able to defend himself from Mikkik's power. Perhaps Eldaloth's return would come swiftly enough to render Chertanne's weaknesses irrelevant.

Pushing aside his doubts and concerns, Gen found peace enough to sleep.

The camp was quiet save for the steady patter of rain and the occasional splash of a sentry's boot. Gen wrung out the hood of his cloak again, wondering why he bothered.

The rain hadn't so much as favored them with a minute's respite, and the Puremen found themselves in the service of those catching sick due to constant exposure to the dampness. The overcast sky plunged the camp into pitch darkness when night fell, and no one dared light a lantern for fear of archers in the dark.

Geoff had stopped by early in Gen's watch to congratulate him on winning the Lady Fenna. While the flashy bard tried to appear nonchalant, Gen knew better. The slight strain in the voice and eyes as he talked about it revealed his feelings on the matter. Gen fought against an urge to hurt the bard by rubbing it in, choosing instead to offer a simple thanks.

Mirelle had also stopped by briefly but left upon finding her daughter asleep. Gen wasn't sure if she had forgiven him for his 'little outing,' as she and Fenna now called it, and the First Mother's face bore more worry upon it than usual. She and Ethris engaged in many conversations with each other that evening, and whatever they talked about discomfited them both. Gen had to admit to a nagging worry festering within him, as well. The enemy, far from being disorganized and incompetent as they had previously thought, was instead calculating and prepared. The Uyumaak and their masters had laid a plan, and there seemed little they could do to disrupt it without exposing themselves to even greater danger.

"Gen?" The Chalaine's voice startled him as she had been asleep since before he came on watch.

"Alumira. What brings you awake this time of night? Are you well?"

"I slept most of the day. The clouds make it even darker in here than usual, and the sound of the rain lulls me to sleep. I have never really been outside in a rainstorm like this before. It makes the little rain we received at Shroud Lake a drop in a pond."

"Most storms aren't this bad or this long."

"Fenna told me what you'd learned about the rain. And while I mention Fenna, I must congratulate you. You certainly turned that situation around in a hurry."

Gen couldn't tell if she was genuinely surprised or probing because she suspected something. "I was almost a bard," he returned. "I do have some skills with the fairer sex, whether you believe it or not."

"You must be powerful in your arts, indeed. Just yesterday I don't think she would have given you an affectionate kick in the shin, much less accept the idea of marrying you without some serious, prolonged groveling and repentance on your part. Then she shows up this morning with nothing but good things to say about you and face glowing with anticipation over your upcoming nuptials. I simply must know how you affected this reversal."

Gen knew she was suspicious now. "Well, if you must know, I think she changed her feelings when she saw me take my shirt off after my watch. I may have the personality of a dog carcass and the charm of a bloated tick, but you will have to admit that I do look good with my shirt off. As far as I can tell, my muscular chest dismantled all her remaining concerns."

The Chalaine laughed, an alien sound in the benighted camp. "Oh, do go on. Was she speechless? Did she just melt into your arms? Surely Fenna is intelligent and stalwart enough not to fall for such base charms."

"You know Fenna well. I thought I was going to lose her for a moment, but then I started flexing my chest muscles one at a time, first the right, then the left. No woman can resist that, especially when combined with a few well-crafted expressions of undying devotion."

"I see," the Chalaine smirked. "So a muscular display and a few sweet whispers in the ear, and Fenna toppled. I had thought she would hold the fort longer. I shall have to revise my high opinion of her willpower."

"Do not be so quick to judge! Don't think that just

because you're the Chalaine that you're the only one that has irresistible charms."

She chuckled. "I see. I must have missed that part of the prophecy—the Blessed One, the Chalaine, the Ilch, and the soldier with the irresistible chest. So your role in our epic history is what? To make all women dissatisfied with any other man?"

"Sadly, yes."

"To what end?"

"To make all men angry with me, I think."

"Really?" The Chalaine's mirth subsided and she dropped her voice to a whisper. "Then you are fulfilling your role well. By all reports, both Kimdan and Geoff were in high dudgeon all day. Geoff, I can understand, but Kimdan's displeasure angers me. Fenna was giddy about him for years and he wouldn't so much as be polite to her. He only became interested in her when he realized she was taken with you. Losing Fenna serves him right."

"I don't much care what either one of them thinks."

"I didn't think you would. I do want to congratulate you. Fenna is a wonderful woman and I'm happy she found someone like you. She has grown since she began her association with you. I can't help but feel a little envious of her. Of course, my heart belongs to Chertanne. . ."

"Don't say that!" Gen protested with sudden heat. "Not even in jest. That your person belongs to Chertanne is bad enough. Let your heart rest on something or someone else."

The Chalaine was silent for a long time. Gen started to apologize when she spoke. "It does, Gen."

"If I thought there was any chance you'd be happy with him, I would encourage you to love him wholeheartedly, but I can't. You must do your duty, and I will see you through it no matter how bitter I may feel about it. I shouldn't have said anything. What you decide to do or feel is your own and I am sorry."

"Do not be sorry," the Chalaine whispered. "You know as well as I do that Chertanne doesn't love me. And you know that I could never love him. The only comfort for me is the long history of women who have for political expediency or family station been forced to do the same as I."

"History is poor comfort."

"Poor comfort is better than none, but I have also been fortunate to have people around me that do genuinely care for me."

Not for much longer, Gen thought, *unless this plan works.*

The Chalaine sighed. "But please, Gen. Do not dwell on me. Tonight is your night. Yours and Fenna's."

A hue and cry halted their talk. Gen drew his sword, thinking that the Uyumaak were up to some mischief again, perhaps firing arrows in the dark.

"Lie on the floor of the carriage and stay away from the windows," Gen ordered, though he thought it was probably unnecessary; previous nights of terror had taught her the lesson. Gen could see little, but several soldiers ran by in the darkness, and after a few minutes, someone lit a lantern near the tents where the soldiers' commanders slept. A great number of men were gathering around the lantern until a stern voice—Captain Tolbrook's—ordered them away. More lanterns were lit inside the caravan circle, the reflected lights dancing in the puddles, as nobles, Magicians, and Churchmen awoke at the alarm. Several messengers from the soldiers' camp pushed their way into the circle, soldiers from the Rhugoth and Aughmere seeking their respective leaders

A cry of anguish rose above the splashing, wind, and rain, and Gen knew the voice, as did the Chalaine.

"Mother!" she cried. "Something awful has happened. Gen, let me out. I must see her."

"No, Chalaine," Gain said. "Get back down! There is danger about."

In the circle of lamplight, he could make out Mirelle donning her cloak and leaving her tent escorted by Cadaen and Ethris. They didn't come near the carriage, choosing the direct route to the soldiers' encampment.

"What is happening, Gen?" the Chalaine asked.

"I don't know. Something in the soldiers' camp. There are a lot of people moving around, but they seem concentrated around one tent. Your mother and Ethris went there just a few moments ago."

The sound of heavy splashing footsteps coming toward them put Gen on guard. Volney came out of the darkness. In the weak light of the lanterns, Gen saw the haunted look in his eyes. His cloak hood was down, and rain dripped of his ample nose and plastered his black hair around his face.

"My Lord Blackshire," he said, breathless, "he's dead. Regent Ogbith is dead. Killed by an Uyumaak arrow. Got him right in the throat while he slept."

Gen's heart fell, and he sought the stillness of his training, forcing emotion out of his mind so he could think.

"It can't be," the Chalaine said, voice pained. "It just can't."

"An Uyumaak arrow?" Gen asked as the Chalaine sobbed.

"Yes, Milord. A black one. Just like the ones that killed the two soldiers. Quite a shot in the rain and dark, don't you think?"

"Almost impossible, unless and Uyumaak got close to the camp without the outlying patrols seeing it. The Regent's tent is close the wagons, and if he were inside, lying down, then a shot to the throat would be an incredible feat of skill or luck."

Gen wished he could analyze the scene himself but knew he couldn't leave the Chalaine.

"Well, the evil one's about, that's for sure," Volney said, looking around nervously. "I don't think it a coincidence that the leader of the caravan was killed. Ilch's work, for sure."

"Certainly not a coincidence," Gen said. "Go. Find out as much as you can and report to me."

"Yes, sir." Volney saluted smartly and quickly walked away.

"I'm sorry, Chalaine," Gen consoled, but she returned nothing. Regent Ogbith was probably as close to a father as the Chalaine had known, and Gen felt for her. He felt doubly worse for Mirelle, for the Regent had been a longtime confidant and friend.

Gen fought his impatience as people ran back and forth, word of the Regent's death on their lips. Gen caught a glimpse of Maewen entering the tent and emerging some minutes later. She came directly to the Chalaine's wagon in company of Ethris, Cadaen, and Mirelle. Mirelle's deep cowl hid her face. Ethris seemed paler than normal, and Cadaen—who had been Regent Ogbith's best friend—walked with his face to the ground and his hands clenching and unclenching as he fought back tears.

"Does she know?" the First Mother asked. Her voice, while steady, carried a deep sense of loss.

"She does," said Gen. "I am sorry, Mirelle. I wish there was something I could do. He was a good man."

Mirelle embraced him and Gen returned it, wrapping her tightly in his arms. She cried quietly on his shoulder for several minutes while those around her mourned silently.

At length, she pulled away and wiped her eyes. "Let me see her. Unlock the door."

Gen reached into his cloak and pulled the heavy key from around his neck, inserting it in the lock only those with the Im'Tith could see. He helped Mirelle in and closed the door quickly, locking it.

Ethris stood in front of him, eyes alight with fury. "We need to talk, Gen. Soon."

Gen nodded and Ethris left, taking long strides toward his tent. Cadaen sat on the edge of the carriage and buried his face in his hands. Gen turned his gaze to Maewen, who regarded him intently.

"They said it was an Uyumaak arrow to the throat," Gen said in Elvish. "Quite a shot, I would say, in the rain, dark, and wind."

"It was an Uyumaak arrow, but if it was shot by an Uyumaak, then I'm no ranger. There was no hole in the tent where it entered, and the arrow stuck down into his neck at an angle that would suggest it came from directly above him."

"Did someone stab him with it, hoping to make us think it was shot?"

"I would say that was likely, but it went deep enough into the ground behind his head that the force of a bow at close range is indicated. It is an impossible shot. Unfortunately, the gawking soldiers turned the ground around the tent into a quagmire before I could see it, though I doubt there was much to see. I fear magic is involved, in which case, I am less help than Chertanne in a sword fight. A powerful enemy is set against us. If they can kill us in our camp at will, without being seen, then we ought to take the Chalaine and leave, Gen. Our only hope is stealth and speed. If the enemy doesn't know where we are, he can't attack us, even if magic is on his side."

Gen shook his head. "You know I just can't take the Chalaine and run off, Maewen. Which brings up a point. Who is in command, now?"

"You know as well as I that it is Shadan Khairn."

"He's half mad!" Gen exclaimed.

"He is also a military genius. You may not like him, but if you insist on keeping the Chalaine in this doomed caravan, then he is the best chance for its survival."

Gen hated the Shadan but couldn't fault the logic. "I suppose you're right."

An order was passed for the lanterns to be extinguished, and Maewen's face was lost in the night. "Oh, yes," she said, voice tainted with sarcasm. "Congratulations on your wedding. Fenna couldn't wait to tell me, of course. I know what you two—or maybe just you—are up to. Be careful. I think you may be making things worse."

For a minute, Gen thought she might say more, but she left, footsteps so light he could barely hear her. Gen turned his attention to Cadaen who had leaned back, staring into the darkness.

"I will find who did this," he said, voice dead, "and I will kill him."

Gen resheathed his sword and put his hand on Cadaen's shoulder. "And I will help you."

Chapter 41 - Dunnach Falls

The Regent was not buried but placed in an empty supply wagon after the Puremen performed an embalming ritual upon his body. Shadan Khairn, as second in command, took charge of the company. Mirelle emerged from the Chalaine's carriage just before dawn. She comforted Cadaen, sitting by him and draping her arm around his massive shoulders. When Jaron arrived, Gen rose to leave.

"Gen," Mirelle said, "will you watch a few hours with me?"

"Certainly, your Grace."

"Cadaen," she said tenderly, "get a few hours rest. Gen will stay with me."

"But he has watched through the night. I should be with you."

"You have watched through the night, too, and have suffered much grief. I order you to bed. You must put your anger and sadness behind you. You cannot protect me while tired and full of sorrow."

"As you wish," Cadaen acquiesced, barely checking his displeasure, "if Gen will swear to me he won't leave your side until I return."

"I will stay with her," Gen promised. "You can rest in my wagon." Cadaen rose and walked away, shoulders slumped.

Mirelle took Gen's arm. "Come. Let's go pay our respects to Harrick."

Everything in camp moved more slowly than usual as he escorted the First Mother toward the rear of the caravan. People clumped together in the rain, talking in low voices. The Pontiff mandated a morning fast in the Regent's memory, though Gen didn't feel much like eating anyway. Near the end of the caravan two Rhugothian soldiers guarded the covered supply wagon where Ogbith lay wrapped in a white sheet with his sword laid on his breast. Ethris sat by the body, his bald head bowed as if in prayer.

Mirelle dismissed the guards, and Gen turned to stand in their place after helping Mirelle inside, but Mirelle waved him up and ordered him to close the flap to the rear opening of the wagon. They sat together in silence for many minutes, Mirelle leaning against Gen and resting her head on his shoulder.

Shadan Khairn rode up and down the line on his massive warhorse, spurring the numb soldiers and servants into quicker preparations for departure. The rain still fell, and there was a great commotion as soldier, Churchman, and noble alike negotiated the mud and stowed equipment and tents. Mirelle did not speak until the wagon lurched forward.

"Kimdan was here," Ethris finally said. "The boy took it well, though I doubt he will think of much more than revenge for a good long while. He is a strong lad."

Mirelle nodded her head in agreement. "Serena will not take it well. She had a premonition that he would die on this trip, but Harrick ignored it. He kissed her goodbye and promised he'd ride back up to the door in as good a condition as he left in. He told me that the sure word of prophecy meant the trip could not fail. He didn't realize that his name was not mentioned by the Ministrant who saw this day."

"And how are you, Gen?" Ethris asked after a pause, eyes tight.

"I am as well as can be expected. I must admit that I have a growing fear of what we are to face ahead of us, especially if the enemy can kill us so easily."

"That is what we need to talk with you about," Mirelle replied. "Do you want to tell him, Ethris, or should I?"

"I will," Ethris said. "I feel I brought this tragedy upon us. I should have never trusted it to Harrick. It has caused a ruinous turn of events."

Ethris fixed his penetrating glare on Gen. "What I'm about to tell you goes to no one else, not the Chalaine, not Fenna, not Maewen. No one. Understood?"

"Yes."

"Very well. You must know this since you protect the Chalaine. We may have to tell Jaron, but I hope we can avoid it since he is on day watch. Do you know the story of Ordd and Ewen?"

"Vaguely," Gen answered. "As I recall, he was the second Mage-King of Lal'Manar. Ewen was his first Queen. She was killed secretly by her sister, Adewwen, who then became Ordd's wife. He found out later, but she managed to kill him with the aid of some magical device."

"Yes," Ethris said, "and the magic device was also what helped her kill Ewen in the first place. Ordd loved Ewen to distraction, and it pained him to be away from her on his many excursions attempting to destroy the rebels flouting his control. So he created what was at first called the 'Lover's Window,' a small looking glass that allowed him to see and speak to her over long distances. Unlike other similar magical devices, this one actually opened a Portal between them so they could kiss, touch, and pass objects to each other. Quite a powerful work of magic which no one has duplicated since.

"Ewen told Adewwen about the device. After Ordd returned home with the Lover's Window, Adewwen found it and used it to kill her sister. The mystery of Ewen's death was never solved, and Adewwen—who had always wanted Ordd for herself—became his wife after he grieved for five years. The device lay unused for a long while, for Ordd couldn't bear the memories it awoke within him and he hid it away. Guilt ate at Adewwen, and one of her handmaidens heard her confess to the murder while she slept. The servant told Ordd.

"Adewwen found out the guard was coming for her and stole the device. She fled the castle and hid. That night, from a small room in a rundown inn, she called Ordd's name and the glass showed him in bed asleep. From miles away, she reached through the glass and slit his throat with a dagger. It took a long time to track her down, and when she was found by some Puremen years later, she was insane. The Lover's Window was placed in a Pureman's apartments and used as a simple mirror for years until a Magician of Duam's order tracked it down and took it for himself. In time, it fell into the hands of wicked men and was used in many more murders.

"The Church finally confiscated it, but not before it became known as the 'Assassin's Glass.' It should have been destroyed. Instead it was locked away within the great temple at Mur Eldaloth. It was stolen recently and no one's been able to find it. Someone killed Harrick using this glass, someone within the camp."

"Why do you think from within the camp?" Gen asked. "If the story is true, then the assassin could be sitting comfortably around a fire many miles from here. The Uyumaak arrow would seem to suggest a dark elf or some human working with the Uyumaak had possession of it."

"No, Gen," Ethris said. "It is in the camp." He was nervous. "You see, it was I who stole it. It was I who brought it with us. It was I who loaned it to Regent Ogbith so he could get messages from home. Someone stole it from him two days ago while we were on the march."

Gen's mind reeled. "Why did you even bring it? And who would want to kill Regent Ogbith?"

"I brought it because I needed to use it to watch certain people, Magicians and evil men I thought might hinder us on our journey. As to who would want to kill Regent Ogbith, there are many answers, ranging from certain members of the Aughmerian camp to those who seek to capture or kill the Chalaine by weakening the caravan."

Something about Ethris's face told Gen that this was an incomplete answer. "Why tell me?"

"Because the Chalaine is at risk," Ethris said, "and you as well. The carriage is warded against this kind of magic, so I do not believe the Chalaine is in immediate danger as long as she stays in it. I can feel when a Portal is opened close by, so I am relatively safe, as well. But I worry for you and Mirelle. Mirelle will sleep in the carriage with the Chalaine from now on under the pretense of consoling her about Harrick's death. You, however, have no protection and you cannot sleep in the Chalaine's carriage without causing a moral uproar. I can help you, though. I can give you a brand that will 'sting' you if a Portal is opened nearby. As the other brands, it will hurt in the giving but will be well worth the pain. There is a problem, however."

"What's that?" Gen asked.

Ethris leaned forward, lowering his voice. "The other Magicians in camp will know I am performing magic if they are nearby, and if they are close enough, they will know it is a Portal ward branding. If they know that, then they may become suspicious. There is speculation already since the tent bore no hole where the arrow should have pierced it, and, at the worst, one of the Magicians may be controlling the glass."

Gen nodded. "So how will we do this?"

"With the Shadan in charge, the Aughmerian soldiers

now have the lead position in the caravan with Rhugoth's soldiers at the rear. You and I will ride near the end of the line and slip off when we can. The soldiers there will be instructed to keep silence and let us fall back. When we have enough distance and privacy, I will perform the branding. Until that time, I suggest you stay awake."

Mirelle and Ethris stayed with Harrick's corpse for nearly an hour, swapping stories about their friend and laughing fondly to dispel their pain. Eventually, Ethris excused himself, leaving Mirelle and Gen alone. The First Mother leaned on him, breathing in deeply and wrapping her forest green cloak around herself for warmth or comfort.

"I hear you are to be married," she said after some time, sitting up and pushing her blonde hair behind one of her ears. Her face was serious, blue eyes clear and determined.

"Yes."

"In that case. . ."

Placing her hand behind Gen's head, she pulled his face forward and kissed him deeply. Whatever his conscience may have been screaming about propriety was completely silenced by Mirelle's nearness and the overwhelming pleasure of her lips on his. Fenna's kisses were a warm wind, soothing and pleasant; Mirelle's were a primal fire, an impassioned call to run wild from the world and dance in heedless joy around the flames. When Mirelle pulled away, eyes inviting and teasing, Gen sat dumbstruck between a decision to run in fear or to politely beg for more.

Mirelle smiled at his wonderment. "Reconsider. No one loves you better than I do." She pulled the flap aside. "Come. I want to see my daughter."

After helping the First Mother inside the Chalaine's slow-moving wagon, Gen sat on the ledge and put his head in his hands, awareness of his surroundings slowly returning from wherever Mirelle had banished it to. The jarring of the wagon and the cool rain running in rivulets down his face cleared his mind. That Mirelle chose to confess her love in the presence of the body of her trusted and recently killed adviser seemed odd, even morbid, signaling some desperation on her part.

Her emotions are running high and she is confused, he reasoned. *She'll probably repent of it later and apologize. She just wants someone to care for her during a difficult time and is uncertain of herself and out of sorts.*

Gen repeated these thoughts until he almost believed them, hoping he could recover sufficiently enough to enable him to look Fenna in the eye without his face betraying the thrill or the guilt.

At length, viscous sucking mud mired one of the supply wagons, and the caravan stopped. Fortunately, Fenna was preoccupied with Geoff, the two of them talking from on horseback. The rain lightened to a drizzle and the air warmed, the air misty and damp. The caravan had climbed steadily that morning, and all around them hills dotted with stands of cedars or towering pines snuggled against sheer gray cliffs. Flecked granite rocks and boulders, some of enormous size, lay scattered on hills or in great boulder washes in the gullies. Clouds concealed the bald, jagged tops of the Far Reach Mountains they had seen from the plain, and patches of snow still clung in the shadowy recesses and cracks in the landscape.

But no wind blew through the pine boughs. Mist clumped in the low places where swift streams, formed from a mix of melting highland snow and a week of rain, flowed down from the high places and pooled in troubled lakes and ponds. Rock slides had torn gaps in the blanketing fir trees. Gen feared the road ahead would prove a morass of mud and rock, though scouting reports said the road was paved in stones after Dunnach Falls Bridge. Once past the bridge, they would pass a road to the ancient and abandoned stronghold of Echo Hold, a massive fort obscured by the mountains to the east.

Mirelle and the Chalaine talked for some time while Gen waited, Fenna joining them while soldiers wrenched the supply wagon out of the mire with the help of long poles of deadwood. The men tasked with the dirty work grumbled considerably about the Mages not "doing their part," but if any of the Mages heard, they gave no sign that the criticism mattered. Even when the caravan finally moved, it only lumbered on for a short distance before it had to stop where the rainwater had eroded a deep gully in the road.

Tempers flared again as soldiers performed the backbreaking work of hauling stones and wood to form a makeshift bridge across the gap. The Magicians, Ethris among them, huddled together and talked, faces grave. Captain Tolbrook pulled Ethris aside and visited with him briefly before coming to the carriage. Dark circles ringed the Captain's tired eyes. The last few days had aged him.

He acknowledged Gen with a nod. "Jaron, I must have word with the First Mother."

"I am here," Mirelle answered through the bars before Jaron could reply. "What news, Captain?"

"Perhaps I should speak to you alone, Milady."

"Nonsense, Captain. We are all about the same business here."

"Very well. The camp at Falls Bridge is either deserted or destroyed. Maewen says there are signs that the soldiers were there, but . . . but they are missing now. All supplies are gone, and there was some evidence of a fight. It appears that we'll need to tighten our belts for the rest of the way."

Gen sensed the edge in his voice—it was Tolbrook's version of terrified. One hundred cavalry and one hundred fifty soldiers had camped at Falls Bridge with a great store of food. That the scouts could find little trace of them was worrisome, suggesting that something had overwhelmed them and carried off the supplies. The river provided a convenient way to get rid of the dead and dying; just below the bridge the river poured over the edge of a deep canyon.

"Thank you, Captain," Mirelle said, voice tight. "Keep me informed." Tolbrook walked away, boots slipping and sinking into the mud. To Gen's surprise, the Chalaine's wagon hadn't sunk into the muck and barely showed a trail in comparison to the others, which cut deep ruts into the earth. Another of the clever features Ethris had imbued into the wagon.

"I suppose you heard?" Maewen came around from the front of the wagon, soaked and speaking in Elvish.

"Captain Tolbrook just left," Gen replied. "He said the encampment at Falls Bridge was missing."

"He softened it for you then," Maewen said, leaning on her bow. "They were slaughtered. The rain washed away a lot of the blood and feces, but not the bent grass and the spoor. The Uyumaak carted off the supplies and what men and horses they didn't eat they probably cast into the falls."

"It would be a lot of work," Gen said, "and to what end? Seems they would prefer to leave the carnage to torment us."

"I don't know. Either it happened some time ago or they had a lot of help. Two hundred fifty men and one hundred horses are hard to clean up or carry off. They didn't use fire to burn anything. There are places I believe they cut the horses up into pieces and carried them away, probably for food. You may see it before nightfall."

"Captain Tolbrook did hide a lot. He probably wanted to be delicate in front of the Chalaine." Maewen's face settled into a mixture exasperation and contempt.

"Why you hide so much from your women is hard to understand. Knowing the truth, even if cold and disturbing, serves one better than warm and peaceful ignorance, man or woman. You tell her, Gen. They aren't attacking this caravan for our sake, but for her and for Chertanne's. But," and at this she moved closer and whispered, "I think we will be in peril before the sun rises tomorrow. We will likely camp close to the bridge tonight. We should take the

Chalaine and Chertanne, cross the bridge, and leave the road. The Uyumaak have guessed our course, and if we don't deviate from it, we will be in their power. Think about it. They will listen to you."

Gen nodded. Maewen held his eyes a little longer to punctuate her seriousness and left.

"So what did your cute elven friend have to say, Gen?" It was Fenna from within the carriage, trying to be mirthful in the worry. Gen stepped up and peered through the bars. The Chalaine and Mirelle sat on the pillows, hand in hand. Fenna stood by the door.

"I'm afraid the good Captain delivered the most comforting version of the events he could."

Gen related in full what Maewen had told him. When done, he thought the Captain had chosen the wiser path. Fenna trembled and Mirelle wrung her hands together, eyes pinched. In her robes and under her veil, the Chalaine was hard to read, though she huddled closer to her mother.

"Gen," Fenna said frantically, "what are we going to do? Are we going to turn back?"

"We cannot go back," Mirelle said resolutely, standing and straightening her deep blue riding dress. "The Chalaine and Chertanne must be wed in Elde Luri Mora, and we must trust that Eldaloth will protect us for that purpose. I'm coming out, Gen. Fenna, stay with the Chalaine, please."

As Mirelle descended and Jaron relocked the door, the caravan started to move again. A horse was brought for the First Mother, and Gen sat behind her, contact with her luring his thoughts back to their earlier encounter. She was all business, however, riding directly to Torbrand Khairn, who sat astride his horse at the edge of the makeshift bridge watching every wagon wheel and horse hoof cross.

"Gen" he greeted excitedly, ignoring Mirelle. A wild anticipation shone in his eyes. "It seems we shall have a fight after all! Everyone is scared, but not you and I. We were fashioned for this hour. They will watch us fight and know that we two, we are the ones to fear!"

Gen wasn't sure how to respond. He had no enthusiasm for a bloody run in with an Uyumaak horde. Luckily, the First Mother dampened the Shadan's fey mood with a good question.

"Lord Khairn," she demanded, "what do you intend to do?"

The light faded from Khairn's eyes as from a child's when a mother tells him to stop playing and come inside the house. "What choice have we, First Mother? We go forward. In less than a mile we will be trapped against the river to our right and the mountain to our left and will be ripe for the killing. I will do the only thing I can—order a wall of soldiers to the left flank to protect Chertanne and the Chalaine and then fight like rabid dog. I just hope those shifty-eyed Magicians don't take away all the fun."

Seeing that the Shadan wouldn't provide satisfaction, Mirelle turned her horse and galloped off to find Ethris.

"I can't understand that man!" Mirelle grumbled. "He's supposed to be a seasoned general and he's got no plan better than that? Phaw!"

While Gen didn't voice it, he knew Torbrand was right. Their mission forced them to go onward. Getting trapped by the river played into the enemy's hands. They didn't dare split their force lest they become too weak. The narrow road and rocky terrain gave them no alternative routes, at least before they crossed the bridge. They couldn't foray out into unknown territory and mount any sort of serious attack. There was nothing to do but fortify the exposed side and win their way through by force of arms, magic, and whatever good fortune they had left.

It took Ethris telling Mirelle the same to calm her down and accept the Shadan's strategy or lack thereof. As they counseled together, Cadaen arrived and relieved Gen. Ethris had another horse brought up.

"Mount up, Gen," the Magician ordered. "We have little time to finish our business."

As if on cue, a wagon near the rear of the column sank into the mud, horses laboring. In the confusion and messy toil that followed, Gen and Ethris gradually worked their way back toward the rear before volunteering to go search for more poles to help lift and extract the wagon. They rode a little way back and quickly skirted behind a large boulder.

Ethris wasted no time. Gen removed his shirt, casting about for any stragglers that might observe their clandestine meeting. From his voluminous cloak, the Magician retrieved the thin, silver blade with which he had performed the other brandings. With confident strokes he cut a runic pattern into Gen's chest before chanting and heating the blade to sizzling white. With it, he sealed and cauterized the cuts. As Gen slipped his shirt quickly back over his head. A shout from the caravan told them the column was underway again.

"Listen, Gen," Ethris said as they rode slowly back. "If a Portal is opened near you, the branding will sting, but it won't help you know where the Portal is. To be safe, sleep with your back against something, a corner preferably. This will limit where the Portal can appear in relation to yourself and make it easier to find. Remember that a Portal goes two ways. You can use weapons to good effect."

"You think Chertanne controls the mirror, don't you?" Gen speculated. "Is that why you're taking such care to protect me?"

Ethris returned a slight nod that left no doubt as to his opinion.

They rejoined the line of muddy, grumpy foot soldiers and weary horses. As they marched, the rain gradually lessened and finally stopped, inspiring a general cheer from everyone. The river Dunnach roared somewhere ahead of them, and as they turned a bend around a hill, it came into view, wide and swift, rushing down from the mountains to their right and forming a small lake against walls of broken granite. Straggly pines grew in these cracks, and over the years their efforts, combined with those of the ice and wind, had dislodged granite chunks that had fallen down the steep slopes and formed a rough stone beach around the water.

Less than a mile across the water ahead of them the mighty Falls Bridge spanned the river just before it emptied into the canyon. As they pressed forward the clouds broke up, sun streaking into the valley in wide, yellow rays. A rainbow formed in the mist from the falls beyond the river, arching above the bridge as if it had provided a guide for the builders to follow.

Gen realized his imagination of the bridge had greatly missed the mark. In contrast to the sturdy shard-spanning bridges of Rhugoth, the Falls Bridge was chiseled into delicate, thin patterns. Expertly tooled clouds decorated the top of the arch, making the falls' mist seem like rain falling from them. The builders had carved the curved supports so finely they seemed like a frail web a stiff breeze might ruin.

As they traversed the rocky edge of the lake, the ground became less muddy and more firm. The steep hill to their left gave way to a deep green meadow, a welcome relief from the rocky, uneven landscape they had grown accustomed to in the previous days. Here Shadan Khairn ordered a halt, calling an early end to the day's march. Gen knew the meadow would be the most defensible place for miles, providing a clear field for approach and a place where the generals and Warlords could put their horsed knights to good use.

The clouds continued to break and flee, and soon the camp was astir with relieved, happy conversation. For the first time in days, someone laughed sincerely enough to be believed. Looking ahead, Gen saw the Chalaine's carriage opening and Fenna emerging. He rode up quickly and helped her up onto his horse. She kissed him long enough for it to be embarrassing.

"Isn't it beautiful!" she said, eyes alive. Gen shoved aside a tinge of guilt, noticing Mirelle nearby. Fenna smiled. "This almost makes up for the days of rain. Almost."

Gen pointed out the bridge to her and her mouth fell open. "It is the most magnificent thing I have ever seen!" Fenna proclaimed. "The Chalaine should see this! It must have taken ages to make! It must be magic!"

"It did take some time," Gen said, enjoying Fenna's fascination, "but I'd bet the Amun'Mu, the giant builders of the first times, had a hand in it. They were massive yet gentle, created by Eldaloth to build mighty structures and cities, including Elde Luri Mora. They did the rough crafting and dwarves provided the finer detail. Both races, unfortunately, were destroyed in the First War. Men have tried to imitate their work with magic, but I don't think such craftsmanship will be matched again."

"Do you think the Shadan will stop and let us see it?"

"I think you'll have to settle for a quick glimpse as we ride over it. His mood is hard to read, but he expects battle soon, and so do I. I don't think he'll allow much time for sightseeing. And speaking of battle, I would appreciate it if you would catch a quick dinner and sleep in the carriage with the Chalaine."

Fenna gave him another kiss. "As you wish, Milord."

The afternoon waned, and the meadow filled with tents and cook fires. Breezes took up the smell of the fatty meat and tender vegetables, wafting it around the camp, setting mouths to watering. Dried bread, meat, and fruit filled the belly but didn't lift the spirits, and as mealtime neared, a feeling of celebration charged the air.

Despite the sunshine and the promise of a warm meal, Gen couldn't relax. He caught Maewen out of the corner of his eye, scowling as she used to do when Geoff would howl out a tune into the unfriendly night. With a quick word to the Shadan, she ran toward the hill, ducking into the forest to the side before beginning her ascent.

Torbrand watched her go, staring eagerly at the high hill as if impatient for an Uyumaak mob to pour over it so he could stain his blade before nightfall. Ethris and Mirelle disappeared into a tent as soon as they could erect one, and Captain Tolbrook and Warlord Maelsworth stood at the edge of the meadow, pointing to various spots on the field as they planned their strategy for a battle they could sense coming but had no proof of. Gen didn't know how many knew of the slaughter that had recently occurred a scant mile or two away, but a force nearly as large as the one now encamped had been crushed and carted off with little trace.

Gen received his food shortly after servants carried away meals for high nobility and the Pontiff. In short order he and Fenna sat on the back of his wagon, feet dangling over the edge. The food, while not fare for the table of a king felt like a feast. With Fenna beside and the blue sky above, Gen could almost forget the danger all about them and have a moment's peace, but Geoff bouncing up in his green coat and yellow hose ruined whatever good feeling Gen had coming. Geoff's resilient cap feather thrust stiffly into the air as if it hadn't seen one drop of rain.

"Good evening, Miss Fairedale and Lord Blackshire," he said, hat sweeping close to the ground, but not close enough to get dirty. "How do you like the weather now?"

"It has brightened up nicely," Fenna said. Gen took a big bite of a potato, knowing he'd have ample time to chew it.

"Indeed," Geoff returned, face aglow, "it is as I said. A ray of sunshine in the middle of the storm! What a paradise we have found in the midst of our gloom. Why, I'd break out into song if I didn't think Maewen would put an arrow through my throat before the first verse was over. But what a song it will make! Imagine the symbolism! Overcoming hardship, pressing on in our duty through dark and distress, striving ever upward to arrive in a blessed land in the mountains where sunshine and peace prevail. I can feel the words coming already! Tell me what you think:

> *Rain and mud, dark and fog,*
> *Don't look down. Press on, press on,*
> *Drenched gray wood and gloomy bog,*
> *Don't look back. Walk on, walk on.*

"We didn't go through a bog, at least technically," Gen interjected through his mouthful of stew. Geoff turned indignant.

"Surely, Gen, you—you of all people—realize that this song would not be historical but metaphorical in nature. I am trying to represent the journey of life, not merely our travels."

"Forgive me; muse on."

> *While hard the way, steel your heart,*
> *The blessing comes though long concealed.*
> *The rain will stop and clouds depart:*
> *The earned reward to you revealed.*

> *For every step of our distress,*
> *For every hope and smile undone,*
> *God gives to us a sweet redress*
> *Where rivers flow through fields of sun.*

Gen watched bemused as Geoff, lost within his mind, waved his arm around to a tune only he could hear. Fenna covered her mouth to hide grin.

"I've got it!" Geoff finally announced.

A deep thud shook the wagon. Gen dropped his plate. Something big and heavy bounced and skidded by, carrying with it flesh, blood and shards of wood as it rammed into the wagon two ahead of his before landing with a heavy splash in the river. Geoff fell to the ground, hand over his head. Gen jumped down and drew his sword.

Shouts and screams from the camp drew Gen's eyes there. A narrow path, strewn with carnage, showed where the boulder had impacted and hurtled along its deadly course before reducing three tents and a supply wagon to rubble. Eyes darted about for signs of an enemy, but there were none. Shouts of "Catapult!" ran through the camp as Torbrand yelled excitedly for his troops to prepare for battle. Gen knew his duty was with the Chalaine, but Fenna sat unmoving on the wagon.

"Geoff!" Gen said, giving the bard a kick. "Get up! You and Fenna stay in the wagon and keep your heads below the sideboard. I must see to the Chalaine!"

The notion of protecting Fenna infused Geoff with enough iron to get up and help her into the back of the wagon. Gen turned and sprinted forward, watching the sky. Ethris emerged from his tent, Mirelle close beside him, and gathered the Mages to him, barking orders.

"Another one!" someone shouted. Gen looked toward the sky. Arcing over the hill was another boulder of impossible size. Gen knew immediately that a catapult could not throw something so big so far. Men scattered as the massive stone impacted near the front of the caravan, tearing through a line of cavalrymen struggling onto their mounts. The horses screamed and men died as the boulder crushed their ranks. Gen arrived at the Chalaine's wagon to find Jaron standing on top watching the hill closely.

"This is Mikkik's work!" he yelled. "We need to get the carriage back to the tree line."

"We can't go without the rest of the caravan!" Gen shouted back. "Splitting the Chalaine away from the main body could be what they want!"

Gen stood at the side of the carriage, eyes fixed on the hill. The Mages spread away from Ethris at his command, forming a line along the center of the meadow. Ethris raised his staff when they were in position, and they began to incant in unison. As they did, another boulder arced over the hill. Gen readied himself—it careened toward the middle of the caravan. Just before it could hit, a faint wall of air formed ahead of the Magicians, and the boulder slammed into it with terrific force. The Mages nearest the point of impact fell to their knees but held the wall.

The rest of the Dark Guard surrounded the carriage as the Shadan shouted for the caravan to move forward toward the bridge. Most of the horses, however, had been unhitched. Torbrand ordered all empty wagons be left and for all to press on. Slowly, one wagon here and another there, the caravan sluggishly moved.

Another boulder slamming into the magical defense tore Gen's attention away from the road. The Magician there had fallen, exhausted but not dead, leaving a large gap in the wall. A howl, distant, deep and loud reverberated through the camp.

With an earthshaking step, something unfathomably huge crested the hill. A gigantic armored head rose first, followed by a body equally protected. It was muscular and was at least fifteen times taller than a man. Its crude armored shirt had been fashioned from a collection of breastplates, greaves, and helms, all from Rhugothian soldiers. Only its own helm had been tailored for it, the rest of its ensemble dangling hodge-podge about its body. Dark gray splotches spread irregularly over the dun skin of its muscular arms and legs. A heavy brow shadowed deep, large eyes. Cries of terror filled the camp as it bellowed and pounded toward them with steps that set the ground to quivering.

So heavy was the armor upon it, that it slumped and walked slowly. Only its arms and lower half of its legs were free of protection, and as it strode forward it loosed another boulder it had reserved, clenched in its hand. Horses pulled at their restraints and screamed. Again the magical shield held, but already the Magicians seemed spent, all leaning heavily on their staves and laboring to breathe. At the Shadan's command, some twenty mounted knights with lances charged forward, not armored due to haste. They formed a wedge, riding fast. Other knights prepared themselves with all the celerity they could manage, and the foot soldiers sprinted to form ranks behind the Magicians.

Upon seeing the mounted assault, the giant stopped and watched them come with a dull curiosity, mouth hanging open stupidly. To Gen's horror, it simply fell forward onto its stomach when the wedge got close enough. The impact on the ground forced Gen to steady himself against the carriage. All but four of the knights were crushed underneath the behemoth's weight, the other four shaken from their saddles. Horses screamed again, and several bolted, pulling stakes and running wild through the crowd. The Chalaine's carriage moved forward, Ulney fighting to keep the horses under control.

Slowly the giant rose to its feet, chest and legs spattered with blood. Several corpses hung from its armor, and these it wiped off with a broad sweep of its hand. With another howl it came forward, steps thundering ever louder. Gen swallowed hard as it turned its gaze toward the Chalaine's carriage and stepped toward it. The Magicians dropped their shield and pulled back into the ranks of the infantry, all save Ethris, who remained rooted as the monstrosity clanged and lumbered toward him.

Ethris lifted his staff high, and a bolt of white light streaked from the sky and hit the giant's helm. At first nothing happened and the giant continued unabated, coming closer to the carriage and pulling away from Ethris. The spot on the monster's helm where the light was focused turned orange as the white beam heated the metal.

The giant screamed in agony, a sound so terrible that the horses on the Chalaine's carriage bolted, throwing Jaron to the ground. Gen sprinted and managed to grab hold of the bars on the side and hang on. The driver sawed at the reins, trying to pull the horses in, but the animals edged closer to the giant, swerving away from the river.

With massive hands the giant grabbed its helmet, working frantically to pull it off its head as the first volley of arrows from the archers peppered its massive face. Ethris fell to one knee, staff still aloft. The giant continued to bellow, unable to pry the helmet off. In unquenchable pain it fell to its knees, soldiers diving away as it sank down. The horses pulling the Chalaine's wagon, feeling their danger, veered straight toward the river, scattering the soldiers in their path. Smoke poured from the gaps in the giant's helmet, and it pitched forward, finally flinging the white-hot armor from its head.

Gen flinched helplessly as the discarded helmet slammed into the back of the carriage, pitching it forward. His vision blurred as he struggled to hang on to the bars, the momentum finally pulling them out of his grasp. He flailed as he flew through the air, hearing the heavy splash of horse and carriage moments before finding himself in the stiff current of the cool, dark water. Using all his training to stay calm, he fought off the disorientation and found his way up, cresting the water. The Chalaine's carriage drifted slightly ahead of him, floating lightly on the river. Due to its size, the current pulled strongly upon it. The horses and driver floated dead in the water nearby, wagon tongue broken.

With all the strength he could summon, Gen swam for the carriage. The Im' Tith told him the Chalaine was alive and only slightly bruised. He knew the carriage had magical properties to protect its passenger, but Gen was still surprised to see that it appeared as if it hadn't even been struck. It also didn't seem to fill with water, and it outpaced him despite his best efforts. The falls roared ever nearer, carriage drifting straight toward the steep drop.

Gen glanced back at the caravan. The entire line was in chaos. Most of the Dark Guard rode along the shore, keeping pace with the carriage in the water. A single Magician astride a horse flanked them, incanting. Behind them, the situation deteriorated rapidly. While the giant lay vanquished, a large group of Uyumaak poured over the hill toward the shattered camp. Chertanne, Mirelle, the Pontiff, and others galloped along the road away from the meadow.

A cracking noise turned Gen's attention forward. A small island of ice entrapped the Chalaine's wagon. The Magician who cast the spell fell forward on his horse, energy spent. Gen scrambled onto the ice and slipped and slid to the carriage door. The great bridge loomed above them, casting a shadow across the water in the late afternoon. The booming of the falls deafened him. High above them the Uyumaak ran across the bridge toward the fray. They didn't seem to notice the carriage below.

"Chalaine!" Gen gasped as he reached the carriage door. "Are you all right?"

The Chalaine came to the bars. "Get me out, Gen!" she yelled. "Get me out!"

Gen could barely hear her over the rumbling of the falls as he fumbled for the key at his neck. As he pushed the key into the lock, the ice to his left cracked, a large chunk sliding away. Gen pulled the key away.

"Gen! What are you doing?! Get me out! Please!" Gen assessed the situation while the powerful current continued to break the ice. While they weren't far from shore, he knew they could not swim to it. The Chalaine had never been allowed near deep water in her life, and her thick robes would weigh her down in the water.

"Gen!" she screamed. A crack formed at his feet as the entire ice sheet floated toward the falls. Decided, he thrust the key in, turned the lock, and jumped inside, pulling the door closed behind him. He had to trust Ethris's craft.

The Chalaine grabbed him. "We have to get out!"

"We can't! We'd never make the shore. The falls are too close and the current too strong!"

Gen searched the wagon, hastily arranging the pillows and blankets that lay strewn about. Luckily, the large chest carrying the Chalaine's belongings was bolted to the floor. Working quickly, he ordered the Chalaine to lie in the pillows and he wrapped her in every soft thing he could find. Before he could finish, the carriage tilted forward, throwing him against the front wall, the bundled Chalaine pinning him to it. He wrapped his arms around the screaming Chalaine as the carriage fell, tumbling slowly end over end.

Chapter 42 - Mikkik

The ancient boughs of black oaks cast an uneven shadow upon the figure sitting stiffly on bulging roots below massive, moss-covered limbs. The dim of Goreth Forest suited the mood of one who passed his days in unending torture. Here he had hidden for centuries, waiting patiently for the light of Trys to break anew into the starscape above and signal for him to leave his hovel of seclusion and return to his quest.

Mikkik cowered deep within this sylvan fortress he had created to protect himself just before Trys waned fully, the puissant moon's light eclipsed by the power of the meddlesome Millim Eri. Without Trys's light, the creative power with which Eldaloth had endowed him faded and died. How he regretted ever coveting that power. How he regretted his own ambition. But regret accomplished nothing and repentance was impossible. He had to cut the lingering life of Eldaloth out of Ki'Hal, to murder the living presence of the God he had slain but whose essence still lingered in Elde Luri Mora. And he had the means to do it.

He had entrusted only one servant with the fullness of his plan. Only she could approach him here, and she was late, as usual. He desperately awaited her report, as much for the information as for the distraction. In speaking with her he could stifle the continual, aching scream that only he could hear and silence the heartbeat he thought would die with Eldaloth in the Plains of Orentan. The scream was Ki'Hal's unending lament for its slain maker; the heartbeat, the essence of Eldaloth's life that emanated from Elde Luri Mora. They tormented him even here in his fortress of cruel trees. Together, the scream and heartbeat drove him mad like a burning sun that never set.

He laughed to think of the pretentious pride of the nations he had massacred in the first wars, fighting bravely against a foe they thought sought to dominate them. To think themselves important enough that one should wish to dominate them or to think that he would feel any satisfaction in doing so was a joke only he could possibly understand. He did not want their obedience. He did not covet their lands. They held no treasure he cared about save one—the feeble power of their otherwise worthless blood.

The wind stirred the branches of the tree above him, warning him that someone had entered his demesne.

She comes at last!

Mikkik leaned against the trunk and considered the sword lying upon his knees. He had fashioned it a duplicate of the one he had used to cut down his master so many years ago. While the consequences lay torturous and heavy upon him, he could not even fathom contrition, only escape. To that end, before the Shattering, he had pulled the power of the blood of the masses fallen on the battlefield to fashion another weapon, to finish what he had so fatefully started.

The blade was not powerful enough by half yet, and he waited anxiously to raise up more creatures of war and begin the bloodshed anew. With the sword's power, he would level Elde Luri Mora. Then that accusatory finger that he could not slap away would finally fall and blessed silence would balm his weary mind.

Joranne's proximity reminded him of more immediate concerns. The Millim Eri had plotted to return Eldaloth to the world, though he knew it a farce. Eldaloth he had annihilated, and all that remained of him lived on in Elde Luri Mora. When news of the prophecy had first reached his ears, Mikkik had scoffed, for the Millim Eri appeared to be foisting some trickery upon the nations. But he could not ignore their cunning or the power within their blood, and if they could somehow create a being to stand against him, he had to respond to the threat.

To that end he had created the Ilch as they had prophesied, a creature of his own blood and power, a creature to end the threat against him before it had a chance to start. But again the Millim Eri proved cunning, and in his weakened state he had no means to counter their treachery. So now his own device was turned against him, aiding the cause the Ilch had been created to crush.

"My Lord Mikkik," Joranne greeted him confidently, and he could sense an eagerness in her voice. "I have returned with strange tidings."

Mikkik considered her. The travel stained clothes and frail human frame concealed the magnitude of the gifts he had bestowed upon her. Only the Millim Eri masters and himself held greater power than she, and in his current debilitation, it would take all his effort to destroy her.

"Is he dead then, Joranne? I must assume that he is or you would not have dared return to me."

"He is not dead my Lord. He..."

Mikkik gestured and a ring of air constricted her throat and strangled the rest of her words. Joranne's face constricted, turning red. Her thoughts sped into his mind.

Hear me, my Lord! See what the Ilch does!

Hurriedly she unloaded what she had gleaned from Gen's mind into her master's, and as the scenes played before them both, the invisible noose around her throat loosened and then released. For the first time in years

Mikkik stood, kicking away the dry brown leaves gathered about him. A menacing smile broke upon his face.

"You have done rightly, Joranne," Mikkik praised. "I could not have devised a plan so clever. The prophecy is ruined, undone by the very people who gave it! Who could have imagined it? The Ilch has sown more contention and division as a man of principle than the Ha'Ulrich in his pride and folly! I need fear the Ha'Ulrich no more than an insect. Gen, I could fear, but if I meet him, I can undo him no matter where the Millim Eri are hiding his animon."

"What is your command, master?"

"One threat remains, Joranne. The Child. While you may help Gen to unwittingly sow his seeds of dissent, we must destroy the Chalaine. Without her, the Millim Eri will be frustrated. There will be no Child of prophecy and no threat to my work."

"As you wish," she said, "though the Millim Eri are tracking me and making movement difficult. May I suggest something?"

"What more is there to do, Joranne?"

And when Joranne told him her plan, Mikkik's laugh, wicked and joyful, set the trees of Goreth Forest to twitching.

"I see that you approve?"

"Of course. And I will keep my promise, Joranne. When this is finished, you will return to ash no more."

Chapter 43 - Revelation

Gen slammed into the walls over and over, almost losing consciousness as he clung to the Chalaine to buffer her against harm. The carriage revolved and spun unpredictably as it churned in the powerful force of the falling water. He braced himself for the impact he thought might end both their lives, but a light splash was all that signaled the end of their violent descent. The water pounded on the carriage roof until the force pushed them downriver.

Gen took stock of himself, noting a broken ankle and several bad bruises, easy fare for the Chalaine, if she were up to it. He worked quickly to extricate the thrashing young woman from the blankets, sensing through his brand that she had acquired some bruises of her own, but little else.

"We're alive!" The Chalaine hugged him, and the pain from his injuries disappeared. He found himself crying with her, for joy at surviving the fall or for worry about the battle above, he couldn't tell. After several moments, he pulled away, feeling awkward.

"Well, let's see where we are," he said, lifting the key from his neck and inserting it into the lock. The door faced away from the falls, opening to a boulder-strewn river. Mighty stone walls towered above them, casting the canyon into twilight. The force of the falls pushed them near the northern shore, and Gen spotted a sandy riverbank surrounded by maples where the water moved slowly.

"I can't steer the carriage, so we will have to swim for shore."

"But I can't. . ."

"I know. I'll help you over. Is there anything you need from your trunk? Do you have anything suitable for hiking? Be quick."

The Chalaine unlatched the chest and flung it open, pulling out clothes and a wedding dress so ornate Gen could only guess at its worth. Working quickly, Gen fashioned one of her unused dresses into a crude backpack by tying the skirt closed and the sleeves together. After leaning out the door and throwing the pack to shore, he grabbed the Chalaine's hand. Without giving her time to think, he pulled her into the water. The Chalaine gasped in surprise as the cold water enveloped her.

The current, while slow, proved difficult for Gen. His sword and boots coupled with the Chalaine's robes dragged them down, and they only managed to get to the shore with the help of a low-hanging branch. Exhausted, they sat on the riverbank for several moments to recover from the exertion. While Gen could ignore the cold, he noticed the Chalaine shivering in the canyon breeze, wrapping her arms close about her. He retrieved the pack.

"You need to change or you'll catch a chill," he suggested. "Choose something easy to walk in, if you have it. I don't think they'll be able to get to us for many miles. We'll have to walk downriver and meet with them . . . if they survive. Come. There's a good thicket of trees here. That'll give you a little privacy at least."

"Do you need healing, Gen?"

"The healing you did in the carriage took care of the ankle and the bruises. I only wish I could do the same for you."

"I didn't heal you in the carriage."

"Yes, you did," Gen contradicted, "when we embraced. Remember?"

"I didn't, Gen. At least I didn't try to. Healing takes concentration and effort. Were you hurt badly?"

"A broken ankle and some deep bruises."

"I didn't do it. At least I don't think so."

Gen could sense a worry in her voice, but he didn't ask her about it as she knelt down and rummaged in the makeshift backpack, pulling out a black divided riding dress and boots with a matching dark blouse and veil.

"They packed these in case there was need for me to ride in stealth. You and I will match quite nicely in black."

The Chalaine stood and walked into the thicket. "You must promise me that you won't try to look at me while I change."

The suggestion stung Gen's sense of propriety. "I would never!" he protested. "The thought hadn't even crossed my mind!"

"Oh, of course," the Chalaine acknowledged in a strange tone Gen couldn't decipher. Putting his back squarely to the thicket, Gen assumed a soldierly stance and concentrated his gaze on the river's foaming water.

"How was the battle going, Gen? I couldn't see. But I could hear. Could you see my mother?"

"It went poorly. I judge at least thirty men died before we even went in the river. That was before the Uyumaak horde. I saw your mother and Chertanne fleeing the battlefield on horse. The Pontiff and others rode close by. I think the soldiers remained behind to buy them escape time. I think she'll do well if the way before them is clear, though the caravan is done for."

Gen didn't voice what he thought was true. If the Uyumaak had any sense, they would fortify the road ahead of the clearing against escape.

"Are we in danger down here?" she asked.

Her wet clothes sloshed to the ground.

The answer to the question slid away as an overpowering urge to turn and look washed over him. He fought against the sudden, insistent desire, turning his thoughts everywhere, to the danger at hand, to his old master, to Mirelle's kiss, and even to his training with Shadan Khairn. He tried to send the compulsion into the emotional nothingness his swordmaster had created within him. Everything broke against the supernatural and unseen command to look.

Mind sprinting for any fortification, he ran through every logical reason he could muster not to turn around—the danger to the Chalaine, the disappointment of Mirelle, a guaranteed dismissal from his post. Gen closed his eyes, gripped his sword, and struggled for mastery.

"Are we in danger here, Gen?" the Chalaine repeated. Her voice showed she was still unaware of his struggle.

Just a glance, he thought. A quick one.

"Gen?" She knew.

Resistance crumbled. Gen turned.

The Chalaine had dressed completely save for her veil, and her face, open, beautiful, and kind beyond imagination, fixed upon Gen's with an expression of surprise. Wet, blonde curls framed her perfect features, and her pale, utterly flawless face seemed to glow in the dim thicket. Gen could sense rather than see the presence of light about her. Her beauty, both carnal and divine, forged a strange union of passion and worship within his breast.

"Gen!" she yelled as if to awaken him.

He barely heard it. Thoughts of possession invaded his mind, yelling at him to take her, to claim her before someone else did. She was his. Hadn't he earned the right? Had any other man risked so much for her? Would Chertanne make her as happy as he could? *I can give her a life of dignity. Take her pain away.* He would kill Chertanne and marry her himself. She would thank him for it.

He took a step forward and stopped. The Chalaine hadn't replaced her veil or even moved to do so. Sky blue eyes, once filled with surprise, softened to a wanting tinged with fear. She breathed heavily, almost expectantly. Her reaction confirmed his thoughts. She was his. He could take her. The Chalaine wanted him, too. His Alumira'rei Se Ellenwei. The voice that had pulled him from despair and darkness.

And at remembering the name he had given her so many nights ago, the pull of her presence quavered and fell and the urge subsided, leaving him at peace. His face and eyes relaxed, and a sudden joy filled him. He breathed out and smiled at her.

The Chalaine watched him questioningly, a return smile turning up the corner of her lips. While he felt like running, he managed a nice casual walk to stand in front of her, staring into eyes that were clear, alive, and pure. Stooping, he lifted the veil from a low branch where it hung and handed it to her. She twisted it in her hands, not taking her eyes from his face.

She said, "You resisted! What kind of man are you, Gen?"

"Come," he invited, ignoring the question and turning back toward the river. "We need to find a protected place to hole up in tonight and get a fire going. Night and cold will come quickly in this canyon. To answer your question, I do not think we are in immediate danger here."

"Look at me!" the Chalaine demanded.

Gen turned. She still held the veil in her hands. "How, Gen? How can you do it? Cadaen accidentally saw my mother unveiled once and they almost had to kill him to keep him from dragging her off. I affect men more strongly than she ever did and yet you resist. Tell me how."

"I don't know, Alumira. Be grateful I did. I never want to think of you in that way again. You should put your veil back on."

The Chalaine held his eyes, searching for something, and Gen waited as she rifled through his soul for answers. At last, she smiled as if she found one. Walking forward, she plastered the wet veil to Gen's chest.

"You wear it. I want to feel the wind on my face."

"You really should put the veil back on." Gen decided he should say that at least once a day so he could swear truthfully that he had said it when he faced the inevitable inquisition that would come if they ever found the others. He shuddered to think what would happen if Chertanne found out he had seen the Chalaine unveiled—and not only seen her, but traveled alone with her for days.

Gen already knew to expect several intense sessions with the Pontiff and Ethris—if the two older men survived the attack—so they could ply their magic to ensure for the prophecy's sake that he and the Chalaine had behaved according to propriety while they traveled alone. If they found out she had walked with him unveiled, he doubted they would believe him, truth and innocence notwithstanding. As she had done the last three times he had suggested she don her veil, the Chalaine said nothing, choosing instead to flash him a smile that unhinged his knees.

Gen could only marvel at her. Each time he looked at her seemed the first, and while he wished she would replace the veil for fear of what others might think, he also wanted her to do it because she was achingly beautiful. The possessive obsession that had overcome him when he first saw her unveiled did not plague him again, but her glory discomfited him. For three days he fought to keep his concentration on the task at hand, but her flawless and inviting countenance invaded and occupied his mind, threatening to overwhelm discipline with distraction.

Gen tried to use Fenna and Mirelle as his defenses, but with the Chalaine near, he could barely summon either woman's face into memory. In the evenings, he tried to immerse himself in practicing sword forms, but the Chalaine always sat nearby watching every move with wonder and appreciation. He struggled with a man's innate tendency to show off for a beautiful woman and nearly lost. Perhaps he did lose. Thankfully, she never clapped or lavished him with praise. She did ask insightful questions about what certain moves were for or what battle was like. He appreciated the questions. Talking to her was easy; having her stare at him with that affectionate look was hard.

He supposed she would wear the veil if he told her of the feelings that she awakened in him, but he feared telling her would complicate the friendship they shared. Every man who looked upon her would no doubt feel the same way as he—that she cared for him. Try as he might, Gen couldn't imagine her face holding malice or even apathy for anyone. Despite the discomfort and privation of the trail and her worry for the caravan, unhappiness never fully took hold upon her features, outing her native good nature. Each day revealed a vivacious, sweet personality that had been smothered by a lifetime of solemnity and the more recent fear of Chertanne, a personality Gen had snatched glimpses of in the dark hours when Alumira had replaced the Chalaine on the trail.

When he wasn't wrestling with his attraction to her, he found himself staving off feelings of inadequacy. When he saw her, Gen felt ugly inside and out. Perfection exuded from her like light from the sun, and wherever she shined, every shadow was twice as dark. He remembered taking her hand to help her over a tumble of rocks. His tanned, rough hand, marred with a web of scars, seemed like gnarled tree bark next hers—white, smooth, and without a mark or imperfection. Even after three days, she bore no scratch, no bug bite, no sunburn.

It was the morning of their third day together between the towering canyon walls. The trek proved difficult. They encountered numerous reminders of the battle their first day hiking downstream. Bodies of men and Uyumaak, washed over the falls during the fight, peppered the shoreline, and Gen did his best to steer the Chalaine away from the upsetting carnage. He tried interesting her in the plants and vistas around her to distract her mind, initially meeting with only partial success.

The pristine, primitive canyon provided no convenient road or path. Trees, brush, deadfall, and the river itself constantly barred their progress, forcing them to guess which way would present the safest course. They guessed wrong as often as not, forcing them to backtrack over rough terrain. "The trail is longest when first taken," Samian would have said. From what Gen remembered of the map, traversing the canyon, given a good trail, would take the better part of four days. At their current pace, Gen calculated they wouldn't get out for at least seven, if not more—if at all.

The Chalaine slowed them, and Gen knew she felt badly for it. Gen had grown up with the sounds and sights of the forest; the Chalaine had spent her life in what amounted to a dungeon. The memory of their first night by the river would always cheer him, and he hoped he had the chance to tell Maewen. Every flutter, crack, splash, or scratch brought the Chalaine from a dead sleep to a rigid, wide-eyed sitting position with "What was that?" on her lips. Of course, Gen couldn't blame her given the Uyumaak difficulties the caravan had experienced and the threat of the Ilch that had haunted her throughout her life. Gen tried to calm her by telling her he'd seen no sign of Uyumaak, and he hadn't.

Worse than inexperience, however, was her conditioning. She tired easily and needed long rests before continuing. Through the Im'Tith, he could sense her cramped calves, aching feet, and burning lungs, and to spare her embarrassment he would stop before exhaustion forced her to admit she needed a rest. These rests provided ample time for conversation. The first day, she asked questions about the battle repeatedly, wringing her hands with worry. On the second day, she accepted that they would know nothing for some time and resigned herself to the task ahead.

Despite her concerns, the vibrant world around her gradually worked its enthralling magic upon her. Gen enjoyed her childlike fascination with every flower, plant, or bird they passed along the way, and he found her enthusiasm infectious. She had taken well to eating the plants, roots, nuts, and berries that Gen scavenged for their meals from the abundant flora around them. Gen expected the new regimen of food to sicken her as it did most of those new to the wild, but he could not see or feel any discomfort from her. If anything, his own stomach fared the worse.

Gen peered downriver as the Chalaine finished drinking from a still pool formed on the lee side of the immense granite rock they had camped under the evening before. The sun rose between the two walls of the canyon directly into his face, making it difficult to see for any great distance. As yet, the imposing walls and fallen rock had not forced them to cross the river, but from what he could tell the canyon narrowed ahead, and he feared their path would compel them to climb or swim.

"So what are you going to teach me today, Gen?" the Chalaine asked happily, coming to stand in front of him. "I could do without any more talk of how to survive bear attacks. I had the most awful dreams last night."

The Chalaine wanted to know everything about the outdoors and eagerly absorbed whatever he told her.

"I know. You talk in your sleep sometimes. Last night

was particularly bad," Gen commented as he kicked dirt over the smoldering fire.

"Was it?"

"Yes. I couldn't understand most of it, though I definitely heard you say, 'To your right, Gen! A bear on the trail!' Or maybe it was, 'Yes you're right Gen, I'll wear my veil!' Hard to tell with all the mumbling and drooling."

"What I really said," the Chalaine retorted, hands coming to her hips, "was, 'Shut up about the veil, Gen, or I'll bash your head in with a rock and push you in the river.'"

"No. It wasn't nearly that violent. Let's go." Gen walked forward, shouldering the makeshift pack.

The Chalaine took up her position just behind Gen in a reversal of their normal routine when within the castle. "The way you keep begging for me to put the veil back on is starting to make me think you find me hideous!"

Gen shook his head. "You know that isn't true. Chertanne will be livid beyond reason that I'm out here alone with you. I think his head will melt if he knows I've seen you unveiled. Not only that, he'll assume I did what he would do were he in my boots right now. I don't want him to think I would ever stoop to his kind of behavior."

"Gen, I've worn this veil my entire life. My *entire* life! You can hardly imagine how tired I am of seeing the world half obscured. I think I'm even more tired of being the Chalaine. Always mysterious. Always unapproachable. Always irresistible. Finally, I find a man I can look at with my naked face without fear of ravishment, a man who talks with me as he would any other person, a man who isn't afraid of me or mad with desire for me. If I weren't stranded in some canyon miles from home, I'd almost feel like a normal woman! Let me enjoy this while I can."

"I'm sorry, Alumira," Gen apologized. She demanded he use the name he had invented for her. "I suppose I just want us both to be above any accusation. I couldn't bear to have your reputation blemished falsely. Or mine, for that matter . . . for Fenna's sake."

"I understand that, but stop a moment." She grasped him by the arm and pulled him around. "Look at me." Gen did so reluctantly. "Let me tell you something. Chertanne will think you've been out here philandering with me, veil or no veil. Chertanne will also not think better of you for not having done so. I think the fact that you wouldn't touch me is completely beyond his understanding. Fenna and my mother will believe anything I tell them. Ethris and the Pontiff will know the truth regardless of what anyone says. As for anyone else, I care little."

"Provided any of them survived the Uyumaak attack," Gen added darkly, avoiding addressing the Chalaine's point.

"Yes. I have faith they did. Prophecy will be fulfilled, and at least Chertanne must have survived. God's will must be done."

"I'm not so sure," Gen replied, turning away and leading out again.

"How do you mean?"

"There is an elven saying: 'For prophecy there must be two, a god to will and a servant to do.' God's will, I think, is not enough. Many lesser prophecies have failed because of the folly of men. What's to say this one, despite its importance and grandeur, won't?"

The Chalaine considered his words quietly for a long time. Gen chanced a glance at her, finding her deep in thought. "What would we do?" she finally asked. "What would we do if we came to Elde Luri Mora and found that everyone else was dead? What would happen?"

"If the prophecy be true, then Mikkik would have won, and he will do with Ki'Hal whatever he pleases."

"No, I mean what would *we* do? Say we arrive in a few days and no one ever comes. What do we do then?"

"I don't know," Gen replied. "We could try to return to Rhugoth with the bad news, though the Uyumaak would likely slaughter us on the way back. I'm not sure we'll get back, even if half the soldiers we came with managed to survive. If we wanted to live longer, we could stay at Elde Luri Mora, since Mikkik's creatures can't abide it. I'm sure Mikkik would change that at some point, but at least for a while we could sit in relative peace and watch the world fall."

"I still think God will provide. I may be naive, but were Chertanne or I to fail, Eldaloth would send others to take our place."

"You could hope that." Gen studied the canyon ahead; the narrow gap awaited only a mile away. "If I were sure of it, I would hand Chertanne over to the Uyumaak at the next opportunity. Maybe the Blessed One's replacement would be a bit more blessed. I must admit to you that I have grave doubts about Chertanne. I know he can father a child, but wherever Mikkik is, I doubt he's spending a lot of time chewing his fingernails over your fiancé."

"My mother said much the same thing a couple of nights before Regent Ogbith was killed. She didn't say it, but I think she's reconsidering handing Rhugoth over to Chertanne."

"That would mean war. Torbrand would come for Rhugoth just as he did for Tolnor. He thirsts for a fight and will use any excuse to get into one."

"He wouldn't find Rhugoth quite so easy a plum to pick, no offense to your homeland. We are strong and a Portal away from Aughmere."

"That is true," Gen conceded, "but I wouldn't worry about it. I doubt your mother would let it come to war. She loves you more than anything, and if she's willing to hand you over to Chertanne for the prophecy's sake, then I doubt she would hold Rhugoth in higher regard."

"What choice do any of us have?" the Chalaine returned glumly.

They walked in silence over a gravelly part of the river

bed. The Chalaine bit her lip the entire time as if struggling with something. Finally, she exhaled roughly.

"I must confess something to you, Gen. I have never told anyone else, and I feel I should tell you now. I have committed a terrible sin."

He stopped and turned toward her, concerned at her tone. "You shouldn't feel obligated to tell me anything you don't want to, Chalaine."

"I know, Gen, but I have borne this alone for long enough. Just listen, please. In the spring of last year, Dason and I were walking alone in the hallway of my chambers and he asked me to kiss him—on the lips—as a sign of my regard. I did."

The Chalaine waited, avoiding his eyes.

"And . . . ?"

"That is all."

"Did he see you unveiled, then?" Gen asked.

"No. It was through the veil."

Gen burst out laughing, and the Chalaine's head snapped up in surprise. "My goodness, Chalaine," he chuckled. "The way you were carrying on I thought you had done something truly awful!"

"It is horrible!" the Chalaine fumed, annoyed by his untroubled reaction. "I was unfaithful to my calling! It was a grievous mistake, and I have suffered greatly for it."

"I am sorry," Gen apologized. "I did not mean to make light."

"You should reproach me, Gen! I couldn't tell my mother or the Pontiff—to whom I should have confessed—because I was so scared of what they would say or do."

"Then why tell me?"

"I don't know. I suppose I knew you wouldn't judge me so harshly, though I certainly didn't expect you to find my deeply hidden secret so ridiculous."

"Chalaine, you try harder than anyone I know to do

what is right. Indiscretions that skip off of the consciences of most strike deep into yours. The standard of perfection you set for yourself is so high that an unhallowed knave such as myself can only think it ridiculous when you flog yourself for transgressions I find trivial."

She folded her arms. "I am supposed to be holy, Gen. I don't feel it."

"And how does *holy* feel?"

"I don't know. More confident, more powerful, more *good*."

"I cannot tell you how to feel," Gen consoled her, placing his hands on her shoulders and holding her eyes with his. "But I will tell you this: *I* have every confidence in you. You have been stalwart in your duty and courageous in difficult circumstances. You should be proud of what you have done."

"Thank you," she said, smiling softly at her Protector. He dropped his hands and continued forward as she followed after. "You are very forgiving."

"Not really. I'm right in the gutter of depravity with you. I kissed your mother a few days ago, and it wasn't one of those pathetic 'show me your regard for me' kinds of kisses, either."

The Chalaine stopped in her tracks, face shocked but eyes alight with mirth.

"You are a knave!"

"Careful now! Don't add hypocrisy to your list of sins!"

"She initiated it," the Chalaine said, "didn't she?"

"Yes."

"What happened?"

"I don't want to talk about it," said Gen.

"Oh, no you don't! Hey! Slow down! What did Fenna say?"

"Do you really think I would tell Fenna about it?"

They marched on in silence after the Chalaine failed to pry any more information from her selectively tight-lipped

Protector. They passed into the shadow of the canyon as it jogged south and blocked the early morning sun. Birds of prey floated high overhead to catch warmer air, and the Chalaine shivered in the shade. Gen realized the bend in the canyon gave it the appearance of narrowing from a distance when, upon arriving, he found it widened. Unfortunately, the river shore switched sides as the water eroded away the other canyon wall for some distance. The side they traversed ended in a stand of stunted pine behind which rose an impassable gray cliff.

"Did I mention," Gen said, "that there's a real possibility we could be trapped in this canyon forever? I hadn't realized it before, but I haven't seen any signs of big animals, and that means they haven't been able to get down here. And that could mean we'll run into a section of the river too difficult to pass."

"What would we do?"

"At that point we would build a cabin and really hope we liked roots, leaves, and each other. This is a good spot for a little hut, don't you think?"

Gen turned to see what effect his quip had on his companion and wished he hadn't. Her smile and the affection in her eyes set his heart to pounding.

"What is it?" she asked, noticing a change in his mood.

"You're too beautiful for your own good. Seeing a face like yours would make a man think all his dumb jokes were funny."

"It wasn't a dumb joke."

"Yes it was."

"Do you think I'm just flattering you?"

"No, you're just . . . inexperienced . . . in matters of humor."

Her hands found their way back to her hips. "Oh, is that so?"

"Sure," said Gen. "The only men you've known have been soldiers. Soldiers are notorious for their unrefined senses of humor. They think getting drunk and falling off a horse is hilarious. So how could you have learned?"

"So you've thought about this quite a bit, then?"

Gen shrugged. "Now, don't get so upset. It's not your fault that you wouldn't know humor even if it were as close to you as, say, that snake is to your boot."

The Chalaine yelped and jumped backward, eyes darting around on the ground. Gen smiled, and the Chalaine picked up a rock the size of her fist and threw it at him. Gen narrowly dodged it.

"Hey!" he protested, laughing. "You could have hurt me!"

"I would have healed you later. Much later. But if the scholar of humor is quite done with his adolescent little tricks, perhaps he could humor up a way across the river?"

She crossed her arms, but the smile in her eyes betrayed the angry look on her face.

Gen bowed low. "My apologies, Milady. To get to the other side I'll need to find some trees taller than these here. I remember some behind us a ways. If we can get two that are long enough, we should have a wide enough bridge to walk across."

The rest of the morning, Gen labored to find, cut down, and clear two straight pine trees. Aldradan Mikmir's sword made easy work of the cutting, but dragging them and hoisting them upright so he could topple them over the river exhausted him. As the second one fell across the rushing water, his vision blurred and he stumbled; four days without sleep were finally taking their toll.

"Are you all right, Gen?" the Chalaine asked, grabbing his arm.

"I just need to rest for a moment."

"You need to sleep," she scolded. "You haven't slept at all, have you?"

"I need to watch. No telling what is out here. I'll be fine till we get out of this canyon. I'll sleep when someone I trust is watching after you."

"You'll sleep tonight. You said yourself that nothing is down here."

He looked her in the eye. "I will not."

"You will. You'll be no good to me if you can't walk or see straight."

"You can't make me sleep."

The Chalaine grinned in a knowing way and said nothing. Gen wondered what it meant. After resting for several minutes and splashing cold river water on his face, he felt better. Holding the Chalaine's hand, she and Gen walked slowly over the swift, noisy water. The thin tree trunks bent as they crossed the middle, and the Chalaine nearly lost her balance, but with a steadying hand from Gen and a quick scamper at the end, they jumped to the ground safe and dry.

"I'll make a Maewen of you yet," Gen commented as they negotiated a rocky decline dotted with shrubs and loose gravel.

"I'm sure you would like to have her around instead of me by now, though Fenna would no doubt be furious if you spent this much time alone with Maewen."

"She seems quite jealous of Maewen. I don't see why."

The Chalaine laughed. "Oh, don't be so coy. You know why."

"Enlighten me."

"Maewen's beautiful. She's a warrior. Whether you like to admit it or not, you and Maewen have a lot in common. You're both brave to the point of being reckless—or reckless to the point of seeming brave—and neither one of you seems to do well with authority. You both speak languages almost no one else understands. Both of you think you're right all the time."

"We do not," Gen disagreed.

"Yes you do! Name one time since you came into my service that you've honestly said 'I was wrong' to anyone."

"Name one time when I have been wrong."

"All right. When you said you weren't sleeping tonight, you were wrong. When you and Maewen attacked an entire Uyumaak company by yourselves, that was wrong—and stupid. When you were injured in said attack and didn't accept Fenna's offer to help you, instead choosing to let Maewen assist you, that was wrong, so very wrong."

"I think you've strayed from the main point. Fenna. Maewen. Jealousy."

"Yes, well, a minor digression was in order to prove you, well, wrong. Anyway, the point is that Maewen intimidates Fenna. Fenna can't see how you could find her more interesting than Maewen. It might not bother Fenna that much if it didn't seem like Maewen had feelings for you."

Gen shot her a disbelieving look. "Maewen does not have feelings for me, for pity's sake. I don't think she has feelings for anyone, especially anyone human."

"Hmm. I think you may be missing something. Just a few nights ago my mother said to me, 'I don't think I've ever seen Maewen smile, but Gen seems to have the knack of bringing one to her face.' Fenna said much the same."

"I thought we just established that I was the 'scholar of humor' a little while back. Bringing a smile to Maewen's face is only further evidence of my skill."

"There you go again," the Chalaine said, "joking around to avoid facing something you find uncomfortable."

"What do you want me to say? That I agree with you? Well, I don't. I think Fenna's jealousy of Maewen is unfounded. Maewen and I have a . . . professional understanding . . . because we are both charged with keeping the caravan safe. That is all. If Maewen were a big, ugly woodsman with a mustache that smelled like week-old boar meat, then nobody would care whether I made him smile or not. This is all just because Maewen is a beautiful woman."

"Nice reasoning, Gen," the Chalaine returned

sarcastically. "Women don't typically see big, ugly, stinky woodsmen with boar-greased facial hair as competition for men they're trying to woo. Though I suppose your attraction to uncouth woodsmen would explain why you find it so easy to resist me unveiled."

Gen couldn't help but chuckle. "I will concede that I can see why Fenna sees Maewen as competition, but what I am saying is that she isn't." He supposed it wouldn't be a good idea to bring up Maewen's offer to have Gen run away with her after Chertanne dismissed him.

"Fair enough, but just remember what you learned today about being wrong so that it won't come as such a shock next time."

⁂

Drying sweat made the Chalaine's skin feel sticky as the day waned. The hike stretched her endurance to the limit. The river descended through the canyon by way of washing over a number of small drops that forced them to scrabble down steep rock faces, often wet, to get to the next walkable shore. In several difficult places, Gen took time to clear brush to ease her passage. In the back of her mind the Chalaine knew that if the she sprained her ankle or broke her leg, the journey would take weeks.

When they stopped for a rest in the late afternoon, she watched Gen fight to keep from dozing, splashing water on his face and stretching his muscles to resist the temptation to sit and close his eyes for a few moments. Only the river droned on beside them. Even the birds didn't sing, and they hadn't spoken for nearly an hour. A tangible weariness, not of body, but of soul, wore upon her, though she couldn't explain why.

After eating more roots and leaves, they started off again. The shore took them over a long boulder fall requiring them to jump from rock to rock to go forward, and by the time they came to the end of it, the shadows in the canyon had deepened at the approach of evening. Just ahead was another waterfall to traverse, and they went forward to see how difficult it would prove and whether or not they would attempt it before night fell.

To her delight, the waterfall, some twenty feet high, fell into a wide pool surrounded by cedar and pine, and on the other side they could make out a series of small gazebos, crafted from a pale stone lining the water. These were set upon an expansive flooring of interlocking stone so tightly fit that roots and weeds found no entrance into the cracks. A short distance beyond the pool, the river fell through a deep fall in a tight gap of the canyon. In the failing light, they could make out the entryway to an underground cave bored out of the canyon itself, descending into darkness.

"It is beautiful!" the Chalaine remarked, eyes wide. "Should we try to reach it before dark?"

"No," Gen answered. "This is ancient work, though it has weathered unusually well. Almost anything might be in that cave. Bears, Uyumaak, or worse. We'll stay up here tonight. If there is anything inside there, it won't be able to get to us as easily up here. Let's find a place to light a fire and spend the night."

They worked together to drag driftwood from the river's edge to a shallow overhang in the cliff near the waterfall. Exhausted, the Chalaine took one last look at the blue pool below her as Gen worked to light the fire, spinning a stick between his hands to ignite fragile tinder. Her muscles and feet hurt, and whether Gen liked to admit it or not, his every move betrayed his weariness. At length, the flames flickered happily, their welcome heat comforting sore muscles. She waited for him sit down before returning to his side.

While he searched the pack for the roots they had gathered earlier, she inspected his arms. The day's rough hike had ripped his shirt in several places, revealing numerous scrapes, bruises and cuts. He took no notice of them, but she reached out to heal him.

"Save your strength," Gen said. "These are nothing."

"Then hush. Little strength will be required." She touched his arm, but before she could close her eyes and expend any effort, the wounds healed instantly. In surprise, she withdrew her hand and trembled. Frantically, she turned away, digging out her veil from her pocket and securing it over her head. Silently, she shed tears of joy and bitterness.

Gen turned and handed her a root. "Thank you for the healing, though it was unnecessary. And you're wearing your veil! You realized I was right about that after all, then?"

The Chalaine nodded and chewed on the root slowly to gain time to compose her voice. "The gazebos . . . I thought . . . well, we might find someone or something here. Perhaps Maewen knows this place and how to get here."

"Good thinking," Gen complimented her. "Are you hurt anywhere? I did find some herbs that might help with minor cuts a couple of days ago."

"I am well."

"I have a hard time believing you got through the whole day without so much as a scratch. But," he said, examining at the flesh on her arms exposed by ripped sleeves, "I can't find a mark on you! You're better in the wild than I thought."

"I'm afraid not," the Chalaine returned, trying to keep the heartache out of her voice. "Two Chalaines ago, we acquired the gift of immediately healing superficial wounds that might mar our physical appearance. As soon as I get a scrape, a blister, or sunburn, it is healed."

"Very handy," Gen commented, running his hands through his hair to dislodge small bits of detritus it had collected during the day. "I could have used that during my training with Torbrand. All my scars must have seemed horrifying to you when you first met me. Was the first time you saw me in the Great Hall, or did you see me at the Trials with your Walls? I was quite a sight then. Just ask Fenna."

The Chalaine lifted her veil. "Gen?"

"Yes?"

"It's time for you to sleep now." The Chalaine leaned close to him, and running through the incantation in her mind, breathed softly on his startled face. At once his eyes closed and he collapsed. She caught him as he fell. Leaning back against the canyon wall, she cradled him. She knew he loved her now. She had wanted his love so badly, and now that she had it, she cursed herself for letting it happen. Shadan Khairn had wounded his body and she his heart. She had tortured him just as cruelly as his swordmaster, and she had yet to deliver the most painful cut of all—to undo it all.

She removed her veil and wept quietly. Like her mother, she longed for Gen's love while feeling guilty for even wanting it. She suspected his attachment at the waterfall when she healed him without knowing, and now that she had confirmation, the guilt crushed her. Not only had she hurt him, but in her heart she was unfaithful to Chertanne, risking ruination of the prophecy and the world.

I have to make things right again!

She rehearsed the lies she would say and wondered if she had the strength or skill to convince him that any of them were true. The nights spent talking with him from the carriage, the teasing, the arguments, the irreverent jokes about Chertanne, the shared joys and pains of their trail through the canyon ranked as the dearest memories of her life. She wanted his touch, his kiss, his regard, and most of all, his heart. He was the only person in Ki'Hal she felt she could be totally honest and open with, including her mother. Somehow, he understood her completely—weaknesses, follies, and sins—and loved her anyway without expecting anything in return. She desperately wanted to give him everything.

"Being a Chalaine means forgetting yourself," she whispered, remembering one of Prelate Obelard's sermons from when she was young. "While you will be crowned with glory, honor, and the gratitude of all peoples when your work is complete, your life must be your duty, your heart single, and your thoughts ever upon the Ha'Ulrich. Distraction from your purpose is the destruction of the world."

Never had that world seemed so distant or her heart so filled with want. She sat and rubbed her Protector's face, tracing his scars with her finger, his body a parchment she wished to imprint herself upon. Chertanne would never fill her heart or win her regard. Gen had done both. Gen's wisdom and deep devotion made Dason's lively conversation and flirtation seem stupid. That she couldn't love and reward the man who had earned it, that she couldn't kiss him as her mother had, that she would bind herself to Chertanne and not to Gen tore at her heart.

Full dark came. A queasy sickness knotted her stomach and weakened her limbs. A soothing breeze arrived with the night, but it, combined with the steady rumble of the small falls nearby, could not coax her weary body to sleep. As she stared into the utter blackness beyond the firelight, fireflies emerged from cracks in the canyon walls, the first fireflies she had ever seen. She'd read of them before, but seeing them flit about, tiny lanterns in the gloom, brought some comfort to her tormented mind.

At first only a few danced above the falls, their numbers gradually swelling until a great cloud of them cast a yellow glow over where she sat. Then, as if at some prearranged signal, they dove as one over the edge of the falls and into the cove. So great were their numbers that she could still see faintly by their light. Laying Gen's head gently on the ground, she rose and hiked to the edge of the falls. What she saw took her breath away.

Many of the fireflies danced over the pool, their reflection in the water doubling their numbers and their light. Small swarms of others had flown into each of the delicate gazebos, flying in loose spheres inside them, illuminating the cove. In her mind's eye the Chalaine imagined elven lords and ladies, graceful, noble, and festive, dancing and talking together underneath the stars in the soft glow. The waterfall's noise seemed more like music now, and she thought she heard the song of birds in the branches of the trees below. She watched, entranced, until weariness overtook her and she turned back. She thought of waking Gen to show him but couldn't bring herself to face him yet.

After replenishing the fire, she knelt by her Protector and unbuckled his sword belt. She laid the sword and scabbard across his chest as he would have done, and instinctively he wrapped his arms around them. In the weak light, he looked positioned for death.

The Chalaine picked up his hand and held it to her heart. "Please forgive me," she begged. "Happiness with Fenna is still yours to have. Someday, when we are old, I will find you and tell you the truth."

Placing his hand back on his sword, she curled up next to him. Laying her head on his shoulder, she fell into a deep sleep, not caring if danger found them.

The familiar dream came again and she ran. She knew the faces, now, and the names.

Chapter 44 - The Weeper

She awoke late the next morning, the sun already high enough to burn away the canyon mist. Reluctantly she pulled herself away from Gen's warmth and sat up. All at once she felt sick, not daring to look at the peaceful face of her Protector for fear doing so would crumble her resolve. After rinsing her own face in the chill water of the river, she walked along the bank preparing herself emotionally for the loneliness she had committed to pull on top of herself.

Thinking of Fenna smiling at Gen's return helped steel her, and at last she crossed back to where he slept. Incanting softly, she put her face close to his and inhaled deeply, stepping back as his eyes fluttered and opened. He jumped to his feet in confusion, staring at the sky for several moments before settling his gaze upon the Chalaine. She braced herself.

Gen regarded her, face troubled. "What have you done?"

"I made you sleep, as I said I would," she answered coldly. "You needed it, so don't bother offering a protest. Let's eat and leave." Her tone took him back, and expectedly, he controlled his face into a stony mask of indifference.

"I don't suppose you stayed awake to watch?" he inquired, voice empty.

"Does it matter? We're alive. But you've been watching, haven't you?" She was thankful for his irritable mood. It simplified what she needed to do.

"What?" he returned flatly.

"I'll show you what I mean. Give me your knife." The perplexity only showed in his eyes as he removed his knife from his boot and handed it to her. "Now hold out your arm."

As he did, the Chalaine slashed it deeply, blood dripping onto the stones. He didn't blink or even grimace at the wound, a feat that still unnerved her.

She removed her veil. "Now look at me."

As he did, she returned the gaze unblinkingly while his blood painted the stones at their feet. How she wanted to see his eyes smile again, to see them soften with kindness or flare with delight when he saw her. Ruthlessly she shoved down her want and put forth her hand and touched his skin. The flaps of the wound knit together instantly.

"What was that supposed to prove?" he questioned. "We both know you are a powerful healer."

"I didn't try to heal you, Gen; you just healed. Remember when you told me that I'd healed you in the carriage and I had no memory of doing so? That's because I did nothing to heal you. If I touch you, you are healed."

"Interesting. What does it have to do with me watching you, and why does it anger you?"

The Chalaine replaced her veil and swallowed hard. "You know the prophecy well. Do you remember the part about the Chalaine and the Ha'Ulrich walking hand in hand?"

"Yes."

"Recite it, then."

And upon the field of death they shall walk,

Hand in hand.
And about them the fire of war shall burn,
And about them the arrows fall,
And around them the blades cut,
And around them demons rage.

But he bears no burn, no wound.
From his heart to her hand is love,
From her heart to his hand is healing,
Without will, without spell,
Without sacrifice.
Hand in hand. Strength for strength.

"Stop." She waited as he thought. "From the earliest Chalaine to me, woman to woman, was passed the mystery, Gen. He that loves the Chalaine suffers no wound if he stands with our touch. Hand in hand I am to walk onto the field of death with the Ha'Ulrich, and in my hand will be the healing that will keep him alive when the armies of Mikkik wage war upon us."

"Then Chertanne is a dead man. He loves you not."

"But you love me, Gen." It took every ounce of effort to sound disappointed. "I couldn't heal you like that if you didn't."

"So? I think everyone who knows you well loves you."

She could sense the turmoil building in his mind, his confusion. "No, Gen, not in the way you do. I cannot heal Jaron, Dason, or anyone as I can heal you now. You love me as a man loves a woman. You've kept watch over me, desiring me. I *thought* you wanted me to wear the veil for your reputation's sake. Now I realize that you just felt guilty for loving me, felt guilty for looking at me like a man looks on a woman he wants."

His face flamed red with shame and embarrassment, and the Chalaine felt guilty and sick for dredging up an emotion in him he could not suppress. But however cruel, she could leave no thread uncut.

"And you should feel ashamed. What of poor Fenna? She's the best friend I have, and you've betrayed her and fallen in love with another woman. At least Chertanne doesn't try to pretend he loves me. Do you think Fenna will believe it when you pretend to love her?

"I'm saddened that you could do this to her. I suppose I should have known. The same thing was happening with Dason before you replaced him. Dason was falling in love with me, and when I am being truthful with myself, I must admit I loved him, too. He is a handsome, noble man. But if I could not love him or let him love me, I certainly would not love you. Not that way. You've been a good, loyal friend, Gen, but you've let your discipline slip and in doing so have hurt Fenna and made me doubt your heart, which I once thought to be true."

He was broken, face ashen. "Please," Gen pleaded. "I apologize for my folly. I will be true. And you must believe, Alumira, that I would have never done anything to dissuade you from your marriage and your duty. I swear it. I know you couldn't love me in that way. I would never have asked you to love me in return. If it weren't for the healing, you would have never known. I'm not sure I would have known either. It's been so natural and gradual, so easy. Just let me do my duty. That's all I ask. I never wanted to hurt you."

The Chalaine couldn't speak for several moments, grateful the veil hid the emotion on her face. "I will do as you ask unless I see that what you say isn't true. I will help you, though. You must never call me Alumira again or act familiar with me as you have done. Since I know you feel more than friendship for me, those things are no longer appropriate."

"Yes, Milady" he said with a slight bow. "I am truly sorry and I thank you for your forbearance and mercy. I will not fail you."

"Then lead on."

The Chalaine observed Gen closely as he surveyed their situation, trying to fathom what he felt, but he returned his face to the cold, meaningless demeanor he had once worn without reprieve. As they clambered their way down the side of the waterfall and searched for a place to cross the pool, his silence and his reluctance to even take her hand to help her in difficult places let her know she hit the mark she intended. Thinking on how hypocritical, false, and undeserved her words had been set her self-loathing to roiling. By nature, she sought to heal others, and she worked hard to convince herself that she was about that business for Fenna and for him.

At the far end of the pool a slender bridge spanned the river, the roar of the waterfall to their right drowning out every other noise. The quick-moving water converged at a narrow notch in the canyon wall, the constriction choking and foaming the water as it rushed over to plummet hundreds of feet to a narrow rapid below. A cool mist added to the morning chill, rising into the air from the troubled water and dampening their clothes as they traversed the delicate structure.

The bridge terminated in a narrow path that led by the gazebos they had spotted the day before, each beautiful and unique, carved with figures of elves, beasts, and intricate symbols the Chalaine had never heard of or seen. Gen passed them all without comment, heading directly for the cave entrance as if nothing else existed. Every step toward that black hole brought a deeper sadness into the Chalaine's heart. There was no evidence of the birds that had sung so loudly the night before, and what the light of the fireflies had transformed into something so lively now lay dead, dreary, and lifeless.

"We'll need to find something to light our way once we enter the cave, Gen," the Chalaine advised.

He answered nothing but instead went to the entrance and stared into the darkness as if waiting for something. A faint, cool breeze blew out of the cave, smelling musty. A feeling, an almost palpable sadness, seeped from the entrance and discouraged entry. The cave was not really a cave but a finely carved hall still in perfect condition, if dusty.

"Gen?" she asked after a long pause. He raised a finger indicating for her to wait. She squinted into the dark, listening, when she discerned a small light coming toward them, followed by another, and then more. The fireflies. A clump of them hovered in a sphere ahead of them, casting a yellow glow to push back the darkness. As they walked forward into the gloomy hall, the fireflies stayed just ahead of them, providing ample light to travel by.

"You knew about them," the Chalaine commented, trying to force some conversation. "I saw them last night, lighting the water and the gazebos. It was beautiful. How did you know?"

"Just a memory, your Highness."

The Chalaine gritted her teeth at his lifeless tone. Each word was a corpse pulled from its grave.

The hallway sloped down for nearly a mile before leveling out and widening. The floor was made up of small square pieces of glazed marble set into patterns and shapes. Some she recognized as runes. Others were crafted into elaborate scenes of nature, people, and war. At long intervals, the right side of the hallway would open to the outside, revealing striking views of the river and the canyon. As much as she wanted to stop and look, she didn't dare ask Gen to delay. She knew what he would say. He pressed forward unheeding of anything around them, focused on getting out of the canyon and nothing else.

Again the hallway sloped down and into darkness, the natural light from the windows fading behind them. Alcoves carved into the hallway offered convenient places to stop, and after what the Chalaine thought had been an hour, she asked Gen to halt their march so she could rest.

He acquiesced, and she sat on a comfortable bench carved into the wall itself within a recessed arch. Rather than sit beside her, Gen stood at attention in front of her, face stony and cold in the weak light. The Chalaine half considered undoing what she'd done, confessing what she felt and accepting the blame for leading him on.

"We should go, Milady," Gen's voice startled her. "This place has an air of sadness to it, and we would do well to get out quickly."

"I feel it, too."

They walked more swiftly now, a sudden urgency spurring them on as an unnatural veil of melancholy enveloped them. The hallway, once flawless, started to reveal pale moss, cracks, and small pools of water. The Chalaine wrinkled her nose as the smell of must strengthened. The wind they felt earlier dissipated and died, the scrape and splash of their footfalls echoing longer and louder than they had before. The Chalaine edged closer to Gen. Deeper they walked, stepping in stagnant pools of grimy water and slipping on slick tiles.

A loud wail, tortured and long, froze them where they stood. The sphere of fireflies broke and fled, leaving them blind. The Chalaine reached out into pure blackness, reaching for Gen, but her hand found nothing. She stepped forward, feeling about her.

"Gen! Gen! Where are you?"

Something flapped past her head, and she shrieked, fear pricking her skin. She called for Gen with a softer voice, finding the wall to her right and feeling her way along it as she walked. Another moan, now closer, reverberated down the corridor, and she stopped, fearful of what she might find. Ahead of her she could make out a lightening in the gloom, and she made her way cautiously toward it.

The hallway turned abruptly to the right, and she spied a large room filled with sunlight. Voices, one powerful and strong, one hoarse and sad, argued with each other. She sneaked closer for a better look, moving slowly so as not to splash in the pools of water at her feet.

The room, dome-shaped and wide, rose some fifty feet into the air where a hole twice the width of a man had been chiseled, letting in the midday sunlight. The circle of light encompassed a raised pool of water surrounded by circular benches. In the center of the pool the Chalaine surmised a statue had once stood, but instead, a figure sat upon the broken pedestal. He sobbed, his face lowered.

At the edge of the pool, addressing him in an unfamiliar tongue, stood an imposing figure, cloaked to hide his features. Gen lay sprawled and unconscious on a bench nearby, and the Chalaine shrank back, fearing discovery.

"Go forward, Chalaine. You are not unexpected or unwelcome."

The Chalaine spun. The voice was that of a woman, sonorous and strangely accented. She could just make her out as she stepped forward into the light from behind her, and the Chalaine gasped, backing away from her into the room.

She stood at least eight feet tall and was regally built, silver hair falling about her shoulders. Her ears were upswept and her features strong and beautiful. She wore a brown cloak clasped about her waist with a silver belt fashioned with interlocking leaves. Underneath the cloak she wore a dress of forest green that set off the intense gray eyes, eyes that held no malice or treachery, but sadness and years of wisdom. The Chalaine stopped.

"Who are you?" she asked, failing to keep the trembling from her voice.

"Fear me not," she answered. "I am Sarina Kam, and I have longed for the day when I might meet you and see your face. I have longed to bring you before him," she indicated the figure sobbing upon the pedestal. "He has wept for long enough."

"What of Gen? The man protecting me?"

"He is asleep. Come. You will see that no harm has come to him." Sarina led the way forward, walking as a noblewoman would, straight, tall, and proud.

"Are you an elf?" the Chalaine chanced, sensing she was not.

"I am Millim Eri, an elf master and messenger for the Ulrich—the gods—though we have no liege that we choose to serve."

As Sarina approached the pool, the other cloaked figured removed his hood, revealing long white hair and a powerful face.

"This is Sore Kam," Sarina explained, "my brother. The one who weeps is Aldemar. He was once Mikkik Dun, those like us that served Mikkik."

"Why does he weep?" the Chalaine asked, finding it difficult to look anywhere but the floor.

"You will soon know. That is part of why we let you come here, why we protected you from his grief. Without our protection, you would be overcome, as Gen is, and never awake without our aid. Many we rescued from this place in the ancient times. You are the first to enter here in many, many years. But Mikkik's work is at hand. Our salvation from the dark God has come to us in human form. Salvation has come in you. Remove your veil, please."

The Chalaine didn't think to disagree or disobey and lifted it from her head. She saw something spark in Sore Kam's eyes, and he and Sarina stared at each other in silence for several moments before Sore turned his attention to Aldemar.

"Aldemar!" he ordered. "Lift up your eyes and behold the salvation of Ki'Hal. Look!" Aldemar did not stir and continued to cry. "Look!" Sore Kam thundered.

Reluctantly, Aldemar lifted his head, and the Chalaine took a step back as the tormented gaze fell upon her. Aldemar, like the others, was noble in features, but his face exuded sorrow and pain. Tears had stained his cheeks gray, and his eyes were red and ringed in shadow. At once she felt a crushing weight of spirit, a burden centuries old she could not bear. Sarina stepped to her side and grasped her shoulders, the weight easing at her touch.

Upon seeing her, Aldemar's eyes widened, and he glanced at Sarina and Sore in surprise before turning back, eyes settling on her.

"Show her, Aldemar. She needs to see."

Her vision wavered as Aldemar entered her mind. She could feel his pain, ancient and abiding, pressing upon her heart. In her mind's eye, a scene opened before her, and she felt as if Aldemar had spirited her away out of the room and out of time.

She flew over a green field on a clear evening, yellow wildflowers starting to close with the end of day. Overhead, all three moons, Myn, Duam, and Trys, waxed full and beautiful. She breathed in, her lungs filling with clean, cool air. The world was new, innocent, and wholesome in a way she had never felt before. While she couldn't say why, a sense of rightness pervaded everything, and she smiled in spite of herself. Here was peace and a reflection of a beloved creator, and finding happiness required nothing more than setting one foot before the other and reveling in the goodness that imbued the world. Every vista of mountain, tree, sky, and river exhilarated and soothed at once.

Just as the grandeur invited her to a bliss she longed for, the feeling gradually changed as the fields slid by. Curious and disappointed at the change, she lifted her eyes. A throng gathered in a small depression on the plain, their dark clothing offsetting a figure, brilliant and shining, in the midst of them. She flew closer and stopped, hovering above them.

"Behold the throng of Mikkik, glorious Ulrich of Ki'Hal!" Aldemar's voice quavered. *"Look, for there am I."* The

Chalaine found him in the congregation, understanding that these were Mikkik Dun, Millim Eri followers of Mikkik. Aldemar stood among them, eyes worshipfully regarding his God. The Chalaine studied the figure of her enemy, but she could barely perceive his shape, his brightness defeating mortal vision. In front of him he had built a crude altar from stones, and upon it lay a sword, simple in design, such as a common soldier might use.

"It is the first weapon made upon Ki'Hal, though what you will see is not the first time it was used. It is filled with power, for Mikkik discovered a great secret."

The Chalaine wanted to inquire into what Aldemar meant, but below her Mikkik's voice raised in a chant, and the Chalaine recognized the sound and tone of those words, the same language spoken by the demon on the night of her betrothal. Though she understood that what she saw was a memory that happened hundreds of years before her birth, she felt the power of the incantation as Aldemar had, and she trembled. Each word felt of hatred, pride, ambition, and greed.

Mikkik stopped his ritual briefly, barking at the Mikkik Dun around him with one harsh word. At his command, they withdrew knives from their dark robes and cut their wrists, spilling their golden blood onto the waving grass.

The Chalaine felt weak as one by one they slumped to the ground, all but one, who stood facing his master with doubt on his face: Aldemar. Mikkik ignored him, grasping the sword and plunging it into the soil. He incanted again, and in a circle around him, the grass and flowers died, withering black and disintegrating into dust. The blood and bodies of the Mikkik Dun followed, and with each passing moment, Mikkik and his sword increased in luminescence and power until the Chalaine could hardly stand to look upon the scene.

"Prepare yourself, child," Aldemar warned, voice laying open his agony, "What comes now is a crime such as

Ki'Hal has never known. But you must see. You must know why."

The Chalaine felt Eldaloth before she saw him descend from the sky like a burning white star. His presence was warm and electrifying, joyful and perfect. It was he that created the beauty around her, for he was beauty, and all creation reflected his heart and connected to his soul. He outshone even Mikkik, and she could scarcely lift her eyes to the luminance.

Eldaloth thundered angrily at Mikkik in a language she could not understand. Mikkik replied by raising the sword and striking Eldaloth with it. Eldaloth yelled in agony and fell backward, his blood falling on the dead grass.

Immediately, the aura around Mikkik and the sword died and his face registered shock. Stripped of his brilliance, Mikkik shared much in appearance with the Mikkik Dun. He was beautiful and strong in features, powerful in build, and fierce of countenance. Upswept ears held back long flowing golden hair, and on either side of a sharp nose, silver-gray eyes burned with power. The sword he held in his hand turned clear where Eldaloth's blood ran along it.

A reverberation filled the air, and Eldaloth died. The brightness faded and nothing evidenced that the God had even been there, save that the ground, too, had turned to a clear stone where his blood had spilled. Only Aldemar and Mikkik remained. The feeling of rightness on Ki'Hal that had thrilled her had perished with Eldaloth, and she ached for its return as a child seeks the arms of its mother.

The Chalaine found herself crying with Aldemar. Mikkik slaughtered perfect beauty, perfect peace, and perfect goodness before her. Not one Churchman she had ever met could understand. They might preach paradise, but how could they feel its loss when all they had were vague notions and weak words to describe the abiding peace and the enduring rightness of everything that Mikkik annihilated along with their creator? For the first time, she understood her own importance. If the being to be fathered within her could indeed bring a return of that world of natural joy, then every sacrifice she must make, every indignity she would suffer, and every love she had to forsake would be of little consequence.

Below her in the clearing, Aldemar sunk to his knees and wept, and nature wept with him. Clouds gathered, the ground shook, and even the plants drooped and wilted. Mikkik gaped at the sword and examined himself, perhaps surprised at his loss of glory. A violent, wrenching crack split the ground in two at the point where Eldaloth had fallen, the earth collapsing into a deep gorge. Mikkik and Aldemar fell inside, and the vision faded.

The Chalaine wiped her eyes as the room came into focus. Aldemar smiled sadly at her, face and shoulders relieved of their burdens. Sore and Sarina stood behind her, watching Aldemar and witnessing the fulfillment of something they had worked on for years uncounted.

"You do not understand it all, Chalaine," Aldemar rasped. "You know my folly, but not the folly and curse of my people, a burden we yet bear and will yet atone for. But understand that it is your destiny to undo one part of what was done that day, though perhaps not in a way you will understand."

Aldemar turned his gaze to Sore and Sarina, bowing to them and speaking to them in their own tongue, though the Chalaine could discern the gratitude in Aldemar's voice.

Sarina approached. "Chalaine, we thank you for this service. We have long grieved for Aldemar and his sadness, for while he did stand and watch Eldaloth die, he had, at least, the courage and the wisdom to disobey his master when the call came. He was Mikkik Dun, but now he is our brother and our ally. For your service, Chalaine, we would give you a gift, if you would receive it." Sarina removed a small stone of molten glass from her cloak and extended it to the Chalaine. "Take it."

The Chalaine carefully lifted and examined the stone, eyes widening at a flickering light within it. "I thank you, but what is it for? What am I to do with it?"

"It concerns the second gift we will give you. Tell me, if you could kill the Ilch, would you do it?"

"Yes, of course!" the Chalaine answered without hesitation.

"That is our gift. That stone is his *animon*, his life," Sarina said. "He lies there by the fountain unconscious. You can slay him without fear. Just cast the stone to the ground and it will break like glass and finish him."

The Chalaine looked toward the fountain, seeing only Gen upon the ground. "Where is the Ilch?" she asked.

"He is there," Sarina indicated, pointing toward Gen's body. "*He* is the Ilch. Kill him and rid yourself of your enemy and your fear."

The Chalaine trembled, disbelief furrowing her brow. "He is not the Ilch!" she objected. She knew he was an orphan. She knew he was near the same age as she and Chertanne. "It's impossible! He's protected me. Almost died for me. He . . . he loves me. He cannot be the Ilch! He is one of the most noble and decent people I have ever met!"

Sarina took her hand, leading her to where Gen lay breathing shallowly. Sore Kam removed the boot from Gen's scarred left foot. "We burned his foot to obscure the mark."

Sore placed his hand on the instep of Gen's left foot and after several moments the scars faded, leaving in their place a perfect circle—the unveiled moon of Trys.

The Chalaine sat hard upon the stone bench behind her, mind reeling. *It cannot be!* "Why did you do this? What have you done?"

"We have deprived Mikkik of his tool," Sarina answered. "We have weakened Mikkik and strengthened your cause. We took Gen from the caretaker Mikkik chose for him. He was but a child, uncorrupted and innocent. We did not expect that he would ever come to your personal service, but we hoped he would be of some use to you and the world, for he will be powerful one day.

"We wanted to keep him secluded until Trys was unveiled, at which point we were to teach him or destroy him if he refused. But other forces have shifted our plans. He has grown to fame and importance and has served you well, for which we are gratified. But, Chalaine, we give him to you to do with as you please. He was to be your enemy. You can kill him or spare him at your whim."

"How could I kill him?" the Chalaine groaned, head pounding and stomach clenching. "How could I murder him after everything he's done? Who am I to decide and who are you that you can give him and take him as you please?"

Sarina frowned. "The prophecy says he will rend you unless he is killed first. I give you the chance to turn the prophecy to your favor. He is Mikkik's creature. Can you live in peace knowing he is alive and watching over you while you sleep?"

The Chalaine shook her head, tears coming freely now. "He could never hurt me!"

"You care for him?" Sarina asked.

"Yes," the Chalaine answered softly. Sarina's face darkened, and she and her brother shared a meaningful look.

"Then you will not kill him," Sarina stated. "Take comfort, dear. It seems my brother and I have done our work too well. Keep his *animon* so that you may protect yourself from him if you need to, but guard it well. Will you still walk with him? We can keep him here if you wish."

"I want him with me," the Chalaine declared resolutely, a sudden understanding coming to her. "I have no need to kill the Ilch. You have done it for me. He is Gen, my Protector. He has done more in my service than any other man, and if there ever came a day when he would feel to destroy me, then I doubt I would have much reason to live."

Sore and Sarina stared at her for many moments, but their confident, noble demeanor had changed to one of doubt and even a little fear. Aldemar, who watched silently, spoke words in the tongue of the Millim Eri, and Sore and Sarina nodded their agreement.

"What did you say?" she asked, annoyed that they were hiding things from her.

"I apologize, Chalaine," Aldemar soothed. "I will simply say that our people have brought trouble to Ki'Hal by meddling before."

"That you care for this man troubles us," Sore confessed. "For if you care for Gen, can you still love the Ha'Ulrich? Would he love you?"

The Chalaine's face scrunched with displeasure. "Have you meddled so much and yet know nothing of Chertanne?" she answered, feeling upset and ill-used. "It is beyond reason to think anyone as indecent as he is could love anyone other than himself, or that anyone decent could ever love anyone like him."

Sarina frowned. "We have known of his character, and it grieves us. He was hidden away from our watch and our influence until recently. We have hoped, however, that hardship would turn him from his selfishness and set him on the path of his duty. Much depends on him."

"Yes, much. I, too, could hope he would change, but I cannot see that he will. How shall we win on the field that day if Chertanne remains as he is, weak and selfish?"

"You are the Healer," Sarina offered. "Perhaps your greatest challenge will be to work your arts on a diseased soul."

"I have no power over men's souls to heal or help them," the Chalaine argued. "And time is short to change such a wayward heart. I think your meddling will come to naught. It would have been better for Gen to have killed me than for Chertanne and I to march headlong into failure. What am I to do?"

Aldemar stepped forward and placed his hands on her shoulders, locking her gaze to his. "Your Child must be born. There is hope there, no matter how despicable Chertanne may be to you now."

Despair flooded the Chalaine's heart. "Then lend me strength to do what I must, if it is in your power to give it!"

"I can only give you this," Aldemar whispered. "Here is wisdom: never do in duty's name what cannot be done in love. If you but obey this one thing, then nothing more is required of you to do your part. It is what Eldaloth taught. It is all that he would have you do. Remember it well."

Aldemar turned to his companions. "Sore, take Gen, and I shall convey the Chalaine."

Before the Chalaine could ask one of a hundred questions, Aldemar flourished his robe around her, and she remembered no more.

Chapter 45 - Elde Luri Mora

She awoke to the sound of softly running water, calmer than the constant roar of rapids and waterfalls she had traveled by for the last few days. She stirred and opened her eyes, noticing by the deep blue color of the sky and the wisps of clouds that the day had passed to evening. The western edges of the shards sailing above were gilded with the oranges of the setting sun.

Shaking off a mental fog, she sat up to find Gen. He lay unconscious nearby, and at his side sat Maewen, legs crossed. Her travel gear and weapons sat off to one side, including a nearly spent quiver. A gash puckered red and angry on her face, and blood from a wound on her arm soaked through a bandage she had fashioned from a piece of her cloak.

"Good evening, Chalaine," Maewen greeted her without looking up from an arrow she was fletching. "It is good to see you alive and well. It seems you've come through this in better shape than most. Gen does not fare so well as you, I'm afraid."

The Chalaine stood and straightened her veil, taking stock of herself and the surroundings. The river ran wide and shallow, reflecting the soft sunset. The Millim Eri had left them on a quiet, shallow beach on the lee side of a low, tree-covered hill. The Chalaline crossed to Gen and saw the reason for Maewen's concern. Sweat beaded on his pale, haggard face.

"He has a fever," Maewen reported. "I've tried to wake him, but to no avail. Has he been well? Was he hurt?"

"He was hurt, but I healed it. He passed through much toil and has hardly slept since the battle. What of my Mother and Fenna? What happened? Are they alive?"

"I will tell you the full tale when we get moving. Suffice it to say that Fenna and your mother live, as do Chertanne and others. They are not far from this place. But first, can you do something for Gen? I doubt we can carry him any great distance."

The Chalaine knelt by him and closed her eyes, trying to give the impression that she expended effort. She touched him, and his color and breathing improved for a moment, but when she broke contact, his condition remained unchanged. She could find no sickness or illness in him in the way she was accustomed to sensing them. Puzzled, she opened her eyes, finding Maewen watching her intently.

"Is something wrong?"

"I can't find any injury or sickness in him," the Chalaine explained. Maewen wrinkled her brow and the Chalaine crossed to her. "I see you have some injuries. Let me heal them."

"Save your strength; they are nothing to be concerned about."

"You and Gen are insufferable," the Chalaine chided irritably, ignoring Maewen's objections. "You would think you two enjoyed being injured."

"I just don't wish to trouble you. There are others in more desperate need of your aid in the camp, or what's left of it."

"I think you are both proud of the little scratches and scars you get."

The Chalaine took Maewen's hand and concentrated. The injuries were not deep, but a couple had started to fester despite the half-elf's herb craft. It took little effort to heal them.

Maewen thanked her and removed the bandages. "Wounds are to the warrior what wisdom is to the wanderer. I will fashion a litter for Gen, if there is nothing else you can do for him. His condition worries me."

The Chalaine took his hand again. "Gen! Wake up!" she said. "We're out of the canyon."

He stirred, and she released his hand as his eyes fluttered open. He slowly rose to his feet and examined his surroundings carefully, disorientation evident on his face.

"Chalaine? And Maewen? Where are we? What happened? We were walking through the hall and . . . how did I get here?"

"I do not know for sure," the Chalaine replied truthfully. "The same thing happened to me."

"Where are we, Maewen? Did others survive?"

Relief overspread Maewen's face to see Gen up and about, though he still appeared sickly and unsteady. "Let's walk, and I'll tell you as we go. Dark falls soon, but the road to Elde Luri Mora and your companions is close and easy to follow. It wasn't nearly so pronounced last year. The city awakes and invites us."

Maewen led out downriver, the Chalaine following and Gen taking up the rear. Knee-high grass grew between the trees, and the sound of crickets and birds filled the air with evening song. The breeze turned cooler as the sun sank, oranges and purples wavering in the river pools.

"As you probably know," Maewen began once they had gone several hundred yards, "the evening of the ambush I left to scout as everyone set to eating. Once I crested the hill and saw what lay in wait, I turned to run back but was forced to hide myself from two full companies of Uyumaak passing by me on either side, preparing to flank the caravan.

A few minutes later, they unleashed the giant, but I couldn't move for fear of discovery.

"Once the abomination fell, the Uyumaak streamed over the hill, outnumbering us three or four to one. I picked at them from behind until I could win my way to the main force. Those who could not fight or who were important to the mission fled down the road as the fighters and Magicians stayed behind to delay them enough to escape.

"The road was held against the fliers, however, and they had to retreat while the main force of soldiers split. Shadan Khairn led a body of men against the Uyumaak on the road. I've never seen a man wield the sword like he does. He and a score of soldiers won their way through the blockade, allowing Chertanne, Mirelle, the Pontiff, and others to escape. Khairn did not come, however, returning to fight with his men."

"What of Fenna?" Gen interrupted.

"She is alive, Gen. Geoff braved the Uyumaak attack to gather a horse and ride her down the road to safety. He suffered a broken arm from an Uyumaak club, but he still seems jubilant and has already begun composing a song about the whole affair. I'm sure once the Chalaine heals him, he will favor us with it."

"Who are we missing? How many soldiers left?" Gen asked.

"None of the Magicians, including Ethris, have shown up yet. Khairn, Tolbrook, and half the Dark Guard and their apprentices are also missing. If I counted right, we have sixteen fighting men left, and that's including the three Dark Guard that came with us and their apprentices. The Pontiff lives, as does Padra Athan. Jaron lives but suffered several broken ribs and a sprain or two. One of the Dark Guard threw him over a horse during the escape.

"It was through Jaron's and Dason's brands that we knew the Chalaine survived the drop over the falls and was progressing through the canyon. We surmised that you,

Gen, survived if the Chalaine had. We made camp near a ford in the river two days ago. It is close to Elde Luri Mora, and Chertanne and all but the Dark Guard have entered it already for their protection. Athan persuaded Dason to accompany them to Elde Luri Mora to aid in Chertanne's protection, but Mirelle, Fenna, and the rest of the Dark Guard refused to leave until you were found. I've been exploring the area near the river, seeing if I could find a way up the canyon. It is impossible."

"How far to the camp?" Gen inquired, voice weary.

"We will arrive in two hours time if we can keep this pace."

And keep it they did, finding the road before full dark. Despite the road's age, the stones spread before them even and smooth, providing easy walking compared to the tangles of the canyon. The two moons provided ample light to see the way. A dense net of stars and shards emerged in the darkening sky, and the thought that she would see her mother and Fenna soon infused the Chalaine with energy. They talked little as they walked, Maewen telling them to save their tale until all could hear so as not to waste breath on telling it twice.

"Stand fast!" a voice barked from the darkness. The Chalaine startled, coming out of deep thought. A bending bow creaked. "Identify yourselves."

"It is Maewen. I have returned with the Chalaine. And Gen."

"Thank Eldaloth!" the sentry said. "Shall I send a runner back?"

"No," Maewen said. "Use what men you have to keep a watch on this road. We left a lot of Uyumaak alive behind us a few days ago."

They continued on for some minutes longer before the Chalaine could make out a huddled group of bodies just off the road in the dark. They risked no fire. The soldiers came on their guard, but Fenna streaked by to hug Gen almost before Maewen could tell the men to stand down. And then her mother was there, and the Chalaine came into her arms and cried. Fenna wept as well. Reluctantly, she let her mother disengage from her as she went to Gen.

"My turn, Fenna," the First Mother said. Fenna laughed and stepped back as Mirelle gave Gen an affectionate embrace. The Chalaine was relieved to see Cadaen come up behind.

"You are better than a son to me," she said, stepping back and placing a hand on his cheek. "I owe you everything. Thank you for bringing my daughter back to me."

"It is my pleasure to serve you and the Chalaine," Gen stated, inclining his head.

"But you are warm," Mirelle observed. "Are you well?"

"Just heat from walking," he answered as Fenna came up from behind him and wrapped her arms around him, laying her head on his shoulder.

"And," the Chalaine added, "he labored hard to get me through the canyon. He barely slept. He needs rest and a caring hand."

"I am fine," Gen contradicted. "I am rested enough to watch through the night."

"No!" one of the Dark Guard protested. "We have been at camp two days and will watch for you. You have earned the sleep."

"When one of you can kill me, you can take my watch," Gen replied flatly. "It is my duty, and I am fit to do it." His tone left no room for argument. The Chalaine considered protesting but thought better of it.

"None of us will sleep until we hear the tale," Mirelle prompted.

"Gen can tell the tale," the Chalaine said. "I will see to the healing of the wounded."

The Chalaline moved around the camp, tending to Jaron first, his injuries the most serious. Gen's voice, soft and deep in the darkness, told the tale with only the bare particulars, leaving out her unveiling and any mention of their conversations. In fact, the way he told it made her think he didn't enjoy their time together at all, for which she was thankful and angry at the same time.

Everyone expressed concern over their strange experience in the cave and their resulting appearance miles downriver. Maewen expressed a wish to find the cave and the gazebos again once time permitted, and Fenna seconded her desire, mainly to please Gen, the Chalaine thought.

"I wish Ethris were here," her mother lamented. "We need those facts he has stuffed up in that mind of his. Let's all get some rest. Tomorrow we see Elde Luri Mora and the Hall of Three Moons. Tomorrow is the real beginning."

The Chalaine lay next to her mother on a single blanket provisioned for her use. Gen sat nearby, Fenna leaning on him. Jaron and the remaining Dark Guard congratulated Gen for his bravery at the falls and for leading the Chalaine through the canyon. The Chalaine tried to sleep, but even an hour later when Fenna settled in at her side, she couldn't. She was awake when Maewen talked to Gen at some length in Elvish, questioning him, as far as she could tell. The Chalaine wondered what he confided in her.

She finally managed to nod off, but when dawn pried her eyes open her head felt full of sand and her eyes hurt. Seeing Gen in full sunlight shocked her. His pallid skin and dark-rimmed eyes gave him an evil mien, and Fenna went to him immediately, feeling his forehead.

"Chalaine!" she exclaimed, "He is sick! Can you do something for him?" The Chalaine hesitated. She had tried before and failed.

"Do not bother the Chalaine with this trifling illness," Gen told her handmaiden, taking her hand. "If we get to Elde Luri Mora, then she may make an attempt. Until then, she should save her strength for any other dangers along the way. I will be fine."

"We should not encounter any more of the enemy ahead of us," Maewen explained as she donned her gear. "I believe the Uyumaak are behind us, and, as creatures of Mikkik, I doubt they will or are able to come much closer than this to the city."

And then the Chalaine understood. Gen was one of Mikkik's creatures, as well. The holy city rejected him to spite his maker. The Chalaine thought hard as Jaron helped her onto a horse with her mother. Gen rode with Fenna, and Maewen led out, sprinting east into the rising sun. The road led through gentle green hills covered with large, mature trees. Deer regarded them briefly before loping away, and beautiful birdsong serenaded them in the early morning light. To their left the river ran wide and quiet, emerald in color.

The Chalaine watched Gen, worry knotting her stomach. His weariness and pain mounted with every mile forward. He bore up well considering his obvious discomfiture, though Maewen and Fenna shot concerned glances at him with increasing frequency. The Chalaine feared he might be killed if he rode much farther, but she could do nothing but pray he could endure whatever protection the builders of the city had prepared against him.

Before long, outbuildings cropped up along the road, most artistic and beautiful without any obvious, practical function save as gathering places. They passed several gazebos of similar design to the ones by the pool in the canyon. She wondered if they had already entered Elde Luri Mora without realizing it or if the gazebos and hall she and Gen saw were part of some smaller province. Before her, the road descended and curved between steep gashes in the hills. The river separated from the road and disappeared behind a hill farther east as the steady descent finally evened up.

As they rounded another corner, the city sprang into

view and they called a halt. Before them the hills split apart as if hewn by a giant ax. A tall silver gate, untarnished and finely tooled, reflected the sun so harshly the travelers had difficulty inspecting them. One side of the immense gate was thrown open, and the road continued onto a bridge. Elde Luri Mora stretched out upon an island in the middle of a deep, blue lake formed in the womb of tall, fir-covered hills.

Impressively, the city seemed to lay as it first had centuries ago, pristine white buildings trimmed with gold and silver nestled in trees and fields of the richest green. The moons reflected clearly and ominously in the still water, their image disturbed only by wind ripples and reflected sunlight. Flowers and blossoms of every color lined its streets of white granite cobblestones, and as they crossed the long bridge over the lake, the Chalaine felt an air of peace and happiness envelop her, reminding her of the feeling emanating from Ki'Hal in the vision Aldemar had shared with her.

She smiled at Fenna, but her handmaiden had turned to wrap her arm around Gen who flagged, sweating profusely. Her mother noticed his distress and angled her horse closer. As they approached, Gen straightened himself with an act of pure will.

"Press on," he said weakly. "I will rest when we arrive."

Mirelle nodded and guided her horse toward her daughter. "See if you can do something for him, once we get him settled in and away from everyone," the First Mother whispered. "I think he has exhausted himself. You may need to force him to sleep. Do you remember how?"

"Yes."

Geoff, Dason, and a small contingent of Aughmerian soldiers met them on the other side of the bridge, faces happy at their arrival, though the Chalaine noticed Geoff's frown upon seeing Fenna and Gen. She couldn't tell if he were disappointed to see Gen alive or disturbed by his appearance. Whatever he felt, he greeted them heartily, his arm hanging in a sling.

"Chalaine and Fenna and Gen! The sun smiles on us again!" He beamed. "Thank Eldaloth. I shall need the story from both of you, of course! I do not lie when I say this may well be the most interesting book I or anyone else has ever written! But come! The Hall of Three Moons is amazing! You must see it, Fenna. It surpassed my wildest expectations!"

Dason approached, face beaming. He knelt and kissed the Chalaine's hands. "I could feel you coming! I knew you would be safe! My heart nearly burst when I saw you disappear over the falls!"

"I am safe," the Chalaine soothed, finding his affection strangely annoying. Gen watched them both expressionlessly, and she withdrew her hand from Dason's grip, realizing what he probably thought of her. She turned to Geoff, and—to his utter delight—healed his arm.

Maewen urged them onward. As they passed into the city proper, the Chalaine marveled at the grace of the structures around her. Unlike human cities where monuments and buildings were built tall and in spite of the environment around them, Elde Luri Mora accommodated the terrain and the trees. Not one building rose taller than the tallest tree, and everything curved naturally to match the shape of clearings and openings in the foliage. There were no harsh angles anywhere, the polished white stone appearing shaped as clay rather than chiseled. Green vines tinged with silver and red snaked up the sides of white walls, accenting rather than overwhelming the architecture.

The silver and gold trim imitated the shape and size of thin-leaved creepers, reflecting the sunlight. Instead of groomed beds of flowers or well-pruned shrubs and trees, everything was let grow in its place without the governing of a gardener's spade or woodsman's saw. Crystal chimes rang in the pleasant breeze, and blossoms of pink, white, and yellows swirled thick about the road, exuding a scent that relaxed the nerves and set the mind to pleasant thoughts.

Since everything appeared so new and inviting, the Chalaine half expected the tenants of the buildings to emerge from the doorless thresholds. But the city's denizens had indeed abandoned it, and it had sat hidden away in the hills for years until the Shroud Lake shard had been discovered and the road found again. Maewen was the first to find and enter it, and she told them that the road to the city practically rose from the ground to meet her feet as she walked.

The Hall of Three Moons stood in a clearing near a high hill, the tallest structure they could see from their vantage point. Towering trees abutted it from every side but the front. A border of pink and white flowering bushes ringed the building, and patches of purple and red wildflowers encroached upon the thin walkway that led to a wide, arched entrance with no door. The building itself was a wide dome, stretching some hundred feet into the air. Smaller domes were attached to four sides of the circle, creating an appearance of four corners. A semicircle patio extended away from the door, and Chertanne waited there, Captain Drockley at his side.

The Chalaine swallowed hard. Her fiancé was travel stained and unkempt, face unsettled and maybe even a little scared. Jaron came to her side, Gen slightly behind, sweat beaded on his forehead. Fenna took his arm and held tightly.

"Chalaine," Chertanne said, voice ingratiating, "it is good to see you again." Chertanne walked around Jaron to stand in front of Gen, hands on his hips. Gen returned the stare without blinking.

"You look simply awful," Chertanne remarked disdainfully.

"He has slept but one night in the last five, your Grace,"

the Chalaine quickly explained, "and was greatly taxed escorting me through the canyon."

Chertanne ignored the Chalaine, eyes fixed on Gen. "I want you to know something, Gen," and for half a moment the Chalaine thought he would thank him. "I will expect you to submit to the Pontiff for a full examination of your actions while you were alone with my fiancé. If I find out that you so much as. . ."

Chertanne's last words were cut off as Gen's free hand shot around Chertanne's throat with such speed that those around him startled. Captain Drockley drew his sword and started forward cautiously.

"Don't!" Gen ordered, face livid. "I won't kill him." Drockley held back. Chertanne's eyes bulged, face turning red. "You listen to me, Chertanne. How dare you question my honor or the Chalaine's after you visited every brothel and bawdyhouse in Mikmir! If you ever question her or me again, you had better be prepared to pick up a sword and fight. No one can keep me from you—not your guard, not your father!"

"I withdraw my statement," Chertanne gagged, naked fear on his face. The Chalaine glanced at her mother, finding her face expectant, almost elated.

"Good. And one more thing." Gen freed his arm other from a shocked Fenna and lifted his shirt to reveal his brandings. "Do you see this branding? It lets me know when the Chalaine is in pain. If I ever feel or discover that you hurt her in any way, I will come for you and Eldaloth help you when I do!"

Gen shoved Chertanne backward and the Blessed One landed hard on his backside. The Chalaine expected Chertanne to return some epithet. He instead gathered himself and practically ran into the hall. Captain Drockley resheathed his sword and followed after him, throwing Gen a challenging look. Much to the Chalaine's surprise, Jaron patted Gen on the back, and her mother flashed him a smile before going into the Hall. Geoff already had his book out, scribbling intently as he walked. Maewen commented something to Gen offhandedly in Elvish as she passed by, though Gen didn't acknowledge it.

The Chalaine, Jaron behind, stayed with Fenna and Gen, unsure of how to feel. Gen was miserable, and the Chalaine reached out to feel his forehead for a fever. It was hot, but as she touched him, it faded. Realizing what was happening, she pulled her hand away. Gen said nothing.

"What did Maewen say, Gen?" Fenna asked.

"She said I am a dead man."

"Let's find you somewhere to rest, Gen," Fenna suggested, rubbing his arm. "I think the Pontiff will hold the wedding tonight. He said there was no time to lose, and he is not faring well. You should visit him, Chalaine."

"I will."

They went inside the hall, finding the other soldiers who had survived gathered there. The Hall of Three Moons stunned the Chalaine. A wide, oval window in the ceiling—glass tinted light blue—framed the three moons and cast a pleasant hue on everything below. On the north end of the hall stood a great throne elegantly carved from a pale wood. Three thrones sat one level below it, all carved of the same wood, though one was charred black. A raised dais encircled the room, and above it was a balcony with a bench offering a perfect view of the floor on which was painted a perfect replica of all of Ki'Hal before the Shattering. Softly arched doorways draped with a soft red cloth led into the smaller domes accessible from the dais.

Dason led them forward. "The Pontiff and the Ha'Ulrich have taken the domes closest to the main entrance. We have been given the one to the right of the throne."

"Very well," Mirelle answered. "You should all take your rest, you especially, Gen. I will visit you by and by."

The Chalaine observed Gen as they crossed the floor,

wondering what had inspired his sudden outburst against Chertanne, especially considering what she had done to him. He stumbled more than once as he walked, always catching himself. Sweat ran from him in rivulets as he concentrated, trying to fight off the pain. Fenna supported him along the way.

They found that the smaller domes contained separate chambers made private by curtains of the same cloth as the entrance. To one of these they led Gen, helping him onto a single red cushion placed on an outcropping of stonework from the wall. A series of small oval windows opened to the outside, and a simple chair sat beneath them. Gen removed his shirt and lay down heavily.

"What is wrong, Gen?" Fenna asked, face concerned.

"I am so tired. My head aches and I feel dizzy and hot."

"Can you do something for him, Chalaine?"

"I hope so," she said. "If you could go fetch some water, Fenna, and some food, if there is any." Fenna nodded and left.

"And Jaron?" the Chalaine asked. "Could you wait outside and close the curtain?"

He complied without comment. The Chalaine came near her Protector and incanted again, breathing on his face. Immediately he fell asleep, though an uneasy one. She reached out and took his hand, and immediately he relaxed, face easing and clenched muscles releasing. When Fenna returned, the Chalaine pretended to concentrate.

"Is he going to be all right?" Fenna asked.

"It is a strange sickness, magical, I think," the Chalaine lied. "As soon as I do the healing, it comes back. I will need to stay with him as much as I can."

Fenna nodded and sat as Jaron brought her a chair from an adjoining room. The Chalaine sat as close as she could to Gen, finding ways to touch him surreptitiously to maintain the healing effect. She marveled at how it drained nothing from her to do it.

She ate and drank what poor provisions there were—hard rolls and leathery meat—and after some time her mother arrived, Maewen in tow.

"Jaron, Cadaen, come in here," Mirelle ordered. "Did you put him to sleep, Chalaine?"

"Yes."

Fenna's eyes went wide. "You put him to sleep?"

"It is a talent the Chalaines have had for some time, among others, Fenna," the First Mother replied. "It was necessary to get him to rest. He is stubborn and would insist on watching until he killed himself. We need to plan, however. The marriage will happen tonight, and after that, Chertanne will rule all kingdoms and we will be honor and faith bound to obey him. I fear what he will do to us, and Gen most of all."

"Is there still no sign of Ethris or Shadan Khairn?" Jaron asked.

"I'm afraid not," Maewen answered. "I just talked to the scouts, and they have found no evidence of either one. I find it hard to believe that they are dead. Both are powerful in their respective arts, but both stood in the thick of the fight. We can only hope they return soon. Besides Gen, Torbrand Khairn is the only one Chertanne fears."

"Nevertheless," Mirelle said, "they are not here and cannot help us. Maewen, has the Ha'Ulrich discussed what he intends to do when we leave? What path we will take?

"He has not," she answered, "but I would guess that he will follow my lead. We really have only two choices since we must stay off the road. We go northwest, which is the fastest, or northeast and then west, which will allow us best use of the horses but is significantly longer."

"Which will you recommend?"

"Neither road will be easy. The northwestern passage—since it is our most probable route—is the most likely to be blocked by the Uyumaak that followed us and whatever reinforcements they managed. We no longer have any force large enough to confront them, and they will no doubt be thick enough to trap us if we try to slip through unnoticed. I would recommend going northeast into the hills."

Mirelle nodded. "Whatever he decides, we will need to follow and try not to upset him. Criticizing him or flouting his commands will only bring us misery. I had hoped Chertanne would have enough intelligence to leave Gen as the Chalaine's Protector since he is the best fighter we have, but after the confrontation in the courtyard, I think the Blessed One will see Gen dead at the first opportunity. Gen undermines his authority and turns people against him, and if I were in Chertanne's place, I would want him gone. I, however, want Gen to live for my own reasons, and he must hide outside of Chertanne's reach to do so."

"I agree," Maewen said.

"As do I," put in Jaron.

"What can we do?" Fenna asked, face worried. "I think Gen suspected he would be dismissed from service, but not killed. He thought all the Dark Guard would be relieved of duty."

"Before the Uyumaak attack, I think that might have been true," Mirelle argued, "but Chertanne's guard was decimated, leaving him only Captain Drockley and six others. He needs what's left of the Dark Guard now. But as I said, Chertanne will see Gen as expendable. I am sorry, Fenna. He must leave us."

Fenna's face was steady and calm. "I feared it would come to this. I am ready," she stated resolutely. "But he won't leave the Chalaine's side without being forced to. Will anyone go with him?"

"No." Mirelle answered flatly. "We cannot spare anyone. He will do fine on his own. Both Maewen and the Chalaine can attest to his skill in the wild, but we must all work to convince him to go. Maewen and I have worked out a plan. We will keep Gen asleep through the wedding and tell Chertanne that he is too sick to attend or watch over the

Chalaine tonight. While Chertanne and the Chalaine are . . . well . . . during the night, all of us save the Chalaine will ride Gen to the end of the bridge. I will wake him, and we must all do our best to force him see reason. If he disagrees, I'm not sure what we'll do. You will be the most important, Fenna. Prepare your arguments well."

"I will, Milady. I think we will succeed. He expects this, as I said."

"Very well. The most important thing is to keep him away from Chertanne and those loyal to him until we can get him away. Chertanne will find out what we've done, but at that point it will no longer matter. Now I must go. If you talk to anyone, just mention that Gen isn't well and that he is being attended to. I will return in the evening to prepare you for the wedding, Chalaine."

Chapter 46 - Trys

The day passed slowly for the Chalaine as she sat nearly unmoving at Gen's side. Fenna went to another room to nap after midday, leaving the Chalaine alone to fret over the wedding and over her sick Protector. The thought of Gen leaving upset her deeply, compounding her sadness. She wondered if the Millim Eri would find and aid him, as they said. Their reactions to what she felt for him had surprised them in a way they did not expect or like.

As the room grew warmer, the Chalaine found she could no longer keep her eyes open, and, despite her mounting anxiety, she dozed off. She dreamed that she was back in the canyon, falling asleep to Gen's voice as they talked of plants, animals, and politics. She dreamed of waking with him standing so his shadow kept the sun off her face. She dreamed of a crude cabin between the river and the canyon wall, Gen returning in the evening with freshly caught fish clutched in one hand. She smiled at his return and he reached out to touch her unveiled face.

"Chalaine."

She opened her eyes, finding her head on Gen's shoulder. Her mother stood at the curtain regarding her softly and sadly. The Chalaine righted herself and reached under her veil to rub her eyes.

"Is it time?" the Chalaine asked.

"Nearly. How is he?"

"Not well. I must heal him frequently. The sickness returns upon him if I don't. I think there is some evil influence working upon him, perhaps from the cave. It started after that."

The Chalaine was relieved that her mother appeared satisfied with the explanation. "We'll wake Fenna to watch over him while you're away. I want you to see if you can do anything for the Pontiff. He has no injury that Padra Athan can detect, but he is not well. After that, it will be time to prepare you for the wedding, though without a brush or your wedding dress, I suppose there won't be much to do."

"I have the dress," the Chalaine said. "Gen fashioned a makeshift backpack and I put the wedding dress in it. It will be wrinkled."

"Still, it is something."

They left their smaller dome and made their way around the dais. Chertanne was nowhere to be seen. The soldiers present bowed to her as she passed nearby. The room inspired such reverence that those inside talked in subdued tones, and the Chalaine thought it a perfect place to marry, even if she must marry Chertanne.

The Pontiff lay on a bed similar to Gen's and appeared as sickly as her Protector. Padra Athan stood nearby, attending his every need. The Pontiff's staff of office stood propped in the corner.

"I rejoiced to hear of your arrival. God indeed favors us," the Pontiff said weakly, managing a smile. "I know you've come to heal me, but I am old and the rigors of the journey have weakened me. If I live to do but this one act, then I will count myself most blessed."

The Chalaine took his hand, healing what she could, but finding his words were true—she could not cure old age, and his time neared. He regarded her affectionately and worshipfully, wrinkled face and wispy gray hair lending him a grandfatherly look.

"Is everything prepared, First Mother? What arrangements have been made?" the Pontiff asked.

"All is in readiness, Holiness," she answered. "We will make the wedding as traditional and festive as we can in our circumstances."

"And the marriage bed?"

"We have prepared one of the outbuildings for that purpose. The Child will be conceived under the first light of Trys, if the moon cooperates."

The Chalaine tried to blank out the thought of her marriage bed and was determined not to think of it even when in it.

The Pontiff relaxed, his voice tired. "It will, Mirelle. It will. We have come to it now. The moon will herald the most blessed of events and the most troubled of times."

"And have you given thought to who will succeed you when you die, Holiness?" Mirelle inquired. "I had not heard as yet that you had chosen."

"I will announce it tonight after the ceremony."

Mirelle kissed his hand. "Very well. We must prepare." The Chalaine followed suit before leaving, the Pontiff favoring her with a smile.

Upon returning to Gen's room, they found him resting uneasily, Fenna dabbing his face with a cool cloth. The Chalaine retrieved her dress, finding it a little dirty and very wrinkled.

"Come help us, dear," Mirelle said to Fenna. "I will have the Chalaine see to him again before the wedding."

During the next half hour, the Chalaine stood numb and unmoving as her mother and Fenna pulled, straightened, and dusted her dress into its best possible condition. Without a brush, they settled on running fingers through her hair, letting it hang loose about her shoulders. The dress held an earthy scent of the roots and leaves she had eaten in the canyon, and the Chalaine found her thoughts wandering back to her dream that afternoon.

At last they declared her ready, and the Chalaine returned their embraces stiffly, mentally bracing herself. Duty finally came to collect its due, and she steeled herself to the purpose. She was the mother of God, given a divine calling, and she would not allow Chertanne to degrade her. She would stand dignified, if unloved, by her husband, and bring God back to the world. While she did not love Chertanne, she loved many besides, and in that love she would find the strength to obey her calling.

As she made a last pretense at healing Gen, she was happy he would be spared watching her wed Chertanne, knowing it would cause him pain. She hoped his exile would not last long, and if bearing Eldaloth back into the world meant nothing else, it would mean Gen might at last find the justice and reward he deserved. That thought steadied her.

They walked into the Great Hall, and Maewen handed her a bouquet of flowers she had gathered for her. To her delight, and the delight of her mother and Fenna, fireflies filled the room, casting their light as they danced about overhead.

"Have you ever seen anything like it!" Fenna exclaimed. "It is beautiful."

The Chalaine nodded, finding more memories of Gen surfacing in her mind. The bedraggled soldiers formed a line down the center of the hall. Others carried the Pontiff out on a litter and laid him at the base of the dais before the throne while Chertanne waited astride his white horse at the Hall entrance. The men had labored to scatter blossoms on the floor, but it was too immense and the men too few to blanket it well.

The Chalaine stared at Chertanne as she approached him, facing down her fear and loathing with stalwart resolve. He wore his travel clothes, his equipage lost in the

Uyumaak attack, though he had managed to comb his short blond hair and shave. He appeared happy and eager despite their poor circumstances.

"You managed to save your dress despite it all. How excellent," he commented pleasantly. She curtsied to him as he cast his eyes about the room. "But where is Gen? It is his time to watch."

"I'm afraid he is still unwell, Milord," Mirelle explained. "He is unable to watch tonight, so Jaron will take his place."

Chertanne shook his head. "Oh no, he will watch tonight of all nights. By God, he will! Wake him and get him out here!"

"Please, Chertanne," the Chalaine pleaded. "Let him be. I cannot heal exhaustion. Only rest will help him, and we need him strong for the return journey."

Chertanne's accommodating demeanor changed back to its natural, petulant state.

"This wedding will not continue until I see Gen at his post. I insist and will not give way. Get him. Now!"

"I will fetch him, Milord," Mirelle acquiesced, and the Chalaine saw her mother's face drain of blood as she turned away and hurried back into the lesser dome. Cadaen walked at her side, whispering furiously to her. Jaron fingered his hilt, and Fenna bit her lip, face worried. Maewen stood calmly just outside, though the Chalaine could sense her tension. The wedding hadn't started yet, and already their plan was falling apart.

"Of course, you, Chalaine, understand why we must have Gen, don't you?" Chertanne teased in the interim. "If the Ilch is to level a blow at us, then surely he would strike at our wedding and our marriage bed, would he not? Best we have our most skilled man close by tonight. Surely you can't blame me for fearing the Ilch's treachery tonight of all nights?"

"Truly, Milord, I cannot."

Gen opened his eyes, summoned from sleep by Mirelle's spell. At once the splitting pain in his skull returned, and he fought hard to open his eyes at all. Even the weak light of the fireflies swirling in a globe above Mirelle's head hurt to look at, and his stomach balked queasily at the movement.

"I am sorry, Gen," Mirelle apologized, straightening his hair. "We'd hoped to let you sleep and let Jaron take your place. But Chertanne insisted that you watch."

"She put me to sleep again, didn't she?" Gen growled angrily, coming to his feet and fighting the dizziness and disorientation.

"Again?"

"Yes," Gen said, mentally chastising himself for saying too much. "Yes. She did it once while we were in the canyon because she thought I was too exhausted. Well, let's get to it. It is my place to watch."

"You are not well," Mirelle stated firmly, she and Cadaen trailing behind as Gen walked slowly forward, buttoning his black coat.

"Be that as it may. Tonight is the fulfillment of prophecy. I want to see it, and I want to be there to ensure that Chertanne behaves himself."

"You must have care, Gen," Mirelle whispered pleadingly as they entered the Hall. "I fear he will seek your life."

"Chertanne can do nothing to me."

"Not yet, but remember he will be endowed with power, and I believe before this night is over. For pity's sake, Gen, you are needed too much to be wasted. My daughter will handle Chertanne."

"No," Gen disagreed. "She will not handle him, for she does not have the feel of the rein for one as wild as he. She will endure him. She will suffer at his hand. And whatever she suffers, I swear I will visit on his head tenfold!"

Their proximity to Chertanne ended the conversation. Gen called up every last shred of control he could manage. The pain and the fever in his body urged him to leave, to flee Elde Luri Mora, and he knew why. But he would not abandon the Chalaine in her moment of triumph and misery.

"Chalaine," Gen bowed. "It is my honor to serve. Jaron, you are dismissed." Jaron nodded and stepped away to join the rest of the assembly.

"My, you do look rather sickly, I must say," Chartanne commented. "Of course, the ladies are too easy on you. A little exhaustion couldn't keep you from such a momentous event as this! At last I will be out from under your little challenge and be your King." Chertanne looked at Gen expectantly, but Gen just stood at attention behind the Chalaine. "Well?" Chertanne said.

"Did you ask a question, Milord?"

"Do I need to? You're usually so full of comment that I can scarce wait for you to shut up. You truly must not feel well. Well, let's be at it. Really, I must admit that I am anxious for the pleasure of seeing what no man has seen! Thanks to you, this is one of the few pleasures I've ever had to wait for, and I must admit that the waiting has only whetted my appetite! The road has been a lonely and long one, and the end holds the best refreshment I no doubt have ever tasted!"

Gen ignored the bait with effort, and at last Chertanne helped the Chalaine up onto his horse and started riding forward down the line. Gen walked to the right of the animal while the First Mother, Fenna, and the Dark Guard formed a circle around it. At once the familiarity of the scene struck Gen. Two years ago he had watched a beautiful woman he cared for and a buffoon astride a horse starting their journey toward betrothal while he stood by powerless to stop it. That marriage was a mismatch of intellect while this one was a mismatch of morals.

But he wasn't powerless anymore. The training tortured into him ran through a hundred ways to escape safely with the Chalaine. He wouldn't even have to kill Chertanne to do it, though his reasons for not killing him fell in clumps like the bricks of a mortared wall hit with a battering ram. Only Dason and Jaron would know the direction he took the Chalaine, and he wondered if they would keep silent on the matter.

An intense wave of nausea and pain weakened his legs, and he stumbled, the effort exerted to avoid falling tiring him. His planning fled as he fought for control of his agony. Fenna stared at him sadly.

Simple, soft Fenna, he thought. He could not leave her. If the power came to him as it did Chertanne, then he had to stay, had to use what time he had to work Trysmagic upon his friends against Chertanne's folly.

Upon reaching the dais, Gen stood behind the Chalaine, Mirelle and Fenna flanking him. Opposite, Captain Drockley and two other Aughmerian guards surrounded Chertanne. The Pontiff smiled weakly at Chertanne and the Chalaine, instructing them to hold hands. Padra Athan, eying Gen askance, lay a purple ribbon over their wrists, and the Pontiff spoke, voice grainy.

"Chalaine, Chertanne, as Eldaloth's hand and voice, it is my greatest joy to perform as almost my last act in the body your union in the sacred bonds of matrimony. A long time the world has waited, and it waits no longer. Tonight is the beginning of Incarnation, the return of Him whom evil slew to spite every good thing and bring all into subjection. Blessed are all of us who see this day, and more blessed are those who have fought, bled, and died to bring it about.

"But I am weak and must not multiply my words lest they fail me completely. I, Pontiff Beliarmus the Third, having received authority through long lines of succession back to Pontiff Alabain, who received his authority in vision from a Ministrant of Eldaloth, pronounce the fulfillment and sealing of the betrothal that took place in the fall of the year past and pronounce binding all covenants you made one with another in that ceremony. You, Chertanne, and you Chalaine, are hereby pronounced man and wife. It is also under my authority, Chertanne Khairn, to proclaim you King of Nations, three now one under your rule, the Chalaine as your Queen. Present yourselves to the assembly."

The Pontiff slumped back onto his litter as Chertanne presented the Chalaine to those gathered. Gen couldn't sort his feelings out. He watched the Chalaine as Chertanne led her off the dais and through the congratulatory crowd, noting her stiffness and the slight tremble of her hand. As they passed under the oval window he saw it; the eclipsing circle over Trys slipped ever so slightly to the left, revealing a slender crescent of Trys's bright circle.

The ground shook for just a moment as the new light broke into the sky, and immediately a power and a joy suffused him, his whole being coming alive and temporarily free of pain. Chertanne exclaimed out loud, releasing the Chalaine's hand and dancing about with his arms raised in the air to an audience of questioning faces.

"Don't you feel it?" Chertanne exclaimed to everyone. "It has come to me! Come! Watch!"

Chertanne bent down and retrieved the marriage ribbon that had fallen when he let go of his bride's hand. Crumpling it so it would fit in his extended palm, he concentrated and the ribbon evaporated into black smoke. Even this simple task tired Chertanne, his breath laboring. Hoping he would fare better, Gen thought he'd best be about his own work, for the pain was returning and he needed his entire concentration.

Reaching within him, Gen pulled forth the power, and running over his mind the spell for protection, he cast it upon the Chalaine, who stood just in front of him. It took time to properly ward someone against transmutation, and Chertanne, fortunately, was too enthralled with himself to bother moving the procession forward. With the last drop of the energy he could find within him, Gen activated the ward, teaching the very elements of her body to reject change. The Chalaine paused as if surprised, and Gen fell, strength gone.

The Chalaine crouched by him, feeling his forehead. Fenna knelt and took his hand.

"Chertanne!" the Chalaine shouted, voice the sharpest Gen had ever heard it. Chertanne, who was about to convert a button into smoke, stopped. "Chertanne, he cannot go on! We must let him rest. Jaron is rested and ready to watch, as is Dason. That is protection enough."

Chertanne slipped the button into his pocket and walked over, face amused. "What say you to that, Gen?" he mocked, hunching over. "A bit too tired to keep watch?"

Summoning all his strength, Gen stood, ignoring the protests and the restraining hands of the women caring for him. Both steadied him, and Gen was thankful for the Chalaine's touch, for it took away the pain and allowed him to stand at all.

"I will watch," Gen said.

"Very good, indeed. Cormith used to be the one to guard me while I was abed. Since you killed him, it is only proper that you take his place. And you should know, Gen, that I kept my part and did as your challenge required. She is my wife now, and nothing you say is, or ever will be, binding on me again. I am filled with power and am the King of all nations. Tonight, I command you to watch, but little will be required of you thereafter. Come away, Chalaine. We'll let Dason help him to the marriage chamber if he needs it. Miss Fairedale, Lady Mirelle, you will stay here with the rest of the assembly. I will return anon."

Fenna released Gen's arm and kissed his cheek, and he smiled at her as convincingly as he could, assuring her he would be all right. Mirelle's mouth was turned down with concern, and Gen remembered her warning. Now that he knew the cost in strength to protect someone, he wondered how long it would take before he had the energy to perform it again.

Chapter 47 - Discipline and Breakdown

All of Chertanne's remaining personal guards followed the anxious, long-striding King out of the Hall of Three Moons. He hummed a catchy tune and danced about in an air of jubilee, oblivious to the somber mood of the train behind him. Gen walked behind the Chalaine, proud to see her unwilted, shoulders up and head high, walking slowly as if to show she were the Queen, to lay claim to what power and dignity were hers by title. Gen thanked Eldaloth that he could at least cast the ward upon her, though he doubted Chertanne would hurt her, at least not until the Child was born.

The temporary relief that the infusion of power had given him was nearly spent, the fever rising and aches returning. He surveyed the situation quickly, noting the seven guards around him. Killing them would be difficult in his condition, but in the surprise he thought he could cut down at least half before they managed any kind of defense. He could take the Chalaine and run. But her resolution and determined walk—her dedication to duty—put these thoughts out of his mind as he opened his heart and let an unspeakable loss enter in.

He watched her only, trying to capture her as she was, pure, innocent, and beautiful, imagining her as he saw her in the canyon, unveiled and happy. As they approached the building outfitted as a wedding chamber, he felt he should bid her farewell, for the woman he knew would change, would enter that room and emerge a new creature. He hoped she would find the strange strength of the truly great who grow even more beautiful in a poor spot of ground. Leaning forward, he put his hand on her shoulder and whispered in her ear.

"Do not let him change you." She did not acknowledge the comment, and Gen did not press to talk with her further. She kept silent and dignified, disappearing into the firefly-lit building as Chertanne held the improvised curtain over the door aside.

"Gentlemen," he said, smiling grandly, "I want Captain Drockley, Dason, and Gen by the door. The rest of you fan out around the building. Captain Drockley, should Gen make a move to enter, kill him immediately. Well, I had best not keep the lady waiting!"

After Chertanne entered, Gen crouched and ran his fingers through his hair, wishing he was anywhere else. The fever returned full force, sweat running down his face despite the cool breeze. He felt unsteady and in pain, but his thoughts centered on the Chalaine and on the brand that linked her to him.

An exclamation of surprise and delight signaled that Chertanne, at last, had laid eyes on his unveiled bride. From that point on Gen did what he could to disconnect himself from everything, trying to drown himself in his own pain, his own sorrow, and his own discomfort. He tried to forget the Chalaine, throwing his memory back as far as he could, to times when he did not know her heart or her face, when she was someone distant and inconceivable. But her pain, her sorrow, and her discomfort drew him back like a lodestone that would not let him or his thoughts escape from Elde Luri Mora.

Drawing his knife from his boot, he rolled up his sleeve and cut shallow incisions in the underside of his arm, trying desperately to distract himself from the Chalaine's agony. But Torbrand Khairn had trained him too well. His mind effortlessly and unconsciously pushed aside every pain he felt, every pain but hers.

"What are you doing?" Dason hissed, and in a heartbeat Gen found himself hauled up pinned to the building wall, Dason's forearm in his chest and face close. Captain Drockley watched the entire affair, face bemused and mocking. Gen hadn't the will to resist as Dason stripped him of the bloody knife and threw it to the ground. Dason's sympathetic eyes bored into his.

"Listen to me, Gen! Listen!" Dason whispered fiercely. "I don't like it any more than you do, but you are important now. I didn't like losing the Protectorship, but you did the right thing that night and I did not. The First Mother did the right thing, too. You are the better man, Gen. That you feel for her so now does you credit. But harm yourself no more!"

Dason suffered, too, and for all the distance between them, Gen found comfort in a companion who sorrowed with him. Somewhere Jaron experienced the same. They three were the solemn, personal witnesses to the beginnings of the Incarnation and the shame and condescension that it necessitated. Gen nodded his understanding to Dason, and Dason released him, returning to his post. Gen retrieved his bloody knife from the ground, cleaning it on his pants before returning it to his boot. Seeking discipline, he stood straight and attuned his senses to the night.

"Unbelievable, gentlemen!" Chertanne announced as he emerged from the tent some time later, arms above his head in a gesture of victory. "I truly feel sorry for you all. For me to have such beauty in my possession is an undeniable sign of favor from Eldaloth. Well, I won't make you all jealous with the particulars. There are many tidbits of business I must attend to in the Hall. Gen, bring the Chalaine when she is ready. Dason and Captain Drockley, come with me."

Chertanne waddled off, tucking his shirt back into his pants, Dason in tow. Gen took up position at the threshold of the door, standing with his hands clasped behind him and the curtain at his back. The Chalaine stirred inside, and after a moment her footsteps approached, and he reached out to move the curtain aside for her.

"Keep it closed, Gen. I am not ready to leave yet." Her voice was resigned, but firm. "Guardsman!"

An Aughmerian guard emerged from the shadows. "Yes, Milady?"

"You and your men will leave and return to Lord Khairn. Inform him I shall come within the hour."

"As you wish." In moments, the guards trailed off into the darkness toward the Hall of Three Moons.

"How do you feel, Gen?" the Chalaine asked quietly.

"I should ask you, Lady Khairn."

Hearing her title momentarily silenced her. "Put your hand inside the curtain."

"I am well, Milady. There is no need."

"Do as I say, Gen! Please. I am your Queen now, and you are honor bound to obey me." Gen acquiesced, leaning against the entryway and putting his arm behind the curtain.

"Your sleeve is soaked with blood! What have you done to yourself?" The Chalaine took his hand and the pain ignored in the back of his mind faded and the sickness Elde Luri Mora put within him ceased. He didn't answer the question, and he waited as the Chalaine undid his sleeve and inspected his arm. Only dried blood remained after the healing.

"How do you tell the fireflies to leave?" the Chalaine asked, still holding his hand. "I want it dark."

"Emebrí!" Gen commanded.

A stream of the glowing insects flew under the curtain and away into the woods and buildings. The Chalaine held his hand in silence for the better part of an hour. Gen used the gift of a clear mind and strong body to reach within himself and work Trysmagic to protect himself against transmutation. He expected the effort to drain him, but when he finished, he felt undiminished in his power, crediting it to the strength he felt as the Chalaine suppressed the sickness.

"What will you do, Gen?" the Chalaine asked.

"Do about what?"

"Chertanne is going to dismiss you or kill you. I know you know it."

"He hasn't the power to do either," Gen stated firmly. "I can kill his entire guard, and I don't believe the Rhugothians will move against me, though bound to obey him."

"It isn't as simple as that, Gen. He will hurt those around you to manipulate you into doing what he wants. You need to leave to protect them."

Gen shook his head. "No, Lady Khairn, I will not abandon you. I will not tuck my tail and crawl out of Elde Luri Mora like a coward."

The Chalaine squeezed his hand. "I command you to go, Gen. I am your Queen, and you were sworn to obey me even before I bore the title. Leave me now. Flee into the wilderness and hide!"

"No."

"This is treason," the Chalaine accused him, anger rising.

Gen laughed quietly to himself.

"Excellent, Milday," he returned. "You and Lord Khairn at last agree on something. It is good to start your marriage on common ground."

The Chalaine released his hand and punched him in the back. "You listen to me, you bastard," she ordered, voice desperate. "You will go!"

"Learned a few words from your mother, did you?" Gen replied flatly, noticing someone approaching from the dark. "Coincidentally, she is coming. Perhaps she can teach you some better curses. People have called me bastard my entire life and I no longer feel the sting of it."

Gen concentrated on blocking the pain that the loss of the Chalaine's touch brought upon him. Mirelle came quickly, half jogging. Cadaen followed behind, but as they reached the door, she commanded her faithful guard to find Jaron and Maewen. Gen thought Mirelle's face the most enraged he had ever seen it, including the night she reprimanded him for his venture with the half-elf ranger.

"Let me by, Gen," she ordered. She entered, and Gen strained to hear what she told her daughter. They conversed in whispers, and he could only make out the Chalaine's horrified reactions to what her mother told her. After Mirelle left—commanding him to keep the Chalaine there until she returned—the new Queen sobbed for several minutes, desperately trying to do so silently, before collecting herself.

"Give me your hand, Gen," she commanded again, and her tone induced him obey without putting up a fight. She brought it to her cheek. "Oh, Gen. I am so sorry. It would have been better that Torbrand Khairn killed you than you ever fell into my company. I will hate Chertanne forever. I will hate him."

"What, Chalaine?" Gen asked, heart sinking. "What has he done?"

"You will find out soon enough. But I must tell you something. You have to know the truth. I know who you are, Gen, what you are."

"And who am I?"

"The Ilch, Gen. That is why this place hurts you so. Do not startle! Those who turned you from that path revealed it to me. The Ilch is dead as far as I am concerned. I have told no one else. But there is more, I have not been as truthful with you or as just as I should have been. I have not shouldered what blame is mine. When we were..."

"Your conduct has been impeccable, as always, your Grace," Gen interrupted. "You have nothing to explain and no blame in anything, especially when it concerns me. I was at fault and faltered in my duty. It will not happen again."

"No. Let me speak, Gen, and do not interrupt."

Gen turned toward the curtain. "We have no time for this, Milady. You must tell me what has happened so I can be prepared. Is Fenna all right?"

"She is safe, that's all I have the heart to say."

An unreasoning fear for Fenna choked his heart, ignorance of her fate stirring his imagination. Every scenario he could think of sparked rage within him, and he fought to control the impulses that called for violence. Mirelle's return distracted him from his thoughts.

"Already your mother returns," he said, "with Jaron and Maewen now."

As the trio approached, Gen worked Trysmagic to protect them all, each showing momentary surprise at the sensation the protective transmutation caused. Casting the protections did not weary him this time, and he hoped his ability to use Trysmagic was increasing already. The Chalaine released his hand as Mirelle stopped in front of him, Jaron and Maewen on either side.

"I suppose," Gen began, fighting the resurgent pain, "that you are here to convince me to leave. Your daughter already tried and you will not succeed where she has failed."

Mirelle said, "She is more than my daughter or the Chalaine, now, Gen. She is your Queen, and mine. You swore to obey her. You swore it, and it is your duty to obey."

Gen clenched his fists. "He's made her one of his concubines, hasn't he? He's made Fenna one of his harem."

"No. It's not that, Gen," Mirelle soothed. "You must

leave before you are killed."

"I won't leave. I swore to protect the Chalaine, and I will not leave her no matter what anyone says, even her. Anyone who wants my post will have to take it from me, and I am not easily moved."

Mirelle stared at him earnestly for a moment and then stepped toward him abruptly. Gen noticed her intake of breath, remembering how the Chalaine had forced him to sleep. He stepped aside quickly to avoid Mirelle's spell. Jaron reached out and clamped his arms around Gen's shoulders, but with some well-placed elbows and boot heels, Gen managed to slip free and out of the circle they formed around him. The Chalaine, wearing her black traveling dress and veil, stepped out from behind the curtain.

"Gen, you must go!" the Chalaine begged. "He will take everything from you and kill you! Please, run. Stay alive. For me if for no one else!"

"What has he done to Fenna?" Gen asked. "What has he done?!"

"She is in no danger, Gen," Mirelle assured him. "But you are! You have an important work to do still! Do not throw it away for some useless show of pride and bravado!"

"It is not pride. It is not bravado!" Gen argued forcefully. "It is honor! It is duty! You say Chertanne has taken everything, and if I run away then he will have taken those, too. If I die, I die. 'Were there not a hundred for fodder before, and will there not be a thousand after?'" The Chalaine bowed her head at these familiar words. Gen regarded them all, eyes challenging. "I am going to the Hall of Three Moons to hear what Chertanne has to say. Come with me if you will."

Gen turned and strode away, aware of the sounds of Maewen unlimbering her bow. He turned in time to see her loose an arrow aimed for his legs, and he dodged it with effort.

"Have you gone mad?" he yelled at her in Elvish. "You know this bitter fruit comes from the tree I planted. It is mine to eat. That is what Samian told you once. He would understand what I have to do now. He would have done the same thing."

Maewen's face registered shock, and she lowered her bow. Nothing Mirelle could say could induce her to take it up again.

By the time he reached the Hall of Three Moons, Gen glanced back to see the Chalaine leading a dispirited retinue behind her. While touched by their concern for him, he could not bend to their wishes and let Chertanne have the satisfaction of scaring him off. Gen stopped to allow the Chalaine inside first, the rest following behind. Both Mirelle and Maewen were grim and pale. Mirelle regarded him sadly, touching his shoulder as she passed.

"Who are you?" Maewen asked, stopping next to him.

"There is a lot to tell, and I may not be granted enough breath to tell it."

"But how could you have known my father?"

"Is that Gen, my Queen?" Chertanne boomed, halting Maewen's inquiry. "Let him approach."

Gen turned to where Chertanne stood in front of the thrones, hands on hips and bulbous lips turned up in a confident sneer. The Pontiff reclined on a litter nearby, Athan still attending him.

All eyes fixed on Gen as the crowd of soldiers split for the Chalaine, who crossed the distance to stand by her husband. She said something to him, but he ignored it. Dason, who moved to stand behind the Chalaine with Jaron, was visibly disturbed. Fenna he could find nowhere. Gen walked forward casually, Chertanne ordering him to stop halfway.

"That is close enough, Gen. Hear what I have to say. As you have shown quite consistently, you have no fear or respect for my person, my wishes, or my commands. You have crossed me so many times in the last year that I cannot with a view toward my own safety and the benefit of this world let you continue on as you are. Your actions are against faith and against the code of law that outlines obedience to one's superiors.

"But I will not trifle with you. I have earlier stripped you of the rank most undeservedly given you by the former First Mother of Rhugoth. You are again the commoner you were, where you should have stayed. Having recently been appointed the Pontiff of the Church, it is also in my power to excommunicate you from the Church and seal damnation on you, which I also did previously.

Gen reeled. Chertanne named Pontiff? Had Beliarmus been coerced or had old age finally stripped him of reason?

"Now, Gen," Chertanne continued, "you are sentenced to death for your crimes. I cannot have you dogging my every step while I try to unite the world and lead them to battle. I think you can understand this. But to show you I am not a vengeful man, I want you to know that I have cared for those you love best. I will return Dason to his post as Lady Khairn's Protector in your absence, a man whom the Chalaine prefers for his refinements. Jaron will remain in her service for the time being. Mirelle will replace Fenna as Lady Khairn's handmaiden. I know Mirelle likes me not, but it is always good to have your enemies nearby. Let's see, have I forgotten anyone?

"Oh, yes! Miss Fairedale. You will be gratified to know that I have seen to her care as well. I know you intended to wed her, but your station and impending execution will intrude upon those plans. I know she was fond of Geoff, so as my first act as Pontiff and High King, I wed them! By my order, they are now, no doubt, enjoying the same bliss as I did this evening, though I believe I had the sweeter portion."

Gen felt sickness compound upon sickness, his stomach a stone. His anger and shame cut through his pain, clearing a fogged mind. He knew what he had to do. He had to trust the prophecy, had to trust that the Child was indeed conceived under the light of Trys by the one intended for that purpose. But he would not tolerate Chertanne any longer. He had already hurt everyone Gen loved, and would hurt countless others if permitted to live.

"And now to the matter of your death," Chertanne continued.

"Yes, Chertanne?" Gen started walking forward slowly. "Who, here, do you think can kill me?"

Captain Drockley and Chertanne's six remaining personal guards eyed Gen warily, drawing swords and fanning out before their King, Captain Drockley in the lead. Gen considered killing the Blessed One with a simple spell, but he thought better of it, fearing exhaustion and exposure. A quick flick of the blade would do just as well.

"No, no, no!" Chertanne laughed whimsically as Gen advanced. "Let him approach! I expected this." Gen drew his sword and continued forward as Chertanne's guard parted.

"Behold the power of the Ha'Ulrich!" Chertanne yelled, and with a great display he stretched forth his hands. "We shall turn him to wood to match his personality."

As he crossed the intervening distance, Gen felt the transmuting power wash over him as Chertanne's eyes narrowed and teeth gritted in concentration. The protection Gen had cast upon himself was more than equal to the challenge. Chertanne's face drained of blood and he concentrated again, closing his eyes and breathing heavily. Gen sensed Chertanne frantically trying to break down the transmuting ward, but the attempt was feeble, even pathetically so.

"Someone has protected him!" Chertanne shrieked, spent, sweating, and scared. "Kill him, kill him!"

Gen started into a dead run toward Chertanne as the Ha'Ulrich's guard formed a protective wall in front of him.

Blade whistling, Gen didn't even slow as he cut through the center of the defense easily, sending Captain Drockley and one of his soldiers to their doom. Chertanne turned to run as Gen closed upon him, unheeding of the Ha'Ulrich's whining entreaties for him to spare his life. Gen was resolved. Chertanne tripped and fell before the thrones, bringing up his hand to fend off the blow. Gen raised his sword to strike.

An enormous thunderclap split the air and Gen felt something slam into his side, picking him up and throwing him halfway across the enormous room. He hit the stones hard and skidded through the blossoms on the floor until the short wall beneath the raised seating stopped his slide. Scraped and bruised, Gen tried to lift himself, but some unseen power pinned him down. Although his vision swam, he could see the former Pontiff struggling from his litter with the help of Athan.

"Kill him now!" Chertanne bellowed. "He is defenseless." Gen blinked his eyes to clear his vision. Chertanne's four remaining guards jogged toward him. Gen fought desperately to move but could not. Focusing on his executioners, he prepared a spell, but as he watched, an arrow caught the lead soldier in the throat, killing him instantly. Maewen knocked her bow again as she ran to Gen's side, and the advance stopped. The remaining soldiers turned to King Khairn, who had soiled his pants but regained his feet by the thrones.

"Call them back, Chertanne!" Maewen shouted. "I can kill them all before they get within ten paces of me."

"I command you to stand down, Maewen!" Chertanne ordered. "He is sentenced to die according to the laws of my people."

"I am not yours to command, leader of men. I am Maewen the half-elf, who, by wish of father and mother, was bound to the will and way of the elves. I give Gen asylum under the name of Tumerath Se'Reinan, leader of my tribe since before the Shattering. He will only be delivered from asylum by Tumerath's will, for which I act in proxy. Tell your men to stand down or you will find yourself walking home with only angry Rhugothians for company, if they'll have you."

For the first time, Gen thought he saw an expression on Chertanne's face that indicated he understood that he had gravely miscalculated a situation.

"Guards, return to me." Chertanne's manner and expression turned from argumentative to ingratiating. "Will you guide us, Maewen, to return me home? If you love any of these people, you must help us, for none knows the way."

"Help them, Maewen," Gen pleaded with her in Elvish.

"Will the Pontiff release you?" she asked.

"I do not know, but if I escape, I will shadow your camp."

Maewen looked at the Athan and the Pontiff for a moment. "I had hoped to take you to elf-home after Unification, a place where you could find rest. I have many questions to ask you. The affairs of this human are offensive to me and I fear I will not be able to abide him."

"Do it for the Chalaine. She must be protected."

"Yes, you see your folly now. The Chalaine must be protected, but leaving you behind goes contrary to what wisdom I have."

Maewen turned back to Chertanne. "I will go on the condition that Gen is left unharmed and released."

Chertanne raised his hands in a placating gesture. "I cannot speak for the former Pontiff in the matter of his release. But I will not seek his death unless he is caught near my person."

The old Pontiff, who had returned to his litter, whispered to the attending Athan who spoke for him. "The former Pontiff will remain here with Gen when the company leaves and will only release him once and if his conditions are met. He would prefer that the entire company leave the Hall immediately after which I am to seal it against exit and entry."

"I cannot. . ." Maewen protested.

"No, it is good enough, Maewen," Gen interrupted. "Accept it. Get them safely home. I will come when I can." Maewen frowned, expressing her displeasure to him in Elvish before speaking to Chertanne again.

"Very well. I agree to these terms."

"Thank you, Maewen," Chertanne said, face relieved. "I order everyone from the Hall save the former Pontiff."

One by one those in the ragged assembly gathered their gear and filed out of the door. Everyone glanced at him before leaving, some in anger, some in pity. The Chalaine and Mirelle left slowly, heads bent together in conversation. Soon only Maewen remained at his side. After searching the ground near where he lay and retrieving something from it that he could not see, she gathered her gear and knelt by him.

"Is there anything you would wish me to relay to your friends?"

"Just my regret. They were right. I should have left." Gen felt drained of will and energy. His actions seemed like those of a madman. "And thank you, Maewen, for keeping me alive."

"You have too much to answer for yet for me to let you die. I hope we meet again."

"There is one thing I want you to get for me," he said. "In my coat pocket there are three stone necklaces. Tell the Chalaine to wear them. They will help her. Tell to keep them secret, especially from the Aughmerians."

Maewen retrieved them as Padra Athan and the old Pontiff watched from the dais. Once she had secured them in a leather pouch, she loped off through the doorway and into the night. Gen watched as the Athan said his farewells to the Pontiff, warded the only exit, and left. Giving up his struggle against the spell trapping him to the floor, he relaxed and wondered what the world would be like if he were ever able to escape.

Chapter 48 - The Ilch

They gathered on the street outside the Hall of Three Moons, sitting on a low wall or on the ground in silence. No one possessed the will to speak. Only Chertanne stood, pacing up and down, acting as calm as he could and mumbling to himself from time to time. The Chalaine found herself glancing back at the entryway of the Hall, hoping but not expecting to see Gen's familiar silhouette outlined in the light of the fireflies.

Fenna and Geoff had not returned from their marriage chambers, and the Chalaine desperately wanted to be with her friend for her own comfort and to give whatever comfort she could provide. Chertanne had dealt cruelly with Fenna to spite Gen, and the Chalaine didn't think she would ever scrape together enough good will to forgive her husband for his crimes.

Dason sat silently behind her, and, despite his previous service, having him at her side did not feel right to her anymore. She wanted Gen back, for he understood duty and pain and therefore understood her; and while Dason and Fenna would provide comfort, Gen was the one person she knew loved her perfectly, and his counsel, protection, and company she valued above all others. Most of all, she wanted to undo the hurt she purposefully inflicted upon him to ensure his loyalty to Fenna. The lies served no purpose anymore. In her wedded loneliness, she would have given anything to hear him call her Alumira again and talk to her about anyone and anything deep into the night.

Chertanne finally broke the silence. "Maewen, when do you think we should begin our journey? Do you think we should wait a few more days for others to arrive?"

"No," Maewen answered, sounding distant. "Our best chance to avoid the Uyumaak is to travel in the higher places and along unexpected paths. We had best leave tomorrow, for snow in the high places of the Far Reach Mountains during the early autumn is common. If we can make it across and into the plains heading east, it will be a sprint to the lake, for the Uyumaak would be fools indeed not to cut off our retreat."

"We will leave tomorrow, then," Chertanne said. "Everyone take your rest where you like. Meet here at dawn, and we will proceed. Chalaine, we shall quarter where our marriage bed is laid. Come."

"I will stay here and wait for Fenna. I would ask you to clean your soiled pants before retiring, as to not befoul the bedding."

"Guards, with me," Chertanne ordered, voice strained.

The Chalaine waited until Chertanne passed out of earshot before turning her attention to the Athan, who stood apart from everyone else.

"Padra Athan, you did the former Pontiff excellent service during this difficult journey for him. We commend you for it. I command you, however, to release the ward on the Hall."

"I will not, Milady."

"I am your Queen. Release the ward!"

"I am of the order of the White Stone, Lady Chalaine. We are not oath bound to Kings or Queens, only to the

Pontiff and to God. My former master and my new one would not want me to destroy the ward. I beg forgiveness if this offends you."

The Chalaine cursed inwardly. So far her supposed authority as Queen hadn't served any purpose at all. "Very well, though I express my displeasure at your refusal and will not forget it. Under what conditions will the former Pontiff release Gen?"

"I do not think it likely Beliarmus will released him at all, Highness. He tried to kill the Ha'Ulrich, which is punishable by death according to the law of the Church. Still, the Pontiff did favor him, and I do believe he thinks Gen's cause was just, if misguided. However, the Pontiff sees Chertanne as the key to this world's salvation and would not willingly place him in danger."

"Will the Pontiff kill Gen, then?" Mirelle asked.

"There is no need. Gen will remain trapped to the floor until the Pontiff dies, and then he will be trapped in the Hall of Three Moons until he starves to death, someone removes the ward, or the ward fails."

Until you die, the Chalaine reasoned. She hoped she would not have to use the knowledge. She didn't know if she were capable of using it. Her mother, however, who watched the conversation coolly, was. Athan did not know of Gen's magic, and the Chalaine hoped Gen would devise some way of his own to leave. She would try to help him as best she could until then.

"Kimdan?"

"Yes, Highness?"

The Chalaine measured up the young apprentice. Naked anger and sorrow played on his features. The journey had proven costly for him—he had lost his father and he also cared for Fenna.

"Stand at the door of the Hall and watch Gen. Give me a report of any change in his condition."

"Your will, Lady Khairn." Kimdan bowed and jogged

back up the hill.

"The rest of you, find your rest, save you, Mother. Watch with me for Fenna's return."

Fenna and Geoff walked up the moonlit avenue long after the rest of the party had retired. The Chalaine stood, watching as she and Geoff talked for a moment. Geoff nodded and, slump-shouldered, ambled back the way he had come. In moments, Fenna rushed into her embrace. The Chalaine invited her to sit with her mother as they told her everything that had happened to Gen. She cried, wringing her hands on her lap.

"Is there any hope of his escape?" Fenna asked.

"Some," the Chalaine said. "Some. We must be patient. It may be a long time before we see Gen again."

"Even if he did escape," Fenna continued, "what would he do? He would be a fugitive. He could show his face nowhere, and his face is easily marked—especially after all the stories told about him."

"He will not be a fugitive in Rhugoth," Mirelle said firmly. "Chertanne is not held in high esteem there, and he may even find himself despised after word gets out about his treatment of us all. Gen will sooner rule Rhugoth than Chertanne."

"But Chertanne does rule Rhugoth," Fenna said. "Gen could not be safe there. Chertanne will no doubt have spies and supporters everywhere."

Mirelle regarded Fenna with determined eyes. "Chertanne will be far from Rhugoth, but make no mistake. I am Rhugoth. And while I will be trapped in Aughmere for some time, my arm is longer than Chertanne knows."

"But what of you?" the Chalaine asked her handmaiden. "What are you and Geoff to do?"

"Chertanne appointed Geoff the new Lord of Blackshire to spite Gen. We are to return there. He has exempted Geoff from service in any war and commanded us to have many children."

Mirelle shook her head. "The Rhugothians will be outraged, if the truth about this night is ever told."

"There is the problem of Cheratanne fomenting falsehood about Gen," the Chalaine added. "Fenna, do you know what Geoff has recorded of the events between Chertanne and Gen? Whom does it favor?"

"I cannot say."

"If Geoff's account does damage Chertanne, you may find yourself in danger, Fenna," the Chalaine whispered. "If so, make for the castle and Mikmir and secrete yourself in my quarters there. Only those who are your friends have the ability to enter there."

"How cruel this has turned," Fenna mourned, head in her hands. "Oh, Chalaine, Gen and I made our announcement knowing that Chertanne would try to send Gen away. We thought if we announced our marriage that he would keep me with you to hurt him. Now I can't have Gen, and I won't be with you. How Gen must suffer!"

"Gen knew, I think, that Chertanne would do far more than send him away," Mirelle added. "In his own way, Gen was trying to see that you and the Chalaine would be together and provided for at his death. There is nothing any of us could have done to make this night turn out well."

"But I love Gen!" Fenna cried. "Geoff is a good man, but it is Gen that I wanted, that I worked for. How am I to get along with another?"

"Did you consummate the marriage?" Mirelle asked.

"Yes. Chertanne sent a soldier to tell us he would kill Gen if we did not."

"Then divorce is impossible, and probably for the best," Mirelle counseled, placing her hand on Fenna's shoulder. "You must try to put Gen out of your mind, my dear girl. We all should, for now. He is beyond our help, and fate will do with him what it will. He played his role, and if it is done, it is done. If God sees fit for him to do more, then he will help him and we may see him again. You can take some comfort, at least, in being wed to a man who cares for you and who is decent and honorable. My daughter received no such mercy."

Fenna nodded, wiping her eyes. The Chalaine found no tears at all, rage at Chertanne for his treachery unseating every other emotion. To see Fenna in pain awoke thoughts of violence the Chalaine had never felt before. Unlike Gen, Fenna was harmless, and any suffering she endured, she endured unjustly and undeservedly. The Chalaine had never considered herself a vengeful creature, but in her mind she resolved to make Chertanne regret every right he had wronged. The feeling was cold, but it filled the gnawing emptiness within her.

She comforted Fenna for some time, but Fenna finally left to rest. Her mother sat by the Chalaine and leaned close, whispering so that even Dason could not hear.

"I will work to help Gen," she said. "You must have no part of it. I know you are hurt, but you have a high calling. Let me get into the mud with Chertanne and Athan and do what must be done."

With a comforting hug, Mirelle signaled to Cadaen and went with him into the night.

The Chalaine thought of retiring but was too furious to even consider sleeping. She took to pacing the avenue in front of the Hall, thinking and plotting, glancing up the hill at Kimdan. Three hours had passed since he started his watch, and still no report. Though she didn't know if she could bear to see Gen again, she marched up the path, Dason silent behind her.

The doorway appeared as passable as it always had, but when she approached, Kimdan stopped her before she came to close.

"Do not approach it, Lady Khairn. The sensation is unpleasant and painful."

The Chalaine peered inside and her heart fell. Gen's

boots and socks lay in a heap by his feet. The Pontiff slumped against the wall next to Gen, and upon seeing her at the door, waved her away. Gen's face, pale and sweating, was also toward the door, and she saw him mouth something. As he did, the fireflies that lit the Hall streamed out through the narrow windows, casting the Hall into darkness.

"You are relieved, Kimdan," the Chalaine ordered. "Get your rest."

"I would prefer to watch, Milady."

"There is no need. We can help him no longer. Rest. We have a long day ahead of us tomorrow."

"Your will, your Grace."

The old Pontiff said little until the morning. Gen heard him fall asleep or perhaps unconscious after the Chalaine had left. The ward held Gen down, helpless. He had hoped the Pontiff's worsening health would release the spell. The sickness and a sleepless night left Gen as weak as his captor looked when he finally rose in the morning. Gen doubted that he himself would fare much better in a mirror.

"Free me, please," Gen pleaded. "I must protect her. The way home is treacherous. I can help!"

"Quiet, Ilch," came the raspy reply. "You will not leave this place if I can prevent it. Mikkik nearly fooled us all. He is clever, indeed, to have put into play such a devious plan! How could we be so blind? But then again, how could we not? They checked for the mark when you entered service, did they not?"

"The Millim Eri concealed it, and they turned me from Mikkik's way! Chertanne is more his creature than I! You must see that."

"The Millim Eri are dead, Gen," the Pontiff said,

"whispers of the past. You were created for one purpose—to stop Eldaloth's work. Mikkik saw the corruption of the Ha'Ulrich. What better enemy of corruption than honor! Your very destiny is to kill the Ha'Ulrich, regardless of the circumstance. You nearly did it. Mikkik shaped you, turned you into what he needed you to be in order to accomplish his purpose—kill his ultimate enemy. Because of your goodness, or perhaps our ongoing disapproval of Chertanne's behavior, we turned a blind eye to the enmity growing between you."

"I am not about Mikkik's business!" Gen exclaimed, writhing against the power the held. "I could have killed the Chalaine and Chertanne a hundred times over, and instead I put myself to the hazard for them! Mikkik's work was done when no one countered Chertanne in his ways, when he was left to self-indulgence! The Church worked to shape the Chalaine into the very image of godliness while letting Chertanne run with free rein toward moral dissolution! You create a hen and a fox and expect miracles to make the one love the other when you throw them in the same cage!"

"You have a tongue, but not the understanding to go with it," the Pontiff wheezed. "The Church tried to harness Chertanne as we did with the Chalaine, but Aughmere is not Rhugoth. In his homeland Chertanne is adored as a God. Unlike the Chalaine, he wandered where he would, and all the instruction in the world cannot change what pride and selfishness the worship of the people planted in him."

"Be that as it may," Gen argued, "but his wickedness is no work of mine! Even if I had never met the man, the world was undone. Chertanne will fall before Mikkik without so much as a whimper! He has no will with which to work strong magic, and the Chalaine does not love him and never could, so he will not be protected from harm. Chertanne alive will have no more success than Chertanne dead when Mikkik stands across from him on the field of battle!"

The Pontiff's eyes softened. "I know Chertanne is weak, but there is yet time. Responsibility is his, now, and he cannot ignore it. The burden of Kingship and the office of Pontiff will change him. There is redemption and change. If the very Ilch can learn honor, love, and obedience, cannot the Ha'Ulrich do the same? I never thought that goodness could be turned to do Mikkik's work, but in you it has. The last revelation of an old life."

"Did he act any differently after the attack at his Betrothal?" Gen asked. "No. After the massacre at Dunnach Falls? No. I do not have faith that he will change. He will use what power is his to hurt those I care for. He has and will."

"He hurt them for your sake, Gen. Now that you are dealt with, there is no need for him to bother with them further. Your death will be the best way to protect them. I tried to kill you last night but could not bring myself to do it. You could kill me with Trysmagic if you wanted, couldn't you?"

"Yes," Gen replied.

"I think you will not have to do it. I'm am short for this life. Athan's ward will keep you here after I am passed away. You may be able to keep yourself alive for some time with your power, but this place is poison to you and will do its work ere long. I have but to send a message to Athan and my work will be finished. The people must know you. They must learn the lesson I have learned."

The Pontiff died that evening and the force that bound Gen to the floor dissipated. Before the old man passed, he chanted his message: *Gen is the Ilch. Publish it abroad.*

Be sure to catch the entire Trysmoon Saga!

Trysmoon Book One: Ascension
Trysmoon Book Two: Duty
Trysmoon Book Three: Hunted
Trysmoon Book Four: Sacrifice

Get more information at briankfullerbooks.com